They that have fallen . . . .

On the very edge of the town, down a sleepy road of middle-sized, family houses, just as our fears were beginning to subside, a single, sharp, arresting sound shattered the air around us. Gunfire. Cal reacted immediately, swinging the horse sharply off the road and crashing into a nearby garden. I kept so close to him our knees were touching. Chewing up an unkempt lawn, we collided to a halt behind a shield of fir trees. Cal hauled me to the ground. At first we could hear nothing.

"We should have the weapons ready all the time!" Cal hissed, speaking more to himself than to me.

"What now?" I asked, rubbing the rein-burns between my fingers.

"Men or Hara?" Cal muttered, ignoring my question.

"They must have been watching us. Damn! I should have known. It was too quiet. Pell, find out. Help me put out a call."

Now was the time for me to put Lianvis' tuition to the test. A call; to men it was a science fiction of telepathy. To Wraeththu it is just another way of communicating, conveniently without sound. If it was somehting other than Hara out there, the chances were they would not pick up on it. We clasped each other's hands and focussed a channel of receptive thought out onto the street. I could feel Cal's nails digging into the backs of my hands; his arms began to shake with effort. We amplified the force, but nothing came back— at first. Then, I could hear it inside my head . . . .

STORM CONSTANTINE

THE ENCHANTMENTS OF FLESH AND SPIRIT

The First Book of Wraeththu

A TOM DOHERTY ASSOCIATES BOOK
NEW YORK

All characters in this publication are fictitious and any resemblance to real persons, living or dead, is purely coincidental.

Reprinted by arrangement with Macdonald & Co. (Publishers) Ltd.

A TOR Book
Published by Tom Doherty Associates, Inc.
49 West 24 Street
New York, NY 10010

ISBN: 0-812-50554-9 Can. ISBN: 0-812-50555-7

First Tor edition: January 1990

Printed in the United States of America

0 9 8 7 6 5 4 3 2 1

This book is dedicated to the almond eyes . . .

With thanks to Dave Weight for liaising,
Heidi for her incisive vision,
The Closets of Emily Child for music to write by,
Gillan Paris for the loan of a 'Forever' surrogate to photograph
and Jag for the sake of his art and being harishly beautiful.

Our next meeting will be in the lodge, where,
beneath the soft radiance of the everburning flame above you,
and with the light upon the altar casting
its wavering radiance upon the symbols thereon, you will take the
Oath of the Mysteries, and I, ruling in the East,
will accept that oath, and, by virtue of my office, bring you
into our brotherhood.

The gates stand open; enter into light.

W.E. Butler
(Apprenticed to magic)

Introduction

Today: a perfect day for thinking back. It must all be said, now, before time takes an axe to my memory. Outside, on the balcony the air begins to chill. The season changes. Curled leaves, brazen with death, scratch along the marble terrace and the clear, golden sunlight is rustling with ghosts. Remember: laughter; fear; delight; courage. I walked out to the balcony to write. It was difficult to begin. For some minutes I sat gazing at the distant mountains, smudged in a lilac haze. Someone has turned all the fountains off. Below me, the gardens are mostly silent.

They say to me: 'What tales you could tell', and if I tell them; 'again, more. There must be more.' This may become a history book, but remember, it is only my history.

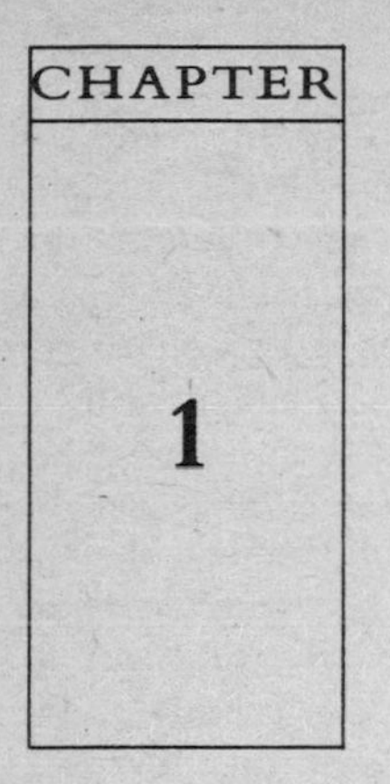

CHAPTER 1

He faces northwest, the direction of the unknown

My name is Pellaz. I have no age. I have died and lived again. This is my testament.

At the age of fifteen, I lived in a dusty, scorched town at the edge of a desert. I was the son of a peasant, whose family for centuries had worked the cable crop for the Richards family. Our town was really just a farm, and to call it that lends it an undeserved glamour. Huts upon red dirt; there is little else to imagine. The cable crop, a hardy, stringy, tasteless vegetable, used for everything from bulk food to bed springs, straggled meanly over the parched ground. It did not grow high and its unattractive, pitted fruits burst with a sound like gunfire to release pale seeds in yellow jelly and fill the air with the odour of putrescence. The grand house of Sefton Richards, a stern, northern man, whose reclusiveness was supposed to shelter insanity, squatted against the horizon, far from our own humble dwellings. Every year, ten of us were summoned to the Great House and ordered to whitewash it. Through the windows, we could see that it had very little furniture inside.

We lived in a cruel, bitter, petty country and it was inevitable that we shared many of these characteristics. Only when I escaped did I learn to dislike it. Then, I existed in a mindless, innocent way, ignorant of the world outside our narrow territories and content to stretch and pound the cable fibre with the rest of my kind. I don't suppose I ever did really think about things. The closest I came to this was a dim appreciation of the setting sun dyeing all the world purple and rose, lending the land an ephemeral beauty. Even the eye of a true artist would have had difficulty in finding beauty in that place, but the sunsets were pleasantly deceptive.

We first heard of what were timidly termed 'the upsets' by travellers passing hurriedly through our lands. Nobody liked to stay long in this part of the country, but my family were an affable, hospitable crowd; and their hospitality was difficult to evade. They loved visitors and entertained them lavishly, and it would have taken a hard brute indeed to resist their advances. The trouble had started in the north, some years ago. Nobody was exactly sure when it had begun. Different travellers opined different reasons for its cause. Some favoured the spectre of unemployment and its attendant poverty; others waved the flag of continuing moral decline; others claimed power plants were responsible by insinuating noxious fumes into the air that warped the mind. 'The world we know is disappearing,' they ranted. 'Not the final, sudden death we all envisaged, but a slow sinking to nothing.' Squatting in the dirt, I felt none of this would ever touch me. I listened to their tales with the same ghoulish pleasure as I listened to my grandmother's tales of werewolves in the desert.

It was said it had started as small groups of youths. *Something* had happened to them. Perhaps it was just one group. Perhaps, once, on a street corner of a damp, dimly-lit city suburb, an essence strange and huge had reached out from somewhere and touched them, that first group. A catalyst to touch their boredom and their bitterness transforming it to a breathing, half-visible sentience. Oh yes, they changed. They became something like the werewolves my grandmother remembered tales of. Spurning the society that had bred them, rebelling totally, haunting the towns with their gaunt and drug-poisoned bodies; all night-time streets became places of fear. They dressed in strange uniforms to signify their groups, spitting obscenities upon the sacred cows of men, living rough in all the shunned places. The final act of outrage became their fornication amongst themselves amid the debris they had created. The name that they took for themselves was Wraeththu. To distraught mothers and splintered communities, this spelt three things: death, rape and darkness. The Wraeththu hated mankind. They were different; on the inside and on the outside. Hungry, baleful fire smouldered in their skins, you could see it looking out at you. They drank blood and burned the sanctity, the security of society, infecting others like a plague. Some even died, it is said, at their touch. But those who survived and joined them were strong and proud. Werewolves really would walk the desert again.

Listening to all this no invisible wind prickled my skin. I never shivered and looked nervously out at the vast stillness of the desert, wondering. One man who came to us warned my father he should chain his sons to the hut at night. We all just laughed. Nettled, the man pointed out that others, families in villages further north, did just that. No, no-one had actually been taken, but it was only a matter of time. I looked at my brother, Terez, and we rolled our eyes and giggled. The man turned on us swiftly. Death looked Mankind in the face, he cried, and we were too stupid to save ourselves. Would I laugh as the Wraeththu corrupted my body and destroyed my mind? Would I laugh as I watched my mother and sisters slaughtered? I turned away from him, stung by humiliation for a moment. No, not even then did I stop and feel Fate's breath on our necks. I took out my sharp knife, a cruel little thorn, and declared this was what any of these weird types would get from me, if by some mischance they should wander so far south, and I stabbed the air explicitly. My father smiled. He patted my arm but his eyes were troubled.

After our visitor had gone, my sister Mima asked our father what he thought of these tales. He told her he believed them to be wildly exaggerated. Rumours such as these have been circulating for many years: 'Wraeththu they say! If the world sinks, it is not because of them!' Mima and I must have looked unconvinced, so my father smiled. 'We are far from the northern cities here,' he said, his voice gentle with logic. 'A gang of unruly, discontented boys has grown into a pack of demons somewhere between the minds and tongues of travellers. They think us fools, easily fooled. No, the Wraeththu are the payment we receive for food and lodging. People on the road have little money, but they have plenty of imagination, that is all. We have nothing to fear. It is all too far from us.'

Mima and I walked in the cable fields that evening. Everything was beautifully red and purple, Mima a stunning raven-haired wraith in the half-light. We talked again of the Wraeththu.

'What would you do, Pell, if they did come here, if just one of them came here . . .?'

'And I fell under their terrible spell?' I butted in with a laugh.

Mima did not laugh. 'You are not quite a man, Pell. You act so young sometimes. I know you would be vulnerable.'

I felt I ought to be annoyed with her. 'Mima! I am nearly sixteen years old. I'm really not such a baby. Anyway, they will never come here.'

'How do you know? You can't be sure.' She squatted down among the cable stalks, her beautiful dark eyes almost wet with tears. Sometimes, she made me ache to look at her, yet I never really noticed girls. I was very backward in that respect.

'Mima, you're over-imaginative,' I told her.

'I wish you'd believe me,' she said, under her breath. But that was an end to the subject for quite a while.

The season had changed, and it was a gloomy day when Cal first came to our home. I was sitting in the doorway, sharpening my mother's knives. The silvery, grating noise I made suited well the warm, clammy air. Nothing could take the metallic taste from my mouth. The skies were overcast, the ground damp and steaming, insects sheltered miserably under the eaves of the hut. He rode in alone on a fine-looking pony. Later I learned it was stolen. I watched him come slowly down the muddy road towards me; past the other huts where other families looked out, past the lithe figure of Mima who was hurrying home through the stream. She stopped and looked at him, enquiry written all over her, but he never looked, just came straight on down to me. He wore a rust-coloured poncho, that covered his knees and most of the pony's back. Suddenly a knife-like depression entered me. The world seemed to change before my eyes. All the huts looked empty and sad, the dampness stung like acid. I think I knew then, in that brief instant, that my destiny had been set. Already the land around me had acknowledged my farewell. Then it had gone, that lightening realization, and I looked up at the rider who had halted in front of me. As he leaned down from the saddle, I noticed he was deeply tanned, with wild, yellow hair flattened by the humid air, and blue, almost purple, eyes. He leaned down and held out his hand to me. I took it.

'I am Cal,' he said and then I knew what he was. I could not hide my fear, my eyes were as wide as a kitten's.

'I'm Pellaz,' I told him and added rather fatuously, 'Are you a traveller?' His mirthless smile told me I did not fool him.

'Of sorts. I've been travelling across country for about a week, I think. Time's gone crazy. I have no money ...'

This was familiar ground. At once I offered him the hospitality of our home.

While we ate that evening, the rest of my family treated Cal with wary respect. They felt he was different from the usual wanderers we encountered. For one thing, his manner seemed quite cultured and he treated my mother and sisters with flattering courtesy. My father, being overseer of the farm, owned a hut more splendid than the rest. Separate bedrooms and a water tap in the wash-room. Because of the weather, my mother had laid out the meal indoors. We sat around a large and worn wooden table, our faces softened by the flickering lamplight, flasks of wine stood empty round our plates. Cal hypnotized us with his voice. I watched him very carefully as he talked. His face was lean and very mobile, emotions flowing across his features like the movement of moths. He told stories exceptionally well and spoke of things he had seen in the north. Everyone wanted to know more lurid tales about the Wraeththu. Only I knew he was one of them: his hands were never still, and I could tell half the things he said were lies. But that was what they wanted to hear, of course. He never told us why he was travelling or where to. He told us nothing about himself. My sisters were especially enchanted by him. He was typical of the strange, fey, yet masculine beauty I learned to recognize as Wraeththu. (That look, so disquieting; it made me uncomfortable to glance at him.) They were very selective in their choice of converts, I presumed. My father asked him about his family. He was silent for a moment, troubled, and then the warmth of his smile moved the silence.

'You are very lucky, sir,' he said smoothly. 'Your family are all with you and in good health, and,' (his eyes flicked for the slightest instant at me), 'they are all very fine to look upon.'

We all laughed then, and respected his reticence.

Mima and I carried the dishes out to the wash-place after the meal. From the main room came the faint sounds of people bidding each other goodnight. The washroom was dark and we did not light the lamp. Only the special light of the sky spun whitely, palely into the little room as we washed out the pots. We habitually washed up in the dark when it was our turn. It was easy to confide in each other then.

'I have heard folk call you beautiful,' she told me in a vaguely troubled voice and reached with damp fingers for my hair, tracing its length over my shoulder. 'Hardly even human, are you ... a changeling child.'

I smiled at her, which she did not return.

'There's something strange about that boy,' she remarked to me, rolling up her sleeves with wet hands and gazing at the dishes.

'Who? Cal?' I answered her without looking up.

'You know very well!' she said sharply and I glanced up at her. In the half-light her eyes were knowing and showed traces of contempt. She looked much older than her seventeen years. I shrugged and attempted to change the atmosphere with a smile.

'Don't!' she snapped and then, 'Oh, Pell, I'm afraid for you. I don't know why. God, what is happening? Something is happening, isn't it?' Suddenly, she was young again and I put my arms around her.

'I'm afraid too,' I whispered, 'And I don't know why either ... but in a way it feels nice.' We looked hard at each other.

'No-one else knows,' she murmured in a small, husky voice. How lost she looked. She always hated not being able to understand things. Our mother just called her nosy.

'Knows what?' I wanted her to say something definite. I wanted to hear something terrible.

'That boy ... Cal. I don't know. It's the way he looked at you. He's barely human; so strange. It's almost as if he's finished his journey coming here. Pell, I'm sure of it. It's you. It has to be you. The stories are true in a way. They do steal people. But not in the way we thought. They're very clever ... I'm not prepared. I have no defence for you... Pell, is it just me? Am I imagining things?'

I turned away from her and pressed my forehead against the window. Was it just Mima's imagination? I felt numb. My fate was no longer in my own hands, I thought, and I did not really care. I strained to be truly frightened but I could not. For a while the only sound was the clink and scrape of Mima cleaning the pots by herself, until I said; 'We have to go back in there.' My voice sounded like someone else.

'You do,' she answered. 'But I'm not going to!' Wiping her hands, she started to leave the room in the direction of the small bedchamber she shared with two of our sisters. At the doorway she paused. It was so dark I could not see her properly. Her voice came to me out of the shadows. 'I love you, Pell.' Husky and forlorn.

I waited a while before going to my room. Cal had been offered a place on the floor there and when I went in, he was lying under a blanket with one arm thrown over his face. Terez and I slept on an ancient wooden bed that groaned as if in pain whenever one of us moved. Terez had waited for me to come in before he put out the light. We did not speak afterwards, because of Cal being there. Lying there in the muted owl-light I dared not look at him. I knew I would see his eyes glittering in the darkness and if he saw I was awake he might say something. I had to prepare myself. I was feeling scared now. Presently, Terez's gentle snores came from the other side of the bed. I lay and waited, knowing that if nothing happened now, tomorrow Cal would be gone, no matter what Mima thought. It had to come from me. He would say nothing otherwise.

My right arm lay outside the coverlet. It felt cold and sensitive and cumbersome. For a moment or two I clenched my fingers with reluctance before letting it move slowly by itself towards the edge of the bed. I must have been bewitched. I was normally such a coward. We had laughed at the tales we had heard. Now I wanted to be part of them. I was excited and curious. In my head I had already left the farm and carved a highway of adventures into the wilderness. My hand hit the wooden floor without a sound. What could I do now? Prod him? Wake him somehow? What could I say? I want to go with you. What if he did not want anyone with him? What if he laughed at me? My toes curled at the thought of it.

I lay, tense and still, my mind racing, and, as I struggled with a hundred impressive words of persuasion in my head, he curled his fingers around my own and gently pressed.

I did not dare look down at him and stayed like that for what seemed hours until my arm screamed for release. Until Cal pulled my hand towards him and I slipped weightlessly to the floor. He wrapped his blanket round us and told me where we would go tomorrow.

'At the moment, I belong to no particular tribe,' he told me. 'Most of my people were murdered by soldiers in the north. Few of us escaped. I'm making for Immanion. That's where the Gelaming, a Wraeththu tribe, are building their city. The Gelaming are powerful and can work strong magic. I will take you there. What have you heard about us?'

I could not stop trembling, so he put his arms round me as Mima had done earlier. 'Come on, speak, speak. Tell me, what do you know?'

'Only what travellers tell us,' I replied through teeth clattering like stones on a tin roof. I am half dead, I thought. Shrivelled by the touch of his almost alien flesh: a wolf in man's clothing, something beneath the skin. His smell, pungent, alien, stifling the breath out of me, like a cat over the face of a child.

'And what do the travellers tell you?' Wicked amusement. (Here I have a child to pollute, torment, seduce.)

'They said it was a youth cult, and then more than that. Like a mutation. They said Wraeththu can have strange powers, but we didn't really believe that ... They say you want to kill all mankind ... They say you are fearless warriors ... that you murder all women. Many things like that. Not all of it is true ... is it?'

'How do you feel about women?' he asked abruptly.

'I know what it means to be Wraeththu,' I murmured, hoping that would suffice.

'Answer!' he demanded and I was afraid Terez would wake.

'I've never known them,' I spluttered quickly. 'I never think about things like that. Never. It doesn't matter. Inside. Nothing. It doesn't matter.' I struggled in his hold.

'It will,' he said quietly, relaxing his grip on me. 'But not yet, and certainly not here. You will be Wraeththu. Perhaps you always have been, waiting here at the end of the world. You've just been asleep, that's all. But you will wake, one day.'

We lay in silence for a while, listening to Terez rattling away on the bed. For the first time I opened my eyes and looked at Cal. He noticed and smiled at me. I did not feel strange lying there with him. He was like an old friend.

'For now, I shall give you something very special. It is a rare thing among us and not given lightly. You will learn its significance as time goes on. I'm doing it because you fascinate me. Because there's something important inside you. I don't know what it is yet. But I know it was no accident I found you.' He leant on his elbow, over me. 'This is called the Sharing of Breath. It is sacred and powerful.'

I was nearly sick with fright as his face loomed above me, satanic with shadows. I closed my eyes and felt his breath upon me. I expected a vast vampiric drain on my lungs, pain of some kind. I felt his lips, dry and firm, touch my own. His tongue like a thread of fire touched my teeth. He called it a sharing of breath. My arms curled around his back, which was hardened with stress and muscle. He called it a sharing of breath. Where I came from, we called it a kiss.

Before dawn, before anyone would notice our leaving, Cal and I went away from the farm. Cal was riding the pony and I walked beside. I have never been far into the desert before and the vast stony wilderness spread out in front of us appalled me. We had filled every available and portable container we could find with fresh water and I had plundered my mother's larder mercilessly. I asked Cal why we had to branch out into the desert, why we could not follow the road. I did not think anyone from home would come after me. I felt sure Mima would stop them, somehow. Cal only replied that there was only one way to go and we were on it. He seemed to be in a bad mood, his voice was terse, so I did not press him further.

After maybe half an hour of walking, I stopped and looked back for the first time. On the horizon, the Richards' house bulked huge and desolate against the faintest flush of dawn. I could not see my old home, but I knew that presently Mima would be stirring. Would she know immediately what I had done? That I had realized her fears. I felt a needling pang of remorse. Maybe I should have left her a farewell note, some kind of explanation. Only we two had ever been taught to write; our father had known us to be the brightest of his children. Whatever I could have written for her would have been understood by her alone; a last shared secret between us. But it was too late now. Cal called me sharply. 'Regrets already?' he asked cruelly, but his eyes were amused. I shook my head.

'This is probably the last time I'll see this place. I've never lived anywhere else ...' I finished lamely and began walking again.

The desert had a peculiar barbaric beauty. Grey rocks rose like frozen dragons from the reddish, stony ground, and sometimes, strange warped plants sprouted rampantly like unkempt heads of hair or discarded rags. Lizards with flashing scales skidded away from us and wide-winged carrion-birds rode the hot air high above. By noon, it was too hot to travel and Cal unpacked a blanket to make a canopy. I was drenched with sweat because I was wearing all the clothes I owned. It was easier to wear them than carry them. The only shoes I possessed were canvas plimsolls, which I envisaged dropping apart after about three days. Luckily, the feet inside them were quite hard-wearing. We stretched out under the shade of the makeshift canopy and ate sparingly of the food we had brought; cheese, fruit and bread. All our water tasted tepid and sour. Hungry insects gorged themselves dizzy on our blood.

I was still very wary of Cal. He appeared cheerful and easy going most of the time, but other times he drifted off into tense, quiet moods, when he stared fixedly at the sky. I could only guess at what he might have suffered in the north. Perhaps he had witnessed things I could not even imagine. Northern society had been disintegrating for years. Even we knew that, safe in our far-away farms. The people now had Wraeththu for a scapegoat. I could almost visualize the brutality that must go on in those grey, mad cities. The people must see Wraeththu as perverted wretches sinking further into decay. Perhaps I too had thought that for a time. Panic and fear blinded them to the cleansing fire that Wraeththu could be. From the ashes new things would grow; not quite the same as they had been before the fire. It annoyed me though, when Cal ignored me and angered me when he would not discuss his life with me. He thought I was naive and sheltered, I supposed, and had no experience to console him. At first, I also dreaded any physical contact with him. In the dark, in the middle of the night, his unexpected kiss had seemed a fitting start to my grand adventure. Here, in daylight, things were different. Most of my reticence, I admit, was due to a fear of making a fool of myself. I was not sufficiently bothered by sex to find him either attractive or repellent. I would accept Wraeththu proclivities because it was necessary if I wanted to be with them; it really did not arouse my interest. Perhaps Cal knew this. On that first day, it was as if what had happened in the night had never been. In my innocence I thought I understood the context of Wraeththu sexuality. It was this way or that way; nothing abstract. 'Cal is strange, being around him feels strange, because he craves the bodies of his own kind,' I thought cleverly. 'That's all it is.'

Once the sun had begun its way back to the horizon, we packed up our things and headed out further into the desert. Far away, bony mountains rose like black spines into the lavender haze. Beneath our feet the ground had become more uneven and sharp stones plunged into my feet through my thin shoes. Cal rode ahead of me, staring into the distance. Annoyance and finally anger gradually unfurled within me. I was carrying a heavy bag of food; my back ached furiously, my ankles were grazed and bleeding and my skin was rubbed raw by sweat and sweaty clothes. There was no way I had begun this journey just to be Cal's unpaid servant. Caught up in a storm of selfishness, that was how I felt. Foaming with wrath, I threw down my baggage, which clattered onto the rocks. Surprisingly, Cal reined the pony in immediately and looked at me. I ranted for a while about my discomfort, feeling both hopeless and abandoned. Sheer willpower kept the tears inside me. 'Pellaz, I'm sorry,' Cal interrupted me. 'Sometimes I don't think. We will take turns upon the pony. Come on.' Stunned into silence, I sheepishly hoisted myself onto the animal's back, who immediately sensed an incompetent rider and began tensing its haunches. Cal swung the heavy bag of food over his shoulder and, holding the pony's bridle, walked beside me.

'You must forgive me for being insensitive,' he told me. 'I've been alone for months now. It's easy to forget how to share things.'

I was going through a phase of being uneasy with him, which came about every two hours, and struggled for something to say. Eventually, 'Where have you come from?' burbled out. He ran his hand down the pony's sleek orange neck, his face troubled.

'About ten miles north of your place, I came to another farm. It was huge, expensive. You know – palm trees verandas, drinks on the terrace, that sort of thing. They were into horses in a big way: and I was in a bad way. God knows what they thought when I lurched into their polite little tea-party! My arm was cut to the bone and stank like a carcase. I was sweating, swearing, hallucinating!' He laughed and so did I, but I did not think it was funny. 'God, I was nearly dead,' he continued. 'Two days before that I had been travelling on the road with a friend. We stopped while I went into the bushes. We had a car, you know, and a whole tank of petrol. Anyway, I was only gone for a minute or two, but when I went back, the car was on fire and my friend was lying beside it – what was left of him. Raw meat! God! Two men, a woman and a child were watching. They didn't smile, not anything. But their hands were red with his blood . . .'

I did not like him talking like this. My heart was beating fast and I wanted him to stop. I did not want to hear any more. It made me nervous and sick. He spoke of the life I had now chosen. I was so fickle; one moment I begrudged his silence, the next I loathed his confiding in me. He did not see me though, did not see my discomfort, just kept stroking and stroking the pony's neck and carried on exorcising his bitter ghosts.

'I ran and I ran and I ran,' he said, his voice getting fainter, 'and I fell, got up, ran and fell again. That's how I hurt my arm. I can't remember doing it . . .' He straightened up and smiled. 'Anyway, I was lucky, the fine people at that very white, clean, prosperous farm weren't prejudiced. They knew I was Wraeththu, but they were only curious. Wonderful liberals. Fools. They cleaned me, fed me, healed me and then, can you believe it, even offered me a job! Decorative as the palm trees, that's me. It would have been easy to stay, forget who and what I was for a time, but I had to keep going. I couldn't stay. So I repaid their hospitality and kindness by stealing this very expensive pony – and money. Look.' He burrowed in his shirt and held out a crumpled bundle of paper. Silver stripes in it caught the sun.

'You said you had no money!' I gasped in one of my common moments of pathetic innocence.

'I know,' he said wryly, smiling, and put it away again. 'We'll need money later, really need it. I wasn't going to waste it.'

After that, the atmosphere between us improved greatly. He had not crossed the gulf, but at least he had thrown me a rope.

For many days we travelled towards the mountains, conserving our supplies as best we could and resting only when absolutely necessary. We were lucky to find water on several occasions and the pony was content to pick at the sparse vegetation along the way. On the evening of the seventh day, we clambered through the foothills of the crags. Plants were becoming fewer, so we gathered as much as we could carry to feed the pony later on. Cliffs reared black and gaunt in impressive silence towards the darkening sky. Splintered rocks littered the ground, and strangely, brackish, milky pools of water lay in the hollows of them. Cal warned me not to touch it. As there was neither brush nor wood to gather, we could not light a fire when we camped for the night. We huddled uncomfortably under a blanket, too tired to keep going, too discomforted to sleep. For the first time since that first night, Cal deigned to touch me. We sat with our backs pressed into an overhanging rock with the blankets swathed round us. Awkwardly, Cal had put his arm around me, more because he was feeling miserable than because he wanted to hold me, I think. I realized that now I was absurdly disappointed that he had initiated nothing physical between us. It is difficult to work out why I had changed my mind about that. I thought that Wraeththu were on the way to not being exactly human, and it was part of their glamour, I suppose, that forbidden and secret sensuality they shrouded in ritual and reverence. Cal had spoken only briefly of such things and then only dropping meagre hints; to test my reaction, I think. He once said, as we lay in a sandy hollow at night, that I possessed a rare and stunning beauty. His words had come to me out of the darkness, I could barely see him, and I had laughed, too loud, immediately, in sheer embarassment.

'Don't be ridiculous!' I had cried, more aggressively than I had intended, because I felt nervous, and just a little scared. He had smiled in a horrible, sneery way.

'Pell, that's one thing about you that is unattractive,' he said. 'You must know you are beautiful. It is more conceited to deny it. If you think that kind of modesty is becoming, you're wrong. It's just pathetically human. When someone tells you you're beautiful, you don't have to say anything at all.'

I squirmed in humiliation for hours afterwards, and would not speak to him, but I knew he was right. Mima and I had always thought ourselves superior to all our peers, and not just in looks. But I had always thought it ill-mannered to let people know that. Cal was of a different world. His kind are proud of themselves and because none of them are truly ugly, Wraeththu are never ashamed to admit they are beautiful. Only in a world where ugliness prevails is it a shame to be vain, a cruelty to appreciate loveliness in oneself. Just being around Cal kindled my sexuality. I must admit this worried me. Had I possessed, unknown within myself, the inclination to desire another male? Perhaps I was being subtly brainwashed, and yet … sometimes, when I looked at Cal, out of the corner of my eye, in the evening, in the red light, it seemed a woman stood there; a woman who might have green hair or wings; something strange, unearthly. Sometimes I was frightened, sometimes just confused. Was my mind losing its grip on reality? The heat of the desert …? I was in awe of Cal's magic; that which I could sense beneath the surface and his precise yet languid movements; his cat-like pride in himself, called to me, softly but insistent, like an enchantment. His eyes mirrored an intimacy long-gone, but it was caught within him for ever. That night, crouched under the gaunt, black cliffs, I longed to touch his face, to make him look at me, instead of the middle distance where old memories replayed themselves on the night, but I could not bring myself to move. My previous life had been cut off and had floated away from me, Mima's face was fading and her hands were mere wisps that reached for me, but I was still young, inexperienced and frightened. The beast slept within me but I was not ready to wake it.

The next day, we made our way up into the mountains. Starting at dawn, we followed a winding, stony path between the rocks, always travelling upwards. Cal told me he thought that once water had flowed down the mountains and had cut this convenient little road for us. In that time, the desert would have been lush and fertile. People would have lived there. I wondered how long it had been since others had climbed this path. It might have been centuries. The mountains had been attacked by huge pressures. We passed through a canyon, so deep it seemed we walked underwater and, looking up, we could see stars. The sides of it looked as if they had been hacked by a giant axe. Huge, scrawny birds, wheeled high above us in the light, their ragged voices reaching us as mournful cries.

'They are lost souls who cannot give up this world,' said Cal. 'They will not pass to the other side.'

I shivered, even though I felt he was joking. 'Will we have to leave Red behind?' I asked. By this time, our pony had a name.

'Oh no, it's not very far now,' Cal replied vaguely. 'Look at this.' He had found a fossil in the canyon wall.

A thought struck me. 'Have you been this way before?'

'Yes. Once.'

My theory of us venturing into territory untouched by man for centuries abruptly evaporated. 'Are we near Immanion, then?'

'Oh no, nowhere near.' He was now sorting through some interesting stones that glittered pink and blue along the path. 'Look at this. It could be anything.' He held a rough crystal up to me. I was riding the pony more expertly now and it stopped when I wanted it to.

'Cal!' I said with a slight whine in my voice. 'Where are we going?' My trousers had ripped at the knees because I had fallen over earlier in the day. While I waited for an answer he thoughtfully licked his forefinger and rubbed the graze on my knee.

'Hopefully, by tonight, we will reach the end of this pass. We will come to what looks like a vast moon crater mostly filled with a rather unpleasant soda lake. On the shores of that lake is a rough little Wraeththu town called Saltrock. It's been there about eighteen months, and yes, I have been there before. I have friends there. Good friends who have pioneered their way to this hellish spot to build a safe haven. At the moment it's not much, but it will be ...' He was annoyed with me. I can see why now, but at the time I went sulky. 'Is that all you want to know?'

I shrugged in the most irritating way I could. Was that all I wanted to know? I wanted to know everything and he told me as little as he had to. I was a willing convert to the way of Wraeththu, yet I knew so little about them. Cal's alien strangeness had become familiar because I was used to him, not because I understood him.

By twilight, the cliffs suddenly fell away beneath us and we stood at the lip of what once must have been a waterfall. Two figures, almost completely covered in sand-coloured cloth, appeared in our path. They were armed with long knives. I felt as if my heart had leapt into my throat and I jerked Red's head savagely. But Cal spoke softly to them and they melted away again. For once I held my tongue. A path had been hewn out of the rock to the valley floor. It was narrow and difficult to follow. A strange, acrid stench reached my nostrils as we descended. Only when we reached the bottom did I dare look up. Ahead of us a vast sheet of what looked like molten gold reflected the sinking sun. Steams and vapours coiled and leapt off the surface. Everywhere, grotesque mineral deposits stood like sculptures, the models for which I would not care to meet. The lake was ringed by mountains and not too far away I could see fresh water cascading down the black rock. Saltrock town, a ragged silhouette in the twilight, was lit by flickering yellow and orange fingers of flame.

Someone came to meet us. A thin, rangy horse galloped towards us along the lake's stony shore. Cal stopped dead. He was smiling.

'Behold exotica, Pell!' he exclaimed, with a grin from ear to ear. He who rode the thin horse skidded it to a halt in front of us. Pebbles flew everywhere. When he leapt from the animal's back, it was in a wild tangle of flying rags, tassels and flying red, yellow and black hair. (Another reality shift shocked me cold as the sexes mingled. Was this creature male or female, or could it be both . . .?!)

'Cal! They signalled it was you!' he cried and, with restrained enthusiasm, they embraced.

In the twilight I could just see his amazing, purposefully tattered clothing and incredible hair. If Cal had ever seemed alien to me, there are no words to describe my first impressions of the second Wraeththu I had ever met. A twinge of despair wriggled through me as I waited, small and silent, while they greeted each other. Fumes rose off the lake like ghosts and the smell was making me feel sick. Cal suddenly remembered me. Partly disentangling himself, he said, with a wave of his arm, 'Seel, this is Pell. I abducted him from a peasant farm.' (Laughter). Nettled, and feeling this was wildly exaggerated, I moved my head in acknowledgement. Seel assessed me in an instant, fixing a huge, disarming grin across his face. 'Welcome to Saltrock,' he said in a way that let me know I was irrelevant. We strolled towards the town. Seel linked his arm through Cal's and chattered continuously about things and people I did not know. The horses plodded behind. Seel overwhelmed me. He burned with an undeniable dynamism, eclipsing even Cal's charisma, although he was not as tall. When he noticed I was trailing behind, he decided to make a good impression on Cal. I was swooped upon and wrapped in leather-strapped, metal-studded arms. 'You look so tired. It's not far. Lean on me.'

It pains me to remember what a bad-tempered wretch I was then. The only thing that kept me from shrugging Seel off with a curse, was that I lacked the guts.

Saltrock was my first true encounter with the Wraeththu way of life. I cannot deny it astounded me. I cannot remember what I was expecting, but Saltrock was a real town, or the beginnings of one. Admittedly the buildings were constructed of a mad variety of materials, with seemingly little organisation. Some were quite large and made of solid wood, others little more than thrown-together metal sheeting or mere tents of animal hides. Light was provided by flaming torches that gave off an oily reek, hurricane lamps and thick candles. The inhabitants, creatures as startling as Seel, exuded spirit and energy. Many recognized Cal as we passed among them. Everywhere the drabness and disarray was disguised by gaudy decoration. Wraeththu boys of bizarre appearance with painted faces strutted through the crazy streets; some were still working into the night. There was a sound of hammering. All carried guns or knives. I once caught a glimpse of a rusting, flashy car sagging in a sheltered corner and a corral with a high fence teeming with restless horses. Nobody looked at me and the atmosphere, though strange, did not feel hostile.

Seel's house was a little way out of the centre of Saltrock, set apart from the other buildings. It was an incredible sight; a large wooden, gothic anachronism. Only skilled carpenters could have produced such a thing. The doors were not locked. Seel said to me, as yet unaware of the simplicity of my origins, 'Sorry, we have no electricity here yet.' Someone, with a crazy, spiked mop of black hair, had taken our horses from us. I had seen the whites of his eyes, like a mad beast, gleaming and the grin he had fleered at me was nothing other than feral.

We went into the house. 'Eventually, we'll get some kind of generator,' Seel continued conversationally, 'but it takes time. We have to steal things bit by bit. We don't have much to barter with as yet.'

The entrance hall was fairly bare, but smelt of clean wood. Stairs led to an upper gallery with doors leading off. Three more doors led off the hall. A boy, who looked a little younger than myself, sauntered out from the back of the house, wiping his hands on a cloth. He was very pale, almost white, with an exquisite pixie face. His head was shaved, except for a long black pony-tail growing from the top which fell over his shoulder.

'Flick, where's the food? Cal's starving. Get back in the kitchen,' Seel ordered with a dismissive wave of his hand. The boy retreated with a shrug.

'Equality, equality,' Cal said, rolling his eyes.

'Oh, I know, I know. I'm an ill-humoured bastard who should make a living out of slavery,' Seel replied with humour. 'If he wants to live here, he works. He's lazy as fuck half the time.' He ushered us into one of the rooms. 'My nest,' he said. We dumped what luggage we were carrying in the hall and followed him in.

'Seel, you Sybarite!' Cal exclaimed with a laugh. Silks and tassels hung everywhere. Lights, suspended from the ceiling in bowls of intricately worked oriental metal, threw out a dim, cosy glow. Perfumes smouldered in corners, exuding a silvery smoke.

'Sit down, sit down,' Seel urged impatiently. He tried to hide from us that he was proud of his home and pleased that Cal had admired it. Cautiously, I lowered myself into a heap of black and gold cushions. Protesting, a Siamese cat wriggled from underneath me and shot out through the door. Incense burned behind me with a perfume so strong it made my head ache, although the soda-stink still burned my throat.

'I'll get you some refreshment,' Seel told us. Moments later, we could hear him arguing with Flick in the kitchen.

Left alone with Cal, I did not know what to say to him. The last half-hour had passed like a dream. I was dazed. Cal looked awkward.

'Well!' he began, with a pitiful attempt at forced heartiness. 'Seel has improved this place since I was last here. He was living in a tent then! What do you think of him?'

He did not look at me when he said it and did not see me shrug helplessly. I was thinking, 'Oh God, he's wishing he hadn't brought me here', and decided I knew now why he had never touched me. He had been waiting for Seel. I had a lot to learn.

'Seel's the top dog around here,' he said. 'This place wouldn't exist if it wasn't for him.' He stood up and walked around the room, examining things. 'God, it's good to be back!'

Seel came back in clutching a bottle in one hand and three long-stemmed glasses in the other. 'Champagne, gentlemen?' he queried.

'Seel, how do you get this stuff?' Cal asked him, impressed.

Seel winked at him. 'Treachery, corruption and thievery of course, how else?'

He offered me a glass. I had never even heard of champagne and did not like the taste much. It was very difficult not to keep staring at Seel, but he did not seem to mind. He was dressed mostly in thin, torn leather and had the same build as Cal, sleek and fit, and that same shifting male/female ambience. His olive-skinned face was almost inhumanly symmetrical and the almond-shaped eyes were lined with kohl. Inadequacy swamped me. It was inconceivable I could ever feel equal to Wraeththu strangeness, and, as fear prodded me sharply, I wondered: 'How did they become so alien?' Presumably, most, if not all, had come from humble origins like mine once. Something other than human blood coursed through their veins now, I concluded. A thought that proved uncannily perceptive.

'Colt and Stringer might call in later,' Seel told Cal. 'But if you want to crash out somewhere, that's OK.'

Cal rubbed his face. 'No. I'd like to see them again. Just kick me if I drop off.' The wine had got to him. His eyes were half closed.

Seel looked puzzled about something, as if he had only just thought of it. 'Cal?' A careful question.

'What?' Cal suddenly looked defensive.

Seel's eyes flickered over me. 'I've a feeling you're going to hate this, but what happened to Zack?' It would have taken more than a knife to cut the atmosphere. I cringed in discomfort.

Cal made a strange, hissing noise through his teeth. 'Not now, Seel. Not now,' he replied, his voice strained and tired. Never had I felt so out of place. I should not be there. Another's place, not mine.

'Hell, I knew I was going to regret that,' Seel sighed, smiling ruefully at Cal. He deftly changed the subject, talking with wit and vigour. Saltrock gossip. I did not really hear him and neither, I think, did Cal. Zack. I had a feeling he was the one who ended up as raw meat.

Flick brought us food. I was hungry but still shy and only nibbled at what was offered; chunks of meat cooked in herbs, and baked potatoes. Hot, melted butter spiced with garlic dripped over them. I regretted my throat was closed. Seel kept glancing at me. 'Flick, go talk with Pell,' he said, after a while, and turned back to Cal. Flick threw himself into the cushions beside me. He was dressed in ripped jeans and a tattered tee-shirt and looked absurdly graceful. He regarded first my mussed plate and then my flushed face.

'Finish your wine. Come with me,' he whispered. 'You need some air.'

The wine hit my stomach like hot ashes. The room lurched as I stood up and I bumped into things as I followed him across the room. I was grateful to get out although I was convinced Cal would start talking about me as soon as I was gone. Half-drunk, I could not be sure if I was really there. Maybe it was a dream and we were still in the desert. Soon I would wake and Cal would be staring at the stars, dead people in his eyes.

Flick steadied me and led me out into the open air. We were in a kind of courtyard. Low buildings shambled around its edge and the air stung my tongue anew with the faint acridity of soda. Above us the sky was rich, dark blue, vividly studded with stars. The eyes of the dead. Raw meat. Dreams. To my left the roofs of the buildings were touched with a weak luminescence that rose from the lake. An underground, sulphurous light. My chest was tight with painful, intoxicated misery. Flick hovered like a phantom, watching. I sat down heavily on the sandy ground. I could not contain it. Like a burst abscess my fear and discomfort spurted out of me. I wept and wept, hearing my sobs echo like the cries of a child waking from nightmare. I hated this place. The strangeness, the stench, the outlandishness of the people. They are not people. Something else. I was alone. Cal was a stranger, remote and calculating. I had been a fool to go with him. Why had I not thought of what I was getting into? I could never be one of them, never. I did not trust Cal and was terrified of what might happen to me. Raw meat. Into the soda, into the limepits. Curling up as tight as I could, trembling animal howls shuddered out of me. And then, there were arms around me. Then the warmth of another body, a living thing, dream whispers in my hair. No language I had ever heard. Flick, an unlikely comforter, crooning reassurance.

'Come on, come on, get it all out,' he urged, as if I was being sick.

Through my tears, I managed a bleak laugh. It was the first time in my life, however, that I had wept and not felt ashamed. Flick asked me what the matter was.

'Scared,' I bleated, and all my fears tumbled out, mostly incomprehensible, even to myself. Flick listened patiently, saying nothing, until I had finished.

'Many feel like this at first,' he told me. A wistful smile quivered across his face. 'You have given up everything you had, everything you knew. It's bound to feel strange. Look at it like this: you come to the world of Wraeththu as naked and helpless as a human baby. You will learn, gradually, just as babies do. Don't expect everything to happen at once. It takes time and there are reasons for that. The Wraeththu are mostly good people. Here at Saltrock they are; you are safe. They will not harm you, especially as you're with Cal.'

I thumped the ground angrily with my hand. 'Cal!' I spat bitterly. 'Safe? With him? He doesn't even live in this world. I hardly know him. My welfare is nothing to him!'

Flick's face was perplexed. He could not think of anything to say. I thought it was because he presumed Cal and I to be closer than we actually were. 'He and Seel are laughing at me!' I announced, hating the petty whine in my voice, but powerless to control it.

'No, they're not!' Flick answered sharply. His eyes looked hurt. 'Why should they?' He thought I was an idiot.

'Because ... because I'm nothing, a peasant. I know nothing, and because I was fool enough to let Cal take me away from home ... and for what?!' I was so angry I could not keep still. I stood up, unsteadily, to continue my ravings. 'Why did he do this? Why did he entice me away with him? I don't understand. I'm no use to him or to anyone here. I have no skill to offer you.

Cal won't even listen to my questions half the time, let alone answer them. I want answers! What happens next? Where do I go and how do I live?'

Flick would not shout back at me. 'You must trust Cal a little more,' he said quietly. 'He won't abandon you, if that's what you're frightened of. There's so much you don't know. Ignore the fear, it's nothing. I know Cal better than you. He's sick. He's not himself. Give him time.' I shrugged and glowered at the floor. 'Look, I can't tell you the things you want to know, Pell. It's not my place to. All I can say is that Cal wouldn't have brought you here unless he was sure you were the right person. You must learn to be patient.' Looking at his face the anger went out of me. I knew I had made a fool of myself, and was thankful only Flick had witnessed it. 'You OK now?'

'Yes.' My voice was a sulky mumble. 'I'm sorry.'

'Forget it. You're tired. You're wrecked. Moan again tomorrow and I'll break your head.' His smile, so genuine, I felt like crying again.

Wraeththu; growing. Something great stirring. My perspective was all wrong. Self-centred. I had to learn, or unlearn, my own importance. Only then, could I begin to see. Only then could Wraeththu touch me.

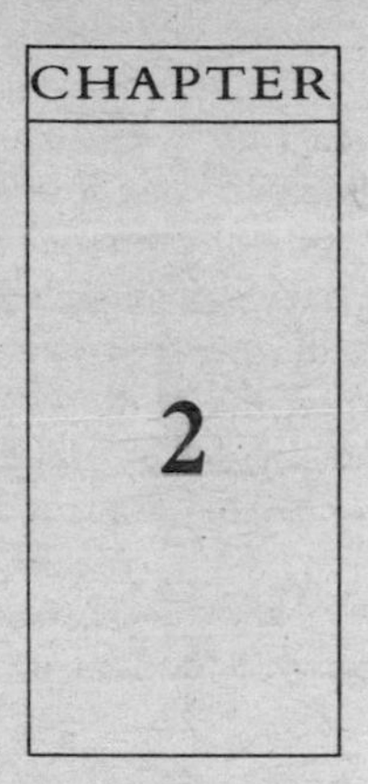

CHAPTER 2

The light beneath the door

Self-discipline must be the hardest principle to master. Second is tolerance and then acceptance. That first night at Saltrock, I began my education. Something that Flick had said to me made me face myself; a facet of maturing I might never have encountered at home on the cable farm. Wrapped up in the small bit of the world that our ego experiences, it is easy to lose track of absolute reality, to warp actual events to suit ourselves. Wraeththu have an almost clinically straight view of things; from the very beginning they strive to rid themselves of self-delusion. Once this has been accomplished one's instincts are infallible, the mind is finely honed for survival. The first law of Wraeththu is selflessness. It is true that not many can perfect this in themselves, (as became all too clear later on in my life), but as a personal goal it is very important. When faced with the hostility of enemies however, there is no more ferocious killer than the Wraeththu warrior. Therefore, I think the second law of Wraeththu must be physical perfection. The body must run like a well-tended machine; be as trustworthy as a blade or a bullet.

Colt and Stringer, those people that Seel had mentioned, were as close to these ideals as it is possible to get. At that time I was under the happy delusion that all Wraeththu must be like them. When Flick and I went back into the house, they had already arrived and were speaking in low voices to Cal. I realized something that had gone over my head in the desert.

Cal was weary and shaken to the core of his being. Only now, as he relaxed, was it truly apparent. His friends could sense it at once; their whole manner towards him was one of calm and healing. How my sniping temperament must have chafed at his nerves during our journey I could only guess. How lucky I was he had not throttled me! Me: so used to being the centre of attention. The beautiful, cherished brother of Mima, the adored, bright son of my doting parents. Now I had to learn that respect had to be earned.

Flick and I sat apart from the others. They barely acknowledged my presence. Flick told me it was because I was Unhar and of no caste.

'What is Unhar?' I asked him.

'You will learn that later,' he replied. 'I really can't tell you. But I am Har, and my caste is Kaimana. My level is Neoma. Cal and Seel and the others are Ulani; that is a higher caste. I'm not sure, but I think Cal's level is Pyralis, that's second level Ulani. He would be known as Pyralisit. Do you understand?'

'No,' I said, 'but I'm tired and the wine was strong. Tell me again tomorrow.'

Flick laughed in a strange, shy way. 'Perhaps,' he said. Some moments later, he offered to show me to my room. As we left, no-one bid us goodnight. Cal did not even look up. It annoyed me but I tried to ignore it.

'I expect you'd like to take a bath first,' Flick remarked casually, as he led me upstairs. 'Some things we have to do without, but we do have hot, running water here.' I was obviously meant to be impressed by this.

My room was palatial compared to what I was used to. Goatskins covered the floor, opalescent lamps glimmered in corners and the bed was enormous. Thick, striped blankets drooped to the floor on either side and swathes of netting formed a nebulous curtain to keep insects away. Luxury indeed!

'The bathroom's over here,' Flick instructed, indicating a door on the far side of the room. 'There should be towels in there. I'll give you half an hour or so, then I'll bring you some coffee up, OK?' Once he had gone, I just stood in the middle of the room, marvelling.

Later, Flick not only brought me coffee, dark as sump oil but with a surprisingly mild flavour, but cigarettes as well. I rarely smoked at home, but this was a luxury not to be foregone. Feeling clean and relaxed I sat on the bed while Flick brushed out my wet and tangled hair. I began to tell him about the cable farm (how fascinating) and afterwards he told me he had come from a city farther north. His family had been quite rich and he had brought a lot of money to Saltrock with him. Seel had put it to good use, he said. (Yes, I thought, looking again around the room.) I wanted to know what had induced Flick to run away from a home that had obviously been so comfortable, to join the Wraeththu and live rough by comparison. His mouth twisted with thought. 'It just seemed ... I don't know ... right. As if I had no choice. I had to do it. Surely you know what I mean.' I did. The Wraeththu of Saltrock seemed remarkably adept at procuring luxuries. Flick implied to me that a lot of what they had was stolen, groups of Saltrock inhabitants going out into the world beyond the desert on looting forays, or else commodities were brought into the community by newcomers. I also felt impelled to explain, with much stammering, just what the extent of my relationship with Cal was. Contrary to what I expected, Flick was not at all surprised. 'Of course, you are Unhar,' was all he said. Some demon made me ask; 'Flick. Cal ... Seel ... you know ... Are they ...?'

Flick gave me a guarded look that melted to a smile. 'Now why should you want to know that, Pellaz?' I shrugged helplessly, wishing to God that I had not opened my mouth. Flick patted my face. 'Classified information at the moment,' he said with a grin.

Once Flick had gone, and I had settled, almost purring, into the canopied bed, I thought about Cal. I was wracked with guilt. I had not noticed his exhaustion, his torment. Perhaps Seel was soothing him now. I could not bear to think about it. Seel and Cal. But it was not my place to wonder. I was Unhar. I was nothing.

I awoke from habit just after dawn. Outside, Saltrock was stirring. I suppose I must have thought, 'What am I doing here?' Thoughts like that did cross my mind a lot at that time, but I became adept at ejecting them. Pale, lemon light filtered in through the gauzy curtains. I lay there, revelling in the comfort and warmth. Only when something moved and touched me did I turn over. Cal was asleep beside me, two cats slumbering contentedly on his chest. It made me jump. I am not a heavy sleeper, yet I had not heard him come to bed. He was frowning, arms thrown up over his head. He always slept like that. I could see the long, white scar on his arm. It was the first time I had looked at him for so long. Usually, he caught me doing it and I turned away. I desperately wanted to talk to him and spoke his name. Wrinkling his nose, he only mumbled and twitched. Never had he looked so perfect.

'Cal,' I said again. He groaned, half-conscious. 'I was talking to Flick last night. Listen!'

He sighed. 'I am.'

'I've been a brat. I'm sorry. Flick told me what I am: Unhar, uncaste. I've been so selfish ... oh Hell!' I could not find the words for what I wanted to say. It all sounded so trite.

Cal was looking at me now, thoughtfully, 'Pellaz, shut up. Come here.' I put my head upon his chest and clung to him. The cats half rose, looking at me with disgust. 'Look, I don't keep you in the dark about things out of spite. In two days time, you will take the Harhune. Then you will be Har. Then you can begin to learn, but not till then.' His arm tightened round me, the muscles trembling.

'You're sick,' I looked up at him but he would not meet my eyes.

'Like hell. I'm tired, that's all. Don't start, Pell, I can't stand it. And lie still, or you'll be out of that window in a moment. Just go back to sleep, OK?'

We slept till noon.

We breakfasted, or more truthfully, lunched with Seel and Flick in the kitchen. It was a low-ceilinged, dark room dominated by a huge, black cooking-range. We ate fried chicken and salad. I was curious as to how Saltrock obtained vegetables and Seel explained they had one or two acres of irrigated land behind the town where it was possible to grow things. Flick said it was more like a jungle of exotic flowers; they thrived horribly on the mineral cocktail in the soil. It was true that the food did have a faint acrid tang to it. Flick asked me if I would like to ride out along the shores of the soda lake with him and I accepted with enthusiasm. I had decided to goad him for information.

Saltrock, by day, was revealed to be a lot shabbier than I had first imagined. However, everyone I saw seemed to be engaged in some kind of purposeful activity; there were few loiterers. Flick took me on a tour of the town, before we headed out along the shores of the lake. There were no proper shops to be seen, but some of the wooden and corrugated iron dwellings had items for sale spread out beside their doors; mainly mismatched clothing, rather tired-looking canned food with faded labels or crude utensils for the home. I was curious about what was used as currency and Flick explained that nearly all trade was conducted on a barter system, for the simple reason that the majority of Saltrock's inhabitants rarely ventured out into the world to places where money was still used. I realized, with a pang, how isolated my family had been (and still was, no doubt), living obliviously at the edge of the desert, happily unaware of the huge changes stirring across the face of the world. Sefton Richards, of course, must have felt it; locked away in his great, white house; he must have had accurate news of what was going on. Eventually, the crops we'd grown must become unsaleable. What would happen then? I thought briefly, painfully, of Mima and the others and pushed it out of my mind. I was now in Saltrock, a different reality, my life had changed or begun to; the past was gone forever. Flick called out to people that he knew who would raise their heads from whatever work they were engrossed in and wave. Very few of the buildings were anywhere near as grand as Seel's residence, most being sprawling, single-storied and obviously occupied by large groups of Wraeththu. We passed one large, church-like construction in the middle of the town, but Flick seemed reluctant to discuss its function. It was surprising how many people appeared to be hurrying around, laden with building materials or driving animals here and there. What drew them to this place? I wasn't yet sure whether I liked Saltrock or not.

It was very hot outside and the fumes stung my eyes. Red made anguished noises through his nose. How exhilarating, though, to gallop through the brittle sands. Strange, lumbering lizards heaved themselves from our path and honking flocks of wading birds lifted from the surface of the lake in alarm. Everything sparkled and crystals of salt formed in my hair. Flick told me I had better make the most of it.

'Of what?' I enquired, shaking the salty locks off my shoulders, making the air glitter.

'Your hair, you peacock! You won't have all that for much longer!'

I yanked Red to a reluctant halt, fighting with his head. 'What?' My hand fluttered up automatically to touch it, my crowning glory. 'Why not?'

Flick looked furious with himself. 'Oh, don't worry, I spoke out of turn.' I must have looked demented; I dreaded being disfigured in even the slightest way. 'Oh well, I don't suppose it will do any harm; what I meant was, they'll cut your hair. It's part of the ritual, the Harhune. Like mine, not all of it.'

'Why?' I squeaked, aghast.

'As I said, it's just part of the ritual, that's all. You can grow it back afterwards.'

'Oh. I see.' My hair ... I could remember in the evening, back home, my sister Mima brushing it out for me. 'A hundred strokes to make it shine', she had said. Once she had caught me looking in her mirror, admiring and swishing the tumbling blackness, and I can still recall her laughter. 'God, you should have been born a girl, Pell.' There was a bleak echo to those words now.

I pressed Red with my heels. He put his ears back as he skipped sideways into a trot. There was a strained air around us now. I was so prickly, and unconsciously, so vain.

Finally, I relented and spoke. 'How long have you been … Har, Flick?' My voice sounded imperious and prim even to me.

Flick suppressed a mocking smile. 'About a year, I think. I progressed from Ara to Neoma pretty quickly. I had a good teacher.' I did not ask him who that was as I was obviously supposed to.

'What is Harhune?' I said instead, to be awkward. I guessed he was forbidden to answer.

He pulled a face. 'Pellaz, I wish you wouldn't ask me things. It's so horrible when I can't tell you. Seel would have my skin if I did.'

Rage ignited in my throat. 'Oh, for God's sake!' I cried. 'Why is everything so damn secret. Don't tell Pell this, don't tell him that! He mustn't *know* anything. It's pathetic!' I was sick of the constant air of mystery; I thought it such a pose.

'Look,' Flick strained to be patient, 'tomorrow you will begin Forale. It's a day of fasting before the Harhune. Seel or someone will instruct you then.'

'Why didn't anyone tell me?!' I raged. 'If you hadn't, would I have woken up tomorrow and stuffed myself rigid before anyone mentioned I was supposed to be fasting? Hell, Hell, bloody Hell!!'

'No, no, tonight – they'll tell you tonight!' Flick was unsure of how to handle me, my tempers could be very colourful. I was pleased inside though. The end of my frustrating, innocent un-Harness was in sight. I had an idea what the Harhune actually was and I told Flick about it. He denied it vehemently.

'Oh, come on,' I goaded mercilessly, 'it's sex, isn't it. That's what it is.'

'God, Pell, what cloud are you on?! Sex is important, yes, but it certainly isn't the be-all and end-all of our existence and it definitely isn't what the Harhune is all about. Stop provoking me; I'm not going to tell you.'

He kicked his pony into a scrabbling canter and darted away from me. Red bucked as I made him catch up. Flick's pony was no match for him. Ahead of us the black cliffs reared to the sky and water thundered down their glistening flanks. Steam roiled about us like smoke.

'Flick! I want to ask you another question!' I shouted.

Flick screwed up his face again. 'Oh no!'

'It's not a forbidden one.' I sidled Red up against Flick's pony so I would not have to scream at him. 'Did you ever meet Zack?'

Flick gave me another of his strange, guarded looks. 'Yes. Why?'

'I'm just curious, that's all. What was he like?' I tried to keep an insouciant note in my voice.

'What was he like? Wild ... wild and reckless. Witty, courageous, fierce, gorgeous ... do you want me to go on?'

'Yes. What did he look like?' My heart was thudding; I felt breathless. Flick had warmed to the subject.

'He looked like ... like, I don't know. He was a bit like Cal, only as dark as Cal is fair. High cheekbones, sulky eyes. In a way you remind me of him; the same temperament I think. That's probably why Cal is kelos over you. He and Zack were chesna.'

'Flick,' I said, shaking my head at him. 'What the hell are you talking about. You must know I don't understand half of it.'

He grinned. 'Yes, I know. Kelos is crazy, chesna is ... well, more than friends.' A fatuous smile spread across my face. I could not get rid of it.

'Cal is not ... not kelos, crazy about me, Flick. Surely I'd know if he was.'

'Sure. Like you know everything else about Wraeththu.'

I could say nothing more. With an ear-splitting screech, I panicked Red into a mad gallop; the stinging, flying air lathering my exhilaration. Tomorrow, tomorrow it would begin. My un-Harness would soon be nothing but a frustrating memory. The consequences? Oh, I banished them, what I knew, banished them from my mind. It was too much of an exquisite torment to think of them.

Supper was a subdued affair. I avoided looking at Cal, and Flick avidly watched what I was doing. Seel smoked cigarette after cigarette, I had never met such an addict, and Cal looked so glum he did not even notice I was avoiding him. Not exactly a party atmosphere. Surely, we should have been celebrating my approaching Harhune. When we had finished eating, Cal and Flick discreetly left the room. We were in Seel's exotic little salon.

'Pellaz, we have to talk,' he said gravely.

I was feeling edgy and hysterical and wished he would smile. I half knew what he wanted to say, but I still felt stricken, petrified inside. He took my hand. His was cool, long-fingered and dry; mine was shaky and sweaty. He turned it over and half-heartedly examined the palm as he spoke.

'You want to be Wraeththu, don't you?' It was not a question and I said nothing, but swallowed noisily. 'Tomorrow you can begin your initiation into our way of life. I have to warn you, it will not be easy, and for that reason, you must be absolutely sure you want to go through with it.' His dark eyes seemed enormous; I was hypnotised. They stared right into me, peeling away the constructions of ego. I nodded.

'I'm sure. I've come this far ...'

'That was nothing!' Seel snorted and let go of my hand, which hit the table like a dead fish. He leaned back into the cushions. I felt foolish. It was all so unreal. I longed to laugh whilst still stretched transparent by nerves. 'You know very little and, frankly, that is the best way to be. I expect you find it very irritating.'

'Yes. A bit,' I confessed in a quiet voice.

'Hmmm. Well, at midnight, tonight, I will take you to the Forale-house. The Forale is what we call the day before Harhune. You will be cleansed and given instruction. You must eat nothing. Do you understand?'

'Yes.' He was so cold, so unlike the Seel I had come to expect over the last day.

'Now, all you need to know is that the Harhune itself is painless. You don't have to be afraid.' That was one thing I had not anticipated: pain. It unnerved me that Seel should mention it. 'Just think of it like this. In a few days' time it will all be over and you'll know everything you want to. Now, you have an hour or so yet. Do you want to see Cal before I take you away?'

His voice was less harsh.

I glanced up at him; a face inscrutable with restrained amusement. 'Yes ... please.'

He laughed then and patted my shoulder, reaching for another cigarette. 'Treat him gently, he's as nervous as you are.'

Yes, I thought, probably because he knows what is going to happen to me.

Cal slunk in like a guilty dog and Seel left us alone. When our eyes met it was like being scalded and we both looked away quickly.

'I brought you into this,' Cal said with a grimace and a weak attempt at humour.

As usual, all the wrong things started pouring from my mouth. 'I don't know what's happening, but the way everyone's carrying on, it must be worse than I think. Unhealthy for me, anyway!'

Cal sat down beside me. 'Oh, fuck! Fuck! Fuck!' he profaned. I had never heard him swear before; he was so fastidious. 'Oh, God, I don't care what the law says. I'm not supposed to tell you anything but, yes, in a way, it is unhealthy. You must have heard the stories; some of them even died... It's not all exaggeration, you know.'

'Oh Cal!' I gasped. 'Thanks! Thanks!' I put my head in my hands, arrowed by shock. Possible death was a consequence of becoming Wraeththu I had not considered.

'You had to know. There is a risk, but I think knowing that will make you stronger. You are strong, Pell.' I looked at him through my fingers. He was sallow with worry. 'It's necessary,' he said. 'We cannot afford to carry dead wood.'

'I know.' I straightened my back and closed my eyes. I could feel my hair, soon to be gone, heavy on my shoulders; the first time I had even noticed its weight. 'I want to be Wraeththu,' I murmured.

'I want you to be as well,' said Cal and inevitably we fumbled towards each other. Nearly every time we had touched, I had clung to him like a mewling brat. Tonight was no exception. He wound his fingers in my hair and stroked my neck. I could feel him sighing. His smell was clean and musky, like new-mown hay.

'You've only known me a week, or so,' I said.

'A week, a lifetime; what difference?' He held me so tightly, I nearly choked.

Seel walked in and found us like that, just holding onto each other as if for the last time. He passed no comment, but he obviously did not trust Cal not to blab everything to me. We had been alone for about ten minutes.

Just before midnight, Seel stood up and signalled to me. 'Now, Pell,' he said.

'Just bring him back in one piece,' Cal told him, not smiling.

'Oh come on, Calanthe, my dear, you'll be there, watching, I know you will.' Seel started herding me towards the door. As we left, he called back over his shoulder. 'Just start thinking about aruna, Cal!' And he laughed.

'What's that?' I asked him, not really expecting an answer.

'The finest time of your life, little Pellaz. If only I could be you.'

A sentiment I was not averse to sharing, adding drily, 'If I get through the Harhune, of course.'

Seel made a small noise of annoyance. 'You're not safe for a minute, are you. I might have known he'd tell you something. Cal's so emotional, I sometimes think he's still half human.'

There is a point when facing the unknown stops being a longed-for adventure and becomes a terrifying reality. When you are young, it is so easy to blunder into situations when misplaced heroism is no substitute for good sense. As I followed Seel to the Forale-house, I started doubting. I had no idea what they would do to me. I had given myself into the hands of strangers with no assurance that they were concerned about my well-being. Cal had glamourized me. His wistful and haunting beauty, his mysterious and perhaps violent past, appealed to me, an inexperienced and immature boy, as make-believe superheroes had appealed to young boys throughout the ages. As much as I realized my impulsive folly, I also knew that it was too late to back out. I would never have been able to find my way home, even if the Wraeththu had allowed it. Perhaps, too, I now knew too much, little as it was, for them to let me go. As Seel opened the door to my fate, the brief intimacy with Cal and the way I had felt about him, had faded. All I knew was that stultifying, indescribable sensation that is the one true fear.

The light inside was dim, but I could make out a bare room, furnished with as little as was practical. A narrow bed stuck out from the far wall. There was a strong smell of creosote. All I wanted to do was curl up on the floor and shut my eyes tight until everything went away.

'Pellaz.' Seel's touch on my shoulder brought me round a little. His eyes told me all I needed to know. Once, he had been in my place. Once even Seel had stood at the threshhold of acceptance, doubting. For the first time, I noticed the faint lines around his eyes and the shadow within them that told of the fighting, the struggle. What were Wraeththu?

'Pell, this is Mur and Garis. They are here to help you through the next few days. They will attend to you.'

Two figures were standing in the doorway to another room. Neither looked at me with sympathy, only a kind of resigned boredom. They moved, with slouching ennui, to either side of Seel, sharp and angular strangers, dressed in dull grey. Seel lifted his head, his face shadowed yet luminous in the yellow light.

'Pellaz Unhar, now is the time of your Inception. It is decreed that you shall be prepared in your physical, mental and spiritual states for your approaching Harhune. Do you deliver yourself into our hands for this time, your Forale?'

'Yes.' My voice was faint, but what else could I have said.

'Then we may commence.' He relaxed and rubbed his face, casting off the incongruous image of high priest. Normally, I would have laughed at it all; arcane words and special effects. At the time, it was deadly serious.

'Garis and Mur will bathe you now,' he said. 'I can promise you, by the end of all this you will hate the sight of a bath. See you tomorrow.'

Without a further glance at me he went out, letting the door swing shut with a horrible finality behind him.

'This way,' the one called Garis drawled at me. Grey shirt, grey trousers, iron-grey hair, like the colour of a horse, half plaited and held up on his head with loose combs. His feet were bare, the toe-nails more like claws. Mur was similarly attired, only his hair was dyed black, mostly cut short and spiked everywhere except at the nape of his neck, where it was braided to below his shoulder-blades. I followed them into the other room which was lit more brilliantly. Two lamps. It was a bathroom that looked more like a dissecting chamber. Two scrubbed tables, a deep, narrow bath and a sink that looked like steel. All that was missing were the knives and the rubber gloves. Chatting to each other, not even looking at me, Mur and Garis pulled off my clothes. I stood there, shivering and naked, while they busied themselves about the room. Even if they had actually shouted, 'Pellaz, you are absolutely worthless!', it would not have been more clear. Thoughts of my old home echoed through my mind. Mima's smile, a dim colourless replay; squeaky sounds I could not understand. Somewhere nearby, Cal was sitting or standing, talking, drinking. Laughing? Did he think of me? Tears of a child dewed my lashes but did not fall. I let the strangers put me into the bath. Salt water licked at all my old cuts and scratches. Garis wrenched my arms as he scrubbed at me. It felt like they were rubbing slivers of glass into my skin.

At the end of it, I was lifted out, impersonally, and dried off with a coarse towel, red and smarting from head to toe.

'Here, put that on!' Garis threw me a bundle of cloth. As I struggled wretchedly to dress myself, the other two laughed together. I dared say nothing, but I hated them. The kind of hate you can nearly see, it is so strong.

'You can go to bed now,' Mur mentioned, throwing a cold glance over his shoulder as he folded the towels. Garis leaned against the sink, preening his fingernails, looking at me through slitted eyes. He held me in utter contempt. I burned at the humiliation, the unfairness. They had several days during which to torment me. Hitching up the unflattering robe I was wearing, I shuffled back through the door. They started talking as soon as

I had gone.

'Human bodies are so disgusting, like animals,' Mur said.

'How lucky for you you never had one!' I heard Garis remind him sarcastically. Disgusting? Animal? To me I looked no different from them.

They extinguished the lamps before they left. Not a word of farewell. I huddled on the hard bed trying to warm myself with the thin blanket that covered it. Rough material chafed my skin and scratching myself only made it worse. A window, high up, showed me a perfect sky sequinned with lustrous stars. Moonlight fell across my face. I wanted to weep, but I was numb. Why were they so cruel? I could not understand, innocent as I was. Nobody had ever been actively hostile to me in my life before. Too beaten to be angry anymore, I sank into a restless sleep and the dreams, when they came, were ranting horrors, perverse possibilities.

I had been awake for what seemed hours when Seel sauntered in. He gave me a flask of water, and did not ask how I was feeling. Already my stomach was protesting furiously at not being fed. I had eaten poorly the day before and regretted it deeply now. Sitting dejectedly on the bed, still scratching, I sipped the water.

'Pellaz thinks he's in Hell.' Seel regarded me inscrutably. I said nothing. 'I can remember,' he continued. 'One day, perhaps, you will be in my position. Soon, you will see . . .'

'It is necessary,' I said dully.

Seel chewed his cheek thoughtfully. 'You must be purified. To do that you must suffer humiliation. Only from trial may the spirit flower,' he quoted, from something.

'Is this a lesson?' My spirit was far from flowering.

Seel raised an eyebrow. 'As a matter of fact, yes. Someone else is coming to instruct you fully, though. He's a high ranking Ulani, called Orien. Don't antagonize him, Pell. He may turn you into a frog.'

I could see he was struggling to be patient with me. I was supposed to be the abject supplicant awaiting enlightenment, but at the moment, I was slipping the other way.

Orien, however, did much to dispel my petulance. He was blessed with the kind of manner that instantly lightens the atmosphere. His clothes were threadbare and his hair, half tied back with a black ribbon, was escaping confinement over his shoulders. He rarely stopped smiling. Before beginning my lessons, he told me we would meditate together. 'Try to empty your mind,' he said, as we sat cross-legged on the floor. For me, that was an impossibility. I did not really know what meditation was and my mind was buzzing like a nest of wasps. I could not keep still. After a while, Orien sighed and rummaged in the bag he had brought with him. 'Put out your tongue, Pell.' He touched me with a bitter paste from a tiny glass pot. I grimaced and he smile at me. 'Come on, swallow.' My throat burned, but in a short time a pleasant coolness seeped through my limbs and crawled towards my mind. 'Now, we shall try again.'

This time it was easy. Gradually, I was eased into a white and soothing blankness and I began to drift, high above my troubles. Intelligence welled within me, as my situation hardened into sharp focus in my brain. I was so earthbound, so wrapped up in myself, I was blind to essential truths. Emotion filled me. It was there; the truth was within my grasp. The door was opening to me …

Orien's hands snapped together sharply. The wrench of coming back took my breath away. 'You are privileged, Pellaz,' he said, nodding. (What did he mean?) 'But you have a lot to learn. It is all strange to you and you have so much to overcome. Human prejudices, human bonds, human greed …'

'Human frailty,' I could not help adding. I remembered it from church.

Orien reached out to ruffle my hair. 'Pretty child, yes, that too,' he laughed. 'Now. Tell me what you think Wraeththu is.'

I was totally unprepared.

'Well?'

'I … I don't know.' It was feeble.

Orien was exhibiting that unfailing Wraeththu patience. 'Oh, come on. I can't believe you haven't thought about it. Tell me what you think.'

Next to him, Seel shifted his position on the floor and cleared his throat. He was either bored or embarassed.

'Well,' I began, leaning forward to clasp my toes. 'I suppose I think it started like a gang of boys ... I don't know ... something like that, and then it just grew. You don't think of yourselves as human though, do you, but I'm not sure what the difference is ... You all seem so ... so ... *old.* It sounds stupid ... you look young, but you're not ...' My mind was full of ideas but I did not have the words to voice them. I shook my head. Orien did not press me further. 'Old? I'm twenty-one, Seel's nineteen, aren't you?'

Seel did not look amused. 'No, twenty now, if it really is that important.'

'How old were you ..." I began, but Orien waved his hand to silence me.

'Questions later,' he said. 'Now, I am going to tell you exactly what you are getting into.'

Some years ago, in the north, a child was born. A mutant. Its body was strangely malformed in some respects. As it grew, this child exhibited many unusual traits that foxed both its parents and the doctors they consulted in their concern. Their son conversed earnestly with people they could not see; some of their neighbours' dogs feared him; other children shrank from him in horror. His mother complained she simply did not like the child; he was unlovable, withdrawn. Even as a baby he had snarled at her, refusing the breast. Once, some years later, as she had prepared his dinner, all the saucepans had risen off the stove and flown at her. Turning round, a silent scream frozen on her face, she had seen him standing in the doorway, watching.

On reaching puberty, the boy disappeared from home, and despite massive police investigation (accompanied by an insidious sense of relief experienced by the grieving parents), no clue to his fate was ever found ... for some time.

Months later, officials were baffled by a bizarre murder case in Carmine City. A young man, apparently having been sexually assaulted, had been found dead in a disused building. But it was far from the simple case it appeared; such killings commonplace in the city. The young man's insides had been eroded away as if by a powerful and caustic substance. Post mortem investigation revealed the presence of an unknown material in the body tissues, something that kept on burning even as it dried on the dissecting table. Under the microscope, it teemed with life like sperm, but unlike the sperm of any creature the scientists had seen before.

A mutant runaway had come alive in the city; alone, frightened and dangerous in his fear. He had learned just how different he was. His touch could mean death to those that offered him shelter, the sub-society of the city. He kept away from them, hiding in the terrible gaunt carcases of forgotten tenements; on the run, shivering in the dark.

Freaks roamed the steaming tips, the rubble. One came across him as he slept; lifted aside the foul sacks that covered him; gazed at his translucent glowing beauty. The veins on his neck showed blue through pearl, pumping with life. Some people are so far gone they would do anything to eat. One more day on the planet, one more day for the fleas, the rats, the sores. Freak lips on a mutant throat, broken teeth to tear. The mutant opened his eyes, relaxed beneath the lapping suction. He did not want to die. He knew he could not die.

For three days the freak writhed, gibbered and screamed on the soiled floor. Passively the mutant watched him, faint interest painted across his bland face. On the third day, the filth peeled away and the mutant was given an angel. An angel like himself, brimming with mysteries that alone he had had no inclination to explore.

The rest of it is now the legends of Wraeththu. Wraeththu, born in hate and bitterness, flexing their young, animal-strong muscles in the cities of the north. Always learning, always increasing their craft and cunning. Increasing. It was inevitable that eventually it touched someone who had the curiosity, the intelligence to probe within the mystery. Wraeththu lost its ungoverned, adolescent wildness; it became an occult society, hungry for knowledge. But what they found within the Temple appalled them; its vastness scared them. Some broke away from the search for truth and fell back into the old ways of fighting and living for the day. Those that remained faced the unavoidable truth: Mankind was on the wane, Wraeththu waxed to replace it. The first mutant faded into anonymity. Nobody was quite sure what had happened to him, but he had left strong leaders behind him. Now he had become a creature of legend, revered and feared as a god. Wraeththu did not believe he was dead, but that he'd elevated to a superior form of existence, monitoring or manipulating the development of his race. The Wraeththu grouped into tribes, each ascribing to varying beliefs, but all united in the Wraeththu spirit. They had the power to change the sons of men to be like themselves. As with the first, within three days of being infected with Wraeththu blood, the convert's body has completed the necessary changes. Many of them develop extra-sensory faculties. All are a supreme manifestation of the combined feminine and masculine spiritual constituents present in Mankind. Humanity has abused and abandoned its natural strengths: in Wraeththu it begins to bloom. Wraeththu are also known as hara, as Mankind are called men. Hara are ageless. Their allotted lifespan has not yet been assessed, but their bodies are immune to cellular destruction through time. As they are physically perfect, so must they strive towards spiritual perfection. If power is riches, then the treasure-chests of Wraeththu are depthless. Purity of spirit is the key; few ever attain it. But one day, when the ravages of man is just a memory, then the Few that have succeeded shall be the kings of the Earth.

I learned later on that all of this was Wraeththu perfection as Orien saw it. At the time, I believed all that he told me of Wraeththu's potential greatness because he seemed infinitely wiser than me. Only bitter experience taught me that he was misled, if not misleading himself. Nothing can be perfect in this world. I was curious about the different Wraeththu tribes, although Orien's knowledge on this subject was far from comprehensive. Owing to varying degrees of civil strife across the country, it had been possible for determined groups of

Wraeththu to seize towns from humans or else take over towns that had been deserted. Some had maintained a serious belief in occultism and were interested in furthering their powers, whilst others (and these Orien mentioned only briefly) were not so concerned about this aspect of themselves. What they *were* interested in, he neglected to mention.

The sun had travelled to its zenith; I was approaching mine. When Orien ceased speaking the hush still throbbed with his words. What I have told you is only the essence of it; there was much, much more. There was no question of my disbelieving him. To be there was to believe. My doubts were quenched.

'Tomorrow, Pellaz, a Wraeththu of Nahir-Nuri caste, the highest caste, shall come to Saltrock. He is known as the Hienama and it is his task to initiate new converts. A Hienama comes to Saltrock about twice a year. This time there will only be one conversion: yours. At the Harhune, he shall infect you with his blood. That is all. Admittedly, the whole thing will be dressed up in a lot of ritual, which gives everyone a good spectacle.' His voice was dry and I smiled at his irony. 'Now, do you have any questions?'

'Which hundred do you want first?' I replied. We all laughed, me louder than the others.

'Just start at the beginning,' Seel advised.

'Right. Why must I fast today?' This was punctuated by a timely growl from my stomach.

'So that your body will find it easier to cope with the Harhune. For medical reasons.'

'And how will I change?' I could tell this was the question Orien liked least of all. He twisted his mouth and looked at the ceiling.

'I must admit, I prefer this question to be answered by experience. I don't want to alarm you.'

I looked at him steadily. 'Please. I would prefer to know.'

He sighed. 'Yes. Very well. Most of the changes are internal. You must have realized that Wraeththu can reproduce amongst themselves (I hadn't), but not in the same way as humankind do.

It involves the physical union of two hara, yes, but to conceive life takes more than mere copulation. Essentially, our young are not formed within ourselves in the accepted sense. Only those of high caste may procreate. Sex is also important for reasons other than reproduction. We do not even call it that. When hara have a high regard for each other they can take aruna: that is pleasure, the exchange of essences. Grissecon is a communion of bodies for occult purposes, but I doubt whether that will concern you for quite some time. Inside you, new parts will begin to grow and externally, your organs of generation shall be improved, refined.'

I felt faint. Images of castration brought a taste of blood to my mouth. Orien smiled grimly at my pallor. 'Now you may wish you had not asked. But there is nothing to fear; it is not as bad as you imagine. Nothing will be taken away; nothing. One thing you must realize, Pellaz; what you will become is not Man, it is something different. Male, female as separate entities must lose its meaning for you. You must stop thinking of yourself as human.'

I barely heard him. I was still listening to what had been said before, wanting to shout, 'Show me! Show me!', but lacking the nerve. What was hidden from my view? Repulsion filled my throat, but I swallowed and closed my mind: from this point there was no returning.

A knock on the door signalled Mur's arrival bearing a flask of saffron-water for me to drink. I was shaking so much I could hardly manage it. There were no more questions inside me. Nothing seemed important now; my elation had dissipated. I needed to think. Sensing my inner turmoil, Orien and Seel exchanged a glance and stood up. Seel yawned, stretched and turned away from me, no doubt already thinking of his lunch. At that point I realized how much I envied him, simultaneously remembering his words: 'You may be in my position one day.' I could not imagine it.

'We shall leave you now,' Orien announced. 'Think about what you have learned.' It seemed they could not wait to get away.

Left alone, I gave myself up to grief. Harhune. Wraeththu. Much more than I had imagined, so much more. It was impossible my sobs could not be heard outside. I was held fast in the jaws of the trap, awaiting only the heavy, inevitable tread of the hunter. What was beyond the darkness? I fantasized Cal bursting in. He would tell me we were leaving, now, and our flight would be speed-trails of dust to the south. But Cal was one of them. A freak. One of them. Human once. Was he? Was he? I had touched him. Arms around each other like creatures that are the same. (Male, female; which one? Both?) Bile scalded the back of my tongue. Cal. A monster who had brought me to this. At Seel's house, he had known. He had known and he had not told me. It was a wicked, evil trick. I would avenge myself, avenge the humanity within me so soon to die. Death. I even contemplated it, looking wildly round the room for some tool of self-destruction. But they had foreseen that, hadn't they? Did they trust me not to destroy myself? I curled tight on the floor. Tight. Into the darkness. Whimpering.

That was how they found me at night-fall. Mur and Garis. They lifted me up without warmth. 'Drink this.' I swallowed and tore myself away, wretching and coughing. Steel-strong hands clamped the back of my neck. 'Drink it all, damn you.' My throat worked. Liquid spilled over my chin. Almost immediately, the drug began to work. I was calm. Light-headed, but lucid. Scrambling, I made my way to the bed and sat there.

Garis, hands on hips, shook his head as he looked at me. 'You can hate us all you want, little animal,' he said.

'Shut up!' Mur snapped at him. 'Get him in the other room.'

I would not wait for them to force me. I stood up and stalked through by myself, submitted myself to their attentions without a sound. As they would not look at me, so I did not look at them. They did not mock me again.

Seel came in to see me later on. I had been half-dozing on the bed, lulled by the philtre I had been given. There was no grief left inside me, only resignation. All I retained of myself was dignity. Whatever they took from me they could not destroy that. Pride that was the essence of me. 'We will come for you mid-morning,' Seel said, pacing the room. He smelled of nicotine, wine and, faintly, of cooking.

'I wanted to kill myself this afternoon,' I remarked in a flat voice.

Seel stopped pacing and looked at me. 'You didn't though.'

Angrily, I turned over so I could not see him.

'Pell, I know all this. Every little goddamn bit of it. It may only be a small comfort, but once I felt just as bad as you do now.'

'Small comfort,' I agreed.

'I was fourteen,' he said. 'Incepted in a filthy cellar, my arms cut with glass. You don't know how lucky you are!'

I said nothing. I did not care.

Seel decided to continue with his instructions. 'The Harhune will take place in the Nayati. That's a kind of hall . . .'

'Yes. Yes. Thanks for the vocabulary,' I butted in coldly. What did I care what the damn place was called. Abattoir was enough.

'Look, you wanted this!' Seel erupted. I turned back to look at him. His face said: spoilt brat. He was tired of me.

'Did I?' We stared at each other and it was me that relented. 'Yes. Yes I did.'

Seel's shoulders slumped and he sighed through his nose. 'Don't be bitter, Pell. You will regret nothing, I promise you.'

I could not tell whether he wanted to console me or justify himself. But, of course, one kind word and my control began to slip. I began to shake uncontrollably. Seel was beside me in an instant. I could imagine him wondering how he had come to be shouting at me. It was not part of the ritual.

'Seel', I said, 'if you mean that . . . about no regrets . . . you must tell me again and again and again. Make me believe it. But it has to be the truth.'

He held me in his arms and told me and told me and told me. I had led a sheltered, barricaded life, and was young for my years in so many ways. I cannot stress enough how ignorant and confused I was. One minute the Wraeththu seemed to me like sassy street kids, just dressed up and then the next minute they were creatures I was afraid of, inhuman monsters, speaking words that sounded old. The truth was they were actually both of these things. They did not know themselves exactly what they were or would become. All I needed at the time, though, was what Seel gave me. Comforting arms and proof that Wraeththu were warm with real flesh and real blood. He must have stayed with me until I fell asleep. I did not wake till morning, and when I did I was alone.

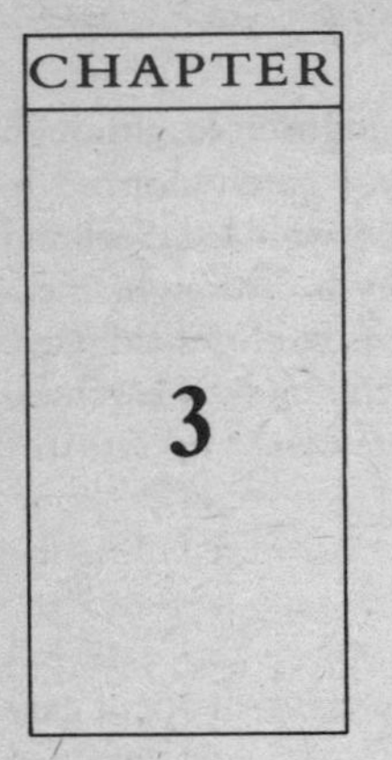

CHAPTER 3

The gates stand open, enter into light

The greatest virtue in Man is his undying sense of hope. A hidden reserve of optimism woke with me that day. I would not dishonour myself. My life was caught upon the Wheel of Fate, but I would face my future with dignity and strength. I was apprehensive, yes, but still almost light-hearted by the time Mur and Garis came to bathe me for the last time. Gone was the corroding salt, the rough towels. I was sluiced with hot, smoky perfume and patted dry with purified linen. Aromatic oils were kneaded into my skin, gold powder shaken onto my shoulders and my hair brushed and brushed until even the split ends shone like dull silk. A new robe, of sombre black, was wrapped around me; eyes were dabbed with balm to take away the swelling my tears had left behind. Mur and Garis, almost pleasant with the sense of achievement, stood back to inspect their work. I was ready.

When Seel and Orien arrived they were dressed splendidly for the occasion. They seemed taller than I remembered, proud and graceful, and treated me like a bride, which I supposed, in a sense, I was. Seel put white lilies in my hair, avoiding my eyes, and offered me a goblet of blue glass. The liquid inside it looked murky and tasted foul. I downed it as quickly as I could. They would take no chances with me; I would be drugged almost senseless.

The white light outside stung my eyes and I winced, although the taint of soda no longer bothered me. I barely noticed it. Before I could take a single step forward, I wobbled. Seel and Orien swiftly took hold of my arms. They had brought me a chariot, strewn with flowers and ribbons; pale horses fidgeted, festooned with colour, plaited with silk and tassels. Wraeththu had already gathered to line the streets we would take to the Nayati. An air of festival vibrated up the sky; they all shone, these supernatural, hypernatural folk, and strange, ululating cries fluted round our heads. Otherworld melodies, and the horses pranced forward, sand skirling in our wake. The hot breezes were intoxicating with the fresh, green smell of cut garlands, petals crushed beneath the capering hooves. I was wedged upright, but nobody could see that. My hair streamed back like a black flag, dappled with fragments of crushed blossoms, palest pink, white and lemon-coloured. Exultation fountained through me. I felt like a king.

Shallow white steps led to the main doors of the Nayati. Petals still danced in the hot air like confetti. The moment my feet hit the ground I felt like I was walking upsidedown. Only willpower kept nausea where it belonged, in my imagination. I had never been really drunk, but thought it must have been like that. Nothing mattered and responsibility had been taken from me. We walked into the solemn and sacred gloom of the Nayati. It took some moments for my eyes to adjust to the poor light, but soon the high, narrow hall materialized before me out of the gloom. Tiers of seats reared into the shadows on both sides; from flank entrances the Hara of Saltrock filed into their places. All voices were muted, but the whispering quiet could not hide the mounting fever, the heights of expectation implied by half-seen movements above me. I stood between Seel and Orien at the threshhold. Light streamed in behind us, dust-moted bars. Gilden metal flashed in the dimness beyond. Seel lifted a long, carven staff from a bracket by the door. He struck the ground three times and the congregation rose, rumbling, to its feet. 'Harhune! Harhune!' It began as a soft crooning, and we advanced among them. And then it was a mighty clamour, my skin prickled, voices ringing like clarions as they bayed me forward. I? I was not there really. I was someone else's dream carried forward on the strength of their tuneless cry.

We came to a place where patterns had been chalked onto the floor, and they pushed me to my knees. White dust sprayed my robe, and Seel spoke; softly, it seemed, but his voice filled the hall.

'Today we witness the inception of Pellaz Unhar. He is deemed fit by myself, Seel Griselming and my colleague Orien Farnell.'

He raised his arms above his head and the soft white cloth of his sleeves slipped back. Henna patterns were painted on his skin; designs similar to those beneath my knees. 'Does the Harhune take place?!' he demanded and a mighty, 'Aye!' shook the walls. They blessed me with fire, with water, earth and air, ripped my robe to below my shoulders and wrote on my skin. Henna again, aromatic and gritty. Seel's voice was gutteral; I could not understand what he said, but the crowd were mouthing silently along with him, howling the responses, half-rising from their seats in excitement. I hated to think of Cal being one of them, but he kept creeping into my mind. I kept thinking, 'They want my blood, they want my blood', but, of course, the opposite was true. They wanted me to have theirs. This was their ceremony. Mine was yet to come.

Hours later, moments later, two young hara, sparkling in white and gold, came out of the smoky dark at the back of the hall. Soft cloth falling to their feet made them glide like ghosts. One carried a shallow metal dish, his companion holding out the instruments of my hair's death. Seel was before me. He raised my head with a firm hand. 'The Shicawm, Pellaz. Be still.' I could not shudder but my teeth ached, I had clenched them so. Cold metal touched my brow and I shut my eyes. The sound was terrible, sickening. I could feel it all falling away and hear the silvery swish as it landed on the shallow dish. So quick. It was gone. 'Open your eyes,' Seel told me, barely audible. It was like looking at an execution. Under my nose, long black locks spilled over the plate, still adorned with waxen, wilted lilies. I half expected to see blood and a thread of hysteria cracked the numbness. It was an effort not to reach up and touch my head. I started to shiver then.

Hands were upon my shoulders and I shook beneath their warmth. Light flared up ahead of me and the dark rafters of the Nayati loomed above, suddenly visible, encrusted with gargoyles who laughed and screamed forever in silence. Tall metal stands made an avenue, topped by filigreed bowls of incense; smoke so heavy it drifted downwards in matted shrouds. At the end a white table gleamed like marble; and beyond that?

A slim reed of light opening out like a flower. Tall. A halo of fiery red-gold hair. An angel. A demon. The hienama. (I heard Seel gasp: 'Him? Him?!', urgent with surprise, and Orien's sober answer: 'I know.') The congregation crooned once more, upon their knees, and the hienama moved; arms peeling out from his sides, one stretched straight, the other slightly curved, his body half turned towards me. I should have known then who he was. But it took years and years, and even then somebody had to tell me. He never tried to deceive anyone, they were just blind, I think. Looking back, it was obvious. He was more than all of them, and he knew about me. He put his mark on me that day, made me his pawn, but, like I said, it took years for him to put me into play.

I was lifted to my feet. Led forward. No, carried. My legs would not work and my feet dragged as if my ankles were broken. As we went towards him, he grew. Not in actual height, but in magnificence. Slanting, gold-flecked violet eyes lasered straight to my soul. Fire seemed to burn in his hair and flicker over his skin. Nahir-nuri. He had the compassion of a vivisectionist.

They lifted me onto the stone table and all I could do was look at him. (Cold bit into me; the caress of a sepulchre.) His voice is almost impossible to describe. It was full of music but with darker tones, like the sound of gunfire or shatterable things that were breaking. 'Welcome, Pellaz. I am Thiede.' Like night falling, black draperies softly descended. There was a sound like falling snow, hardly a sound at all, more a feeling, and the crowd could no longer see us. Only Orien and Seel remained. He signalled to them, tying his own arm above the elbow with a knotted cord, always looking at me, inspecting me carefully. I had seen that expression before, a life-time before, on my father's face as he chose a mule for himself. The dealer had been untrustworthy and he had not been sure if the mule was sound. I doubted that Thiede often made mistakes, though. His assessment of me was realized in one short glance.

'Don't be afraid,' he said indifferently. 'Seel, prepare him. Hurry up.'

The veins on my arms stood out like cords. They took away my robe and Thiede looked me up and down with the same indifference, and then he smiled at Seel.

'Yes. Very good.'

Seel moved half of his mouth in response. He did not look comfortable.

Thiede's glance whipped back to my face, the movement of a snake. 'You know what we're going to do?'

I blinked in reply.

'Are you here of your own free will?'

I think an insignificant 'yes' escaped the constriction of my throat.

Thiede nodded, stroking his arm. 'Give him the dope', he said, which I found incongruous. He turned away.

Something sharp slid into my arm, an unexpected medical shard in this arcane setting, and the cold poured into me. I had not expected that and was grateful. I thought the last thing I heard was 'Open his veins and drink from his heart,' but common-sense tells me it was something else. There was no pain.

By late afternoon of the third day, my fever had abated. I was still weak, my eyes hurt most at first, but I was alive. Mur and Garis, in attendance once again, sat me in a chair by the window while they stripped and changed my bedding. I mulled over what I could remember of the last three days.

It had been early evening of my Harhune day when I

regained consciousness, not knowing who, where or what I was. I had stared at the ceiling, breathing carefully, aware of pin-pricks of pain, like flashes of light, darting round inside me. Red light streamed into the room and a dark shadow hovered at my side.

'Pell, can you hear me?' Flick's voice.

It was all over. I was back at Seel's house in my own room.

'Pell?'

I could not move, my throat felt sewn up and I could not rip the threads. Flick pressed a beaker against my lips. It tasted like sugared water, warm, and my shrivelled mouth turned to slime.

'How long?' I croaked.

Flick dabbed at my face with a wet cloth smelling of lemons. 'About six hours or so. Do you feel any pain?'

'I don't know.' My body was still numbed by drugs. I might have imagined the pricklings. 'I can't feel anything.'

Flick sat down on the bed and examined my face carefully, pulling down my eyelids. I did not like the expression on his face. It was worse than I felt.

'I've seen quite a few through althaia,' he told me. 'Don't worry.'

I had not, till then. 'Althaia ...?'

Flick sponged my face again. 'The changing. It will take about three days. The thing is, Pell, when the drugs wear off, you're going to feel quite ill.'

'And I may die.'

Flick started to clean between my fingers, concentrating hard and not looking at me. 'A small risk, but you're a fighter. I told you, don't worry.'

My eyes felt hot. I closed them and tried to swallow. Flick offered me a drink. 'Where's Cal?' A sudden, irrational terror shot through me that he had left Saltrock without me. I tried to sit up and my limbs shrieked with pain and displeasure.

Flick pressed me back into the pillows. 'Stop it! Don't move!'

I struggled, oblivious of the discomfort. 'He's gone!' I half moaned, half screamed, threshing against Flick's restraining arms.

'No! No. It's alright. He's here. In the house. Downstairs. He's here. But you can't see him yet.'

Still fringed by hysteria I stopped moving, slumped beneath Flick's hands, which were hot and trembling. It was almost as painful to be still, but the struggle had tired me out. I had to close my eyes, and when I did, the darkness was shot with vague, pulsing colours.

'There, that's better. Lie still, Pell and rest. I'll be back later.'

I heard Flick leave the room, slowly. I heard him close the door, oh, so quietly. He would have run down the stairs.

Inside me, irreversible processes had begun to work, yet I could not feel it. No churnings, no bubblings, no strange movements. A sigh escaped me, high and lisping, and childhood tunes scampered from my memory. Now I skipped naked in the red dirt of the cable fields, Mima at my side, both of us laughing. Now the pink sky arced over us, a symbol of innocence; the dark was beneath the horizon.

The first assault, when it came, hurtled rudely through my half-sleep. It felt like a knife turning in my stomach, wrenching, pulling, tearing. My entrails were being torn from me. I shot upright in the bed, the room filled with a high, unearthly sound. My own scream. Half-blind with pain, I squinted at my stomach, terrified of what I might see. Nothing. No blood, no spilling, shining ropes. With sobbing breath I lowered myself back under the blankets. Tears ran down my face. The room was so quiet, not even an echo of my cry. Only quick, shallow breaths hissing in my head. As soon as I shut my eyes the invisible weapon plunged into me again. My body threw itself to the ground, arching in agony. Lights zig-zagged across my vision. I clawed the floor, the edge of the bed, myself, anything. (Stop this. Stop this!) A hard surface, cool and smooth, slapped against the back of my hand. I heaved myself forward and rested my cheek against it. (Somebody come. Somebody please come!) Eyes open, movement on the edge of my vision. I turned my head quickly, and looked. Looked into the hideous face of ... Something. Oh, that something! A fiend. A creature; ghastly. Screeching, I backed away, flailing my arms, falling, helpless.

Oh God! The grey-faced demon did the same. Mimicking, mocking. And then I realized. No demon, no creature. Hallucination? No. Just this: a mirror. That is all. As the pain ebbed from me once more, sick fascination made me look again. This ...? This! Whimpering, I crawled closer to the glass my half-naked scalp gleamed damp and white, a long matted plume of hair fell over my face. My face! Bloated, grey, the eyes rimmed with red, the mouth wet, purpled and slack. My body was bruised and discoloured, the left arm nearly twice its normal size. I could look no more. Crumpling onto the floor as a new spasm of incisive pain ripped through me, upwards, from my vitals to my throat. Mucus and blood and frenzied sound sprayed from me. My eyes were blinded by black, marching shapes and ziggurats of light.

Suddenly, activity, voices. 'Get him back on the bed!' Strident, unrecognizable. A softer tone: 'It's started.'

Hands lifted me and where they touched, raw skin seemed to be peeling away like charred paper. Distorted faces peered down at me, eyes like saucers. And then a thin trickle of bitter juice was forced between my swollen lips. My jaws were clenched so tightly, someone had to hit me hard to force them apart. The agony was indescribable. Death would have been preferable, and fight to the death it was. Thiede's blood and mine, and if mine won I knew there would be no me left. As suddenly as it came, the pain shot back to a hidden place to brood. The room flickered, lurched and then settled, perspective see-sawing back to reality. I was gulping breath, swallowing foulness.

'A short respite, Pell.' Seel's face hovered over me, disembodied, pale. 'This is just the beginning, but we are with you.'

Smells of fading years, years of innocence, came back to tease me. An untimely stillness of Autumn changed the room. Mellow light. The changing; it had begun. My changing. Within myself, within myself.

That was the last thing I could remember clearly. Afterwards, it was horror, pain, fever, filth and sickness. Occasionally, I would feel lucid enough to understand what was happening around me, usually in the afternoon or dead of night. Then the stillness would make me weep as they changed my bedding yet again with weary, fraying patience. Faces haunted my delirium: faces of the future and the past. Sometimes they fought beside me, hands on the same torn banner, but sometimes they only chittered on the edge of my awareness, mere observers.

Mur rubbed my flaking skin with balm. Weeping sores and blisters burst beneath his fingers. He never spoke, only pushing his braided hair back over his shoulder when it fell forward, a frown between his eyes. Once, I remember, vomit flew from my mouth in a great arc and my body constricted like a bow. I was shrieking, 'I'm full of insects!' or some such nonsense. Another time, I was convinced the room was alive with squeaking bats, or something like bats, and I was afraid they would settle on my face to block my nose and mouth. Every time I awoke the room was completely different. When the bats were there, it looked just like a cave. Often I hit out at those who tried to help me. Garis lost his temper when I blacked his eye and smacked me across the face. When he did that, the room exploded with stars and I spiralled, laughing hysterically, like a helix-shaped atom on the air. Sometimes, if they left me alone for even a second, I would get out of bed and crawl, gibbering round the room. I kept wanting to get in corners because I felt more comfortable with walls on two sides of me. They would find me, crouched and demented, blood and bile running out of me across the floor. That was some of it. There was more, perhaps worse; thankfully, most of it now forgotten. But I lived to tell the tale, coming out of it; exhausted, wasted, yet alive.

Mur and Garis whispered about me across the bed. I felt they no longer despised me but their presence was still no comfort. A cat jumped in through the window with a musical greeting and leapt into my lap. I tensed, but there was no pain. The animal crawled up my chest and butted my chin with his head, purring rapturously. I hugged him fiercely and he did not struggle. Then I dared to think it: why had Cal not been to see me? A thought I had been rejecting for some time. Was the althaia so repulsive to him? On reflection, it was probably better that he had kept away. Sleek Pellaz of the desert journey was no longer in residence. I had zealously avoided glancing into mirrors because I was sure my appearance still bordered on horrific. I had still not examined my body for outward changes. When Mur, or one of the others attended to me, I kept my eyes shut. I really did not feel any different, apart from ill. I knew I would have to face Cal again soon and it filled me with different tremors. Fear, anger, pleasure and, something else. Something I examined least of all.

The chair was uncomfortable. I squirmed. Mur was beside me. He was kinder towards me than Garis, less harsh, although just as quick with sarcasm. Because of my condition any riposte I attempted was usually embarrassingly feeble. Though I now knew that their cruel treatment of me had been for a purpose, that of bringing me down to a level from which I could rise afresh, they never completely warmed to me. Could beings as perfect as Wraeththu were supposed to be behave in such a way? Part of my ignorance was that I never questioned this.

'Pellaz, try to stand,' he told me. I just looked up at him stupidly. 'Come on!' He stood in front of me, offering his hands. Stand? My legs felt as supportive as thin gristle, but I clasped the arms of the chair. It wobbled beneath me as I struggled to rise. The room swerved around me and nausea punched my ribs.

'I can't!' Sweat bubbled from my pores.

'Yes you can. Come on, you have to walk to the bathroom with me.'

No mercy, as usual. He held my elbow. 'Lean on me.' I did not feel pain exactly, but the sensation was sickening. All my guts seemed loose and my loins tingled. Mur half dragged me across the room, accompanied by Garis' spiteful amusement.

I was bathed again. Mur laughed without cruelty and told me to open my eyes, but I would not.

'You should wash yourself now,' he said. 'Stop trying to be ill.' He left me sitting there in the cooling water. 'When you've finished, call me,' he remarked over his shoulder. 'Don't be scared, it's perfect.'

Blood scorched my face, but he did not see. He was already

complaining to Garis in the other room. 'Help me, will you!' The rustle of my sheets being bundled into the linen basket.

I sat there for about five minutes before I dared to open my eyes. Even then I stared at the wall for a while. It was getting dark. Goose pimples invaded my skin. 'Hurry up!' Garis called. I could smell food cooking somewhere below. Horses neighed outside, in the distance. All the light was dim and the air was fragrant with herbs. I looked, and looked, and looked again. There was no damage, no scars. Just this exquisite instrument of magic and pleasure. Not changed too much, just redesigned. An orchid on a feathered, velvet shaft. It is something like that. When I touched it, it opened up like a flower, something moved in the heart of it, but I had seen enough for now. I knelt up in the bath, shivering and called, 'Mur!' When he stood in the doorway, our eyes met and a great sense of recognition went through me. That which marked us more indelibly than anything else as Men, a crudity, was transformed in Wraeththu to something alien and beautiful. If it is hidden, it is not from modesty or the fear of giving offence, but because the revealing of it is that much more delightful for its secrecy. Men did not know about this, but we knew. Mur smiled. Relief melted something hard and cold inside me.

Back in the bedroom, Mur and Garis set about pampering me. They massaged my skin with oil, fluffed my hair, scented me with pungent essences and disguised my eyes with kohl.

I was a little suspicious. 'What is all this for? More rituals?' I think Garis would have liked to have given me the back of his hand, hard, across the mouth, but he contented himself with ignoring my questions and curtly silencing Mur if he opened his mouth to answer me.

Tidying away their things, Mur said, 'You must rest now, Pellaz. Go back to bed. Don't overdo it yet.'

I felt he was trying to communicate something to me without Garis knowing, but I could not fathom it out. Mur was beginning to like me, or feel sorry for me. He arranged the pillows behind my shoulders before he left.

Once alone, I struggled out of the blankets and weaved over

to the mirror. Spots of light speckled my vision, but when the dizziness cleared, I could see myself. Once I would have been ashamed at the rush of pleasure my own reflection gave me, but Cal had done something towards dispelling that attitude. Now, I instinctively drew myself up taller, throwing back my head, gazing haughtily back at myself. I liked the shape of my head, and the sides of it shaved, and the shape of my jaw. I looked leaner and somehow older. Ironically, I remembered my sixteenth birthday had past forgotten two days before. Was I now a woman, a woman who needed no breasts to nurse her young, no swelling hips to carry them? And was I not also a man, a man that needed no woman? They had told me there was nothing to fear; nothing.

A knock on the door made me jump. I did not want to be caught posing, and scrabbled, panicking back to the bed. I was beneath the blankets by the time it opened. Then fear and awe and shyness converged within me; it was Thiede. He was standing there in the doorway, so blatantly, unashamedly inhuman, a towering monolith of potency and power. He flicked his fingers and Mur hurried past him into the room, carrying a tray of food. He virtually threw it on the bed and rushed out again without speaking. Thiede closed the door behind him. I cringed beneath his stare, unable to look away. He was, and always is, marvellous to look at. He prolonged the silence, maybe unintentionally, just gazing at me implacably. When he spoke, his voice made me jump again. 'Well. How are you Pellaz?' 'Oh, fine.' I could not clear my throat properly and my voice sounded squeaky. He nodded disinterestedly, turning away, examining the room. How could he be curious about it? 'Eat, eat!' he said, waving his hand. I looked at the tray of food with aversion. Thiede's presence did nothing to stimulate the appetite, but I obediently picked up a hunk of bread. It turned to glue in my mouth, and I struggled to swallow.

'Pellaz, now that you are har, there is one final ceremony to be undergone. A ceremony that will make you truly har, and one, I might add, that will make permanent those transformations that have taken place within you.' Where was this leading? 'They will have told you what aruna is,' he stated flatly. A dreadful suspicion flashed through me. Not him! He knew what I was thinking, of course, and fixed me with an indignant scowl.

'No,' he said, drily, and then with humour, 'not that I wouldn't like to, but in your present state, well, I do not want to be responsible for your death ...'

He came to sit on the bed and I hated him being so close. It was like a fear of being scorched.

'You're so quiet, Pellaz, and so scared. Terror of the unknown, I suppose, and so attractive in the newly har.'

He settled himself more comfortably.

'My task as hienama is to prepare you for what comes next. We shall have an intimate little talk, Pellaz.'

I still could not speak. Surely he could hear my heart.

'Aruna: the exchange of essences. First you shall be soume, shall I say the least demanding role? Accept the essence as an elixir; you need it ... I am pleased with you Pellaz, very pleased.'

He stretched out a hand to touch my face. I could understand nothing of what he was saying.

'Now listen to me carefully,' he continued. 'Aruna can be a powerful thing. It is not merely the basic thing it appears, but a coming together of two dynamic beings, a mingling of their inner forces. A drawing together. Hear this, Pellaz. One day a stranger will recognize you and you shall recognize him. You will both *know.* Inexorably you will gravitate towards each other and only in aruna express your innate need. Not only the exchange of essences, achieved through that elevating state aruna is, but something more. One day, your seed will become a pearl in the nurturing organs of another. Then you will sire your first son ... then. But for now ...' He stood up again, smoothed the soft material of his trousers, shook out his hair and turned to look at me again. 'Do not confuse what may happen to you with the self-destructive emotions of Mankind. They once called it love, didn't they? So true, so special, so rotten. Hara may come together for aruna; their friendships may be loyal, but there is never the greed of possession to blacken the heart. Never. Does it frighten you to hear me say we can never fall in love?' I shook my head, wishing he would leave. 'I'm glad you understand me. They have chosen for you, Pellaz. You are in good hands, or so Seel tells me.' He was no longer looking at me, walking to the middle of the room. 'Surpass yourself, Pellaz. Take hold of the life I have given you.'

I had not spoken once. Perhaps drowsiness overtook me, perhaps the door opened, perhaps the air fractured around me ... The next time I looked at that place in the room where Thiede had stood, he had gone. I tried hard to think about what he had said but could not understand most of it. I shivered. Aruna. The word that sounded whispering, blue-green, shadowed. I put the tray of food down on the floor and lay back on the bed. Outside, the sun sank lower and lower until the light in the room had nearly faded away. No-one came to light my lamp or to take my tray away. The house felt empty. Not even a cat to keep me company. I kept thinking of Thiede and suddenly the gloom frightened me. I jumped off the bed too quickly and reeled over to the table. Dizzy and shaking, I fumbled with the matches, heart pounding. As a welcome petal of light bloomed in the glass the door opened behind me.

I felt it rather than heard it, expecting 'What are you doing? Get back on the bed!' or some such outburst, but it did not come. Before I turned, I knew it would be Cal. His face was a mirror: me in the caressing lamplight.

'Oh, it's you.' My voice barely shook. I could not bear to look at him and went back to sit on the bed where the light was dimmer. Actors on a stage, playing out this premeditated performance. He knew his part well. I did not even know my lines. Anger made me itch. I wanted to look up at him with welcome in my eyes, but shyness and embarrassment had frozen all sensation. Encased in ice it glowed there inside me.

'Hello, Pell,' he said, in a voice which told me he knew I was going to be difficult.

Fists clenched in my lap, I launched into the attack. 'Well, as you see, I am alive. Had they told you? I thought, perhaps, you'd left Saltrock.' I had my back to him, but could vividly imagine his eyes rolling upward in exasperation. No reaction. I brought out the big guns. 'Why are you here?'

'It's my room. While you were ill, I was sleeping elsewhere. I'm moving back in now, if you don't mind.'

Well countered, I thought. His voice gave nothing away. I wondered how long he would wait. Was he ordered to produce results? He sauntered over to my window chair and flamboyantly threw himself down in it, steepling his hands, tapping his lips with his fingers, staring passively out at the yard below. I would have given anything for Thiede's talent of perception. Cal's thoughts were barred by stronger locks than I could break through. Huge, white moths batted moistly against the window, trying to reach the halo of my lamp, or the halo of Cal's bright hair. I wanted him to beat down my defences, but guessed instinctively he never would. Cal was a great believer in letting other people take the initiative. He made them work for him, just conceited enough to know that they always would. (How could I have known that Cal's darker side went a lot deeper than mere conceit?) Sitting there, sparring and sniping and circling each other, we both knew what the score was. It was just a question of who would back down first. It might easily have gone on for days. I wanted to say, 'Cal, look at me. I am Har. I am one of you. We are equal, you cannot treat me as less.' My mind was racing in the awkward silence. He would say nothing. I would have to provoke him again. 'Cal,' I began, and his eyes lashed up and caught me, calculating, without warmth, challenging. The merest implication of a smile hovered over his face. 'Go on,' he was thinking, 'go on.'

'I …' (Oh God, what?), 'I still get tired easily. Thiede was here … I'm … well, goodnight.' I could feel him studying me as I burrowed into the blankets, lying there, heart pounding, reciting childhood prayers; I think those few moments are among the worst I have ever lived through. Something hit my pillow, softly. Through slitted eyes I saw a single perfect crocus inches from my nose. Deep purple fading to lilac at the petals' tip, an aching yellow flame within its heart.

'Where did you get it?' I asked. No answer. Seel's flower

garden, I thought. His ritual flowers. I felt Cal sit down heavily on the other side of the bed, humming quietly to himself; thuds as his boots hit the floor. I could not resist looking at him. He was lifting his loose white shirt over his head, brown skin and white linen, standing up to finish undressing. He had his back to me, stretching like a cat. All the Wraeththu things inside me that needed aruna were going berserk. He looked over his shoulder at me and I shut my eyes. I heard him laugh, quietly. My body felt uncomfortable. I wanted to run away. I wanted Cal. I could not cope. He could so easily have put me out of my misery with a single word of reassurance. When I could bear it no longer and looked at him again, he was lying beside me, some distance away, arms behind his head, just gazing at the ceiling.

'We were friends once,' he said, conversationally.

'You didn't come . . .'

'I couldn't. You should know that.'

'Why?'

I heard him sigh.

'Because . . . I had my own rituals to go through.'

'Cal.'

He looked at me and laughed. 'Oh, I know, I know. I'm sorry. Why do you make me so angry? I know. You make me feel inadequate, can you believe that?' I shook my head, confused. 'Oh, God, you're incredible. I can't get used to having found you. Come here.' He pulled my nightshirt over my head. 'There, that's better. Skin to skin.' His hands stroked my back, while I clung to him as usual, scared to move. 'It is an enormous privilege to share breath, Pell,' he told me. 'You can even get power over someone that way.'

'How?' I could only say the right things. He made it happen that way.

'Oh, like this.' Now I was no longer Unhar, it was different. I could taste his soul. I knew then that we had not shared breath before, no matter what he had told me that first night back on the cable farm. It had been nothing in comparison. Would it have poisoned me then if we had?

'Even aruna is not quite like that,' he said, 'What do you think?'

'What do *you* think!?' We laughed, hugging like children, sharing our breath again, getting mixed up in each other, like overlapping colours, tasting each other; his a taste of ripening corn and sunlight on fur. He pulled away to look at me.

'In the desert, I nearly killed you. I nearly jumped on you,' he said. 'You're exquisite. The crocus. Let me look at you; all of you.' He tossed back the bedclothes and cool air hit my skin with his eyes. 'Thiede is interested in you,' he remarked. 'He knows something about you. Too perfect. What are you?'

'Yours,' I told him, making him laugh.

'Oh, I don't think so. But just for now I'll happily believe that.'

I asked him, 'Cal, why have I done this? What made me do this? Was it Fate that I've become Wraeththu? Did I have a choice? Will I . . .?'

'Hush,' he answered. 'If there are a thousand reasons or only one, the outcome is the same.'

'Is that an answer?!'

'Not really,' he said, smiling. 'Believe the answer is merely that I wanted you, that I bewitched you into coming with me. Perhaps you didn't have a choice . . .'

'Are you telling me the truth?'

'Perhaps.' He laughed and folded his arms around me like wings.

I never asked those questions again.

There is no coupling in eternity that can rival aruna. After a while we did not talk again; there was no need. Thoughts transferred between us like kisses. It was like dreaming and being in someone else's dream all at the same time. A star of pain inside me shot out light like a comet. It was a signal. His face was serious, but he did not speak, just culminated our foreplay by laying me back gently on the pillows. I was in agony, but for a while he did nothing, almost afraid. Feverishly, I reached for him, calling his name. End this torment. Dark flower. Touch. The star of pain fizzed wildly and went out. Tides of another ocean washed me delirious. Inside me, deep inside me, a nerve, a second heart, throbbed, itched, desperate to be stilled. Something snaked out from the heart of the flower and licked it like a bee's tongue. The heat of liquid fire engulfed us, sizzling our sweat and I cried out. Aruna. Ecstasy that can kill. The poison fire that is narcotic. I could never have imagined so much. The finest time of my life? There was something in what Seel had said. Later, others would bring sparks to my eyes, but that time, that first time . . . I could speak of it forever and never fully convey the magic, the power, the union that makes us strong. Nothing like the affairs of men: it is quite different.

We recovered and Cal said, 'Be ouana for me, Pell,' shining, lazy, passive. We blazed again, and I bloomed within him. When the dawn came, we slept, but even in my dreams, it was the fires of aruna flaring and flickering, a dense inferno, the heart of the volcano, flowers and ashes.

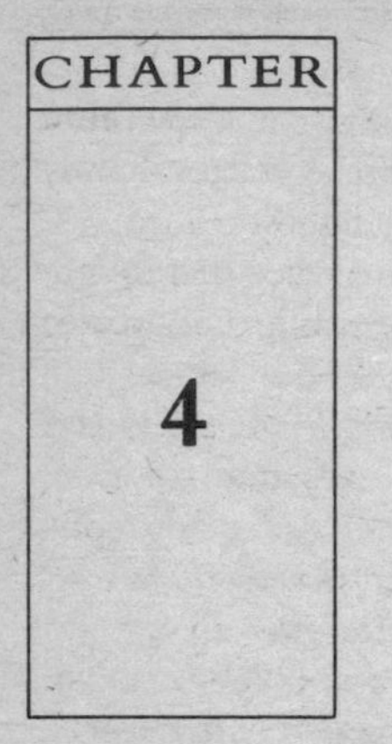

CHAPTER

4

On the learning of craft, and beyond sanctuary

My caste was Kaimana, my level Ara. The beginning. Kaimana progresses through three levels; Ara, Neoma and Brynie. Ara means altar and signifies a time of learning and preparation. I had many things to learn; basic occultism as I found out later. Its strange and lavish ritual intrigued me and I took the Oath that bound me to secrecy. There have been books based upon the codes of our religion. This is not one of them. As I speak to you directly through these pages, so I take heed of my vows. To those who already know the truth, there is no need for me to enlighten them. At that time, I had also to come to terms with the biology of my body, to understand its limitations and abilities. I learned to flex the muscles of my mind, so long unused.

Cal and I lived in Saltrock for about eighteen months and during that time I progressed from Ara to Neoma. Everything I learned came mainly from Orien, a patient and wise teacher. Seel taught me the mysteries and uses of plants (that knowledge was invaluable), whilst Cal, never less than that first time, explored with me the horizons of my sexuality. I suppose I was living in a kind of comfortable vacuum. Saltrock is cut off from the real world in a sense, if only by its location. Often, Wraeththu from other places would make their way there, some hideously scarred in mind and body by the wars and skirmishes beyond the mountains. One thing was clear: Wraeththu was becoming more powerful and Mankind responded valiantly to its threat, but the old world was disappearing fast.

We sometimes heard tales of the Gelaming; they that fought hardest of all and were rumoured to have the most sophisticated technology known on Earth.

'At the beginning,' Cal told me, 'Gelaming were the finest, the brightest; in secret, so long ago. Men did not know about us then; that came later, with the killing. They may never know our true nature. (It was incredible to you too once, wasn't it?) They that joined us, the lucky ones, will be the only survivors.'

Immanion reared, splendid and shining, somewhere faraway. One day, Cal vowed, we would find it. Saltrock, meantime, grew more solid, more stable with every day that passed. As Seel predicted, a generator was somehow procured and flickering electricity soon lit the lengthening streets and sturdier houses of the town. Saltrock would never be a proud and haughty temple city like Immanion, but it became a place, where even to this day, I could go to find peace and good company.

During that time I heard no more from Thiede. Sometimes, if I stopped to think about it, a threatening prickle of apprehension would scare me. Thiede had made no secret of his interest in me and he was stronger and more dangerous than we all knew. Several weeks after my Harhune, I was talking to Flick about Thiede's visit to my bedroom and how it had disturbed me. For a moment or two Flick looked at me as if I was mad.

'You must have been hallucinating still,' he said. I laughed, although a little annoyed that he did not believe me.

'It's true,' I insisted. 'Thiede did come to see me and he said strange things. I wasn't hallucinating. Mur was there as well.'

'But, Pell,' Flick replied, his voice beginning to falter with bewilderment. 'We all saw it. The day after your Harhune. Thiede left Saltrock. Everyone turned out to see him go; he rode away on a great, white horse . . .'

'Then . . .' My skin freckled with goose-bumps and Flick rubbed his bare arms as if he were cold.

'Then . . . well, he is Nahir-Nuri. That's all there is to say.'

But it was more than that. Thiede is a law unto himself. It is possible, though difficult, to handle him, but not an exercise I would recommend. At that time I looked on him as a kind of god, now I know better. He has his limitations; they are just farther than everybody else's.

One day, a young emaciated Har stumbled, half-dead, into Saltrock. His body was in an appalling state and those proficient in medicine were perplexed by its cause. Orien read the crystals to find the answer. Oh, the ways of Men. How they revel in destruction. Now they had discovered a virus lethal to Wraeththu-kind and had lost no time in exploiting it. I was terrified. I thought it would be the end of everything.

Cal laughed at my fears. 'It is a mere tick on the skin of Wraeththu,' he professed.

I was amazed at his optimism. 'How can we combat such a thing?' I argued.

'Simple,' he told me. 'Our strength can eradicate it easily.'

We had to wait for the next full moon. A week and a half. During that time, three hara of Saltrock fell sick with the killer virus. The carrier could not be saved; he was dead two days after his arrival, already two-thirds decomposed.

One day Cal said to me, 'Tonight, Grissecon shall be performed. Then you shall see. There is nothing men can throw at us we cannot handle effectively.'

He had taken me to the shores of the soda lake to tell me. Instinctively I knew there was something more.

'Why bring me here to tell me this?' I asked. He put his hands upon my shoulders.

'I'm not sure how you'll feel about this. It will be Seel and myself who will perform the Grissecon.' For a moment I did not realize what he meant and stared blankly at him. 'Pell, you would have to face this sooner or later. We cannot be selfish with each other. Here, in Saltrock, it is easy. Many Hara are paired off... but this, this is different. Orien has told me it will have to be Seel's essences and mine. We are the only combination here that will work.'

He did not know that I had been anticipating something like

this happening for some time. Cal often expected me to react in a humanly jealous way to a lot of things. Probably because my temperament had made such an impact on him before my Harhune, in the desert, when he was still raw from what had happened in the North. I was different now; almost detached from emotional matters. I felt a lot for Cal and always will, but I was not possessive about him. Outside, a lot of Wraeththu have degenerated from the True Spirit, and are once again the prey of their own emotions. Thiede's blood ran in my veins, his words stamped indelibly in my head. Unbeknown to anyone, I was more Wraeththu than most, and my emotions were slave to me rather than the other way around. I put my arms round Cal's neck and kissed his cheek.

'Your essence is healing,' I told him. 'I know you will destroy this curse.' I could feel his relief like a golden rain in my eyes. I would watch him work magic with Seel and be proud. Grissecon, simply, is sex magic. Power is a natural result of aruna, which is normally wasted, dissipating into the air. Now I would have the opportunity of seeing this power harnessed, the potent essence of Seel and Cal combined, taken as a living force and directed back against those that cursed us. Somewhere, a resistant pocket of humankind had combined their own efforts in an attempt to destroy us, ignorant (as indeed I was at first) of Wraeththu's ability to fight back.

Saltrock has a sandy central square. It is often used for various meetings or ceremonies, and also for social gatherings. Everyone clustered there that night. I went with Flick. Seel and Cal had been absent from the house for two days to undergo purification. We all sat in a wide circle around a central fire. Orien, as shaman, conducted the preliminaries and we all chanted along with him. He threw grains into the fire and it flared up blue. When Seel and Cal were brought out to us, magnificent and clothed in gossamer, everyone cried out. We were drunk on excitement and pride. Seel's hair had been unbound from its usual rags and ribbons confinement and it seemed to me as if it had a life of its own; all those different colours catching the light of the fire. Cal was simply the primeval embodiment of Wraeththu, his violet eyes shining like midnight from the first days of Eden. By the light of the sapphire flames and the star-crusted, indigo sky above, Cal and Seel sank down together in the dust. They spoke the language of angels and their draperies blew away, into the fire, crackling up into the air like will-o-the-wisps. The throbbing of drums, hand-beaten, rose up behind the crowd; a deep, passionate growling like thunder. We, the gathered, thumped the ground with our fists, our bodies aroused in tune with the workers of magic. When the moment came for the flower to strike, Seel uttered a cry, strange and echoing and I seemed to see it drift from his mouth like an azure smoke, glowing as if a strong light shone through it. Did I see that? I saw Orien hold aloft a glass ball and the blue vapour seemed to coil into it. Cal stood up. In the flickering shadows, Seel still writhed on the sand, half replete, his hair lashing like angry snakes in the dirt. Orien's acolytes rushed forward to milk his essence into a curling glass tube. Cal and Seel mixed. When they held the tube out for us to inspect, I could see it glowing gold and red and purple. Then Orien took it away. He would use this elixir to work on the bodies of the sick and send the soul of the sacred seed speeding out on the ether to do battle. Everything has a life-force; even evil sickness conceived beneath the long eye of the microscope. Back in the square, we thought no more about it for a time. Seel had clawed Cal back to his arms and around us everyone fell to the same activity. I looked at Flick, his little anxious face looking up at me. Only a short time ago, I had felt inadequate beside him. I cupped my hand behind his neck and he closed his eyes.

By morning, it was as if the sickness had never been. I had been shown a little of what we were capable of. In a way, it was hard for me to grasp what I had witnessed, hard to believe that it was real. Did I possess this power too? Was it waiting within me? The sickness had gone. One death to remind us; that was all.

As I had pointed out before, I had no particular skills to offer the Hara of Saltrock, yet I could not expect to live there without making some contribution towards the town. I turned my hand to many things: working in the strange, lush gardens under the black cliffs, where vegetables and flowering plants grew with grisly splendour and hugeness; assisting in the construction of new buildings (gradually the tents and makeshift cabins were disappearing); grasping the rudiments of vehicle technology (we had several ailing cars to work with, but lacked many of the tools needed to make them run, and what fuel we had was precious). Sometimes, I would climb alone to the lip of the glossy, dark cliffs, the staunch wall of Saltrock, and gaze out over the landscape. In the distance, rough abandoned farmland wrinkled the surface of the Earth; a pale road cut through it. Beyond that I would often see lights winking in the haze or vague movements. One day I would pass that way, and when I thought that, a deep and thrilling wave would shiver me.

In the mornings I worked, but most afternoons were set aside for study. Orien's house was made of stone, small inside and dark. He lived alone. It was rumoured that when the first Wraeththu had come to the soda lake, this little stone building had already been there. Lost, abandoned; who had lived there? No bones had been found, but several fine cats were existing comfortably in what was left of the sparse furnishings. Orien said it was improbable that they had built the place. When I laughed at this, I had the uncanny suspicion that he had not been making a joke. Orien often came out with outlandish suggestions that I later regretted having been amused at. Anyway, since the beginnings of Saltrock, the cats had mysteriously multiplied in numbers. By mysteriously I mean that it happened too quickly to have been by natural means. They are now the familiar spirits of Saltrock. When other Hara came bringing with them other types of animal, the cats showed no hostility to the invaders of their territory. How they had lived untended in that cruel, barren countryside, with so little to hunt and eat, is an enigma, as is their philosophical tolerance of other animals. That was the first thing that Orien and I talked about.

He would give me books to read and then ask me later for my opinions of them. Often I had had difficulty with the language; some of the books were so old. He studied me very carefully as I talked, watching my face more intently than listening to my voice, I thought. Something puzzled him and he told me about it.

'I get a feeling about you, Pell. What is it? What's so different about you? I've instructed dozens of newly-incepted Hara, but you ... Your beauty is uncanny. It's more inside you than on the surface.'

I still could not accept such talk without embarrassment. 'No, no, not more than many others,' I pointed out quickly. 'There is nothing different about me. I was born a peasant ...'

'You do not talk like a peasant,' Orien suggested, awaiting my response.

Something made me say, 'It is Thiede,' and Orien raised an immaculate eyebrow.

'Perhaps?'

'What is he?' I asked, somehow frightened, like looking into a huge space, dark and cold; somehow sure Orien would know the answer.

'No-one knows for sure,' he said, guardedly. 'Thiede is certainly *different* to any other Nahir-Nuri I've met. Sometimes he seems barely even Wraeththu. But then, we are a new race. Those of Nahir-Nuri caste are relatively few at present. One day I shall understand perhaps. However, Thiede has only been here twice before and then never as Hienama.'

I was shocked. 'You mean I am the first ...?' (A memory: Seel surprised. 'Him?!')

'Yes,' Orien confirmed. 'He has never performed a Harhune here before. Yet here he was, as if by magic, when you were ready for yours. Pell, I feel I should warn you, but I don't know what against.'

As if by common consent, Orien and I never mentioned Thiede again to each other. By now, I realized it was important to progress, for my own protection perhaps. Aspects of my training would often leave me unnerved, like waking from a bad dream. The first time, for example, that my own unsuspecting mind made contact with another's, filled me with disquieting anxiety. Orien spoke to me without words. He touched my brow lightly and I heard him say, 'Rise, Pell, rise …' His lips never moved. I tried to communicate back and he laughed and stepped away, telling me that my thoughts were as confusing as a whirlwind. It took time for me to relax enough to touch his mind with calm and confidence. I learned also how to manipulate matter to my will, the concentration for which is exhausting. Many times, I was at the point of giving up, only Orien's soothing encouragement keeping me going. The first time I managed to shift a small cup along a tabletop by sheer willpower alone, I nearly wept with relief. I was learning to flex my muscles, the muscles of my own power. Lack of confidence was the worst handicap, and the first that Orien was anxious to help me overcome. To his credit, through patience and understanding, he succeeded. I studied hard and within six months passed to Neoma. Then Orien told me that I would have to continue my studies elsewhere to ascend to Brynie. Saltrock did not have enough Hara of third-level Ulani to conduct the ceremony. I did not want to leave. My life at Saltrock had been nothing other than blissful. I had learned many things and made many friends. When we worked together, I revelled in the shared sense of achievement. I did not want to lose that. Yet I also knew that I must go on. Neoma was not enough. It was obvious to myself and to everybody, that I had great reserves of ability. I had no intention of letting it atrophy from disuse before I even discovered it fully.

Cal was still obsessed with finding Immanion. Often, when we lay in the afterglow of aruna, curled around each other like sleepy snakes, he would relate at great length all he believed Immanion to be. A place of great beauty, calm and symmetry; certainly a place where Wraeththu had disassociated themselves from the violence and chaos of the world and had built up a superior society, tranquil and affluent. It would be a place of soaring crystal towers, glistening in the brilliance of perpetual sunlight. Cal thought it was somewhere all Hara should naturally head for. I was shrewd enough to realize that the Gelaming hid its location because they preferred to seek out themselves the people they wanted within its walls; nobody would ever find it by chance. However, I humoured him. It would have been presumptuous of me to contradict him. He would say, 'Don't get uppity, Pell, you've seen nothing yet. Saltrock's a haven,' if ever I did pass an opinion he considered was founded on imagination. I knew I had acquired knowledge Cal could never learn, and I also knew where it sprang from. Something made me hide it; respect for Cal was not the least of the reasons.

One day Seel had to go to another town for supplies. It was decided Cal and I would go with him. The time had come for us to go on. We would not return to Saltrock with Seel. On the last night, we had a farewell party in the square. I was nearly heart-broken. It was possible we would never see our friends again; anything could happen Outside. Everyone was there. Mur and Garis, lean, gothic and sharp as needles to the end. Mur shared breath with me and I could taste ice and metal. Flick, I could only hug to me, genuinely sorry to leave him. His was a taste of welcoming fire in a cosy room and soft animal fur. He was a true friend, and when the time came, I turned the world upside-down to find him again.

The fire had sunk low and nearly everyone had drifted back to their homes when Orien bid me farewell. He gave me a talisman, which I still have, of a sacred eye.

'Be strong, Pell,' he said, and I could feel tears behind my eyes. It was difficult to speak.

'Only you know ...' My voice quavered; I could not help it. Orien nodded, firelight shining through his hair, his face in darkness.

'Be wise as well,' he said. 'The time will come ...' I threw myself against him, my chest tight with grief.

'I know, I know!'

Orien knew more of my fate than he cared to tell me, but he could not see all of it. Somewhere, out there, my future hovered like a poison insect. Orien let me weep out my fear.

'After this time, Pell, never show your tears. Never! You are a child no longer.'

It was advice I took to heart.

In the cold light of pre-dawn, I saddled up Red outside Seel's house. All the windows were dark with farewell, as if we had already gone. Cal had used a little of our money to buy another horse off Seel, bigger and showier than Red, but not as hardy and, surprisingly, not as fast. Seel had been going to use a pick-up truck for the journey, but because we were going as well, and on horseback, he settled for a covered cart drawn by two heavy horses. Because it was a slower and more vulnerable method of transport, he took three armed Hara with him as protection. All our good-byes had been concluded the night before, and no-one came out to see us off. When I had come to Saltrock my clothes had been barely more than rags covering the gangling awkwardness of youth. Now, when I caught a glimpse of myself in Seel's windows, I realized I had changed beyond all recognition. Gone was the tatty-haired, grubby child with the luminous eyes, bony knees and bony shoulders. I was a year and a half older and a year and a half taller. My hair was still cropped close at the sides of my head, but long down my back and combed high over the crown and wisping into my eyes. Clad in leather and black linen, silver hoops hung through my hair, three in each ear. I spared a thought for Mima and the rest of my family. Would they have recognized me? No. For the essence of the Pellaz they had nurtured had gone. All I retained of my former self was the memory of it.

I had had to leave most of the belongings I had collected behind. Cal refused to waste money on a pack horse. Also, it would have slowed us down. I had not got much, but I was sad to leave it at Saltrock and reluctantly gave it all to Flick. We set off at a brisk trot, down to the farthest shore of the lake where a guarded pass led to the outside world. The rising sun gilded the sulphurous surfaces of the lake; drowsy birds clustered on crystal spars, gaunt, black shadows. Behind us, a dog barked to greet the morning. I did not look back; never again did I look back.

Greenling was not strictly a Wraeththu town. Men existed in surly, wary alliance with Hara. We arrived there, mid-afternoon, three days after leaving Saltrock. The land around it was dry, with desert encroaching from the south, but grudgingly fertile and the Wraeththu folk much more urbane. Two women were walking down the road towards us and one of them recognized Seel. She waved and ran over to us. Seel, being the charmer that he is, has an easy, friendly manner with humankind. The woman jumped up on the cart beside him. I realized with some amazement, even disgust, that they were flirting with each other. The men of Greenling, whether by accident or by commonsense, were clever in their acceptance of Wraeththu. Although their kind were dwindling, they would carry on unmolested and in peace until the end. Needless to say, this was not a common circumstance. In other areas humankind would not give up the idea that they were meant to rule the world. In those places, men and Hara fought each other like dogs for territory, for commodities, for fuel. Not many places had the calm air of Greenling, where the two races existed alongside each other, somewhat reluctantly sharing resources.

Seel called me forward. 'Pell, this is Kate. I usually stay with her family when I come here.'

She began to smile, then looked alarmed. 'We haven't got room for all of you!'

'I know, I know,' Seel teased her. 'We'll put up at Feeny's place. Anyway, your father would see us off with a shotgun. He can only handle Wraeththu when they're in a minority.'

Kate's smile came back again then and she relaxed against the seat, proud to be seen with us.

Feeny's was a small hostel-come-bar and seedy in the extreme. The proprietor, a large, oily man and an apparent stranger to the concept of hygiene, grumbled at having to find room for six. While Cal organized our rooms, Kate grabbed my arm and flounced me off to buy a drink. She bought me a beer (uncannily enough one of the first things she did next time we met). Boyish in her manner, barely older then myself, she sprawled on a stool like an ungainly colt, appraising me with green eyes. 'I curse the day I was born a woman,' she told me.

'I can see that,' I muttered drily. She unnerved me because

she reminded me of Mima, although in appearance they were entirely dissimilar. Kate had blond hair, the kind that is almost green, and not such a bony face as my sister.

'It's so unfair,' she continued, wiping her mouth with the back of her hand (a hardened beer drinker!), 'I know I would make a brilliant Har.'

What could I say to that? I could not tease her like Seel. She could sense my discomfort and hated it. She asked me my name, how old I was, where I was born, even how I did my hair!

'Why me?' I asked her, attempting to stem the flow of her questions. 'Have you pestered all the others like this?'

'Oh no!' she exclaimed with an endearing innocence, and shaking her head vigorously. 'You were the most beautiful.'

'I shall have to wear a mask then,' I laughed, 'Otherwise I might be hounded by inquisitive girls to the ends of the earth.'

'Wear a mask?' she grimaced with a careless wave of her hand and taking another gulp of her drink. 'What makes you think that will hide it?'

There was some truth in what she said. It wasn't beauty that marked me though, but something else. Something that would draw trouble towards me like a magnet when the time came.

As the sun sank, Greenling Hara came to drink at the bar. Sultry and rather unsociable creatures, festooned with decoration; heavy earrings, thick bangles laced with spikes and chains. Seel and Cal and I sat apart in a corner. Tomorrow we would part and there was little conversation between us. Cal reached out and curled his fingers round Seel's arm where it lay on the wet tabletop. 'Stay with us tonight,' he said. He kicked me on the ankle, sharply, pressing me to silence. Seel said nothing to Cal but turned to look at me. I briefly touched their hands where they lay.

'We both want you to,' I said, not really sure if that was true. I still had fears of showing myself up. Cal and Flick were the only ones I had taken aruna with. But I need not have worried. Seel wanted us to remember him. It was the only way to say farewell.

It was decided we would travel south, back into the Desert.

Out there, hidden in the dreary scrub, bleak dunes and rocky terraces dwelt the Wraeththu who could take me to Brynie. The desert people: Kakkahaar. I had been told of their cautious instincts, their preferred solitude. It would not be easy to find them, even less so to enlist their help.

Once again, Cal and I had to stock up on supplies and Seel advised us to purchase things that the Kakkahaar might find appealing. Runes, incense and coloured scrying beads from a Wraeththu shop in Greenling centre. We also bought weapons, long knives that were expensive but essential, from a surly, lank-haired man in a cluttered shop reeking of human sweat. Afterwards, we loitered round Feeny's till noon, drinking sour coffee at the bar and laughing at our occult purchases. But our humour was underscored by sorrow. That afternoon, we would make the final break with Saltrock and sanctuary. I think in our hearts, both Cal and I longed to say, 'Damn it, Seel, we're coming back with you.' But to do that would have been to go against destiny. There was no way back; for me especially, and Seel, beautiful Seel, who in times to come became a great leader, a tactful and trustworthy politician, his future too would have been spoiled had we returned to Saltrock. It is also true that someone else was marked for death that day.

When the bar began to fill with lunchtime patrons, both human and Wraeththu, Cal and I prepared ourselves to leave. Outside, we blinked in the brilliant sunlight. Red and the other horse, Splice, were already loaded up and waiting, sleepily kicking the dust.

'Greenling might be the last peaceful place you'll visit,' Seel said, musing aloud. Leather creaked in the hot sun and we gathered up our reins.

'Goodbye Seel.' I reached for his hand. Splice's head went up, ears flattened, as Cal made him prance into life.

'Come on, Pell!' he said irritably, and his horse sprang forward, halfway up the road in seconds. I looked at Seel but he shook his head.

'It's alright. Go on.'

And so we left him, Cal galloping Splice into a lather, an

expression like fury on his face.

Two miles into the desert's perimeter, a jeep screamed out of a dust cloud and swung to a halt beside us. Red stood stock still, ears pricked, muscles tensed, while Splice made a scene, side-stepping, half-rearing. Someone jumped out of the driving seat, leaving the engine running. It was Kate.

'What the fuck do you think you're doing?!' Cal exploded at her, attempting not too successfully to get Splice under control. Kate came straight to me.

'Pell, I'm sorry, I meant to catch you earlier. I went to Feeny's but you were gone. I've got something for you.'

She pointed to the jeep and I followed her over to it. 'Here,' she said. 'Guns.' She was smiling up at me with that deceptively innocent expression, holding out the weapons.

'Where did you get them?' I had never handled a gun before, but I knew weapons were probably the only thing that would ensure our survival, and bullets were more effective than blades.

'My father,' she explained. 'He deals with many things. He'll probably miss them, but what the hell. It'll be too late then.'

Cal snatched the other gun from her hands, weighing it up, gazing over the barrel. Kate frowned at him, not really understanding his ignorance. She handed me a peeling box of ammunition.

'Don't mind him,' I said, nodding at Cal. 'Thanks anyway. How much do you want for them?'

She laughed. 'What? Oh, nothing, nothing.'

'We'll think of you, then, when we're fighting for our lives,' I joked and she nodded.

'Till we meet again,' she said, swinging back up into the jeep, 'and I'm sure we will.'

'I fucking hope not!' Cal replied, thankfully drowned out by the roaring engine.

As we rode away, he said to me, 'Don't be like Seel. Don't bother with men and their bitches. Remember, they'd kill us all if they could.'

'I'll remember that with the first bullet I fire,' I answered. Cal gave me a sour look but said nothing.

It seemed we travelled in circles. The ground underfoot was too stony for us to go faster than a walk and the landscape so monotonous, it was difficult to tell which way we were going. I thought of Saltrock, where everyone would be sitting down to eat after a day's work. Cal and I did not feel hungry and certainly did not feel inclined to stop and make camp. We would have felt vulnerable and unsheltered trying to rest out in the open. The light had gone from the sky by the time we found a tall, stark rock poking without welcome from the dry stones. Grumbling and unhappy, we tried to make ourselves comfortable beneath it. I felt guilty. If I had not been so insistent about the Kakkahaar, we could have travelled east, where there were other Wraeththu settlements, though small and of low caste. I had discovered that the majority of Wraeththu rarely passed to a higher level than Acantha, which is the first of Ulani. I could not progress without the aid of adepts, the knowledge-seekers. In a fit of self-pity, I started apologizing to Cal. It was my fault. We could have stayed in Saltrock for longer. The desert might starve us to death. Something of the old Cal broke through his reserves of grief at leaving Seel and the miseries of our position. He held me to him.

'Oh, Pell. Don't ever think me selfish. Never. I knew the moment I saw you, you were special. Brynie you shall have to be, and more. Tomorrow we shall set out and find the Kakkahaar. Without fail!'

It took slightly longer than that, however. We wandered about aimlessly for three days, eyeing our dwindling water with concern. The only pool we had found had been in the process of dissolving the carcase of an unspecified animal. Large, scraggy birds trailed us hopefully; flies appeared from nowhere, clustering like grapes around the animals' eyes, leaving unbearably irritating bites on our faces, hands and ankles. We were so dejected, we did not even notice the Kakkahaar had been trailing us along with the birds for about forty-eight hours. They made their presence known in the late afternoon of the third day.

CHAPTER 5

The inverted pentagram

They rose up out of the sand, unfolding like dune snakes ready to strike. Faceless, hooded, motionless. Cal drew Splice up sharply, biting his lip. He had no experience of the Kakkahaar and was unsure what our reception would be like. I was feeling dizzy with heat-sickness and in no mood to put up with any ritual feinting. Something made me draw Orien's talisman out of my shirt. I lifted its leather thong over my head and held it up for all to see, urging Red forward at a walk at the same time. The nearest figure strode towards me, his robe blowing all about him, the colour of the desert.

'What is your business?' he asked in a low, rasping voice.

I could see little of his face; a moving mouth, a strong, well-shaped chin. 'We are from Saltrock,' I began. 'The shaman, Orien Farnell has bidden me seek out the Kakkahaar.'

'For what purpose? Why tempt danger in the desert?' He spoke as the wind speaks, whistling over the shifting sands in the dead time before the dawn. A dreadful cold that changes the desert to a different kind of wilderness.

'I am Neomalid,' I answered. 'I have to pass to Brynie. There are not enough Hara of Algoma level at Saltrock ...'

Red was sniffing the stranger's robes, inquisitive. The whites of his eyes were showing.

'Give me your hand.' I leaned over and reached down. His fingers were dry and hard, and from that position I could see his eyes sparking beneath the folds of his hood.

'There is more.' His voice was little more than a whisper now; his followers still as sand-stone behind him.

'The one named Thiede incepted me.' There was no choice. I had to tell him, even though there was a risk that that information might go against me. I had no way of knowing what the Kakkahaar thought of Thiede.

The stranger drew his breath in sharply and stared at me intently for a moment. 'We are a nomad people.' He stepped back a pace or two and with careful grace, lifted both hands to his head to throw back his hood. 'Our camp is not far from here. Welcome. I am Lianvis.'

The Kakkahaar are steeped in mysticism; there are few amongst them less than Ulani, although they keep a choice selection of Aralids as servants. I expected them to lead an austere life, but in fact found them to be a luxury-loving tribe. They loved to be waited on, hungered for comfort and trinkets; their Ara attendants were dressed in diaphanous silks and heavily hung with gold adornments. I could tell Cal disapproved. He thought the Kakkahaar treated their Aralids like women, and although I could not disagree entirely, at no time did I meet anyone in the camp dissatisfied with the arrangement.

Lianvis, asking us polite questions about ourselves, but not too prying, led us to a tasselled pavilion; his home. Inside, it reminded me of Seel's living-room, though Seel would have been sick with envy had he seen it. The colour scheme was dark bronze, dark gold and black. Tall, decorated urns spouted fountains of peacock feathers, canopies hung down from a central pole sparkling with sequins. The tent was so large it had several different rooms. A near-naked Har with hair to his thighs bound with black pearls, rose from the couch. A book lay open there beside a half-eaten apple. He bowed before Lianvis. 'Ulaume, barley-tea for my guests. They need refreshment.' The Aralid looked at me from beneath long, thick lashes. His dark eyes looked bruised, his lips full as if aruna was never far from his thoughts. Never had I seen such a breathtaking, sulky beauty. Lianvis caught me staring. 'Magnificent, isn't it,' and then ushered us to be seated. I would not help but remember, with amusement, Seel's introduction of Flick. Enormous cushions, slippery silk and satin, littered the floor. We sank down into them and Lianvis sat down in front of us.

'I know of your Orien,' he said. 'A well-respected Har among Wraeththu-kind, though it is some time since we met. How are things at Saltrock?' All the Kakkahaar wear their hair incredibly long. Lianvis' pooled about him, the colour of honey.

'It progresses in leaps and bounds,' Cal told him. 'The terrain is difficult, but at least they can grow things.' Lianvis leaned back sighing.

'Ah yes. They work hard at Saltrock. Not the life for me, I fear. Not a day passes that I do not give thanks for how we earn our living.'

'How's that?' I asked, hoping it would not sound impertinent. Lianvis smiled, tapping his head.

'This. We are seers by reputation and people pay highly for glimpses, hints of their future. Men and Hara alike.'

Cal shook his head. 'You amaze me and I respect your genius.'

'Oh no, not genius, my dear Cal, oh no. Shrewdness, sharpness, cunning and a good sense of the dramatic.'

'You don't fool me,' Cal said with a smile. 'The Kakkahaar are full of genius. Cunning, maybe, but extremely clever cunning.'

Lianvis was enjoying himself immensely, lapping up the compliments. Ulaume brought in the barley-tea and a silver plate of thin-cut aromatic bread spread neatly with butter. Cal and I were so famished we fell upon the food like wolves.

Lianvis was apologetic. 'How foolish of me, you must be ravenous. Ulaume, something a little more substantial, if you please.' Cal slid an embarrassed smirk at me but we made no comment. 'The desert is an unpleasant road to suffer if you are improperly equipped. You have no pack-horse, I see?'

We both had our mouths full and there was a strained silence broken only by the sound of chewing. Cal wiped his hands on his knees.

'No. We wanted to travel swiftly,' he said.

'Oh, but we have brought you something,' I put in quickly. 'Cal, where are they, those things . . .?'

'Later, later, please,' Lianvis urged, but looked interested.

Later, while he watched contentedly as we feasted ourselves on the meal Ulaume had prepared, I asked him how long it would take for me to be ready for the ascension to Brynie. He told me that they would assess me in the morning.

'Business tomorrow,' he said. 'You are tired and need to relax. Ulaume shall make ready a bath for you both.' He immediately made us conscious of our travel-stained, unwashed appearance.

Ulaume led us to another room. Cal's trousers were ripped across the backside. I thought it looked very becoming, but Ulaume snatched them out of his hands with a quick murmur about laundering and sewing. We splashed into a huge, dark-wood tub together while Ulaume hovered around, eyeing the rest of our clothes with aversion.

'I'll find you something else to wear,' he said finally, scooping them up distastefully and marching out, holding them at arms length. I laughed, hoping Ulaume would not hear. I did not want to be cruel.

'Pell, you're so beautiful,' Cal chanted, feeling sensual in the scented water. There was hardly enough room and most of the water fell out onto the floor, soaking the scattered goat-skins. We were half-drowned, high on aruna, when I noticed Ulaume watching, half concealed by the door curtains. Inscrutable, he caught my eye, twitched his mouth and walked out. What the hell. The Kakkahaar thought we were barbarians. Now Ulaume would tell Lianvis we coupled like animals, when the mood took us. I spent several minutes mopping the rugs with the towels afterwards. It took some time for me to discover what true barbarism was.

We spent a couple of hours with Lianvis after our bath, conversing freely on a superficial level. Our host amused us with tales of people who had sought out his talents.

'Of course, all that men want from us is our secrets. They think we drink from the fountain of eternal life and that is what they crave more than anything. As their women are drying up, so too must the well-spring of their race; they know this ...' Lianvis told us airily. On his fingers, rings set with huge tiger's eye gems shone dully in the lamplight. He asked me where I came from and I told him hurriedly; it was not a subject I cared to dwell upon.

He eyed me shrewdly. 'Peasant stock, eh? Strange, Pellaz, I could have sworn you had an educated air.'

'My father taught me some things ... and he had the priest to teach us the rest. You know, reading, writing and of course, God's message. He had a lot of books ...' I could not understand why he should think I was lying, and tried to make light of it. Cal was abnormally quiet beside me, never taking his eyes off Lianvis. He had a brooding, thoughtful look on his face.

'For a tribe that makes its living out of other people, you have an unusual reputation for solitude,' Cal said after a while. Lianvis shifted his attention from me, smothering a sharp alertness that flashed across his features.

'It's all part of the allure,' he said. 'It makes our prophecies seem that much more real ...' That made Cal laugh. It was not a pleasant sound and it embarrassed me. The tone was not lost on Lianvis.

Later, once we had retired to the chamber Lianvis had prepared for us, I tackled Cal about his behaviour.

'I'm not stupid enough to trust anyone as soon as I meet them!' he snapped. 'And our charming host is far from trustworthy. Can't you see that?! He lives on deceit.'

I did not argue, but dismissed his suspicions in silence.

Some moments afterwards, the curtains twitched and Ulaume insinuated himself into our presence, carrying two steaming tankards. 'Lianvis sends you spiced wine,' he murmured, holding them out to us and glancing at me with those unnatural smouldering, smoky eyes.

'Put it on the table,' Cal said. He was sitting on the low, fur-strewn couch and did not look round. Ulaume put one cup down, and with fluid grace, held the other up to my lips. I sipped, spell-bound.

'I can stay,' he said, his voice soft and husky. Oh, the promise! I half reached for him.

'No,' said Cal, 'that won't be necessary.' His smile, as he turned, had the hard clarity of diamond. Ulaume slowly raised one dark, curving eyebrow, still transfixing me with his eyes.

'Another time, perhaps,' he said.

By the time I realized he had gone, I had finished my wine. Cal was smirking at my awed stupefaction. 'God help you, Pell,' he chuckled, 'you are easy game – too easy!'

'But he's incredible,' I protested.

'Perhaps, but he's a lamia all the same. Share breath with that and you'll be so much dried gristle hanging from the nearest tree.' He had pulled off his Kakkahaar garments with some distaste.

'What do you mean?' I asked, still staring at the midnight blue curtains where Ulaume had vanished.

'I mean Wraeththu have many interesting variations. I suspect Ulaume is one of them. It's obvious. Aruna is only food and drink to him. He's Lianvis' pet and should be kept chained up!'

But I was not convinced. 'You're so suspicious,' I grumbled, as he pawed at the fur blankets, grimacing.

'That's why I'm still alive!' he retorted. 'It's a bad old world out there. God, these furs stink!' He reached for his wine, wrinkling his nose. 'This is foul as well.'

Now I know better. Now I keep things such as Ulaume in pretty cages to amuse my guests. Then I still saw good in everyone.

We slept late into the next day and then both woke with headaches. I groaned and burrowed back into the blankets. Our journey must have exhausted us more than we thought.

'Do you realize,' Cal announced, 'that we used to wake up from a bed of stones with a bellyful of dehydration feeling better than this?' We looked at each other, both thinking the same thing.

'Of course, how stupid!' I cried, sitting up in the bed and slapping my head; it was too late to knock sense into it though. 'The wine! It was the wine, wasn't it? But why . . .?'

Cal curled his lip. 'Perhaps Lianvis prefers to have any visitors dead to the world at night. Knock them unconscious; keep them neatly in bed. Other reasons, though?' He made a noise of disgust. 'Watch me shudder!'

'If we get wine offered to us again tonight . . .?'

'Oh, it goes without saying, doesn't it. God, Pell, I know you need these snaky types for now, but tread carefully. Accuse me of paranoia, even hysteria, if you like, but there's more to this cosy little set-up than meets the eye.'

I dropped back down onto the pillows, screwing up my eyes to ease the pain. 'It would help, Cal, if I knew what ascension to Brynie involved. God, it could be so easy for them to . . . take control . . . let *something* in . . . you know.'

'Mmmm, that's not impossible, of course. Look Pell, I've been through Brynie; I can tell you some things. That's highly irregular, but at least if there's any drastic deviation in the procedures, you'll know. Only ignorance makes you vulnerable.'

All power lies within the mind. If it is said: 'there is no magic', to a degree this is true. Magic is will. Will power. Ara and Neoma are concerned with the search for self-knowledge that is necessary before progression. (Try exercising your will without it! You can't.) I had learned how to discipline my mind, how to believe in myself. Brynie is the expression of this knowledge. Cal's memory of the actual rituals involved was sketchy but I gathered enough for what I hoped was safety. Perhaps we were being too cautious. I could not see what Lianvis would have to gain that was worth taking the risk of perverting my ascension.

Although I had been told my assessment would begin in the morning, it was not until the afternoon that Lianvis asked to speak to me. After lunch, Cal and I went to attend to our horses. They were looking tatty in comparison with the polished steeds of the Kakkahaar. At the back of Lianvis' tent was a cooking pit and a canvas-draped pit that served as a toilet. We tethered the horses there. I counted ten other large pavilions and several smaller, shoddier dwellings. From the outside, all were of a neutral-coloured material that blended effectively with the surroundings. There was not much noise, not enough for a camp of that size. A sense of vague, unseen activity around us, but done silently. Sometimes, the warm breezes carried scents unidentifiable and unpleasant. Both Cal and I started to get paranoid, especially when Red or Splice threw their heads up in alarm and nothing was there.

I was squatting at Red's heels smoothing his legs, when something made my skin crawl. I glanced up quickly, and fell into the unwavering gaze of slumbering menace. Ulaume. He stood, half-wrapped in the door curtains at the rear of Lianvis' tent. All I could see of his face was his eyes and I did not like what I saw. It was a look to inspire fear and dread, even to one hardened by scepticism, and yet, there was an undeniable fascination. Ulaume wanted something of me, and because half of me wanted him back, I was powerless. 'Lianvis has sent for you,' he whispered and from ten feet away his voice was as clear as a bell. I stood up, dizzy in the hot light.

'Yes. I'm coming.'

'Pell.' Cal's voice reminded me of the warning. I raised my hand in a gesture of complicity and followed Ulaume into the tent. Inside, it was dark and hot, endless corridors of drapery. I could not see very well. The odour of heavy perfume masked other, earthier smells.

'Your friend does not like me,' Ulaume murmured, somewhere ahead of me, his body luminous through a veil of hair.

'He thinks you are dangerous,' I said, wishing I hadn't as soon as it came out.

Ulaume only laughed; a tinkling, restrained parody of amusement. 'He is jealous.'

'And what's that?' I sounded sharp. Jealousy, in that sense, was a word erased from the Wraeththu catalogue of emotion. He must have realized his mistake. There was a slight rustle and then his warm, mobile arms were around my neck, his breath disguised with the perfume of mint, close to my face,

'I shouldn't have said that. He's right; I am dangerous. I can be. But you are safe; you know you are. I can smell the power in you. It smells like fire!'

'Ulaume ...' I half-heartedly tried to break away, attempting to resist the onslaught of musky, sinuous allure. The heat and the gloom were claustrophobic; sweat began to creep from my skin.

'Are you really afraid to share breath with me?' His face was so close, we were nearly touching. I could see small, neat teeth shining like nacre between lips that were as well-shaped and smooth as swollen petals. A muscle twitched uncontrollably along his jaw. Part of me was still repulsed (the hint of the tomb ... something), but I could not stop myself; the pull was too strong. He was a well and I was thirsty, it was as simple as that. His taste and his power poured into me. First the darker tones of earth, then hissing sand; sand harvested by the hot, desert winds; the metallic wings of the element of air prevailing. Ulaume: a dark vortex. But whilst I floundered on the edge of the maelstrom, afraid of slipping, of losing myself, exhilaration spumed through my blood. He tried to drag me down, take my soul, but I could match him. We embraced; we fought. He did not want to kill me, not that; it was a little violation he wanted. To rape my soul, perhaps; feel him there lapping at my strength. He had said he could smell my power but he was confident his own was greater. Now I could feel him scared, his heart pounding, his hands claws upon my chest. I could feel the weight of that waist-length hair shifting, lifting with a life of its own, lashing with reptile spite. There it was, tight as ropes around my wrists and whipping round my back. I tore myself away from his mouth, barely able to lift my head. Horror fizzed in my throat. Trapped, I was Ulaume's prey. We were so close; locked together in an embrace of tangles. There was only one way out for me. I looked once at his face; a pale and challenging oval suppressing its fear. One look, and then, with that supernatural strength I hardly knew, I directed one blasting surge of will at the strands around my left arm. Be free! Be free! With a screech and a smell of burning hair, Ulaume stumbled backwards. On my wrist, red weals began to rise where the hair had bitten into me. I could hear him swearing at me, low and guttural, but not quite a curse. He had that much sense, at least.

'Snake!' I cried, and hit him, hard, with the back of my hand across the face. He snarled, dropping to all-fours, bearing those immaculate, child's teeth, head thrown back; a neck of white cords. Then there was nothing. Then a shrinking howl; Ulaume vanished; upwards, sideways, backwards, in the smoke of his own hair.

For a moment or two I had to lean down; put my head between my knees. It was the first time I'd really tried to put into practice all that Orien had taught me. Supervised exercises, like moving a glass along a table-top are nothing in comparison. It was the difference between drawing a picture of killing someone and stabbing someone to death in cold blood. Although I had been trained to believe in my natural powers, some part of me was still surprised that it had worked. It felt like I'd been running. My chest ached, my heart raced and every breath was an effort. Blood had begun to bead on my wrist where Ulaume's hair had whipped around it. Lianvis, where are you? I wondered. Stumbling, absently licking away the blood, I went to seek him out.

Lianvis' pavilion was like a maze of shrouds. It seemed larger on the inside than it looked on the outside. Sometimes there were dark, deep-piled carpets underfoot, sometimes only sand. I felt disorientated with shock after my struggle with Ulaume. I was not used to dealing with such things, and knew I should have taken more notice of what Cal had said about him. At the same time, however, I was glad that I had found out for myself. It had also proved to me just what I was capable of. I had needed that moment of danger to channel my powers. It had been that or defeat.

Lianvis let me search for him for several minutes before he guided me to the inner chamber. It was draped in the darkest, non-reflecting black, and decorated with esoteric symbols. The curtains dropped behind me as I stepped into the room. I was still sucking my wrist which had begun to throb and prickle ominously.

'You did well with Ulaume.' Lianvis' voice came out of the shadows. I could see him sitting on the floor on the far side of the chamber, cross-legged, robed in silvery grey, his hair pooled around him like molten metal, in the metallic glow thrown out by a single lamp that was on the floor somewhere behind him. Shadows arched and flickered among the curtains like mocking spirits. 'Was that a test?' I asked.

Lianvis beckoned me to him. 'Sit.' I did so. 'A test? Yes, of sorts, I suppose it was. I have been watching you Pellaz, while you slept, just now with my little pet, and I have reached a conclusion.'

'Oh? You admit to drugging us then? Last night?'

Lianvis gave me a rueful smile. 'Oh Pellaz, don't look so fierce. I only talked with you.'

'I don't remember.'

Lianvis shrugged. 'Of course you don't. Now listen. My conclusion is this: it is not Brynie that you want or need.'

'Why?' I could not hide my disappointment. I had been feeling good about myself, now this.

'Don't jump to conclusions. It is this. I shall raise you to Acantha, nothing less.'

'But Acantha is Ulani!' I cried. 'I'm not ready!'

Lianvis flapped a hand at me, leaning behind him and producing a long, carved wooden box. He opened it with leisure and drew out two long, slim black cigarettes, passing one to me.

'Your excitement is uncalled for,' he remarked, lighting his cigarette from a smoking taper of incense. Heavy browny-grey smoke plumed from his nostrils. 'I have examined you. I am of Algoma level. Therefore I know. We have heard of Thiede here. Few in the world of Wraeththu have not. He is a potent force, neither light nor dark, but something of both. Only a fool would not fear him. You say he incepted you, and from what I have observed I see that you are telling the truth. You have great power Pellaz, but you must learn to harness and use it correctly as of now. Brynie would be a waste of time for you. A redundant exercise. You already know that much. Few of Acantha level could have managed what you did with Ulaume. He possesses an untramelled elemental force.'

'I could feel it,' I said in wonder.

Lianvis nodded. 'There is more. Sometimes even I am wary of aruna with him, Pellaz. He is what is called Colurastean. His tribe are the Colurastes; sometimes called the snake people, though that is a deceptive term. They have nothing to do with reptiles.'

He remembered my unlit cigarette and leaned forward to light it for me. The smoke was acrid and burned the back of my throat although the aftertaste was pleasant.

'You do not trust me, do you,' Lianvis remarked, without rancour.

'Not really,' I admitted.

He smiled. 'No. A little wisdom on your part perhaps, or your friend Cal's. Kakkahaar have somewhat different ideals from those of the Wraeththu of Saltrock. We travel different paths. But I shall help you if you wish it to be so.'

'I have little choice. As you said, I can't waste any more time. The basic rituals must be the same . . .'

'Yes. That is only a formality. I shall instruct you as impartially as I can, but,' here he leaned forward, just a little, 'in my opinion, you would benefit from learning a little of the darker side of Wraeththu power. With abilities such as yours, any experience can only be advantageous.'

I was not so sure about that. 'Are you trying to glamourize me?' I asked him.

He feigned surprise. 'Pellaz, please!' he exclaimed, throwing up his hands.

'Lianvis, I'm not a fool, not completely. Inexperienced, yes, but not stupid enough to stray off the path now. I know the dark exists, we all do, but you cannot convince me that looking into it will benefit me.' I stood up. 'I have to get this wrist seen to . . .' and made as if to leave.

'Pellaz, sit down!' His voice was an order, but I avoided his eyes and remained standing. He sighed. 'Alright, alright, sit down. You'll have the straight ascension and nothing more. Now, show me that wrist.' I sat down again and held it out to him. Three short strokes, an unutterable word. He wiped his hands. 'There. Is that better?' I looked. There was no sign of injury.

'Fine,' I said, gazing at it, flexing the fingers.

'You could have done that yourself,' he told me. 'Now, to work together, you'll have to trust me a little.' I narrowed my eyes at him. 'Look,' he continued, 'your friend is Pyralisit, is he not? He will watch out for you. He can attend your instruction if you wish ...' I relaxed.

'Very well. I'll trust you a little.' And I indicated how much with my finger and thumb.

'That much, eh?' Lianvis was amused. I raised my eyebrows at him and he said, 'Ah, well, I suppose that is enough.'

It did not take me long to realize that Lianvis had been astute in his judgement of me. He gave me instruction for two weeks, and during that time I was surprised at the ease with which I handled his complicated teachings. It seemed I only had to hear the words once or twice for them to lodge ineradicably in my memory. It was no problem for me to recite them at will, no difficulty for me to muster my strengths and utilize them. Once, back home, the old priest had told Mima and myself that one day we might find the knowledge we had acquired a burden, more than anything else. 'Where will you use all this that's in your heads?' he had wondered. I feel sure he would have violently disapproved of the direction my search for knowledge had now taken and been horrified that the foundations he had laid within my head should support such timbers of information as Lianvis now imparted, but I, at least remembered the old man with thanks at that time. Without that first teaching, none of what followed would have been so easy, if at all possible.

Lianvis once told me I was 'primal'. He said this in a very grave and humourless tone, so that I was impelled to ask what he meant.

'Simply that,' he answered, smiling. 'Your aura is primal – back to the beginning ... I get a feeling about you. Obviously, you'll have heard of the first Wraeththu; well, one of his names, used for invocation, is Aghama – that is an arcane word for 'the first', literally, primary. His essence must be very strong because it is so pure. I sometimes get a whiff of that about you ...'

'Is it possible to invoke the first Wraeththu then?' I butted in impatiently.

Lianvis sighed wistfully. 'It is possible to try,' he said.

Lianvis told me that two other Kakkahaar as well as himself would conduct my ascension ceremony. It would take place on the next night of the new moon, out in the desert, among the grey dunes. Only one thing bothered me. Cal would not be present. As he was of a lower level than the others, Lianvis pointed out, he had no place there.

Several days before the completion of my studies, a man came to the Kakkahaar camp. He was accompanied by a fair-sized entourage, all muscle-swamped, trained killers from the look of them, and they travelled in an impressive cavalcade of heavy duty vehicles. We had been sweating in Lianvis' inner sanctum when the approach had been noticed. One of the Kakkahaar Aralids had burst into the room (that alone was unheard of), and announced, 'Tiahaar Lianvis, Mr Shasco is here again!' An expression of unbridled avarice transformed Lianvis' face from adept to merchant in the space of a single second. He rose quickly in a flapping of garments and rushed outside. Cal and I raised eyebrows at each other. This was something we had to see.

Outside, the unrelenting sun flashed with the strength of white fire off the glittering chrome of Mr Shasco's vehicles, that creaked as their engines tried to cool. Cal and I stood in the mouth of the tent, shading our eyes against the glare. A fleshy, red-faced man was descending from a hatchback, puffing with exertion and dressed in dripping khaki. He petulantly shrugged off assistance offered by his henchmen, and staggered forward; in appearance uncannily like an aggressive bulldog.

'I need your help again,' he rasped at Lianvis, lurching past him into the tent, not even looking at Cal and myself.

Lianvis followed him, more slowly, grinning gleefully. When he saw us, his mouth pursed. 'Pellaz, Cal, I'm afraid I have business to conduct now. You'll have to carry on without me today.'

'But I can't!' I protested. 'I've learnt the preliminary exercises, and the responses. I can't do any more without you.'

Lianvis clenched his teeth. I knew I should have said something like, 'Oh, it doesn't matter, we'll carry on tomorrow,' but I could not resist being awkward. I disapproved of what he was doing anyway.

'Go back inside,' he said impatiently. 'I'll find you something to get on with.' He tried to hurry us past Shasco who had sprawled uncomfortably into the floor cushions and was fanning himself with his hat.

'I'll be with you in a moment, Mr Shasco,' he said unctuously. 'Ulaume! Refreshment, hurry up!'

I had never seen Lianvis so agitated. Money sat fanning itself in the main salon, of that I was sure.

Within the inner room was a black chest bound with iron. From this Lianvis produced a dense and ancient tome of thaumaturgical lore which he thrust into my hands. Decrepit leather flaked through my fingers. 'The third chapter, read it and I will test you later!' he exclaimed with triumph.

'I will test you later,' I mimicked, once he had gone, passing the book unceremoniously to Cal. Cal grinned with wolfish humour.

'Fuck this, my precious,' he said. 'I think now is the time to indulge in a little casual eavesdropping.'

'He'll hear us!' I pointed out, none too keen. I was still sensibly wary of Lianvis, despite the amount of time Cal and I spent ridiculing him or lampooning his flamboyant mannerisms. I did not think he would take too kindly to us lurking in the draperies, listening to whatever transaction he was conducting with the corpulent Mr Shasco. I felt sure he would catch us.

'He won't know,' Cal argued. 'Come on, where's your spirit? We might learn something useful.'

'What, Mr Shasco's fortune?' I asked scathingly, but followed him anyway. We crept stealthily back along the curtained corridors. I can recall, even to this day, the singular, pervading smell of Lianvis' tent. It was a burnt perfume smell, almost electric and hung like invisible curtains in the hot gloom of material curtains. Tendrils of less savoury aromas mingled with it from the toilet facilities outside. In fact, we did not have to get too close to the main salon to be able to hear their voices. We could hear Shasco saying, '... superior quality. You can expect nothing less. The best; baptised, virgin ...'

'And this *impediment* you mentioned. I trust you have brought some trifle, some personal trinket, with you.' That was Lianvis talking. We could hear rustling.

'Yes,' Shasco answered him. 'I knew you'd need something of the kind. Here, will this do?' A moment's pause.

'Ah, yes. A ring. Yes, I can still get the feel of him.'

'Lianvis, it is vital this matter is dealt with immediately. God knows what mischief has been afoot whilst I've been travelling here ...' I could detect a note of panic in Shasco's voice, and could visualize Lianvis' expression of icy politeness.

'But of course, Mr Shasco, of course. Don't worry, it is of minor concern. Rest assured your enemy will trouble you no more. Now, once again, as to the payment ...'

'It is as I promised. When, where, shall I deliver it?' Shasco's voice was a disgusting wheeze, notes of lasciviousness vibrating within it.

'Tonight. By sundown I shall have concluded your business. After that ... There is a place half an hour's walk from the camp towards the west. There are stones above the sand, big stones. They are visible from some distance away. Deliver it there. Wait for me if you get there first; there are certain preparations ...' Lianvis' voice was terse.

'And ... you will let me stay?' An obscene plea. There was silence and I could sense Lianvis' disgust.

After a short while, I heard him sigh. 'Very well. Yes,' he said.

Cal put a hand on my shoulder and I jumped. The curtains trembled. 'Come on Pell,' he whispered. 'I've heard all I want to.'

Back in the inner room, we sat on the floor and looked at each other.

'God, I can't believe that!' Cal exclaimed, hitting the air with his fist.

'Is it . . . then?' I asked stupidly. Cal did not answer me.

'Lianvis is nothing more than a paid killer, and for *men* too! How could he?'

'Oh simple,' I replied. 'For money. Economies crumble like burnt wood all over the face of the globe, but there's no denying it can still buy a lot . . .'

'Oh grow up, Pell!' Cal sneered at me, making me feel ridiculous. 'You can be really stupid sometimes! There's more to it than that. Didn't you listen?! Since when has money to be' (and here he struck a typical Lianvis pose) '"delivered to the secret place when the moon is high"? Money? God! Pathetic!'

'What then?' I asked in a small voice but I thought I knew.

'Flesh,' Cal muttered, with a grimace. 'Of what kind, I'm not sure, but I'd swear to it. Flesh; Mr Shasco pays in blood.'

It was inevitable that Cal wanted to follow Shasco that night. I knew it would be an expedition fraught with the most horrible danger and told him so. 'You were the one who warned me off Ulaume. You were the one that told me caution had kept you alive. Now this!'

'Now this!' Cal agreed, a fanatical light in his eyes. (A look I came to dread). 'Remember, Pell, you'll be alone with these creeps and in a position of submission pretty soon. How long is it to your ascension ceremony? Two days? Three? Maybe after tonight, you'll decide to forego the honour. Maybe you'll learn something useful.'

'Oh alright, alright,' I said, giving in, starting to flick through Lianvis' book, seeing nothing.

'Look, Lianvis will be busy magicking Shasco's foes this evening. He'll have little time for us. Drugged wine again, perhaps? We'll take a romantic walk in the desert together, before the eminent Mr Shasco trundles forth.'

I could not really understand Cal's zeal for nosing into Lianvis' business. I felt it had nothing to do with us; the only interest I had was simple curiosity.

It was without surprise that we received the news that we would receive our evening meal in our own room that night. Ulaume had been efficient in his attempts of avoiding me since our skirmish, but it was he that brought our food to us. Cal was feeling bored, lying on the bed, and I could see a cruel mischievous light come into his eyes as Ulaume silently laid out our food. He watched the Colurastean for some minutes, various calculations slipping across his features, before uttering, 'Come here, snake-beast,' in a voice like ripping silk. Ulaume glanced up, his hands wavering above the plates. I still thought him beautiful and watched him carefully. He did not look at me. I could tell he was frightened of Cal. He started to back away, but with striking speed, Cal shot up and grabbed his wrist. Ulaume made a pitiful little sound, half whine, half cry.

'I said come here,' Cal hissed through his gritted teeth. 'Where's that offer now? You can stay can't you? Won't you share breath with me, Kakkahaar plaything.'

'No,' Ulaume gasped, trying to prise himself out of Cal's hold with his free hand.

'He's not Kakkahaar,' I said, 'Colurastes.'

'He's Kakkahaar,' Cal spat, shaking him. 'You're Kakkahaar, aren't you, Ulaume. The Colurastes demand respect for their craft. What would your people say if they knew what you are now, Ulaume?' Cal shook him again.

'Cal, shut up!' I cried, afraid he would say too much. We could not risk alerting Lianvis to what we knew.

'It's alright, Pell,' he answered, not looking at me, but the venom had left his voice.

I wished I had not told him about what had happened with Ulaume. Cal could be insensibly vindictive when the mood took him. He wound a handful of the threshing, tawny hair around his other hand.

'Come on viperling. Braid your hair. It gets in the way, doesn't it? It might creep around my neck. It might give my throat a little squeeze, accidently.'

I was expecting Ulaume to muster his defences at any

moment, but of course he knew Cal was Ulani. When Cal let go of his arm, he did nothing but braid his hair. Cal smiled and lay back, arms behind his head. 'Pellaz, commit to memory here another lesson. There is aruna, there is grissecon, and there is pelki . . .'

'Oh!' Ulaume's hands fell to his sides, clenching into fists.

'Oh. Yes. You think the Hara of Saltrock are pious upstanding creatures, don't you Ulaume. But we're not from Saltrock, Ulaume. At least, I'm not. My tribe is Uigenna. Does that mean anything to you?' Cal, with the face of an angel and the sensual cruelty of a fiend.

Ulaume started to shake his head. 'No, no, no, no, no,' he wailed.

Something about this little scenario was beginning to sicken me. 'Cal,' I said, without emphasis. It is horrible when you realize that someone you think you know quite well could very possibly be a complete stranger.

Ulaume seemed to notice me for the first time. 'Uigenna!' he said helplessly.

I could see him shaking. It meant nothing to me. I wanted to say, 'Ulaume, I don't know, I don't know any of this', which I did not, but I stayed silent. Something inside me told me it was safer to remain uninvolved. Let Cal play this game himself. For a while there was a terrible, heavy silence. Cal stared without feeling at Ulaume, and Ulaume gazed beseechingly at me. I don't know why he expected my sympathy. I looked from one to the other wondering what the hell was going on. Suddenly Cal jumped up. Ulaume winced and covered his head with his arms.

'Oh, get out,' Cal told him, smiling. 'I don't have the time.'

Ulaume fled without a further glance at either of us. I could not bear to look at Cal and started picking at the food.

'Don't eat that!' he said. 'Remember the wine.'

'Well, let's go then.' I turned away from him, unsure of why I felt so angry, reaching for my goat-skin jacket; it would be cold later.

'Don't you want to know what Uigenna is?' Cal asked.

'No.'

We went outside. In the distance we could see a smudge on the horizon. 'That way, I think,' Cal said. We trudged along without speaking. Eventually Cal broke the silence. 'You're angry,' he stated. I did not reply. 'Oh, don't sulk Pell! I wouldn't have done anything.'

My voice was harsh. 'Wouldn't you?'

'No, of course not. I was just playing. Getting him back for what he did to you.' He put an arm around my shoulder and kissed my cheek. 'Forgive me?'

'Cal, he didn't *do* anything to me.' It would not do for me to give in so easily.

'God, don't you ever bear a grudge? If you've forgiven the snake Ulaume, then forgive me.' His face was the epitome of innocent charm and I could do nothing but relent.

'Very well, I'll believe what you say.' After a while I said, 'Cal, what is pelki?' I had my arm around his waist and felt him tense.

'You'll be angry again,' he complained.

'I promise not to be.' We both knew I might not stick to that.

'OK, you asked for it. I'll tell you this. I was incepted into the Uigenna. Their belligerence is famous. They are hostile to nearly everyone else on this planet except Uigenna. Pelki is a remnant of man's so-called civilization. It is something Wraeththu hate; it is anathema to them. Some will even deny it exists, but it does. It is rape.' He stared into the distance, avoiding my eyes.

'And Uigenna and pelki are synonymous?' I enquired carefully. I was not as upset as Cal thought I would be.

He shrugged. 'Not really, but it's where I learned the term. Mention Uigenna and most Hara with their heads screwed on start running, though. I was very young when I was incepted: thirteen. I suppose I had a hard time but it all had a kind of grim glamour. Two years later I defected to the Unneah. They are another northern city tribe, somewhat warlike, but honourable enough. I was really too young to be part of the violence of Uigenna, but I witnessed plenty of it.'

'Cal, are you telling me the truth?' I asked him. He looked at me then.

'I've never lied to you, Pell. Never. OK, it might have been wrong of me to threaten even a reptile like Ulaume like that, but sometimes the beast just comes through in me, that's all. I didn't like what happened with you two, really I didn't.'

'We cannot be selfish with each other,' I quoted, reminding him.

'Oh, Pell,' he said, rubbing my arm. 'It's not like that, honestly it's not.' I looked at him archly and he said, 'Oh hell!', and leaned down to bury his face in my hair. I had been given a glimpse of the future, but I didn't know it.

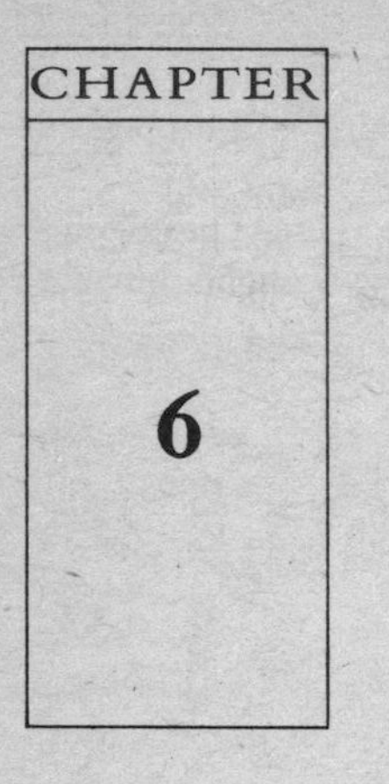

Beneath the sand

The stony sand beneath our feet cooled for the night. Pebbles clicked in the shadows. Out there, in the desert, the cold and the dark creep up on you unawares. One moment it is balmy evening, the next it is a blue, gaunt, werewolf place.

Ahead of us, sand-sculpted ruins poked through choking, powdery folds, their carved summits eroded to formlessness. This must be the place Lianvis had spoken of. I could feel a hundred prickling emanations bouncing off my skin. It was a place that had felt Corruption's gingery touch.

'How old is this place?' Cal asked the darkness, his voice hushed with caution, echoing among the blind stones.

'God forbid it should answer you!' I replied in a quavery warble. 'I think we should hide.'

'We should fear least the creatures we *can* hide from around here,' Cal told me cryptically.

I knew what he meant. Perhaps this jumble of disintegrating stone had once been a holy place. There was something of a feeling like that still lingering. Dark holes that were stone throats led down into the ground. Very little remained on the surface; most of the walls had toppled and the sand had swallowed nearly everything. I did not want to go underground. There were many places where we could crouch unseen (by Hara and men at least) on the surface.

'Don't be ridiculous,' Cal scoffed. 'Nothing will happen out here!'

'We won't be able to see, if we go down there,' I protested as reasonably as I could. It was true there were no lights, however dim, shining out from any of the tunnels.

'Well. Then we shall wait.'

We leant against a half-wall, warmth oozing out from the heart of the cooling stone into our backs. We did not have to wait long. Soon a line of shambling figures folded out of the dusk, lit by the steady, orderly beams of flashlights. We crouched lower as they passed us; four or five individuals. Men or Wraeththu? It was impossible to tell from our position. One of them was obviously Shasco. We could recognize the stumbling step and laboured breath.

'Now we wait again,' Cal murmured, as their sounds disappeared into the earth.

Perhaps you have heard someone say: 'My heart was beating so loud I was sure others could hear it!' and have thought it a colourful, exaggerated way of simply saying: 'I was scared witless'. You are wrong. It really does seem that way. Any moment I expected Cal to say, 'For God's sake, stop making that noise!' There was no logical reason for us to be there. If Lianvis found us, we had no excuse. If I had argued more persuasively with Cal back at the camp, I might have been able to talk him out of this reckless folly. I cursed my weakness.

Out of the darkness came a muffled sound. Soft thuds, faint jangling. Horses.

'Two of them, I'd say,' Cal whispered, lifting himself a little.

'Don't look!' I hissed, pulling him down. 'It's Lianvis!'

He had to know we were there, had to! He was Algomalid. He must be able to sense my fear, at least. We heard them dismount, voices, the words indistinguishable. A horse snorted, hooves dancing on the cracked paving, its bridle jingling. We listened to the voices moving away. I had been holding my breath. Now I let it out, and my stomach ached.

'What now?' I asked.

'Oh, we'll give them a few minutes to get involved in whatever they're getting involved in.' Cal stood up.

'Cal!' I squeaked, tugging his arm.

'It's alright,' he said, 'there's no-one here.'

I stood beside him. Lianvis and his companion had hobbled their horses. They looked at us from lowered heads with troubled eyes and pointed ears, snuffling and backing away. Tassels on their bit rings brushed the ground.

'Which tunnel do you think they took?' Cal asked me, looking round.

'Who cares!' I replied.

'That is not the spirit, Pellaz,' Cal chided me in a voice that betrayed not the slightest hint of fear. 'You must learn to face danger with strength and courage. You won't last long if you don't.'

I will last even longer if I avoid danger, I thought.

'That one looks vaguely lit up,' I said, pointing.

Keeping to the shadows, we crept towards it. No sound issued from the uninviting gloom, but a faint, ruddy, flickering glow. I felt as if we were being watched from every other dark entrance. Cal stepped inside and I followed. Shallow, worn steps, dusted with sand, curled down before us. Many thousands of feet had trod here in forgotten times. It was possible that once this building had been well above ground, perhaps even a tower, before the desert had got to work with its enveloping tides.

We descended for some minutes, progressing slowly. At the bottom a corridor with a damp, sandy floor stretched forward. The ceiling had once been plastered. We could see, from the light of a single crackling torch hung on the wall, that most of it had fallen away. The stone beneath was pitted and cracked, but there was no rubble on the floor. It seemed to indicate that the place was used fairly regularly. Wall paintings, obscured by black mould, depicted orderly rows of figures marching towards the end of the corridor, their expressions frozen in haughty piety. I had expected to hear the sounds of chanting, the preliminaries of ritual, but the single sound that echoed towards us was worse than that, much worse. It was the last, desperate cry of the irretrievable soul, still recognizable as human, or Har; just. I froze in horror, and found myself gripping Cal's arm. He touched my hand. 'Let go. Come on.'

The corridor was not really that long. At the end, the remains of huge, wooden doors sagged inwards. Beyond that, the light was stronger. The gap between the door lintel and the wood was so large, we could look through easily into the room beyond. It was a high-ceilinged chamber, columned, camerated; a temple.

Several figures stood around a central bowl of fire. Lianvis, clothed only in his hair and a black loin-cloth threw grains into the flames, which spurted up, amethyst, sapphire and ruby. His eyes shone like a wolf's in moonlight. Reflective, milky and opalescent. Ulaume, robed in diaphanous grey stood at his left side, holding a metal dish. His face was arrogant, yet dissociated, fronds of hair wafting about him as if in a breeze. There was only one man there and that was Shasco. He stood a little apart from the others. I counted six Hara, including Lianvis and Ulaume. Candles, thick as my wrist, stood upright in thick pools of their own wax upon the floor, illuminating the circle and the signs that had been chalked there.

Lianvis spoke a word of power, and cold, luminous light filled the entire chamber. The candles guttered fitfully as if the luminence choked their flames. I could see then what had passed unnoticed before. Curled up on the ground at Lianvis' feet, moving feebly like a weak puppy kept from its mother too long, was a child, presumably human. Ulaume clicked his fingers and two of the Hara stepped forward to lift the boy; his feet trailed in the chalk as if the bones were broken. When the light touched his face ... God knows I never wish to see such a thing again. He knew he was to die, wretched hopelessness was etched across his features, frozen in a rictus of a scream. It must have been his cry we had heard at the mouth of the corridor. I wondered what they had done to him for him to make such a sound. There was no mark upon his body. Lianvis stepped forward, his head thrown back; a wolf's head, his eyes beacons of destroying power. Ulaume bent to untie the cloth about his master's hips and I could see the corded muscles in his lean thighs straining and trembling with restrained energy. Realization made me utter a single, shocked 'No!' and Cal elbowed me in the ribs to silence me. I did not want to see any more. Lianvis' face was changing into something demonic, the lips pulled back, long teeth shining in the sulphurous radiance, his neck twisting, twisting, his hair lashing like frenzied snakes. The boy began to howl, to struggle, his feet paddling helplessly in the dust, and I pressed my eyes against Cal's shoulder. There was nothing we could do; nothing. Whatever power we possessed was no match for Lianvis in that state. I clapped my hands over my ears, but it could not shut out the sound, the dreadful, dreadful cries and Lianvis' snuffling, guttural snarls.

Suddenly Cal pulled me upright. Whirling noises, shrieking out from the chamber broke up his words, but I made out, 'Now ... now ... the power ... him ... the power ... back! Back!' Reeling backwards, we started to run, the appalling, scraping screeching chasing us down the corridor; the smoke, the stench of burning flesh.

I shouted, 'Does he know?! Does he know?!' as we ran. Cal did not answer.

Blue light flooded the tunnel as we reached the bottom of the steps. Slipping, grazing myself against the stone, I scrabbled up after Cal, his long limbs sure and swift above me. Outside, the stillness of the night was unnatural. Cold air hit our lungs with a breathtaking chill and I gasped, hardly able to breathe. Cal hauled me out of the tunnel, dragged me across the paving and threw me down behind the wall we had first hidden behind, covering me with his body. Arcane words ripped from his throat, his breath wheezing and shuddering. It was a simple protection. I was in no position to augment his strength with mine. I tried only to press myself into the stones, to become invisible. For a second or two there was only silence and then the night exploded with sound and blue luminence. Cal buried his face in my hair. I could feel his heart racing manically in his chest against mine. 'Oh God, Oh God, Oh God,' he kept repeating. I had never seen him afraid. We hugged each other, eyes shut tight. Something formless and huge spurted out of the ground, out of the tunnel. Its light burnt through our closed eyelids. Stricken with terror, I held my breath again, feeling the awesome, devilish fever pulsing round us. Lianvis transformed into elemental power. We were lucky that in that elevated, supernal state we were beneath his notice. With a dismal scream, he shot towards the stars, fizzing and hissing like a monstrous rocket, the air cracking around his phantom shape in shards of lightening. I opened my eyes, looked up over Cal's shoulder. It filled the sky. Lianvis, barely recognizable as he but for the suns that were his eyes. I felt he looked right into me, mocking. He could have reached down and plucked us off the earth. But the night just filled up with his demon laughter and the light that was his greedy soul reached up for the sparkling darkness. He blazed away from us like a comet. A word sprang uncontrollably to my mind. I still don't know why exactly, unless it was some kind of obscure presentiment concerning later events in my life. The word was this: Aghama.

Cal rolled off me and lay on his back, blinking at the sky.

'Your idea,' I said, sitting up and brushing sand off my coat.

Cal closed his eyes and swallowed, clenching his jaw.

'We could steal the horses and leave,' I added, tentatively.

'What horses?' Cal said in a flat voice. I peeped over the wall and could see them lying there; the black humps of their bellies.

'Dead,' I murmured rhetorically.

Cal sighed. 'There's no cover on the way back to the camp. We'll have to wait for the others to leave,' he told me.

I said nothing, although I could see no way we could get back inside Lianvis' tent without being seen.

'Maybe we should just try to get back to our horses and get out of here,' I suggested.

Cal rolled his eyes. 'Are you joking? We have no supplies, no idea which way to go. Lianvis would know then that we'd seen something. He wouldn't let us get away. No, we wait, and then follow the others back. Once we're in the camp, we could bluff our way through if anyone sees us.'

'Cal, he knew we were here, he must have!'

Cal stared at me and then shook his head. 'No, I don't think so, no.'

We lay in the dark, still breathing quickly. After a while I said, 'Cal, what happened in there?'

'Murder,' he replied. 'Murder for power. Wraeththu essence is death to humankind, remember. But it is a sweet way to kill for those on the dark path, a sweet way to feed on souls ...' He motioned me to silence then, for we could hear them coming up out of the ground. I heard Ulaume curse when he saw the dead horses, and that was all. There was no sound of conversation as they headed back into the desert.

I turned to Cal. I spoke to him. I said, 'What are we, Cal? What are we part of?' He did not answer.

After maybe fifteen minutes, Cal stood up. He said he could see their flashlights in the distance and it was safe for us to follow. Luck was on our side. When we reached the camp, sounds of revelry reached us from around a leaping fire by Shasco's vehicles. His men were getting drunk and the witnesses of Lianvis' conjurations, doubtless desperate for a drink themselves, had joined them. As we slipped silently back into the tent, I saw Ulaume standing staring into the fire, a tin cup pressed to his chest. Even in the orange glow I could see his face looked grey.

I still feel that it was by some miracle that Lianvis did not become suspicious of my behaviour from that time on. When, on the following day, Cal and I went to the inner room to spend more time with him on my studies, I could do little more than twitch and mumble at him. Terrible images of a gaping mouth uttering only a heart-rending mewl paraded indelibly across my inner eye. What made it worse was that Lianvis had conducted that ritual for no other reason than sheer, dissipated pleasure. I had thought at first that the whole exercise must have been for Lianvis to gain some kind of extra power, but Cal informed me otherwise.

'What we saw was sheer decadence,' he said. 'Nothing more. Lianvis took life as we take alcohol. The effect is similar, but as you saw,' (and here he smiled), ' so much stronger!'

Now, facing our charming host every day was a nightmare. Lianvis sat, composed and neat upon the cushions, but somewhere inside him the rushing wind spirit, star power, still glowed; a hidden, dense-white core. He had trained me well to focus my strengths; there was little time left to spend with the Kakkahaar and I wanted to make that time as short as possible. I visualized the shining symbols of protection against evil above my head and kept them there. If Lianvis guessed I knew something of his activities, he gave no sign, but knowing his level and his art, I think it virtually impossible that he did not know. It seemed he did begin to accelerate my studies towards their conclusion, but I may have imagined that. Of course, Cal and I had considered leaving the Kakkahaar before my ascension but we did not want to risk making Lianvis suspicious of us. We were afraid of him and it was fear that kept us there beside him.

Two days later he told me that my ascension to Acantha would take place that night. I asked him where and he replied it would be at the ruins some way west of the camp. He watched me sleepily as horror must have thrilled across my face. But that was all. He said, 'It may be a good idea for you to ride out there this afternoon. Look at the place. Take Cal with you.'

Of course, once we were there, in radiant daylight, there was no sign. The underground corridors smelled old and unused. Flaking cobwebs dangled from the crumbling plaster. Perhaps we took the wrong route down. The vast temple chamber was lit hazily by smoking bars of sun. There was no blood on the floor, no marks at all. Cal and I did not speak, but looked at each other in the gloom. Cal moved into the radiance and looked up through the cracked ceiling. It was a perfect picture. I poked among the rubble; not even a candle had been left behind. Nothing spoke to me there; it was thoroughly cleansed.

I had to fast that day. At sundown, Lianvis put me in a different room. He would come for me at midnight, he said. I lay down on the couch, uncomfortable in the hot, close atmosphere of the tent. My mind was in a daze; my ascension seemed something of an anti-climax now. The pleasure, the pride, the excitement had gone out of it. Kakkahaar's noble Hara were bloody with unhallowed crimes. I knew that what we had witnessed under the ruins was no isolated incident. The memory of it would not leave me and I knew it never would until the desert was behind us. One awful thought, that I could not banish, that made me feel sickened, saturated with sickness, was this: me going with trusting innocence with Cal into the desert. Me leaving my home with a stranger whom only Fate had decreed had not been a Kakkahaar, or something like them. Visions of me smoking, writhing, sizzling in the most unspeakable of agonies kept rising before me. Me, unconsciously flirting with Cal, tempting a possibility I could never have dreamed of.

So, here I lay, still in Lianvis' tent, awaiting the hour of my ascension ceremony. I vowed we would leave as soon as I was rested the next day. Perhaps then the bad thoughts would fade. I threw my arm across my eyes and pressed down hard, making the colours come. I knew that outside, in the real outside that is, far beyond the sand, the rocks, the scrub, the world of men still struggled to maintain their supremacy. I knew that the things that had frightened me so far were mere nothings in comparison with what might await us beyond the solitude of the sand.

Outside, muted voices called mournfully on the night air. The sun, a great, boiling, ruby globe, would be sinking in a haze of colours behind the ruins. Bars of light sneaking in through the cracked vaults of that unholy place would be crimson now, the chamber suffused with bloody light. And later I would go there, later bite my tongue whilst Lianvis stands in that same place; different, calmer forces bowing to his touch.

I turned on my side and curled my knees up to my chest. The room looked tawdry, the air stale beneath its veil of incense. I felt hot and dirty, hungry and anxious to be free to leave. The hours till midnight seemed interminable. I rolled around on the couch, trying to get comfortable and reciting rituals in my head until I hated them.

It was almost dark when I heard the curtains rustle behind me. Someone came in on silent feet, bringing with them a hint of the freshness of the air outside. I rolled over quickly. It could not be Lianvis; it was far too early. A dark figure, barely visible, stood at the side of the couch. All I could see was one pale hand holding the folds of its hooded robe together. I made no sound, but waited. The figure pulled itself up to its full height and gradually unfolded the draperies that swathed it, raising its arms above its head. Pellucid skin glowed like phosphorous in the shadows; yet I still could not make out the face. There was a cloud in my head forbidding recognition. I held out my arms and the strange, silent, pliable visitor curled into them. I found a mouth tumid with desire and I drank from it dark and secret things. All the colours around me were mazarine blue and richest purple; a taste of ink. A burst of starfire. I was ouana, violet and gold, tongued with flame, seeking ingress, conquering and revering. Streams of ice flowed from my heart, meeting fiery air, hissing, swirling, making steam. It may only have been an erotic dream; a temptation, an illusion, or it may have been a living, hungry thing.

I was sleeping when Lianvis came through the curtains. He shook me and smiled at my waking eyes. My mouth was dry, my body slippery with sweat. 'Come now,' was all he said. I looked. There was no-one on the couch beside me, though my arms felt cold as if only recently emptied. Lianvis watched me sit up, rub my face, reach for my clothes. His secret smile led me out to the desert.

Perhaps if I had known more of the way things really were in the world, I would not have been so desperately anxious to leave the camp of the Kakkahaar. All things in life are merely relative. The evils we had encountered in the desert were extremely bad compared with our time at Saltrock; later events would make our time with Lianvis seem like days of peace, a holiday. Never, there, had I been under direct threat. Things we had seen had been only an education, perhaps a warning. Then I was still afire with the ingenuous idealism that the haven of Saltrock had formed within me.

My ascension to Acantha had concluded when the first pre-dawn grey had diluted the pristine darkness of the desert night. I did not feel as if my body was brimming with new found power exactly, but what I did feel was an inner kernel of calm and confidence, something that could be called upon, should the need arise. I rode back to the camp with the echoes of ritual ringing in my head; exhausted, but still determined to leave the place that day. Lianvis insisted I broke my fast with him. He told me he could not see why I was in such a hurry to leave.

'Whatever's waiting out there for you will still be there tomorrow,' he said, flinging his arm to the east.

'I don't want to waste time,' I told him, lying glibly.

'You *could* rise to Pyralis here,' he pointed out, avoiding my eyes and picking at the food on his plate.

'No!' I cried, too quickly. 'No, I mean, I mean we have to go on.'

Lianvis shrugged. 'Your choice, of course. Where do you plan to go?'

I looked beyond him, out through the door of the tent. Where? 'Oh, Cal will know. Somewhere.'

'You would be wise to return to Saltrock you know,' Lianvis said, wiping his hands, slowly. 'We are fairly isolated from any trouble here in the desert; it's too far and too inhospitable for us to be a threat to anyone, and Saltrock too, but other places ...' He drew his breath in sharply and shook his head. 'Pellaz, some of the towns north of here are painted with Wraeththu blood. There is hell beyond the boundaries of the wild country.'

I could have told him that even before I was Har I had not seen the towns and cities of men. My experience did not extend further than pictures in books the priest had shown me. Now I wanted to see. But what I said was, 'I do not want to hide forever. There is a world out there and a great war perhaps. Wraeththu will win that war because of the simple fact that they have Fate on their side. Cal and I are going to be part of it ...'

'Why risk your life?!' Lianvis exclaimed. 'It would be more sensible to wait a few years at Saltrock. Maybe, by then, things will be a little more ... resolved.'

I did not think he was right, which of course he was, and I was exaggerating slightly about our sense of heroism. Cal and I had no plans at all. He wanted Immanion and I wanted to live a little. We had not even discussed where we wanted to go next yet.

It was late afternoon by the time we were ready to leave. Lianvis equipped us richly with food and water. He had also donated a pack horse to carry it, ignoring our protests. There was a multitude of useful things: rope, salt, a knife sharpener, clothes and a tinder box. I thought Lianvis was just trying to get round us for some reason (and was probably right), but was grateful all the same. I had given him very little in return for the training he had given me, and now he showered us with gifts. A Kakkahaar guide would take us to the edge of the desert.

As we left, Lianvis came to bid us farewell. There was no sign of Ulaume, which surprised me. Lianvis said, 'You mustn't waste your talents, Pell; try to stay alive until you have matured enough to use them properly.'

'I shall certainly try!' I replied. I gathered up Red's reins and he lifted his head, ready to leave. Cal was talking to the guide some feet away. 'Oh, one thing, Lianvis,' I said quietly, leaning down. 'Last night; was it you who sent Ulaume to me?'

Lianvis laughed. 'I did not send Ulaume to you,' he answered, but his face looked sly. 'You never saw Ulaume last night.'

I was puzzled. 'But his *hair*...' I said.

'No. It was not Ulaume. Farewell Pellaz.' He turned quickly in the usual swirl of sandy cloth and strode back into his tent.

As soon as we rode away from the camp my spirits began to lift. The desert, past its cruellest mid-day heat, shone with barbaric splendour. Red and Splice, rested and well-fed, were anxious to please and light on their feet. Lianvis had given us a tent of sturdy black canvas. When we camped for the night, there were whole chickens to eat and pale, yellow wine to hasten our sleep. The Kakkahaar guide had told us that he would leave us at mid-day tomorrow. In less than a day the desert would be behind us, yet it would probably have taken us weeks if we had not had a guide.

As we lay in our tent that night, Cal quizzed me about the previous night's events. His voice sounded strained and he was lying on his back, not touching me.

'I'm sure all the ceremony bit is just decoration,' I said. 'It's the instruction that's important. That's what raises your level. Look at this!' I materialized a glowing crystal in the air before us. Cal slapped it with his hand and it vanished.

'What is important is common sense, that's all! You are Wraeththu. The power is there anyway. It is in man too, but they ignore it . . .'

'What's the matter with you?' I snapped, leaning over him. His eyes were cold, the darkest violet. He pulled his blanket tighter round his neck.

'Why won't you tell me?' he said. 'I have never kept anything from you!'

'What do you mean?' I had an inkling however. He just looked at me and I dropped my eyes. 'It is no secret,' I said defensively, 'I just forgot.' His expression did not change. 'I feel as if you expect me to apologize.'

One side of his mouth twitched in a tentative grin. 'Forgot? Oh Pell!'

'It's the truth! It all seemed like a dream anyway. I still don't know if it was real. How did you know?'

He raised one eyebrow. 'I know; that is all. I can see it round you; something dark.' The coldness had left his voice and I lay down, resting my head on his chest through the blanket.

'It was all so strange. I don't even know who it was. I did think it was Ulaume, but I asked Lianvis and he said it wasn't.'

Cal said nothing for a while. His hand crept under my hair and stroked the back of my neck. Outside, I heard the Kakka-haar cough in his sleep.

'I know who it was,' Cal said. Something in his voice scared me.

'Don't tell me; don't,' I murmured. 'Just make me Light again.'

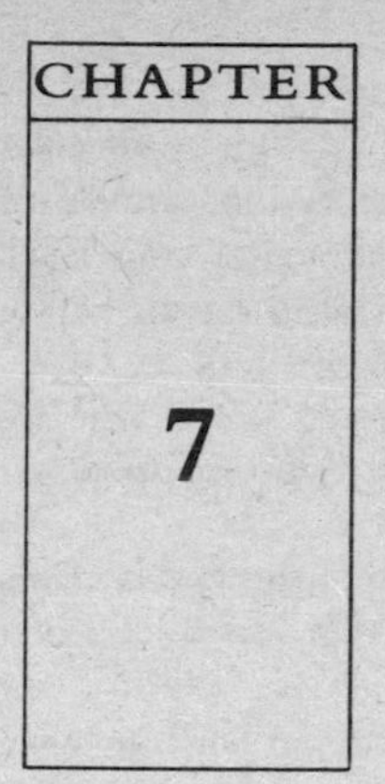

CHAPTER 7

They that have fallen . . .

To the east of the desert, a long, straight road winds straight across an unrelenting plain. There are a few farms there, some dealing in livestock, some in grain. We could see smoke rising thinly from their chimneys. The Kakkahaar had said that we should begin to avoid the habitations of men. There were only two of us and men might be tempted to shoot on sight. Cal said we should forget the road and head north. Although that might mean we would risk encountering danger, there would be more of our own kind that way. We still had plenty of supplies and we could travel fairly fast across the plains.

Now we changed direction again, abandoning our journey to the south and heading north once more, away from the arid country towards greener lands. For several days, we did not meet any Hara or men. In the distance we could see the land begin to rise. There, the blue of the sky started to mist. Cal taught me how to use a gun. We did not want to waste what ammunition we had, but we shot at small animals, which supplemented our diet. Sometimes I would dream of our being attacked by men, (shadowy creatures with pale, dead faces), and not being able to defend ourselves. I was not a good shot. Our horses grew sleeker and fatter on the lush grass of the plains. When the wind blew it billowed like a vast, green sea.

The first town we came to seemed inhabited only by ghosts. Only litter moved on the empty streets; a makeshift garrison sagged unmanned. Cal left me with the horses under cover and went to investigate. I fretted impatiently while he was gone. Surely it should not take this long. I could see him killed a hundred different ways, mostly shot and shot and shot. He returned an hour later, sauntering back to me, biting an apple.

'It's safe,' he said. 'I think.'

I could tell it had not been that long ago that this had been a thriving town. Something had made the people leave. Just the fact that they appeared to have left their vehicles behind (we saw many parked along the streets), made me uneasy. Cal said that wasn't too ominous a sign. Fuel was becoming scarce, after all. I looked inside one of the cars and it appeared long unused, but I was still unsure. Had this place been abandoned or attacked? There were hardly any indications of destruction; what there was could have been caused by neglect. The buildings were for the most part undamaged and we could see nothing of the more grisly remains of conflict; dead Hara or men. Cal showed me the fruit tree where he had picked the apple. It was in the garden of a large, white house. It reminded me of the Richards house back home. 'Let's explore,' Cal suggested, but I was not very keen. As a child I had often dreamed of big, empty houses, and the dreams had never been pleasant. I think that deserted houses have personalities of their own, and once deserted, resent the intrusion of living things. Cal laughed when I told him about it, but he did not insist on going inside. We walked up the wide, main street, where once a community had bustled, ignorant of their fate. The horses hooves made an alarmingly loud clatter, which echoed all around us. I hoped frantically that the town was as empty as it appeared. If anyone did still lurk there, I felt sure it was unwise of us to advertise our presence. But no-one came. The town held its breath or slept or dreamed. The empty eyes of the shops, the cafes and houses watched us implacably until the hair stood up on the back of my neck. Once out of the centre, we remounted our horses and cantered out through the suburbs.

On the very edge of the town, down a sleepy road of middle-sized, family houses, just as our fears were beginning to subside, a single, sharp, arresting sound shattered the air around us. Gunfire. Cal reacted immediately, swinging Splice sharply off the road and crashing into a nearby garden. I kept so close to him our knees were touching. Chewing up an unkempt lawn, we collided to a halt behind a shield of fir-trees. Cal hauled me to the ground. At first we could hear nothing.

'We should have the weapons ready all the time!' Cal hissed, speaking more to himself than to me.

'What now?' I asked, rubbing the rein-burns between my fingers.

'Men or Hara?' Cal muttered to himself, ignoring my question.

'They must have been watching us. Damn! I should have known. It was too quiet. Pell, find out. Help me put out a call.'

Now was the time for me to put Lianvis' tuition to the test. A call; to men it is a science fiction of telepathy. To Wraeththu it is just another way of communicating, conveniently without sound. If it was something other than Hara out there, the chances were they would not pick up on it. We clasped each other's hands and focussed a channel of receptive thought out onto the street. I could feel Cal's nails digging into the backs of my hands; his arms began to shake with effort. We amplified the force, but nothing came back – at first. Then, I could hear it inside my head. Cautious, reticent.

'What tribe?'

Cal was controlling his thoughts with cool dexterity. He answered, 'Saltrock', and did not waver. It is extremely difficult to lie, or even attempt half-truths, when communicating by thought, but Cal could do it easily. There was not even the faintest whiff of Uigenna or even Unneah. Thank God.

'We are Irraka,' came the mind-voice once more, 'You can come out now.'

Cal smiled uneasily at me. 'Let's go,' he said. Our pack-horse, Tenka, had scrambled off up the garden. I could see him staring defiantly back at us with lowered head. Red and Splice, trusting creatures that they were, still stood behind us, breathing down our necks.

'I'll get him,' I said, 'You go and shake hands with the Irraka.'

'Well, thank you Pellaz,' Cal muttered scornfully. He led Red and Splice out onto the street. Tenka decided to be awkward and it was some minutes later that I emerged from the garden. Cal was talking to a tall figure clad in thick, black leather with cropped hair. He had a fierce, sharp face and unsettling grey eyes that were almost silver.

'I am Spinel,' he announced, folding his arms so that the leather creaked.

'Pellaz,' I said, resenting strongly the stripping directness of his gaze.

'I know. Your friend tells me you're heading north.'

I looked at Cal whose face had assumed the blank look he reserves for strangers. 'Yes.' I confirmed. Spinel sniffed and shrugged.

'Brave Hara,' he said with the faintest hint of a sneer. 'Though you'd better learn to be more cautious. We could have finished you easily back there.'

I almost said, 'We thought the place was empty', but thankfully realized the folly of it before I opened my mouth.

Spinel spoke again, 'You're from Saltrock, eh? Everyone's heard of Saltrock. Seems stupid to leave there ...' He did not trust us, that was clear.

'Oh, we have business further north,' Cal told him. I was wondering what this stilted conversation was leading to. Was he going to offer us hospitality or order us on our way. I did not understand why he was cautious of us or that he had good reason to be. He obviously came to the conclusion, however, that as there were only two of us, we were not much of a threat. He raised a hand and snapped his fingers. Instantly, a dozen Hara materialized from concealment, all pointing weapons at us.

'There's no need for this,' Cal's voice was beautifully clear and steady. 'Let us pass. We mean you no harm.'

It seemed ridiculous even saying it. Cal and I; two of us, and a dozen guns aimed at our heads. What did they expect us to do? Shape change into something large and numerous?

'We have to be careful,' Spinel said smoothly. 'As you see, the town is empty. Varrs were here. About a mile out of town, there's a place that's a heap of death. One whole heap of death. Men, women, children. We come from Phesbe; that's a town up there some way.' He pointed. 'We saw the smoke. Investigated. Varrs tried to burn the dead, but there were too many.'

'Oh?' Cal said daintily. 'And how long ago was this?' I caught on to what he was thinking; there was no smell. That much death and no smell?

'Very smart,' Spinel sneered. 'We dealt with it. You could smell it at Phesbe two days ago.'

I could tell Cal was beginning to get annoyed with this pointless altercation. 'We're not Varrs,' he said.

'Varrs have whores,' Spinel countered, aggressively.

Cal just laughed. 'Do they? Saltrock whores even? Oh spare us the shit, Mister Irraka, and good-day to you. Come on, Pell.' With remarkable sang-froid, he put his foot in Splice's stirrup and started to mount. I swung up onto Red's back hastily, hoping Cal knew what he was doing.

'Are you planning on passing through Phesbe?' Spinel asked him gruffly.

'I don't think so,' Cal replied stonily, urging Splice into a trot. I followed.

'They'll shoot us!' I squeaked, catching up with him. Cal did not answer.

Some moments later, I heard hoofbeats behind us and looked round. Spinel and his troupe were galloping towards us on enormous black horses. Spinel caught up easily. His brute of a mount had a huge, curving head with red nostrils. Its mane was cropped, like its rider's.

'You'd be fools to carry on north just now,' the Irrakan addressed Cal. 'Chances are you'll meet the Varrs. We've decided you can come with us back to Phesbe. Wait a couple of days there.'

Cal did not slow Splice's pace. 'So kind of you,' he said. 'Well, what do you think, Pell?'

'It's up to you,' I replied.

'OK, lead on,' Cal smiled at Spinel.

The black horses poured past us, their hooves throwing up grit from the road. They were very impressive, like part of an army. Soon, all we could see of them was dust, but their trail was easy enough to follow.

'I wonder what they want,' Cal mused.

'I won't say it!' I said.

'And what's that; "Oh Cal, you're so suspicious"', he pantomimed, imitating me. 'They probably want to steal all we have and ravish our silky bodies!'

'Why are we following them, then?' I demanded, in alarm.

'Because a thorough ravishing is good for you now and again!' he joked, or at least I hoped he did.

Just before we reached Phesbe I asked, 'Cal, what are Varrs?'

'Oh, they eat Uigenna for breakfast, darling,' he said.

'Be serious for once!' I snapped. He loved to irritate me.

'They're just another northern tribe,' he explained. 'Hideously arrogant and shockingly ferocious.'

'Thank God it was only the Irraka we met then!' I exclaimed.

Cal pulled a face. 'I should save thanking Him for a while yet if I were you,' he said.

It seemed that with each Wraeththu tribe we came upon, we were slipping one note lower on the scale of civilization, comfort and morality. Phesbe was a stinking husk of what once might have been a decent, and fairly affluent, community. Now it was merely a rat-heap of broken concrete spiked with rust, rank, seeding weeds and ungodly stenches. Most of the buildings were crumbling into a rapid dissolution, gaping roofs were hastily patched with flapping canvas. All the streets, mostly insurpassable with rubbish, bore a sad wreath of mulching newsprint nurturing a surprising burst of late summer poppies. I saw two dead dogs and a dripping carcase of what might have been human hanging from a pole.

In the centre of the town a rococco town hall stood bravely and still intact. Spinel had made this his palace. He was waiting for us at the foot of a sweeping flight of steps that led to the hall's porticoed facade. Bitter-looking Hara with cruel faces lounged about him, all dressed in black leather uniform. Many were heavily tattooed, none wore their hair long, and I noticed quite a few had shaved their scalps completely and scored the white skin with black patterns. Their expressions ranged from outright hostility to mere boredom, and I could not suppress a shiver as we dismounted. Spinel snapped his fingers (all he ever had to do to summon his aides), and a skinny Har with pale eyes shambled down the steps to lead Red and Splice away.

'Hold it!' Cal ordered, and removed as much of our luggage from Tenka as we could carry. Why tempt Fate, or indeed the fingers of the Irraka? We followed Spinel into the hall.

Inside, a sickly sweet odour of corruption mingled with a smell of wood smoke. Horses' hooves had cracked the marble floor and it was no longer the least bit white. Tatters of cloth hung without apparent purpose from carvings around the walls. Spinel studied our stunned appraisal of the surroundings.

'We are fighters, not thinkers,' he said bluntly. 'We have no time for Saltrock fancies here.'

Cal raised his shoulders eloquently. 'Quite,' he said.

There was one large room where all of Spinel's immediate retinue appeared to sleep, eat and lounge around. Rags partitioned the room's perimeter into separate sleeping quarters, but there could be little privacy. In one of these makeshift holes I saw a pitiful creature, little other than a skin-covered skeleton, lying on a pallet. Spinel caught me staring.

'Leg broken' he explained. 'The bone came through. Time says he might not heal.'

I felt sick. The Irraka were without hope. They did not have any healers and, as there are few Wraeththu who cannot effect some measure of healing, this betokened more than anything, more than the filth and the squalor, that this tribe had fallen from the path. Wandered off it, more likely. I realize now that they must have been a splinter group of Aralids somehow separated from their main tribe. Without the strength of the higher castes behind them, the troubles they had suffered had dragged them down. They had no sense of productiveness; their fire and imagination had been doused by hardship. Most of them seemed healthy enough, however, in a lean, hard way, and their animals appeared well cared for. Two hounds had bounded over to Spinel and he absently touched their heads as they scrabbled to lick his hands. I dreaded that we might be offered something to eat. The smell alone was enough to turn the stomach. I remembered with regret Lianvis' heavy-perfumed chambers. The windows here were mostly broken and stuffed with cloth. Smoke had stained the ceiling and walls; there was little light.

Cal dropped his luggage onto the floor and uttered a long, low whistle. I knew we still carried bread and fruit and cheese from the Kakkahaar. It may have been foolish to waste it then, but I suggested Spinel should share it with us. Cal obviously shared my thoughts for he agreed immediately. I could only admire Spinel's restraint as we unwrapped the food. The dogs were more honest; they howled to get at the cheese, which was dry, fragrant and crumbling.

'How did you get this town?' Cal asked, tearing at a hunk of sweet bread. Spinel did not seem to hear him; he was chewing with utter concentration. Cal repeated the question.

'Eh? Oh, the Varrs had it first. Took what they wanted and left. We were travelling around. Moved in. The men who lived here had fled to Stoor, the town back there, you know ...'

'What? And they leave you alone?' Cal sounded incredulous.

'Sure. We got nothing they need.'

I could not resist asking, 'Why did you go to Stoor when you saw the smoke? If you thought it might be Varrs, I mean? Would you have helped the men who lived there, if it had not been too late?'

Spinel's face creased with thought. He brooded over this question for a while. 'Fight for men? Help them?' He laughed bleakly. 'By Aghama, men are dead already, but the Varrs are a big badness. They make the sky go black. They should be made gone.' He stood up and the dogs pressed around his legs. He still had pride, if little else, looking down through the remaining mired window-panes at the street.

'Why don't you all leave this place?' I asked him, rather appalled that he had used the name of the first Wraeththu in oath.

'For what?' He did not turn away from the window.

'Things are better elsewhere.' It was so simple and so true I felt foolish saying it.

'Better!' Spinel scoffed. 'Where? All the north is plagued by the Uigenna and Varrs have all the rest. No-one bothers us here. We have nothing. We have nothing for them to take.' Muscles twisted in his face. He looked briefly at the figure I had seen lying on the pallet and then back to the window.

'It *is* safer down south,' Cal put in, in a clear, even voice. He was sitting cross-legged on the bare boards of the floor, unhurriedly rolling himself a cigarette. Lianvis had donated tobacco too, apparently. He looked luminous, soaking up the only available light; almost unearthly; illustrating, by contrast, the dismal squalor of the room. Spinel stared at him stonily. He would never like Cal; Cal was everything he was not.

'There is a town called Greenling on the other side of the desert. If I were you ...' Cal paused, licking the thin paper and pressing it down, 'I'd take my people there. Have you got a light?' Spinel ignored his request. Cal shrugged, turning to search our bags, the cigarette dangling from his mouth.

'There are desert tribes. We could never get across.' Spinel threw himself away from the window and squatted down beside us again.

'Ah, you mean the Kakkahaar,' Cal said with a smile. I wished he would not make his contempt so obvious.

'Look Spinel, we've been that way,' I told him. 'The Kakkahaar are not as threatening as you imagine ... well, nothing like Varrs anyway. There's a Kakkahaar Algomalid named Lianvis. We are known to him. If you mention our names he may well sell you the services of a guide. You could get across the desert that way ...'

Spinel looked at me with suspicion. Though he did not know the Kakkahaar's name, he obviously knew of their reputation.

Perhaps I had been too forward. The patronizing tone of our comments and the implied criticism of the Irraka and their hovel-town did not land lightly on Spinel's ears. He was obviously thinking; 'Who the hell do they think they are.' Cal was grinning happily to himself.

'Some time, perhaps,' Spinel said at last. 'Sometime, we may move on.'

Sometime perhaps. The Irraka would linger in Phesbe until they were all dead.

As the sun sank behind the bones of the town, someone lit a fire in the enormous, soot-coated grate. It filled the room with leaping shadows and smoke, but hid most of the unpleasantness. Spinel left us alone. I guessed we discomforted him. I was annoyed by the waste and apathy we had seen. I could not understand why the Irraka wanted to stay here. They did not want enlightenment, that was clear. There was one thing I *could* do, however. Lianvis had given me instruction on the art of healing the body by force of will. So far, I hadn't had the opportunity to put this talent to the test properly, but if there was a case of having to try, this was it.

Close to, the Har with the broken leg looked even more pathetic. I knelt beside the pallet and drew back the revolting blanket that covered him. He started like an animal and snarled at me. Dirt was scored into the frown of pain on his caricature of a face. I attempted conversation by thought and projected a calming form. Some of the aggressive fear left his eyes. The leg was not merely broken, it was shattered. Shattered and putrifying. 'Why have you no healers?' I asked him. It was all I could say, congested with anger. He stared defiantly at me, a look which told me he was only waiting to die. I put my hand above the wound and my arm went cold. Lianvis had taught me thoroughly the practice of healing. He had been surprised I had known so little. Most Kakkahaar could effect simple cures at Neoma level. I sensed Cal at my shoulder. He threw a shadow over the injured Har.

'Why bother?' he asked, with cruel indifference. It did not deserve an answer. 'I suppose you are going to invoke water elementals to get rid of the dirt?' he continued, with cheerful sarcasm.

I ignored him. First I had to draw out the badness. Cal was right; the wound did need to be cleaned.

'Have you water here?' I asked slowly.

'Don't waste your time playing with me!' the Har croaked at me with surprising venom.

'Find some water, Cal!' I ordered. He did not move. 'Please.' I heard him sigh.

'Alright, alright. If you must. Don't make a habit out of this kind of thing, will you!' He stomped away, still sighing.

'Do you have water in this building?' I asked once more. The Har turned his face away.

'Yes. There is water ...' He looked at me again. 'I despise you! I hate you that you can help me!'

I did not argue. His hopelessness and bitter rage could not be fought. 'Hate me all you want, little animal,' I said.

Cal brought the water and Spinel sauntered over to see what I was doing. I expected him to complain, but he passed no comment, just watched as I cleaned the wound. This was the first time I had ever put these skills into practice and I was not very quick at it.

'The bone is shattered,' I remarked, over my shoulder.

'Yes,' Spinel confirmed.

'How did it happen?'

'In one of the old factories through town. He fell.' Spinel stared into the Har's face without compassion.

'Why have you done nothing for him?!' I demanded angrily. I could not keep my feelings out of my voice.

'That's none of your business.' Spinel did not sound offended. He meant simply that. 'Anyway, you're helping him now.' He went away.

I did what I could. Only time would tell if that was enough. I asked him his name and he replied, 'Cobweb, Cobweb, Cobweb!' straining to lift himself up off the rags to shout in my face.

'You're mad to be in this place!' I hissed at him, casting a wary eye about the room for Spinel. 'You hate us, you say; I know why! You could be out of this. You could be in a tribe, a real one. This is a shambles!'

Cobweb tried to push me away as I started wiping his face with the wet rag, but I was stronger. 'I can't leave. I am Spinel's,' he said.

'What?' I could not help laughing. 'You are nobody's. You're just yours!'

'You don't understand. You're talking shit,' he replied in a dull mumble. 'The Varrs left me behind, 'cause I busted my leg. I guess I was still pretty when the Irraka came, so Spinel didn't kill me. Now I have to die to be free and, thank you, thank you, now it seems I'm not dying anymore!'

'I can tell you're not Irraka,' I said. His eyes appraised me with weary intelligence.

'Yeah.' I offered him what was left of my food and he observed, 'Well, if I'm to live, I might as well eat.'

'You could starve yourself to death,' I pointed out, and he smiled weakly, propping himself up on one elbow.

'Well, maybe life is worth living. Make me stronger and I'll feast on Spinel's guts. He wanted me to host his progeny because my blood is better than theirs, but he's so low-caste he can't, thank God! He wanted me lying here like a crippled brood mare . . .'

I still did not know much about Wraeththu reproduction and was keen to question him, even began to, but he would not listen. How long had he been here, hostile, silent and suffering?

'You're from Saltrock,' he gabbled. 'I heard them talking. They're fucking stupid, all of them. Stupid and ugly. They ought to be afraid of you, oughtn't they? You fixed my leg, didn't you? Why don't you kill them?'

I smiled and shook my head, looking at his leg. I had cleaned it, bombarded it with my strength and splinted it with wood, but I knew it was far from healed. 'Your leg has a better chance of healing now,' I said, 'but it won't take your weight for a while.'

'How long?' I did not know. 'How long?' he repeated. 'Look, I have a chance now. I can get out of here and find my people.' His feverish excitement alarmed me.

'You must eat properly. And exercise the leg.' Privately, I thought if Spinel noticed Cobweb's condition was improving, there was no way he could escape. 'Why do you want to find your people again?' I asked. 'They did abandon you after all.' His face curled into gaunt ugliness.

'What do *you* know?!' he spat at me. 'Terzian did not see me fall. None of them did. It was crazy out there; too much smoke. I heard him call me. He didn't know I was there. He thought I'd got out. I heard him call me, but I couldn't answer . . .'

'He never came back though.'

'No, no; never.' He lay back, grunting with pain as he moved his leg for comfort. Orange, flickering light smoothed the sharpness of his features. It was easy to see beauty had been there once.

'Don't let Spinel know how much you did for my leg, OK?'

I nodded slowly. 'OK.' I stood up. 'Good luck, Cobweb.'

'Luck? Who needs it? I'll bust my way out of here!'

I went back to Cal feeling heavy with depression. Cal had been out to see our horses. They were stabled in an old store next to the hall. He said our possessions seemed to be intact so far and had brought two of our rugs back up with him. We found a corner as far from the Irraka as possible and tried to get comfortable for the night. The fire had died low; we could hear Hara grunting like animals. One of the dogs gnawed on a bone too close for us not to hear the cracking. I thought of Cobweb's leg and pressed my face in Cal's fragrant hair to quell the nausea.

'We're leaving tomorrow,' Cal decided. 'I've had it with this rabble. The Varrs could not be worse. God, I'd sell my soul for a bath!'

We had not bathed properly since we had left the Kakkahaar, but I knew what he meant. Phesbe made cleanliness seem suddenly more important.

'Go on, argue with me!' he said, but for once I agreed with him completely. 'Amazing!' he exclaimed. 'What did the shrivelled one say? It looked quite intense.'

'His name's Cobweb. He's a Varr. Spinel's prisoner, or viciously reluctant concubine! He was planning on dying, only now he's decided on escaping.' I laughed bitterly, dreading the guilt about him that I felt sure would haunt my path out of Phesbe.

'So. He's a Varr, is he?' Cal's voice sounded calculating.

'You don't know everything, Cal,' I warned.

'There's nothing to know but the fact of his miserable existence and, perhaps, possible usefulness.' He propped himself up on his elbow. Faint light from the window spun and glowed in his hair. 'We'll have to take him with us,' he said.

'What?! No!' I protestd. 'No, no, no, no, no!'

'And if we don't? And if we meet the Varrs on the way north? Do you suppose they'll ask us in for dinner?'

'Only if they're cannibal,' I remarked. 'But it's useless. Spinel won't let Cobweb go. He plans to found a dynasty with him.'

Cal laughed at me. 'You're joking! There's no pearls in his loins and that's a fact.' He lay down again, wrapping me in his arms. 'Just leave it to me,' he said. 'Take your cue from me. Tomorrow.'

In the greyness of an overcast morning, the room looked even more dreary than it had the day before. We started to gather up our belongings and before long, Spinel came over to see what we were doing. It was morning, yet there was no smell of cooking or even coffee. Nothing but the filthy stink.

'Leaving are you?' Spinel asked us.

'Well yes,' Cal confirmed. 'We'll take our chances with the Varrs. We can't afford to waste time.' He was squatting on the floor, carefully folding the rugs.

'I see.' Spinel sounded put out. I looked at him hard, pleased to note the trace of weakness in his chin, his small, silver eyes. He stared back at me. 'Him with the leg. How did it go?'

Cal would not let me answer. 'Oh, it's a shame about that. Too late to do much, or enough anyway. Sorry.' Spinel grunted, looking even more displeased. I realized it was not beyond him to blame me if Cobweb died.

'He wants to go back to his tribe to die.' Cal glanced quickly up at him. This was the test, the bait.

'They left him here.' Spinel did not look exactly suspicious but I hoped Cal would not push it too far.

'I know. Pitiful, isn't it. Pell, pass me that bag there, will you. It would be best, Spinel, if you got that Har out of here, you know. The poison's in his blood; he may even contaminate others.'

Spinel's eyes opened a little wider. He knew nothing about medicine or poisoned blood and was in no position to argue.

'Even if he had lived, his essence would have been tainted,' Cal continued smoothly, buckling up the bags. 'Put him outside the town. Maybe the Varrs will find him. Maybe he'll poison them!' He laughed. Cal had lying down to a fine art. Even I was beginning to believe him.

'Hmmph!' Spinel grunted and went back to the fire.

'They're going to try and stop us,' I sang.

Cal stood up and swung one of the bags over his shoulder. 'Possibly, possibly. Get the rest of the stuff, Pell. Come on.'

Our guns were still packed safely in the bottom of our luggage, but we had tucked our knives into our belts. All the Irraka carried guns, of course.

'Now may be the time, Pell, for you to exercise those talents Lianvis has been grooming for you. I won't be able to handle this alone.'

'Oh no!' I spoke to his back. He was sauntering over to the group of Irraka huddled round the fire.

'Right. Thanks for the hospitality,' he said to Spinel. 'We're leaving now.'

'You're mad!' was the reply. 'You won't get very far.' I sensed a growing alertness in the hunched shapes, but I would not look at them.

'Oh, it's not that much of a risk really. We can handle ourselves,' Cal told them. 'Like this!'

One arrow of thought reached me: there! Our strengths mingled. Together, we had no difficulty in bringing down a corner of the ceiling. The Irraka jumped like a pack of dogs. The dust settled; a few more pieces dropped from the ragged plaster.

'You see,' Cal shrugged. 'If the Varrs try anything, we'll turn a few of them inside out. It might dampen their ferocity.' He adopted his most dazzling smile. 'Think about what we said about Greenling, Spinel. Oh, if you like, we'll dump the crippled Varr outside the town for you.'

Spinel only wanted to see us gone. He nodded nervously, his little eyes avoiding Cal's. I went over to where Cobweb lay, watching the show with relish.

'You said you didn't need luck, but you've got it,' I said. 'Come on, we're taking you out.'

Cobweb hid his relief and his gratitude with abuse. 'My leg, my fucking leg. I can't walk!'

'That doesn't matter.'

He was so light, I could hoist him over my shoulder easily. Spinel's crew watched us leave with the expression and posture of beaten dogs.

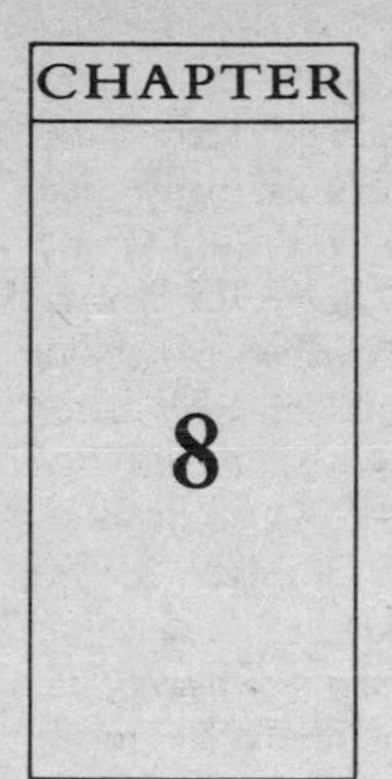

CHAPTER 8

... CHOSEN gods of
carnage voice,
Dictate in etiquette tease ...

North again. The land began to rise and was cut through by the wide, straight roads of men. We passed by several towns during the next few days; some were still smoking. Only one or two still showed signs of habitation. Cobweb, riding Tenka along with the baggage, was fractious with pain. For the first few days he hardly spoke at all; his face set in a sour expression of discomfort. Under the revealing light of the sun, we could see clearly the sad condition he was in. We had no opportunity to bathe and the filth of Phesbe, still saturating his clothes and body, could have done little to lift his spirits. I attended to his wounded leg each evening and morning, but I knew there was little more I could do. Even the most accomplished healer works better under sterilised conditions. At the very least I needed salt water to clean the wound and although we carried both salt and water, Cal would not let me use any of our drinking supply. Cobweb said we would eventually come to a river, and I hoped his condition would not worsen until we did.

There was no sign of the Varrs, other than the dead towns they had left behind them. Cal had told the Irraka we could deal with the Varrs, but that was just another of his convincing lies.

The Irraka had seen us work magic, but the Varrs were a true Wraeththu race, and Cobweb told us they included many Ulani in their ranks. Parlour tricks would not deter them. Cobweb was our only protection. We did not really know if the Varrs were habitually hostile to Hara of different tribes, but it was safer to expect the worse. I worried privately if Cobweb's patron would be pleased to see him again. The Varrs did not seem to be a tribe given to displays of compassion, and Cobweb's appearance was far from attractive. It might be that the mighty Terzian would be happier believing him dead.

The river, when we came to it, bore the signs of heavy conflict upon its banks. The dead were only men. If any Wraeththu had been killed, their tribe had either burned or buried the bodies. With typical inconvenience, dead men littered the stream. We would have to ride some way up the bank before the water would be clean. I was still a stranger to the reality of death, and the sight of the empty, staring bodies, sprawled in unnatural distortions disturbed me deeply. It was unbelievable that those clay-like puppets had ever thrilled with the spark of life; perhaps only the day before, thinking, talking, eating and sleeping. To see the dead like that can leave little doubt in even the most sceptical of minds as to the existence of the soul. Once the soul has gone, the flesh looks barely even human.

That night, Cal looked worried for the first time in ages. He watched me as I bathed Cobweb's leg with the long-awaited salt-water.

'Pell,' he said. 'This land is dying.' The sound of his voice more than the words, sent a bitter chill through my stomach.

'What? Why?' I asked quickly. Cobweb had closed his eyes.

'A few years ago, we came this way. This was man's land; it was full of them. Now they are all gone,' Cal replied.

'Then it is only the men that are dying, not the land,' I argued, with relief. He had painted a terrible, dark picture for me with those words.

'It is closing up. The land is taking over. Once more, as it was a long, long time ago. Can't you feel it Pell? Feel it! Mankind's funeral. You can feel them, can't you? All of them, somewhere around. Empty, but full of them.'

'Shut up, Cal!' I shouted. Suddenly the dark was full of eyes. Unseen at that, which was worse.

'Spooking you, am I?' He picked up a stick and scratched in the dirt round our little fire. The only sound was the comforting crackle of flames and vague animal rustlings in the distance. 'The sky's very high here, isn't it?' he remarked, looking up.

'Cal!'

'It's just changed so much, that's all. And in such a short time. Centuries of civilization wiped out in a couple of years. It's awesome!'

'We knew this is what it would come to!' I retorted, irritably.

'Are you feeling guilty, Cal? Are you thinking of all the pain and suffering and wretchedness of innocents just born in the wrong time and the wrong place?'

'And the wrong body,' Cobweb added drily. I looked down at him. He seemed like an untidy bundle of rags thrown down in the grass. A sudden thought prompted me to speak.

'Maybe they have the choice . . . all of them. Perhaps every man on this earth could be incepted to Wraeththu – even the women! Does anyone really know? Has anyone ever tried to incept a full-grown man, or a woman?'

Cal looked at me with distaste. 'You can be quite grotesque sometimes Pell,' he decided.

To my surprise Cobweb agreed with me. 'No, Cal,' he said. 'It is grotesque to think otherwise. That is man's smallmindedness; man's fear of questioning important issues. You know what I mean.' Cal also looked surprised that Cobweb had spoken.

'Well, I suppose it has a certain grim fascination. Shall we try it on the next woman we find?' His voice was caustic with sarcasm. Female was just a symbol to him of something that made men hate us. Even if it were possible, I do not think he would want to share our Har-ness with women. Cobweb's comments had astounded me too though. The only way I can describe it, is that it had sounded very un-Varr.

'I thought your tribe had dedicated themselves to speeding

up the extinction of Man,' I said.

'They have,' he answered simply. 'But it is different for me. I am not a warrior. The Varrs all have very set roles. I am a progenitor. Killing does not always seem the best way.'

'Yet you were there when your tribe sacked Phesbe,' Cal commented sardonically.

'Yes, I was there,' Cobweb agreed.

'Ah,' Cal began, relishing the moment before the next thrust.

I did not want to give Cal the opportunity to exercise his love of quibbling and spoke quickly to dispel the tension. 'Cobweb, you say you are a progenitor. Does that mean you have actually, er, you know ... reproduced?'

He looked at me blankly for a moment. I could still feel irritation behind me in the silence.

'Yes,' Cobweb said warily, after a while.

'You have Nahir-Nuri among you then?' Cal asked him suddenly, his curiosity overwhelming his desire to argue.

'No, that's not necessary. Given the right circumstances, we've found that Pyralisits or even Acanthalids can inseminate a host.'

'God, that's amazing!' Cal exclaimed. 'No, wait. That must be something fairly new. It must be. How long have the Varrs been practising it?'

Cobweb shrugged. 'I don't know exactly. I came from the tribe of Sulh some eight months back. It was a common thing then.'

'Events are moving even quicker than I imagined,' Cal said softly, with a trace of bitterness. He looked at me. 'God Pell. One year in Saltrock. Time stood still for us, didn't it? But out here ...' He shook his head. I had gathered that the knowledge Cal had of Wraeththu procreation was nearly as sketchy as mine. At the time when Cal had met me, it had been a shrouded subject, relevant only to the Nahir-Nuri. Yes, he was right. Everything was changing, speeding up. I had a feeling that the farther north we travelled, the more surprises would be revealed.

At our backs, the trees. Beyond our fire, the river. All around us a haunted quiet, disturbed only by the water and the flames. Cal spread our rugs on the ground. He had lapsed into a contemplative silence and curled up with his back to me. I sat watching the fire and the darkness over the river. I thought Cobweb had fallen asleep, but I heard him say, 'I have a son.' The tone of his voice made me feel sad. I poked at the fire with a stick, sending sprays of sparks spiralling upwards. Cobweb was not looking at me. I think he should have been weeping, but all I could see was his thin, well-shaped lips twitching as he chewed the inside of his mouth.

'Terzian's?' I asked, and he nodded, once, just staring at the stars.

'I expect he's alright,' I said, wishing I had never opened my mouth.

'Oh, I know that!'

I wanted to ask so many questions but at the same time, did not want to hear the answers.

'I know what you've been thinking,' Cobweb continued.

'Oh?' I was not sure which of my thoughts he had in mind.

'I know what's happened to me. I know that ... In a way I don't want to go back, but I have to ...'

'What have my thoughts got to do with it?'

'Oh, I can see you thinking,' he said with a wistful smile. 'When you do my leg. I can hear you say to yourself: there was beauty here once. We both know where that leads to don't we!' He did not want to say it, make it real with words.

'You're still the same person,' I told him.

He grimaced. 'Pellaz! If all the Hara in the world were like you! They're not though, are they? I know it matters. It matters very much. Perhaps less so in a tribe where there is utter equality of status. The Varrs are not like that.'

'You'll heal, get better.' I did not like any of this. It made the peace of Saltrock seem like a crazed, idealistic dream. This was what was real. It mattered to be beautiful. Spinel had told us the Varrs had whores, and he was right. Where was the proof of the Utopian visions Orien had spoken of? We had seen only the ophidian cruelty of the Kakkahaar, then the sordid apathy of the Irraka, now this. What had really changed since the first Wraeththu had come into the world? One selfish, ignorant race had been exchanged for another, more powerful, selfish, ignorant race. Where was the great tribe of noble and elevated spirits to cleanse the world? Since Saltrock, all I had seen were magicians, villains and killers. Maybe Immanion too was just a hazy fantasy. If it existed at all, it was somewhere far, far away, where none of this sordid mess could touch it. I was overwhelmed by a swelling tide of emotion: anger, indignation and love. Perhaps it would be best to turn back and return to Saltrock. We could take Cobweb with us. Maybe, there, his body and his soul could be healed. The sanity and the care of kindred spirits would make him whole and proud again.

'No!' he said, and I lifted my face from my hands. 'Do not think that, Pellaz.' He was looking at me now, with a great weariness. 'You look surprised. Am I reading your mind? It's there for all to see, isn't it?' I was dumbfounded. Cobweb sighed. 'Oh Pell, it wasn't just for my pretty face you see. That's not just what Terzian wanted. I am Brynie and, they tell me, a gifted psychic. Not that it takes much of that kind of talent to work out what *you* are thinking! You must know you can't go back. You must. It's a wonderful idea, and I'm grateful that you're thinking it, but no. I'm strong enough to take any of the shit Terzian might throw at me, I really am!' He grinned. 'You're tiring me out, do you know that? Tell me to shut up; I'm just moaning. Ignore it. I know I'll get better, and if Terzian tells me where to go, that's just too bad. I'll always have Swift; the son I still can't believe actually came out of me. You want to know about that too, don't you . . . I might scare him though, like this. How am I going to feel if he doesn't even recognize me? Why don't you tell me to shut up? Swift's not very old. Do you think he'll have forgotten me? I've not been gone that long, but, well children are strange, aren't they? *Their* children are strange, what are ours like? I don't know. He won't have to be incepted, will he? I'll have to tell him what men are. Won't it be crazy if he thinks that men and women are a kind of pervy idea? Only

Aghama can help me now, if he's really out there; Aghama or God. Is there a difference?'

'Cobweb,' I said, 'shut up.' He laughed, sort of crazily, and I leaned over him to wrap his blanket more firmly round his shoulders. 'You shouldn't be in this ...' I told him.

'Oh be quiet, Pell. I know what you think. Why don't you let me go to sleep.'

I went back to watching the fire. My people. My race. I felt a hundred years old.

Two more days of travelling and then the spiky outline of a town appeared in the distance.

'This is where we'll find them,' Cobweb said. He looked as if he was scraping the barrel of his strength.

Cal trotted Splice up alongside me. 'Well,' he said. 'This is it. A meeting I would have preferred to avoid.'

'Yes,' I agreed miserably. We had started out from Phaebe regarding Cobweb as protection against a possibility. It had been clear for some days, however, that we had to actually seek out the Varrs. Cobweb was deteriorating. If we did not get him back to his people, the only alternative was to leave him to die. Cal often appeared hard-hearted, but I knew the limits of his coldness. It was a tough, thin shell around an extremely mushy centre. Cobweb could no longer guide us; he lived in a solitary nightmare of delirium. So, without even discussing it, we had begun to look for signs that would lead us to the Varrs rather than away from them. After their ransacking expedition in Stoor, it appeared they had headed back to their home. It was not a difficult task to follow their trail of destruction.

About a mile from the town, a squad of mounted warriors cantered towards us. The horses were lean, breedy and polished; the riders fit, clean and lithe. Like the Irraka they wore mostly black leather, but it gleamed with the lustre of matt silk. We halted our horses and waited for them. Their leader spoke to one of his troupe, who walked his magnificent, mincing mount to within a couple of feet of Red and Splice's straining, quivering noses.

'We would like to speak with the one called Terzian,' Cal explained in his clear, careful voice.

'Why?' There was no hint of either hostility or cordiality.

'The one on the pack-horse back there,' Cal indicated with his thumb, 'he's one of yours. We got him out of a rather distressing situation and he's none too well. I understand Terzian would welcome news of his whereabouts.'

The Varr warrior looked round us towards Tenka and the rigour dropped from his face. 'Oh my god,' he said, almost in a whisper. Cal and I exchanged a comforting glance. 'Follow me!' The Varr trotted his horse back to the others and spoke urgently with the leader. They all looked at us with interest and suspicion. When we caught up with them the leader said, 'We shall take you to Terzian. I am Ithiel.' He held out his hand in a strange, old-fashioned gesture of welcome.

Cal took it and said, 'Thanks,' looking at Ithiel's hand with surprise.

'We had thought Cobweb was dead,' the Varr remarked as we rode towards the town. 'It is indeed fortunate that you ... came across him.' I had the feeling that he was finding all this very embarrassing. I did not know what Terzian was like, but I did not envy Ithiel the task of breaking this piece of news to him.

The town had been renamed Galhea, and was the largest I had ever seen. It was clean and boasted electric power. In fact, little appeared to have changed since Man had lived there. Shops were still trading, only the variety of their merchandise had changed. Music from inns and cafes gave the place an almost festive air. It was nothing like Cal and I had imagined. At home, the Varrs seemed relaxed and unexpectedly cheerful. Nowhere could we see the grim and deadly ranks of Wraeththu armies that we had anticipated. We rode through the town towards a residential area, bordered by tall, clipped trees and hedges of late-flowering orangeblossom. The perfumed air made me want to laugh with relief. It was a fragrance, a memory, of Saltrock.

Terzian's house was white and grand, approached by a winding uphill drive flanked by towering bushes of rhodedendron, rooted in turf as smooth as velvet. Order and cleanliness were everywhere. I did not catch sight of one stray leaf. We could see the house growing out of the top of the hill. It had once been a man's house, and he had evidently been rich. Slim, sparkling pillars framed the back of the building, leading to sloping, terraced lawns. The air held the faintest tang of autumn and the house stood out like a white tooth against the darker clouds of the sky. Inside, of course, it might have shared the same fate as Phesbe's civic hall, but I doubted it. Behind me, Cobweb began to cough. Only yesterday, the poison had reached his lungs. He said the Varrs had powerful healers and I prayed it was not too late.

Ithiel led us round the side of the house to an impressively neat stableyard. As we dismounted, he said, 'Your things will be safe here.' Hara came to lead our horses away and we followed Ithiel and two of his troupe into the house. One of them carried Cobweb in his arms. He looked barely alive, the damaged leg dangling uselessly. I knew how little he weighed. Cobweb; his name was sadly apt.

Dark, wood-panelled corridors wound through the kitchens and domestic quarters. We could see many Hara working there.

'It smells nice,' Cal said.

'Better than Phesbe,' I agreed and we laughed.

Ithiel turned at the sound. 'Phesbe. Is that where you found Cobweb?'

Cal nodded cautiously. Neither one of us wanted to explain too fully about the Irraka yet. It was not inconceivable that the truth could cause a Varr-ish act of retaliation; depending on how Terzian felt about it. Terzian was an unknown quantity to us; we could not guess how he would react. The Irraka were pathetic and we held no sympathy for them, but we did not want to make more trouble for them. Time would see to their disappearance without any assistance from Varr revenge.

We were taken up huge, curving flights of stairs carpetted in dark red, to an enormous suite of rooms approached by white double doors.

'Terzian says for you to make yourselves at home here,' Ithiel said, rather perfunctorily.

'Luxury we enjoy in the gilded chambers of the emperor!' Cal remarked sardonically, touching the heavy, floor-length, velvet curtains that bordered the windows. The predominant colour was palest green; the carpet was like moss underfoot. Terzian, Ithiel informed us, would grant us an audience after we had rested and eaten. 'Where's the bell for room service?' Cal asked him.

Ithiel sucked his breath in heavily, not smiling. 'You will find everything you need in here. Food will be brought up to you presently.'

'God, where have we found ourselves this time?!' I exclaimed once Ithiel had left the room.

'Nirvana?' Cal rejoined.

I looked out through the window. Below me, lawns and trees glowed emerald and viridian in the light of the dying sun. Rain-clouds of deep grey and purple massed on the western horizon. A great forest crept in towards the east.

'Things never turn out as you expect, do they Cal,' I said.

He sighed and collapsed backwards onto the enormous, grass-coloured bed. 'No. The Varrs are very civilized killers,' he replied. 'Have I turned out as you expected?'

I looked away from the window, surprised, but he was not smiling. The pupils of his violet eyes were enormous. 'Why?' I asked uneasily.

He shrugged. 'I don't know ... sometimes it seems ...' He went silent, still fixing me with his lazy, cruel eyes.

I went over and sat on the bed beside him. 'At first, I didn't know what to expect with you,' I said. 'Sometimes you frightened me, sometimes. Perhaps you still do. I get the feeling there are some things you will never tell me. But you are ... Cal, what are you trying to make me say?'

He reached out with one hand and touched my back. 'You're too good, Pell. I hope I don't see that pious, little angel knocked out of you.'

'I'm glad it was you that found me,' I told him, and he smiled.

That look, the fading light, the fragrant air of Galhea; they are with me for always. I took his perfect face in my hands. Our tired bodies, unwashed, underfed; hip bones sharp enough to bruise. We recaptured some of the magic of Saltrock then. Here we were; another oasis to shelter us in the savage waste of the world. It must have been on both of our minds: luck had been with us when Cobweb's had deserted him back in Phesbe.

As with the Kakkahaar, the Varrs brought us clothes of their own to wear. Black shirts of soft cloth and close-fitting black trousers. Boots of thin leather buckled to half-way up the leg. We were taken to Terzian well after the evening meal. Veiled lamps suffused the carpeted corridors with dim light. Downstairs, we were conducted to an enormous drawing-room. Thick curtains shut out the dark. Terzian was alone. He was leaning against a huge, white fireplace, staring into the flames. It was all very self-conscious. He looked up when we were announced and said, 'Please, sit down.' It was clear he was a Har who was used to obedience and more. He was slim, tall, well-groomed and had the refined elegance of a torturer. It was hard to imagine him in the act of killing, but it was easy to imagine him ordering someone else to do it.

'I want to convey my gratitude for bringing Cobweb back to us,' he said in a voice that betrayed no feeling. He asked us our names and where we had come from. Perhaps he had not visited Cobweb yet, or perhaps Cobweb could not talk to him, or he might have done both of these things, but just wanted to hear it from us. We told him anyway.

'Will Cobweb be alright?' I asked him.

'Oh yes. Our people know how to deal with the worst of wounds; they have plenty of practice of course. But for you, though, Cobweb might have died.' He did not ask about the Irraka or even how we had found Cobweb. I do not think he cared. He offered us sheh, a spirit they distilled themselves. We accepted and found it pleasant enough.

'Where are you travelling to?' Terzian asked us.

'North,' Cal replied. Terzian pulled a face.

'There is not much there,' he said. 'What there is, is horribly sordid. Tribes have broken up. Some of the splinter groups are like dogs. Men still have strong-holds in the cities. Time is spent there trying to stay alive by killing. But it's not organized enough. The cities should, in my opinion, be flushed out, evacuated by Wraeththu and destroyed. There is nothing there we really need.'

What could we say to that?

'What of the Uigenna? I understand they had the balance of power in the north,' Cal said.

'The Uigenna?' Terzian uttered a dismissive snort. 'Where have you been? They had internal conflict, to say the least. Their leaders fell to murdering each other; very artistically and no doubt spell-bindingly entertaining for the rest of them. Now, they spend their time bickering amongst themselves, experimenting colourfully with new poisons and ways to torture men and unpopular Hara to death, and have little interest in maintaining order.'

'I didn't realize that they ever did. Chaos was more their style,' Cal remarked drily, sipping his drink. Terzian gave him a hard look.

'Although the Uigenna do have a reputation for a certain ... reckless nature, they at least once had some kind of organization. We never have any trouble with them.' I could imagine Cal saying: that does not say much for Varrs, but thankfully he kept quiet, allowing himself only a private smile.

'How about the Unneah?' he asked.

'I don't really know,' Terzian answered him, moving away from the fire. 'They left the northeast cities. Can't say that I blame them. More sheh?'

'Thanks,' Cal held out his glass. Mine was still three-quarters full.

'You are lucky,' Terzian remarked, looking at me directly for the first time. 'Cobweb gave you a ticket in here. We don't normally tolerate strangers.' All of this seemed very rehearsed to me. 'However, the Hara of Saltrock do command a certain amount of respect. I have never been there.'

I hope you never will, I thought.

'Tell me about it,' Terzian demanded. We painted a glossier picture than reality, but Saltrock deserved it. Violence had no hold there. It was not a place for Varrs and their like.

'They don't live in the real world,' Terzian commented, after a while.

'Perhaps not,' I said, thinking of all we had seen on our travels north, 'but their way of life is something all Wraeththu should want for the future.' Terzian flared his nostrils and looked away from me. I could tell he thought that would be a boring prospect. I wondered what would have happened to me if I had fallen into the clutches of the Varrs for inception. It made me shudder. Varrs lived like men; their culture seemed just like men's. They were living in stolen towns, acting out the lives that had left them.

As we drank more sheh, conversation became easier. Terzian spoke volubly of conditions in the north, the birth place of Wraeththu. Men had fallen because all the might of their weapons could not fight what was meant to be. Tribes like the Uigenna were strong. Weapons could burn like matchwood under the concentration of their force. They had the ability to fill the minds of men with confusion and fear so that their leaders lost control. Both the Varrs and the Uigenna had Nahir-Nuri in the north. Dangerous, black creatures of heartless ambition. They had little time for tribes of lesser strength, in fact, often regarded them as being as worthless as men.

'We must cull the weak,' Terzian declared. Like Cal, he was Pyralisit, unlike Cal, he had bred many sons. 'This is not the time for braying and praying in the temples!' he told us vehemently. 'We need new blood. Young, pure Wraeththu blood, growing up untainted by man.' He stared at us hard. 'You have lost some condition on your travels, it would appear.'

Later, back in our room, Cal said to me, 'Do you want to move on tomorrow?' We looked at each other, honest, and yet not entirely so. I shook my head.

'Not yet, not yet.' I walked over to the window to look once more over the sweeping, lush countryside. 'I think I like it here, don't you?'

'You just like the comforts!'

'Don't you though?'

Cal sat down on the bed, rubbing the back of his neck and looking at himself in the mirror opposite. 'Their culture . . .' His hand touched his throat.

'There is much we could learn here. Maybe I do want the comforts; more than I want to winter in the north anyway.'

Cal lay back on the pillows and closed his eyes. He sighed. 'Something tells me: "Move on!" but I don't want to. It's easy to see why Cobweb wanted to come back.'

'There's nothing for us in the north, Cal,' I said.

'Hold on a moment. This is all presupposing Terzian wants us to stay around. He's said his thank yous; that might be the extent of his gratitude.' Cal sat up again.

'You don't really think that,' I said, rather sharply. Cal did not ask me to explain what I meant. He knew.

I was not surprised when Terzian invited us to his table for breakfast the following morning. Again, he was alone. After we had sat down, I enquired after Cobweb.

'He'll live,' Terzian muttered shortly and dismissed me from his attention.

His attendants brought us eggs, smoked fish and fruit juice served on thin white china. I asked Terzian if he lived alone. He did not answer me for a moment, dabbing his mouth with a starched napkin.

'No, not alone. I have Hara that see to my needs.' He tried to hide the fact that my question had irritated him. I wanted to ask where Cobweb was but feared his temper. After a while he said, 'There is one other.'

Cal and I exchanged a furtive glance across the table. The room was very light. Large windows led out to a terrace, closed against the chill, morning air. Black birds stalked across the tiles looking in at us angrily. Terzian lived like a lord; a warrior prince who had realized his fantasies. I could tell he was observing us, covertly, although he said little.

It was not a comfortable meal. I was trying to eat as quietly as possible when someone knocked on the door. Terzian bid them enter. The door opened a little way and a child ran into the room. It scrambled, chuckling, onto Terzian's lap, and I watched the brooding, sullen expression drop from his patrician face. I could understand, then, something of what Cobweb admired in him. 'Quietly, little one!' he ordered gently. 'We have guests.'

The child turned to look at us with wide, intelligent eyes. He looked about two years old. 'This is Cal, and Pell,' Terzian told him, smoothing his fine, dark hair. 'I'd like you to meet my son,' he said to us. 'His name is Swift.' Not two years old, then; nowhere near that.

'That must be Cobweb's child,' I said to Cal.

'My child,' Terzian corrected mildly.

'How old is he?' Cal asked.

'Six months.'

Cal and I both laughed. Terzian chose to ignore our indiscretion. 'I'm sorry,' Cal explained. 'We don't have much experience of this kind of thing. Swift is the first Wraeththu child we've seen.'

Terzian was not surprised. To him all tribes other than the Varrs were pitifully underdeveloped.

'He is perfect isn't he,' Terzian said to Cal. 'This is our future; perfect and whole.'

It was suggested that we spent the day sightseeing in Galhea. We were to be treated like tourists then.

'You'll find your baggage in the stable block,' Terzian told us. 'By all means, bring what you require into the house, but I would prefer it if you left soiled items outside. My staff will launder anything that needs it. You only have to ask.' He stood up, lifting Swift in his arms. 'Lunch is served at mid-day here. You are welcome to dine again with me, or in the town, as you prefer.' He inclined his head. 'Until later then.' Swift smiled at us over his shoulder as he walked out.

'My God, what is this place?!' Cal exclaimed, pushing his plate roughly across the table. I stared at the wrinkles he had made in the white table-cloth.

'Two centuries in the past?' I suggested.

He grinned at me. 'Two? Two! Three maybe, or three into the future, who knows!' He leaned back in his chair. 'I wonder what they use for currency in this town?'

We had hardly touched Cal's stolen money, but both thought it unlikely we could use it here.

During our meal the previous evening, all our Kakkahaar clothes and any that were still wearable from before that, had been taken away by Terzian's staff. An abundance of Varrish garments had been left in their place. I had noticed that none of the Varrs wore jewellery; only those who we learned were the tactfully-named progenitors wore their hair long.

'Male and female?' Cal queried with his usual acerbity, as we walked along the wide, manicured avenues of Galhea. It certainly seemed that way. 'They are splitting off again,' he continued. 'Wraeththu combined the sexes, but they are splitting off.'

'Is that so bad, so immoral?' I argued. 'Wraeththu combined the sexes by favouring the male. There are too many issues unraised, too many uncomfortable questions unanswered ...'

Cal glanced at me sideways. 'You worry me sometimes,' he said. 'What's going on in that busy little brain of yours?'

'Some things worry *me*,' I replied. 'As time goes on, I get more questions in my head and no-one knows the answers. They don't want to. No-one knows the questions either, come to that. What are we? How? Why? To what end? It is more than just a fun time, running wild and screaming, "Hey, let's get the bastards that fucked the world up!" It has to be. Perhaps the Varrs are on the right track about some things. Let the female side out ... it is in us after all. Oh, I don't know!'

We came, at length, to an inn; old-world, gambrelled, and dark inside. Curious, we ventured through the door, and found ourselves in a large, low-ceilinged room which smelt of wine and food. The tables were highly polished and had lion's feet made of brass. Cal asked at the bar about currency. Could we use our money here? 'You're staying at the Big House. Whatever you want is on Terzian,' was the reply, given reluctantly, we sensed.

'Our fame precedes us!' Cal declared. We ordered food and drink at Terzian's expense. The menu was impressive. Long-haired, soft-footed Hara, veiled and dressed like they should belong to an exotic harem, brought our meal to us. Slim, pale arms sliding from silk; their perfume eclipsing the aroma of herbs. They did not speak to us or even raise their eyes. Cal shook his head, his face grim.

'Cal, the Kakkahaar had Aralids as attendants,' I pointed out, 'and they were every bit as perfumed and delicate as they were.' I indicated the swaying bead curtains that led to the kitchen with a wave of my hand.

'Not like that!'

I could not lessen his disgust. 'What do you think about the child?' I asked, cutting into the fragrant, roasted fowl on my plate.

Cal raised his eyebrows and shrugged. 'It's weird, I'll say that. Didn't Cobweb say he came here about eight months ago? That means it took him roughly two months ... God! I wish I knew more about this. I didn't think it would be important until if and when I upgraded from Ulani. I suppose, deep down, I never really believed it was possible.' He was showing no inclination to begin eating.

'Do you suppose,' I began, trying to quell a rising discomfort, 'that they bear their young ... *live*?'

'What? As opposed to dead? Oh, I should think so!' Cal picked up his fork and started pushing food around his plate.

'Ha, ha! Come on, Cal, you know what I mean.' I kept my voice low, paranoic about anyone overhearing our conversation, even though the place was nearly empty.

'Sorry.' He reached over and touched my hand, lightly. 'Don't look so scared, Pell. I know only this. It's something like an oyster and a grain of sand. You must have heard me mention pearls before.'

I nodded. Cal twisted his mouth before speaking. 'Well, it's like this. The Har who is ouana, his seed is like the sand. The soft, passive, inhuman cavities of the soume; that is the oyster. Something happens that makes the pearl. It's not just ordinary aruna ... something happens. That's all I know. The pearl becomes a Wraeththu child; how, I really don't know.'

'Why have you never told me this before?' I demanded.

Cal gave another of his expressive shrugs. 'The same reason you never asked me! Let's face it Pell. We still think of ourselves as male, totally male; with a few pleasing adjustments, of course. We look male, don't we. We come through inception; wake up and it's just us. Don't you see? You never have to face yourself as some kind of monster. Your head's still the head you were born with; the same thoughts, the same memories. All this, it's a bit scary. It's having to face just how inhuman you are; what inception really did to you. All those female bits lurking inside you, where you can't see them, where you can forget them; but they're there!' Cal always had a way of putting things that opened doors onto a nasty, cold unknown.

'You were the one who was scorning the Varrs for, how did you put it, "splitting off". Are you now trying to tell me you've been actively suppressing half of your nature?' I tried to scoff, but my words sounded empty.

'And you haven't, I suppose?' He poured himself a glass of the pale, lemon wine. His fingers were wet, restlessly rubbing the glass. 'OK, now's the time, Pell. Let's be painfully honest, shall we. When you first met me, your first Wraeththu chum, what did you think? Oh, here's a boy that's into boys, and as I'm an effeminate, spoilt little brat, living a boring life, I'll go along with that ...' He made a hissing noise through his teeth. 'Oh, don't look like that! Alright, that was a bit strong. I know it was more than that – for you. It was an adventure, the promise of life beyond the fields. But it was like that for me, can't you see? That's what I am. If I wasn't Har, I'd be ... you know what I'm saying don't you?' I nodded quickly, unnerved by his agitation. 'But neither of us ever thought of this, Pell, did we? The responsibility of supplementing the race. Living things . . . oh god!' He put his face in his hands.

'Cal, Cal!' I said, reaching for his arm. 'I didn't know it had . . . upset you . . . this much.'

He did not look up. 'Someone gave me a mirror and I saw the future,' he said.

We wandered slowly back to Terzian's house. My head whirled with a multitude of questions and feelings. Cal was silent, looking at the ground, kicking up leaves. I looked around me. How come the Varrs had so much. Did they trade with other towns, other Wraeththu settlements? What did they trade? Perhaps it was all stolen; appropriated during Terzian's foraging tours around the country. As much as I tried to concentrate on how the Varrs obtained their wealth, the words, 'you do not have to face yourself as some kind of monster' kept pounding between my ears. My body felt strange; even hostile. Cal did not touch me as we walked along. Above us, tumescent clouds boiled across a confused sky, echoing my mood.

That evening, after another fine meal at Terzian's table, he asked us how long we planned to stay in Galhea. There was a moment's embarrassed silence and then Cal said, 'Well, that is really up to you, Terzian.'

Our host smiled in a careful, controlled way. 'I hardly think so,' he said. 'As far as I am concerned, you can stay as long as you wish. You can see my house is not exactly overcrowded.'

'I must admit, we don't relish the thought of having to travel further north with winter approaching,' I said, 'And we haven't any plans to do anything else just yet . . .'

'Obviously we'll work for our keep,' Cal put in. He was shredding a piece of bread onto his plate nervously.

Terzian laughed. 'There's no need,' he said pleasantly.

'We can't stay here for nothing,' Cal insisted.

'I don't see why not! But if it will make you feel better, I'm sure one of my farms would welcome your help to gather the harvest. There is one just north of Galhea, not far.' He stood up, neatly pushing his chair beneath the table. 'Now, if you will excuse me ...' Another gracious exit.

I told Cal that I did not trust Terzian. 'He must have something to gain by having us here,' I said.

'It was you that wanted to stay here,' Cal pointed out, still fiddling with breadcrumbs.

'We must be vigilant.'

'But I always am, my dear!' He reached forward to pat my cheek, making an effort to look unperturbed. I wish I had known then, that being vigilant is sometimes more than just having to look over your shoulder.

The following morning, we rode out to the nearest farm to offer our services. Terzian must have told them about us already. They treated us warily and with laboured politeness. Most of the grain had been brought in, but there was still plenty of work to be done. All the Varrs are very hard-workers, whatever else you might say about them. We were hard-pressed to keep up with them.

We did not see much of Terzian during the days that followed. Now that we ate most of our meals at the farm, there was very little opportunity to meet him. On our days off, and during the evenings, we kept to our room at first. Because we were unused to hard work, we were too tired to do anything else. But gradually, as we fell into a routine and began to befriend the cautious Hara we worked with, we took to spending more time in the town at night. Several evenings a week, we would go out drinking with Varrish companions, or visit them at their homes. Most of them were interested in our tales of Saltrock and the Kakkahaar; especially the Kakkahaar. My skin would prickle as Cal made Lianvis, in all his unholy glory, real again. When he finished speaking, we would all feel unseen eyes upon us and revel in the delicious fear.

We discovered that the Varrs had appropriated the remaining human population of the town as slaves. They were rarely seen; but we guessed the bleak nature of their existence; their hopelessness and utter despair was mirrored in the dull and wretched greyness of their appearance.

One evening, whilst we were sitting in a warm inn, quaffing large measures of ale, one of our companions brought our attention to a commotion that was going on outside. One Har stood up to look out of the window. 'They've caught something!' he cried. We all went outside to see. A group of Varrish warriors on horseback were herding a ragged group of individuals up the street. It looked like something from the Apocalypse. There were no electric lights in that area and the scene was lit by torches. Red sparks flashed off the horses' curbed bits and stirrup irons. Metal gleamed along their cheeks and their rolling eyes glowed red; their chewing mouths were laced with foam. The riders were like messengers of Death's angel; faceless and black. They ordered interested spectators to go back into the inns. We all shuffled back a few steps, but nobody went inside. At the end of the street was a small square, probably once used for open-air markets. We followed the procession and it stopped there. I saw Ithiel come riding across from the other side. His uniform was only half fastened, suggesting he had been summoned forth unexpectedly.

'What's going on?' I asked somebody standing near me.

'Intruders. Most likely caught thieving,' he replied, craning his neck to see over the crowd.

'Are they men or Hara?' I wanted to know, shaking his arm to make him listen to me.

'I can't tell from here,' he said.

Cal had disappeared. I pushed through the crowd to get a better view. The prisoners were making pitiable noises; some on their knees. The great, black horses pranced about excitedly. I heard Ithiel say, 'Let me see them.' Horses blocked the spectacle, their hooves kicking sparks off the cobbles. I saw Ithiel frown and shake his head. 'No good,' he said, and turned his horse away. For a moment there was silence as the crowd held its breath. Then the horses back-stepped away and one of the Varr warriors raised his arm. I didn't realise what was going on until six evenly spaced gun-shots cracked the night air. Hara around me began to mumble, turning back to the inns, back to their half-finished drinks, and their half-finished conversations. Perhaps some of them looked over their shoulders at what lay in the square, but not many. I stood frozen by disbelief. Six twitching bodies were sprawled in an ungainly heap near the middle of the square; no, five. One had tried to run. He lay a short distance away. Blood pooled among the stones and the air smelled of sulphur. The warriors dismounted and began to talk amongst themselves. I saw the brief flame of a match. That, then, was the nature of Varrish justice. It was not messy, not zealous, nor even exultant in its savagery. It was merely brutal and to the point and without compassion.

Cal came and put his arm around my shoulder. 'Not for them the fate worse than death,' he said, with disgusting humour. I could not bring myself to speak.

Back in the inn, nobody seemed affected by what we had witnessed. One Har said to Cal, 'This kind of thing often happens. Wraeththu stragglers or small groups of men stealing from the fields. Sometimes not even that. Sometimes they are merely passing through and run into Ithiel's watch-dogs. If they are Har and presentable, or human, young and male and presentable, they are bestowed the privilege of slavery. Most of them end up as progenitors for Terzian's elite guard. If they are not presentable enough ... well, as you just saw ...' He drew his finger across his neck expressively.

'You can see how lucky you were!' another exclaimed with a laugh, fondling Cal's shoulder.

'Luck?! You think it's luck?' the one who had spoken first began to cackle. 'Luck? Huh! Look at them!'

Because of Cobweb (just because of Cobweb?), we were Terzian's guests, and the respect that this situation afforded us made life even easier. Both Cal and I enjoyed working on the farm and liked the hara we worked with. Of course, none of them were in the least bit politically minded and accepted Terzian as their Autarch without question. He was admired, even deified by his followers. Terzian must know best, they thought. The average Varrish Har was neither cruel nor ferocious; just stupid in that they never examined the way their leaders operated. But then, Terzian, to his people and his friends, was nothing other than sympathetic and just. Living inside all this, wallowing in the luxuries of Terzian's grand house, it was difficult to keep our situation in perspective. In a way, we had become Varrs and the Varrish way seemed right. We were protected from what Terzian's armies got up to outside of Galhea. Sometimes, Terzian's superiors would send representatives down from the north to keep an eye on what he was doing. When any of them were staying in the house, we were meticulously prevented from meeting them.

Sometimes, little Swift would escape from the vigilance of his attendants and creep into our room to chatter to us. He was a disarmingly attractive child and very precocious, but not annoyingly so. Cal studiously avoided contact with him, but I liked listening to his childish ramblings and would take him on my knee and tell him stories. It was almost disorientating to think that I held a creature who had not been born of woman or even heard of men. I had long since given up asking Terzian about Cobweb. He would never answer my questions and I did not like to try and ask Swift for fear of upsetting him. I often feared the worst. Perhaps Terzian was reluctant to admit that his celebrated physicians had failed in their ministrations for once.

One evening, after we had been at Galhea for about two months, Terzian sent word to us that he would like us to dine with him in the house. When we went downstairs, we were served the usual sumptuous fare, but there was no sign of Terzian.

'So what!' Cal declared. 'Let's eat.'

We thought he must have been called away to deal with some of his clandestine business. He was forever disappearing from the house for some reason or another; sometimes for days at a time. There was an unusual tension in the air that night, and I remember remarking upon it to Cal. He had rubbed his bare arms and shivered, although there was a huge fire burning in the grate. We had just finished eating when the door opened and Terzian came into the room. He stood there, one hand gripping the door frame, just staring. Cal and I both jumped with surprise. It was obvious Terzian had been drinking and the very fact of it was chilling. He was normally so contained; his every action controlled and precise. I could not think of anything to say and Cal looked cynical. He half twisted in his seat, leaning back, waiting for Terzian to speak. For one brief instant I was crazily frightened for him. Cal bloomed under the right conditions; at that time he was second to none. Terzian knew that, and in his intoxicated state could not hide that he knew. He stepped forward unsteadily and leaned on the back of a chair. I could see he was trembling; it was terrifying.

'Cal, I have to speak to you,' he said. His voice was surprisingly steady. I noticed Cal's shoulders stiffen and I knew what went through his mind. His eyes kept flicking over to the door and back to Terzian. At any moment I expected him to make a run for it. Terzian guessed what he was thinking.

'Cal, please,' he said, very quietly. 'Why are you afraid?'

'Afraid?' Cal sounded dazed. I knew he feared Terzian, or more exactly, what Terzian might ask of him. I could not tell if that was a possibility or not. Terzian tore his gaze away from Cal to look at me.

'Pellaz?' he said, in the same quiet, deadly voice. I pushed my chair away from the table and stood up. There was still a chance he did only want to talk.

'It's OK,' I said. 'I'll leave you to your conversation. I was just going to go upstairs anyway.' It sounded about as sincere as Lianvis at his worst. Cal glanced up at me quickly. I could not interpret his expression, but something said inside me, 'He has been waiting for this.' We both had.

I shut the door behind me and went quickly to our room. Everywhere seemed strangely empty. I kept repeating to myself, 'We cannot be selfish with each other', but it was difficult for me. Cal and I were together nearly all the time. I remembered that night in the desert and a Kakkahaar incubus whose name I dared not guess. I remembered Cal's troubled eyes and the darkness he had sensed around me. It is not easy to be selfless in that way; it is almost unnatural, fighting against an inborn instinct.

I ran myself a hot bath (the water was always hot there), and miserably misted myself up in it. We had heard that Terzian planned to make one more destructive venture into the countryside before the cold season got its claws into the land. I hoped he would leave soon. There was little left in this area for him to deal with. Come the Spring, the Varr armies would trek north for some serious Spring-cleaning amongst the colonies of humanity that still stubbornly held on to their lands. We had overheard talk about it. Cal and I had never seen the warrior quarters of the town but we had heard about it. One of our friends at the farm had told us that Terzian's fighters lived like kings; nothing was denied them. Sleek machines whose only purpose was to kill and make Terzian more powerful. But, of course, he had kept us away from all that. Whatever he thought of us, whatever purpose he had in mind for us, it was clearly nothing to do with the belligerent side of Varrish nature. He admired the way we looked and, I think, liked to have us around the house for that reason. His house was full of beautiful things. I had always known he liked Cal better than me; he never looked me in the eye. Now he had obviously decided to take his admiration for Cal one step further. There had been no hint of it before.

The water had begun to cool and I lifted myself out, reaching for the thick, white towels, wandering back to the bedroom, drying my hair. I had let it grow back again on the side of my head, but still tried to keep it short there. I was still vain, but out of boredom more than vanity, I sat on a stool in front of the mirror and messed up my hair with a comb. Unplaited, it now reached my waist. For convenience, I had adopted the kakka-haar fashion of braiding my hair; there had been little opportunity on our travels of late for preening. Staring hard at myself at the mirror, I remembered thinking: you can be taken for a boy no longer. What you are is Wraeththu; male and female in one body. Then it was just an abstract, but now I know we are made of the hardest part of woman and the softest part of man. Is it any wonder then that we have to fight not to be cruel? Living in Galhea, my eyes began to open, my thirst for knowledge increase. 'What lies outside, outside across the hills, the forests, the abandoned towns? Does enlightenment lie that way? Does Wraeththu shine with a different kind of light that way?' We are made in the image of the First, of the Aghama. If he still watches us, have we lived up to his expectations? I doubted it. Weary with a half recognized depression, I burrowed into my bed.

Sometime, in the darkest part of the night, when everything wears its worst shadows, something woke me. I held my breath and hid under the bedclothes, suddenly conscious of the size of that huge, slumbering house, sentient in its hugeness. That someone, standing in my room unbidden, spoke my name, and it was not Cal. I did not answer. Again, 'Pellaz.' Soft, chiding; it was the voice of someone who saw me as a child, wrapped in the heart-coccoon of blankets. I felt the weight of someone sitting on the bed, and my skin prickled. (This house is so old, so many corridors ...) I thought of a vampire face and hollow eyes. Many faces look that way in moonlight. 'Pellaz, I know you're awake ... look at me.' The voice was familiar and I threw back the covers. At first, I did not recognize him and he said, 'Yes, it's me. You look like you were expecting a ghost.'

'Looks like I've got one!' It was Cobweb. I could only just see him. The curtains were pulled tightly together at the window; very little of that pale light outside shone through. The room felt cold.

'Let me in ... beside you ...' Did he think I knew nothing, that I had not heard the stories of how the night creatures can only harm you if you invite them in? There was only werelight and cold; I was not sure about him.

'No.'

He sighed and stood up, reaching to turn on the lamp by my bed.

'You look better,' I said.

'Mmmm.' I noticed he still limped as he came back to sit on the bed.

'Why are you here?'

He made a short, bitter sound. 'I have not thanked you for

saving my life.'

His face was still too thin; the skin as white and flawless as ivory.

'Terzian sent you.' It was not too brilliant a deduction.

'Well, yes.'

'You don't look too happy about it.' He shrugged and wrinkled his nose, running his fingers nervously through his dark hair, looking fragile enough to break. 'It's taken a long time to heal, has it?'

He nodded. 'Yes, a long time. I still get so fucking shaky, I hate it.' He pulled at his hair again. 'This house is so big, isn't it? I don't like it at night. Creeping along here, I felt like things were looking at me all the time. Lots of people must have lived here ...' He shivered.

'You scared me.'

'It's easy to get scared here at night. Anyway, part of you is still living in that old desert, isn't it. Peasants live on creepy stuff; it's in you.'

'Oh, you've seen the sharp sticks under my pillow then?'

'And the silver crucifix!'

We were both silent for a while until I gave in and said, 'OK, get in.' He was wearing only a long, white shirt and felt as cold as death.

'I wondered what had happened to you,' I told him. 'Terzian wouldn't tell me.'

He crept closer to my side and rested an icy cheek on my chest. 'You're hot,' he said.

'No, you're cold. Are you sure you're not a ghost?'

He laughed, 'No, not sure. Stroke my back.' I could feel every bone in his spine and was unsure whether it was attractive or repellant. He did look like a vampire. The ivory skin, the ebony, bruised-looking eyes; but he was not half as gaunt as the last time I had seen him. I put my hand to his face and tried to draw him towards me, but he pulled away.

'No. Not that. It scares me.'

'Why? I don't breathe poison.'

'Everyone breathes poison. Poison of themselves. It makes me feel like I'm getting lost, all mixed up in someone else; and their breath is always stronger. What if I can't come out again? What then?' I remembered Ulaume and knew something of what he meant. 'Terzian is like that,' he continued. 'Like a big, black cloud filling the sky in the shape of a wolf.'

I shuddered. 'Cal ...'

'I know.' He sounded resigned, and not a little bitter.

Was it within me to warm away that kind of chill? Terzian had sent him to me and I wondered what had made him obey that order. In his position I wouldn't have done.

'I'm no substitute, am I, to either of you,' he sighed.

I had forgotten he could eavesdrop on other people's thoughts. I held his face in my hands; his jaw trembled. 'You are still beautiful,' I told him, 'and so is your son. I've seen him.'

A faint cunning hardened his eyes. 'Love me,' he said.

'There is no love!' I replied.

'Oh, there is!' he said.

Masculinity in progenitors is considered unaesthetic and they try to hide that side of themselves. Aruna was a great skill to Cobweb; he teased me effortlessly. I could not understand why Terzian did not appreciate what he had; wit, sensuality and grace, if a little skinny.

'Why are you here?' I asked him. 'With the Varrs, with Terzian. Why did you leave the Sulh?'

He smiled ruefully. 'Ah, well, it is a simple story. Imagine this: Your tribe are a nomad people; fierce, strong, but not rich. You have travelled down from the north to trade with the Varrs. (Your leader carries a message from the Uigenna; that was our visa). Conditions are bad in the north. It is all dried blood and the smell of burning and horrible black birds everywhere. Galhea looks like heaven and it's full of angels; black angels. One of them, a king of angels, looks at you and suddenly, before you can wake up, your tribe have left town and you're living with a Har who's like the beast in the middle of the maze. At first you don't mind because he's so wonderful, so tall, gold-haired and viciously handsome. He also has a metal heart. He doesn't say much but he knows the right way to touch you. All he wants is sons; he is ouana, never anything else. He takes beautiful hosts for his seed; but of course, you haven't realized that ...' He sighed once more and I could feel his fingers flexing on my chest. 'So there I am, Pellaz; innocent, wide-eyed, loving the warmth, the fine clothes, the rich food ... and then one morning, I wake up retching my guts out, feeling like the sky's falling in. Terzian is actually pleased! He has his staff carry me off to the kitchen table and in a red, red, spiky haze, I know they tear something out of me. It shouldn't have been like that; not that exactly. Something went wrong. God, did I shout! I screamed and swore at Terzian and he told me not to swear. There was blood on the table and he put his finger in it, right as he told me not to swear. I can remember that so well. They carted me back to my bed and fussed around my fever and poulticed my torn parts, and so I got better again. Sometime, about a week later, I think, they came and put Swift in my arms. I didn't know he was mine at first. God, there he is; I can still see him. Perfect. He ate meat from the beginning, like some kind of reptile. A demon child. I wake up again and again and again; it's always real. Once I was human, a human boy with a mother that called me in for my dinner and mussed my hair and called me "honey". Now I'm something else. Maybe I don't even look the same. But you know something, it's a powerful feeling, very powerful. To make life out of nothing ... Terzian. ... if it wasn't for him, I could be happy, I guess.'

'Why aren't you angry?' I asked him. 'Why stay here? You're treated like a slave!'

He laughed at me again. 'You're a real crusader, Pell. I'm lazy, really lazy. Don't feel sorry for me.'

'You're lonely.'

'Not really. Once I'm fit again, I'll start fighting. It takes time.'

'Fighting! For what? For Terzian?'

'What else? He'll want other sons ...'

I could not understand him. 'Terzian left you for dead with the Irraka,' I said, and he turned his face away.

'You don't know what's best for me, Pell. I am the only

progenitor he keeps in the house. I am worth something to him.'

In the morning, I could not face going to the farm and stayed in my room with Cobweb.

'We are on different paths,' he said.

I braided his hair for him, fine as a child's. 'You are a fool!' I told him.

He only laughed. 'Oh, go home, Pell. Sort the world out!'

He brought us food from the kitchens. It was like stealing. It was like hiding from stern and serious things not yet to be faced.

He said, 'Cal will not be with you today,' and I looked at him sharply, gut-cold. 'Oh, you might see his body, later, but I know where his head will be. Far away. Somewhere deep in that wolf-shaped black cloud I told you about. Up there.' He pointed out of the window, where the sky was dark and heavy.

'Cal is not like you!' I answered hotly. 'He can't be mesmerised by anyone. He won't be sleeping until it's too late to wake up!'

'You shouldn't have left him last night.'

'Why tell me this now?'

'Because I'm a double agent.' He put his hands on my face. 'I may be wrong, of course, but I know Terzian. He ensnares people. Locks them away in that metal heart.'

I was filled with a cold, condensed kind of anger.

'You can't kill him,' Cobweb said. His cool, light hands slipped over my shoulders, down my back. 'I am the chalice in the waters of forgetfulness.'

'Perhaps you'd like to be!' I began to laugh. Cobweb had the power to make me forget. I couldn't see it. I should have searched the house, shouting, breaking the enchantment, but Cobweb made me forget. He was the web. He was the spider.

When evening came to draw its shades over the day, I wanted to go downstairs. Cobweb pushed me backwards, back onto the bed, laughing, smiling. His mouth was hot upon my skin and that room became the whole world again. I was hungry. We had eaten hardly anything since breakfast. He said he would go down later. There would be cold meat left from the evening meal. I wondered whether Cal and Terzian had sat, one on each side of the table, to eat that night. Did they talk together? 'Don't think about them,' Cobweb whispered. Cobweb. My head was full of cobwebs. I should have gone down, fought the lethargy, thrown off Cobweb's spidery, wispy magic. But I could not leave him. He could not (would not) satisfy me. I wanted more and more and more. In the dimness, he became more beautiful, more full and the sensations he aroused in me were unimaginable.

In the night, as Cobweb lay curled against my side, breathing evenly in contented sleep, the door opened. I was still awake, having slept for most of the day. I saw Cal walk into the room, without furtiveness, unenchanted, totally alert. He stood at the bottom of the bed, arms folded and slowly shook his head at me. He was smiling in his usual careless way; there was nothing different about him. After a stunned second or two, I hurled back the covers and threw myself at him.

'Cal, are you alright? Are you?'

He held my shoulders, laughing. 'Alright? What do you mean? Of course I am.' He looked beyond me to Cobweb, who had awoken and was crouching like a cat amongst the wrinkled sheets.

'Get back to your master,' Cal chanted to him in a soft, chilling voice.

Cobweb's head went up. 'You should not be here,' he said.

'I am here though, now get out. You've done your part.'

With dignity Cobweb hopped from the bed and went to the door. He had to get in one parting shot. 'I don't know what you think you're doing Cal, but you won't get away that easily. And if you do, you'll be back some day.'

Cal made a noise that was half growl, half laugh and raised his fist. Cobweb closed the door behind him.

Left alone, Cal and I embraced in silence. There were horrible words unspoken and I did not want to hear them. It was a crisis we had passed, that was all. There was no magic, no enchantments; just bodies and clever eyes, that was all. When I looked at Cal's face, his eyes were wet. Only two times, did I see that happen. This was the first.

'We cannot stay here,' he said.

'No,' I answered. My voice sounded as if it came from far-away; an insubstantial thread of sound. Cal let me go and sat down on the bed. He rested his elbows on his knees and put his face into his hands. His hair had grown longer since Saltrock; he had not bothered to cut it for a long time. Where it fell on either side of his bent head, I could see livid marks on his neck. My head went cold; loathsome, unwelcome pictures filled it. But I kneeled behind him and put my arms around his chest. I could feel him shaking. I did not know what to say. Outside, grey dawn started to creep up the sky.

After a while, Cal stood up. He took my hand. 'I'm going to take a bath. A long, hot one.'

'Shall I start getting the stuff ready?'

He paused at the doorway to the bathroom, rubbing his neck. 'Yes, OK.'

'Will we have any trouble?' I heard him turn on the taps.

'No.'

I was anxious to know what had been going on, but also sensible enough to know I would have to wait. With some regret, I started hauling things out of the drawers and cupboards. Terzian had been generous. We would leave Galhea richer than we had found it. Curious. That statement works two ways. Maybe we should have left most of Terzian's gifts behind. Maybe not. We had a pack-horse now. Weight was no problem.

We walked through the great, silent house and met no-one on the stairs, in the corridors. Outside, in the courtyard greyed by mist, Cal turned and looked up. He pointed. 'That's Terzian's room,' he said. The curtains were closed. Red, Splice and Tenka had been shorn of their winter coats. It took some time to find travelling rugs to fit them. The remainder of our belongings we found amongst bags of oats in an unoccupied stable. Everything was floury.

We left Galhea and Terzian's big, white man-house. It was that easy. No-one came out of the house. No-one tried to stop us. The blank eyes of the building watched us impassively;

Terzian's curtains did not twitch. All the time I was expecting somebody to appear; either to impede our leaving or just to watch us, make sure that we did leave. Would Cobweb show himself at an upstairs window to wave or smile or glower at us? No-one did. Something had happened and our presence was no longer important. Terzian, blind in grief, rage or humiliation had turned his back on us.

The horses had been shod with iron and the sound of their hooves echoed too loudly as we trotted out of the yard. Once round the front of the house, we turned them onto the wet lawns and urged them into a canter. Clods of turf flew everywhere, awkward carrion birds flapped up from the dew, complaining hoarsely. When we reached the gates of the driveway, Cal turned left rather than right, which would have taken us into the town.

'Where are we going?' I asked.

'South.' Cal kept Splice at a trot. He could not leave Galhea fast enough.

'South? Again? But why?' Red was trying to go sideways, frisky, with a bellyful of oats.

'It's the way to go.'

'The way to go for what?'

'Immanion, maybe? Who cares!' He looked so angry. I let it go at that. He would not talk, his head haloed by a nimbus of quick, shallow breaths.

CHAPTER 9

Release, resist; you're on a leash

At least if we travelled south again, I thought, to comfort myself, and kept travelling for long enough, we would out-distance the winter. Although the climate was not too harsh in that part of the world, it was very wet, and a misery if you were stuck on a horse all day. At mid-day, the skies opened. Rain slashed down with merciless gusto. We had to dismount and unpack the enveloping cloaks Lianvis had given us. The material had been treated (by some secret Kakkahaar process) to guarantee comfort to the wearer, be the weather hot, cold or wet. We did not want to sleep out in the open and kept riding until we reached one of the dead towns. It was hardly pleasant to stay there. The houses were mostly ruined inside, but we managed to find shelter. There were animals outside, we could hear them; quite large too by the sound of them. Neither of us went to look. Cal built a fire and unpacked some of what little food we had taken from Galhea. I hated the wall of silence he had put between us; it could mean so many things. Eventually, I could contain myself no longer.

'Cal.' I reached for his arm. 'Tell me, tell me what happened.'

He put his hand over mine, carefully. 'It's not that much,' he said, but he would not look at me.

'Is it bad?'

'No, not bad.'

'Did he want to make you like Cobweb?' Cal looked up at me then. His face was strange and guarded in the meagre light of the little fire.

'Like Cobweb?' he laughed cruelly. 'Cobweb's just a plaything to him. No, not even that ... he's looking for something else.'

I could feel myself withdraw as if scalded or pressed with ice. 'I see.'

'Do you?' He stared at me stonily. His hair was wild and matted, his eyes wide; he looked like a lion. 'You don't see Pell. You can't. What I've seen, what I've known ... maybe I'm the only person alive who has and that's it! And I really don't want to talk about it anymore, just now.'

I was horrified. It was like he was slipping away from me. 'Cal,' I said, questioning, sorrowful.

'Oh, it's alright, Pell. It's alright.' He forced a smile and rubbed his face with his hands. 'We'll keep on going. We've learnt a few things, maybe. We're wiser, maybe. There's no harm done.'

For several days he said nothing more about it. We kept on going, as he said, killing small animals when we could for food. Luckily, because of the time of year, there was a lot of fruit around. Leftover cultivations in disappearing gardens raped by wilderness. Red ate too many green apples once, and I had to spend a whole night walking him round to ease his belly. The land around us was eerily deserted. We saw no-one. Nature crept back across the concrete at her own pace.

One day, the sun shone a little brighter and the sky was clearer. The air smelt wonderful, full of mist and ripeness. Cal sang to me as we rode along. I told him he had a good voice. Then he said, 'Pell, do you think we are in love?'

I was so surprised by this that I felt colour rise to my face.

'Orien said there is only one kind of love,' I said quickly. 'And that is the universal kind. We love our race. Anything else is just a state of agreeable friendship coloured over too hard by lust.'

Cal laughed, apparently oblivious of my discomfort. 'Yes, that is Orien talking!'

'Why did you ask me?' I feared for his mind.

'Because ... oh because ... look, I know they teach you at your inception that you should never lay claim over another emotionally. We are encouraged to be independent in that way, aren't we? Wraeththu must be free. We have examples to warn us. The history of Mankind; what they did in the name of love. It can make you kill; because love's shadow is jealousy. Men could not have one without the other. Can we? We claim to be free of such things, but are we?'

Cal did not normally ask himself these kind of questions.

'Cobweb said love existed ...' I said, not meaning to.

Cal reined Splice in to a halt. 'You've said it, Pell, that's it. The Varrs, what are they? Selfish killers, pillagers? To us, they appear to have deviated from the pure beliefs. They do not want to progress spiritually, they are content the way they are, but they do not deny love.'

'Don't you mean "*and* they do not deny love"?' I added cynically.

'Love itself is not a terrible thing,' he said.

'I know that. Orien knows that,' I conceded, 'but as you said, it has its shadows.'

'We must bring it into the light then, where shadows cannot exist.'

'This is all hypothetical,' I pointed out.

Cal laughed, 'Look at me and say that,' he said. What I saw in his face almost frightened me; I could feel a frightening tide in my blood.

'I cannot say that, you are right,' I answered.

'Then it must be true; we are in love.'

'If a name has to be put to it, I suppose we are,' I said.

'Yes, I thought so. Then I made the right decision.'

I leapt off Red's back; he began to eat grass. 'Cal, get down.' He smiled at me. 'I want to know what you're really talking about,' I said.

He swung one leg over Splice's lowered neck and slid to the

ground beside me. We had been riding over wide, sprawling fields; there was no cover. In the distance, trees crept forward from the horizon.

'We shall walk to the wood,' Cal said, 'and by the time we get there, you shall know everything.'

We walked side by side, the horses trailing behind.

'You must have realized Terzian asked me to stay with him,' Cal began.

'I think so,' I answered (untruthfully).

'And you must have realized I was in two minds whether to leave or not ...'

'No! Were you?'

His arm went around my shoulder. 'Keep walking. Yes, I was. Terzian seduced me with the fire power of a volcano.'

'Yes,' I agreed, cynically. 'Cobweb said he could mesmerize people!'

Cal gave me a dry look. 'Oh, I expect he can, but it was nothing like that. Do you want to know?'

'If you like.'

'Well, after you left us at the dinner table that night, he just came straight out with it. "Cal," he said, "I want you to stay here." "But I am," I replied. Then he told me. He had been watching me. He had seen no-one else like me. I was wary of the flattery, of course. It all seemed too glib. All his life, his Wraeththu life I might add, it appears Terzian has been waiting for someone like me. He said he wanted me to share his life, his powr and everything else; for ever. And he meant it, I have no doubt of that. It was all so serious; not just a seduction scene. I think it must have taken tremendous guts for him to say all that to me. He's proud, you know that, and rigidly contained. That kind of demonstration doesn't rest easily on him. We went to his room and for a whole day it was ... just ... it was just ... well, you know.' (The immediate thought, what, better than me? sprang to my mind, but I would not say it.) 'Terzian said, "Cal, we can be great", and I believed him. He was as fine as a panther. I was waiting for him to say something about going that one bit further, further than ever before. That was what we were expecting, wasn't it? All those shrouded conversations. I was dreading it, feeling him there, knowing he had the power to open me up, to touch the place that would open me up and plant his seed there. But he didn't. He must have been sure I would stay, otherwise ... when I think rationally about it, there was no reason on Earth why I should not have stayed with him; it is somebody's destiny after all. My dreams of Immanion are just that; dreams. What am I looking for? What was I looking for, way back, on the road, when Zack ...' His face looked bleak; he turned to me. 'I found something, didn't I, back then? The one thing that made me say no and turn my back on all that comfort, that easy way out of life. I would have missed it had I let it go, that something.'

He waited for me to ask, 'Which is?'

'You,' he answered. 'Simply you. That's what made me think.'

I smiled at him, although strangely, it was hard. 'You know I would have been lost without you, Cal,' I said, which was true in the literal and emotional sense. 'Most probably dead within a week.'

'Most probably. Anyway, it's over now. How easy it is to say that. It was nothing, really; so quick. Now, I just feel one hell of a lot wiser. Some things I'm not ready for. Spawning brats is one of them; you know about that. But one day, when all this (and he flung his arm towards the sky), when all of this belongs to Wraeththu; Wraeththu building new cities here, *sane* people, not the crazy man-killers, there will come a time ... God knows I want us still to be together then. If we are, we can begin new life with each other; I don't want to discover that without you.'

'That's quite a speech, Cal,' I said, embarrassed, but not for him. Seel had once said to me (and it seemed so long ago); 'Cal's so emotional, I sometimes think he's still half-human,' and he was right. What he had not thought of, however, was that we were all still half-human. Perhaps our sons would be for ever. Not all of mankind had been bad. I think humanity's main downfall had been that they had just over-civilized themselves, and as a result, surrendered themselves to isolation. Lonely, solitary creatures trapped in the darkness of their own frightened minds, and cruel because they feared the dark. They forgot how to trust, be trustworthy and how to see beyond the mundane. Because of that, as they slipped further and further away from the Truth, some great thing, the thing they had simplified to God, had made Wraeththu happen. Mankind, you had your chance with the world and you failed. Now it is our turn. And to succeed where Man did not meant there could be no Varrs, no Uigenna, no cruelty. Since Saltrock, the Wraeththu tribes we had encountered did not inspire hope, but this was a big country and we had seen so little of it. One country in a big world.

As we reached the shelter of the trees I asked, 'Why are we going south again? Is there a reason?'

'Oh yes,' Cal replied. 'Terzian told me that beyond the desert, much further south than we've been, there may be a way to Immanion.'

'You still follow your dream then?' I pointed out, rather acidly.

He laughed. 'We have to go somewhere.'

'How can Terzian know of this?'

'How indeed! Who cares? It'll be a hell of a lot warmer down there.'

I said, 'You mentioned Zack back there. You never have done before.'

'Before ... Don't try to draw me out on that subject Pell. Let me forget that.'

The forest was a big one. Matted, heavily scented with evergreen resins; dark and haunted. But we were not afraid. Light folded down into the Earth; the forest vibrated with the sibilances of night. Absorbed as we were in a new process of discovery within our hearts, the darkness, creeping and rustling, could hold no terrors for us. We found a clearing and lit a fire. When Cal reached for me, he drew me towards him in spirit and mind as well as body. We were truly one creature, and fierce and terrible in the strength of that knowledge. His mind was a shining city for me to explore; even the shuttered doors seemed to whisper to me, 'one day, one day'. A lonely voice called at the end of the darkest avenue. If only it did not have to end. If only. The end. Cal. I was soaring like a bird, my nerves bursting with a sizzling, gunpowder radiance. Totally unafraid, elemental, letting go; experiencing the unspoken word, loving him. There blinked the half-closed eye of God. Ouana pressing against the seal to another cosmos. I could have opened up to that strange, new universe, could have. But he ended it there. In a sigh, in the night-time, in the dark, glowing together, by the dying light of the fire.

I should have known. Perhaps I did. It was the last time.

BOOK TWO

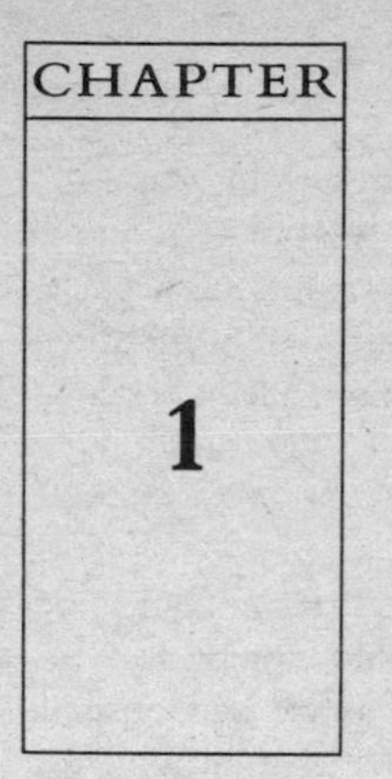

The thunderstruck tower

In the morning, we packed away our belongings, ready for the next day's ride in our journey south. A low breeze, tinged with the promise of ice, fretted the damp ashes of our fire. Daylight stripped the magic from the place where we had lain. The air was moist around us and we both felt sad. Cal held me in his arms beside the snorting horses. It was as if he knew our love was ephemeral. We had given it a name, a substance, and somehow, by doing that, we had condemned ourselves. We did not know the truth, not then, not for a long time, that we had never been alone. Forever at our heels, unseen eyes, all-seeing eyes. The gift of my inception. Cal had become too important to me. To the mind behind the eyes, I was no longer safe, no longer theirs alone.

By mid-afternoon, the trees began to thin around us. Where the horses had once pushed breast-deep in thick foliage, they now trod a sandy soil. Leaves above us tapped to the rhythm of a fine rain. Between the leaves, the swaying black branches, we could see it: a village.

Now is the difficult part. Now. I have thrown down my pen and picked it up again a hundred times. Even now it makes me feel sick and cold to think about it. I can remember the feelings, the smells, the sounds, everything. Just by closing my eyes I can bring it all back.

There were no people there. No Hara. Everything was still, under the whispering mist of the rain. It was an enchanted place, asleep, dreaming, red brick and lush greenness. A place waiting to fulfil its destiny; its one true purpose. Something made me say, 'Cal, let me go first.' My voice sounded slow and deep.

He replied, sleepily, 'There might be danger.'

I looked straight at him. 'Might be . . .'

Pain shadowed his eyes. It was impossible that we could not have known. We knew. Inevitability. It could not be fought. Our mood had become silent and sombre as we had pushed through the trees, because we had felt it closing in around us. Fate. The great invisible hand. I made a clicking noise in my mouth and urged Red forward. My legs were frozen. His neck was up, ears flat. I did not look back, but I could feel Cal's eyes burning into my back.

The woman was crouched in a doorway. I saw her first, but could not stop, my legs still frozen to Red's damp sides. I could not take cover. How her eyes hated me; black, almost blind with hate. She held the gun, really too large for her to use, against her belly, rag covered, twisted with poverty and tongueless rage. She saw me, wretched, weak as she was. Wraeththu, shining Wraeththu. Sleek with health, she saw the blood of her kind light my flesh from within. She struggled with the gun, raised it . . .

The shock came before the sound, the single, rolling, echoing sound. Something cracked against my head. At the front. At the back. There was no pain, no further sound. My body started to fall, but the essence of me still stared out between Red's ears in surprise. Vaguely, like a phantom, Cal flashed past me, red over white, like a scarf on the wind, and the woman died in silence. No resistance. Nothing. Just a weary confusion in her eyes as she looked at the knife. As it rose. As it fell. Slowly. I could see all around, colours bright enough to ache, the sky a white, white light. I saw Cal, his cheek cut by flying bone, stand over the shell that had been Pellaz. Red and white. He could not take it in.

Then he knelt. Warm lips against the cooling flesh. I could not feel it. In his confusion he could not feel me. I did not want to leave him; I could smell his tears. He gently pressed his fingers against the red star above and between my eyes. The ground, Cal's knees, were dark red. So much blood in one small body. One body containing all that red. The horses were shaking, foam along their sides. Cal threw back his head and screamed, howled; an animal cry. All feeling was leaving him; I could sense his numbness, his rage; all of this. For a while, I ignored the insistance, the calling. I wanted to watch Cal. I still needed him. We belonged to each other. If I left, I was afraid he might forget me. Already the scene had become unreal, like watching a moving picture, dusty with age.

The Call. Above the houses, the light had condensed into a star. Not really me, half me, I went up to meet it, I could not resist, and the eyes in the light were familiar, knowing. That was when I wanted to scream, but it was too late. I had no throat.

It was ... rushing. Rushing past me, over me, through me. Moving black air, threads of light; spiralling curls of ether. I felt my murderer wailing at my heels. The soul, no longer she, a nebulous, tumbling light; afraid and screaming the voiceless fear of the newly dead. Our journey; a squealing, aching descent, ascent, through black gulfs and summitless cliffs. We were the only light between obsidian crags that were frozen forever beneath a black sky. No time; the limitless yawning of aeons. And then faster; something zooming in. Gold and shining. I wanted to throw up my arms before my face, but I had neither; nothing to shield me from the brightness. Reality shift. Upsidedown, inside-out. Impossible shapes scored my substance; sickening impossible, zigzag agonies. I was drawn, sucked, inside the golden columns. Inside a temple of light, its glory turned towards the starless dark of infinity. The soul, my companion, denied access, fled shrieking upwards and away. That was all. I can remember only that I remembered. It is no longer real. Like I only heard it somewhere, read it in a book. Do you understand? It was a split-second, a micro-unit, of time that my memory has retained. I can get it to replay, sometimes, on the blank screen between my eyes. I just have done. Do you understand?

It was sound that first came back to me; a voice. I could not understand the words, yet at the same time knew their meaning. It said, 'He is perfect,' and another voice answered, 'Yes, he is.' After sound, I became aware of solidity, my soul again encumbered by flesh. I accepted this without question. Then the flesh gave vent to its pain and poured its torment into my brain; stretching, searing, burning. Tears formed in my hot eyes, my hot, blind eyes. I could sense movement, life, around me, but could not see it. Everything was blank; not dark, just blank. Colour was a concept I could no longer grasp. Voices came at me again, fluctuating in volume and pitch. 'Pellaz! Pellaz!'

No! I tried to move the awkward flesh.

'Pellaz, you are with me. Don't fight it!'

Drenched with recollection, I knew, I knew that voice. I wanted to scream and die.

'Open your eyes!'

I can't, can't.

'Open your eyes!'

No, no, no, no.

Something hard like glass was pushed between my teeth. Sour liquid scalded my sealed throat, but I had to swallow. Coughing, spluttering; liquid in my lungs. Rough, wet cloth scored across my closed eyelids, dabbing, then pulling.

'Open them, Pellaz; you can.'

Fingers prised at my skin; it felt like tearing, the edges of my lids were sealed and gummy. Lashes tore loose and tears poured down my face. Light pushed into me like hot pokers and I cried out. I heard myself cry out. The agony was insufferable. A hot thread pricked the inside of my arm, followed by a cool wave creeping up towards my neck. When it reached my head, I stopped screaming.

'There. Pellaz?'

My mouth felt thick and numb. I could barely move my lips, and my voice, when it came, was like a breeze through tissue, but I said, 'Thiede ...' I could see him. Tall, shining, flames for hair; his eyes were black with curiosity. He wore a white robe that showed his chest hung with pentacled chains; behind him the room was white. I could see his hand, resting against his cheek, long pointed fingernails tapping thoughtfully.

'Thiede, why?' I croaked. He did not answer, but covered me with a fine sheet up to the neck. I could not feel it.

'Rest now,' he said, smiling gently his dragon's smile. 'You must rest.'

'How can I?' I hurt so much; the deepest hurt in my heart. I knew nothing, was incapable of knowing anything; too tired to care, yet my mind churned backwards from a fear of sleep.

'Take this,' he said and his hand arched over me, the nails glistening with the lustre of pearl. 'A temporary oblivion.'

Dust was falling, falling, falling; the dust of centuries. I would fall back into a lighter slumber where dreams would walk once more. Up from the eternal pitch, the senseless peace. I slept.

For days, perhaps weeks, Thiede kept me in a semi-stupor, bringing me back to reality only at mealtimes. Even then, my limbs were too feeble to guide the food to my mouth; others fed me. Half-seen attendants saw to my bodily needs; cleaned me, turned me to prevent sores. My mind was switched off. I thought of nothing; watching only colours behind my closed eyes. My dreams were just of colours. Even so, I was fairly comfortable; just a little stiff. Hara came to massage my limbs three times a day. I could smell the light fragrance of the hot oil they kneaded into my skin. Sometimes, propped up on the pillows, I would stare at the room. It was sparsely furnished, but functional and tasteful. There were no mirrors and the windows were shrouded by gauze; I could not see what lay outside. Concealed lamps comforted me in the dark hours, so that I was never left alone in blackness. Sometimes, I thought I could hear music, wistful music or the tinkling of wind-chimes. It was so quiet there, no voices in the other rooms; the only sound, the only regular sound, was of footsteps outside my door, quick and light. The food they gave me was necessarily easily digested yet tinged with perfume I had never smelt before. Its fragrance would linger in my throat and nose long after the food had gone. After some time, I became alert enough to see properly the Hara that fed me. Every evening, during my massage, a stern-faced, red-haired Har came to look at me. I guessed he was inspecting my progress. Thiede never came; not then. Reduced to the status of a child, I trusted completely my silent attendants. Not once, that I can remember, did I think of Cal.

One evening, the red-haired Har came alone to my room. He brought with him a tray of food, which I obediently began to eat. I was surprised when he spoke. 'Pellaz, do you feel stronger now?' I must have looked startled, jolted out of my mindlessness. I had not thought about myself or my condition since waking up here. He did not press for an answer.

'I am Vaysh,' he said.

'Vaysh,' I repeated, stupidly.

I think it genuinely hurts him to smile, he so rarely does, but he did try for me that night.

'You must bathe,' he told me. Silent-footed Hara drifted into my sight and, at his signal, raised me from the bed. Dizzyness blinded me again. All I could see was flashing light as they eased my arms into soft cloth. 'Slowly!' Vaysh instructed. Slung between them, they carried me off.

When my vision cleared, they were lowering me into a bath set into the floor, steaming with greenish aromas. I know this ritual, I thought. It was all so familiar; only the room was different. Flickering recall of Mur and Garis ... Saltrock ... inception ... Cal ... Then the knife twisted in my heart. The veil in my head turned to glass, thin as ice, and shattered. I made noises, horrible, unintelligible noises and all the time, the ghostly, silent Hara just kept on smiling their soothing smiles, caressing my skin, their fingers lathering my hair. Weeping, in a hopeless, monotonous way, I lay in the bath, salt in my mouth, behind my eyes, saying his name endlessly in the tortured dark of my mind.

They put me back into the bed, oh so gently, their soft sighs filming my pain. So beautiful they were, so beautiful, but surreal and heartless. They laid me naked on the bed, on my back and drew back the light, gossamer linen. The room was warm and I did not shiver. Vaysh was standing at the foot of the bed, clothed in violet, holding a purple, glass vial. He gave it to one of my attendants. 'Make it easier for him,' he said and turned away. I could hear his footsteps, soft as a cat's, fading down the hallway outside my room. I was turned onto my stomach, arranged neatly, and salve from the vial was applied to my body. It felt cold as ice. I was rolled over and the procedure was repeated; I could hardly keep from laughing. Laughter through tears; I kept switching from grief to hysteria. 'Who is it?' I asked, but they would only shake their silken heads, like slender flowers. With a glass rod, one of them filled me with unguent that spread sleepily its insentient cold through my loins. Perhaps they could not speak. Perhaps he had taken that from them. They straightened my legs and flicked invisible creases from the sheet. I was not afraid. Nervous of the waiting, yes, but not afraid. They stood, one each side of me, by my head, their faces turned to the door. I had expected them to leave.

Then there were footsteps outside, faraway, coming down the hall, brisk but unhurried. Nearer they came and it seemed to take forever. I knew. I knew and my heart was bursting. He was coming. Thiede was coming. Yet I was still surprised when it was him. He came into the room and stood there, where Vaysh had been before, arms folded and the disguised light of enthusiasm in his eyes. I spoke his name.

'Yes,' he said. 'Do you remember Saltrock, Pellaz?' I nodded at him.

'I remember.'

'Was it so long ago I wonder? Can you remember the things I told you?'

'No, not now.'

'And the things I didn't tell you?'

'I remember all of them.'

'Am I a god to you?'

'No, not that. I don't know what you are.'

'Are you ready for me?'

'I can't ever be ... can I?'

'You realize what must be?'

'I think so ...'

He wanted to say more, he was enjoying it, but then thought better of it. I could see him, his shining robe shifting with subtle colours, his flame eyes. His lips parted to release a Sound. He began to ... sing? No. A Sound; like a different language of gentle vibrations. His arms dropped to his sides, his head went up. I could see his eyes ... shining. Reflecting light; they were white stars. All the light in the room went dim but for him. My heart! A pounding that sent the blood cataracting to my loins; my heart sucked dry. The Sound filled up the room, rising, becoming louder, more strident. I knew that sound. Knew it, knew it. His face; changing. His neck, cording, twisting, hair writhing, crawling, lifting.

'No!' I whispered, in disbelief, in denial, yet I still felt my body call to him. His teeth, his lambent eyes ... taller. His hair was crackling with orange flames. It could have been Lianvis standing there; the elemental Lianvis of beneath the earth. He was naked, his body coursing with colours; colours I had never seen before, that hurt my eyes. He was above me, hovering, crouching. I tried to move, but his Hara held me down. I could see their teeth; they smiled. I screamed in agony, but then in ecstasy; his smouldering, smoky breath bringing me to the lip of the abyss that was lit at its deepest point by a star of pulsing red. Movement there; bats, ravens, demons, all the creatures of the lake of fire rose up to claw my hair; their talons in my flesh that shuddered to a nameless delight. I wanted the pain, craved it; reduced to an animal fury. He filled me with the hot, smoking essence of his incomprehensible soul. It ripped me, scoured me, ate into me like acid. It was melting me apart, the sizzling rain of hell and I screamed, and I screamed again.

Is it a nightmare, is it? When I came back to my senses, I was alone, and at first I thought, 'What have I been thinking?' But then I saw that the room was full of smoke, and the smoke was full of the smell of seared flesh. Then I began to moan. It was the right thing to do. I called upon God, 'Help me! Help me ...' I was sure I was dying again and it was a slow, lingering death. I did not want to die. Not again, I pleaded, please, not again. I could sense myself ruined. Sense myself used up, burnt out, finished. You have to die! You have to! Vaysh materialized beside me, out of the vapours. His hand hovered over my shoulder.

'Don't try to move,' he said.

I could have laughed. Move? Could this charred remnant move? Vaysh was pushing tubes down my throat. 'Open the window!' he called, over his shoulder. Cold air sucked the heat from the room and blew away the smoke. Vaysh was touching me with one hand, sitting on the bed. I tried to raise my head. One glimpse was enough. The bed, the pristine whiteness of my bed, was polluted with the dark stains of dried blood. It looked like dried blood. My body was purple and black and blistered.

'Don't move,' Vaysh repeated. My eyes felt cracked and shrivelled; it was a miracle I could still see. It hurt to close them, yet I longed to do so.

'I don't ever want to have to do this again,' Vaysh said to someone I could not see. Disgust filled his voice. I began to slip and Vaysh said, 'I'm losing him!' Another voice answered him, calm and confidant. 'It proceeds as it should.' As it should.

Thiede. I contemplated on his magnificence in the higher spheres. He had brought me back to him from death; this personality. Now he had mutilated me; he held me dangling on the end of a silver thread. Why? But I knew he would not let go.

For days I must have hovered on the threshhold of a second death. Vaysh was in constant attendance. He was there to heal me and he succeeded. Thiede knew that. Vaysh is one of his best. My mind was nearly broken and I retreated deep inside myself, seeking once again the comfortable idiocy of my first days in this place. Yet I could not shut out my senses completely. They drugged my body, but not my mind. Even though I feared insanity, I was aware of everything that happened around me, no matter how hard I tried to escape inside myself. My poor brain, exhausted, stunned, but still labouring on. I made an impossible vow never to speak again, and banished all memory of Cal from my thoughts. It was the only way I could cope. When they took away the tubes and tried to make me eat, I vomited with uncontrollable force. The tubes were put back.

One day, Vaysh put his hand on my paralysed legs. 'Tomorrow, we shall leave here,' he said. I whimpered and wept, and he did not comfort me.

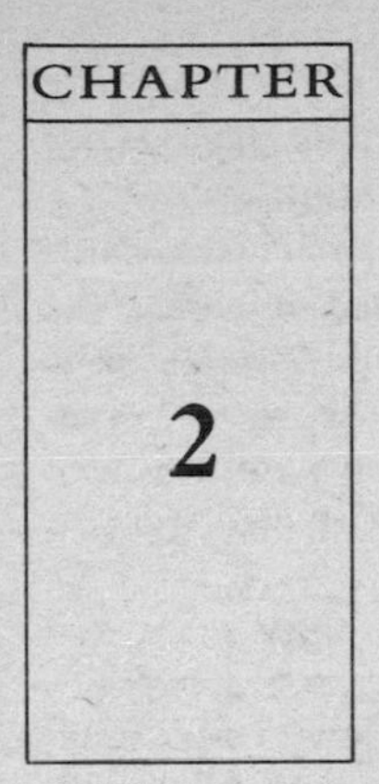

The symbolism of the thirteenth key

Winter; white, crackling, numbing. Vaysh rode a black horse, I was strapped onto a grey. Behind us, Thiede's marmoreal palace reared like a vast, sparkling bird of prey. Before us, dark canyons wreathed in drifts of snow. The sky above was pale. I had no idea where in the world I was. It was the first time I had ever seen snow, the first time I had ever been this cold. I was anaesthetized almost senseless, unaware of where we were heading and for what purpose. Wrapped in thick furs, strapped with leather, lolling with slack face upon the back of my silvery horse.

I had been given no explanation for anything that had happened to me or for what was to come. That Thiede had a definite plan was obvious, but I was only his pawn and as such, it was unimportant that I should know what was going on. I was changed for ever; into what I did not yet understand. There had been no mirrors, no words to tell me. Vaysh hardly looked at me. He had my horse on a leading rein. I could see his long, red hair, powdered with white, blowing back on either side of his fur hood, his straight back; a prince of Wraeththu. All sound was muffled in the pure and crystal landscape. No tracks other than our own marred its virgin shrouds. I sat and dreamed and sat and dreamed, as the sun arched from one horizon to the other. Once darkness fell (but it was never completely dark), we came to a wooden cabin under a sheltering overhang of rock. Icicles fringed its porch; drifts of white fingers reached towards the windows. Vaysh unstrapped me and hauled me to the ground. He had a key to the cabin and dragged me inside, leaving me alone as he went back into the snow to see to the horses. Some of the drugs were beginning to wear off and I began to whimper. I felt so *different*; distorted, heavy. Crippled and tied into the furs.

Vaysh methodically built a fire in the dusty grate and unpacked food to cook. He had paused only to feed me with milk from a beaker that was nearly frozen. Now I could smell rice simmering in a froth of garlic and my mouth filled with reluctant saliva. Once he was content the food was cooking slowly, Vaysh turned his attention back to me. I was lying on the hard, wooden floor, trussed like a chicken. Vaysh moved his mouth a little. It may have been a smile. 'Let's unwrap you then,' he said. It was the first time he had spoken to me that day. It took him some time to undo all the straps and pain was waking up in me with greater and greater strength. I was groaning and trying to twist around. When I was naked, I could see my body had become grey and misshapen like half-worked clay. The sight of it silenced my noises. There was a low, wooden bed, barely softened by a thin mattress. Vaysh lifted me as if I weighed nothing and laid me out on it. They had packed cloth around my loins and I had helplessly soiled it. Vaysh heated water on the fire and silently cleaned me. Incontinent cripple. His eyes held no expression other than concentration for his task. He did not have to offer me an explanation. I was reduced to the state of nothingness; something like before I was Har. But he did speak. Vaysh the cold; Vaysh the silent. My loyal assistant, always; scarred frigid by distant pain. He lifted his head and looked at me with his hard, grey eyes. I saw him properly for the first time. His face almost makes you jump when you see it. A wistful, childlike beauty, until the flint in his eyes makes you look away. He looked so young, yet I had thought him older.

'It will not be long,' he said. A boyish, soft voice, but so cold.

'Three days? Maybe. Maybe four, it's different for everyone.'

I was still adhering to my vow and swallowed the questions filling my mouth. Vaysh stood up and went back to the fire, staring into the pot of rice.

'You must eat some of this. Don't try to be sick, don't try to be awkward; I don't want any of that.'

I moved my head as far as it would turn to look around me. The room was rustic and coarsely furnished, but a haven from the snow. Heavy dark curtains, grimed and colourless with age, hung against the windows and the back of the door. It was becoming quite warm.

Vaysh lifted my head and spooned small portions of rice into my mouth. At first, I refused to chew, like an obstreperous child. Vaysh put his head on one side. 'Damn!' he said, without rancour. 'Come on, eat it. Hurry up; I have to eat as well.' He prodded my lips with the spoon. 'Come on!' Churlishly, I opened my mouth. It did not make me feel sick, but I could manage only half the bowl. Vaysh covered me with a hairy blanket and sat by the fire to eat his own portion. He consumed it as neatly as a cat only without the relish. After that, he spiked my neck and pumped a soporific into my veins through a tube, his face serious with concentration. As I drifted away, I wondered what he was thinking …

I do not really know how long we journeyed for, but from what Vaysh had said, I think it must have been for about four days. Thiede's horses were tireless; we rarely paused to rest them. At nearly the same time every day, sundown, a wooden lodge would appear through the dusk. Thiede's people must often take this path, I thought. I had hoped that my condition would improve, but each day I felt sicker and sicker. By the fourth day, I did not even have the strength to swallow and Vaysh gave up feeding me. He seemed strangely unconcerned. I kept mumbling inside myself: I am in Hell, I am in Hell … I suppose I should have been grateful he spared me any pain (Thiede had supplied him generously with drugs), but I was far from comfortable. Every few hours, Vaysh would dash our water leathers against a rock or a tree to smash the ice, and then dab at my congealing mouth with water and wipe my eyes.

On the fourth day, we rode through a forest of giant firs. In the silence I heard the muted thud of snow dropping off the highest branches. Everywhere seemed devoid of life; an enchanted waste. On this day, we came upon a great abyss cutting deep into the Earth. Black, jagged rocks reared aloft, the haunt of shrunken trees with twisted branches and huge, untidy looking birds with featherless necks, their eyes rimmed with yellow crust. One of them swooped right up to me and screamed in my face. Far below, the thunder and white spume of rushing water careered off the walls of the chasm; it sounded like vast, underground machinery. Rising up from the spray, mid-way across the gap, a single stone tower weathered the torrent. Spindly, wooden bridges swayed from it to either side of the canyon, creaking in a mournful voice. Here we would have to cross. Vaysh shook his head and made a noise of discontent. Icy wind rolled between the rocks, plucking at our hair and furs.

I do not think any horses other than Thiede's, half supernatural as they were, would have dared to set foot on the bridge. But with shaking muscles and tensed haunches, ears and eyes pivoting wildly, they cautiously edged their way forward. Below us, the water roared its anger, flinging up fingers of spray as if to pluck us from our fragile pathway. I cared nothing for our danger. It was all one to me: whether we made it across or plunged to our deaths, but I could see Vaysh's face looking back at me sometimes, his face bleached with fear. Once we had reached the far side, he dismounted and leaned against his horse's trembling flank. I was still slumped as before, strapped upright in my saddle. My horse began to sniff half-heartedly at the stringy plants along the side of the path. Vaysh looked at me for a moment without pleasure. I could see him thinking I was not worth all this trouble. Then, with a sigh, he swung back into his saddle, hastening the pace to a canter.

The road led once more into a forest, but this was a place of sweeping slopes and steep hills. The firs were dense, standing in neat rows and here, the snow underfoot was marked by the tracks of wheels and hooves.

At dusk, the forest fell away beneath us, thinning out to a valley floor, where a long, frozen lake glowed with the night-whiteness of thick ice. A small town curled around its edge. Directly beneath us, rising higher than the sentinel trees, a stone trident speared the heavy sky. 'Phade's tower,' Vaysh told me, pointing, looking round to see if I was interested. 'Oh, what's the bloody point?!' he snapped, when he saw my face. I was looking beyond him, at the lake and the yellow lights of the town, reminded yet again of Saltrock. All memories seemed to lead back there. But here the warmth, the hell-soil of soda had been exchanged for the parchment purity of winter; endless white in a sleeping land. I was lulled by staring at the pale, pale fields and thought with longing of the powdery embrace of the deep drifts, and the sleep that has no end. My existence had become merely discomfort; no pleasure, nor even pain. I wanted only for it to finish, but was so weak, I could do nothing except what Vaysh ordained. He moved my limbs, he kept me alive and I did not question why. I had no interest in the answer.

Vaysh's horse skidded down the slope and mine followed dutifully. Phade's tower. I thought the windows looked like sunken eyes.

It seemed we were expected. Fur-wrapped Hara bearing lights waited for us at the gate. They grabbed our horses' bridles and led us into a cobbled courtyard. Grim, high walls hid the sky all around. Windows in the wall appeared heavily shrouded with curtains. Very little light shone down into the yard, but I could see that large, silent snowflakes were beginning to fall. Hands unstrapped me and lifted me down. Voices to either side of me were cheery with welcome. I could hear Vaysh's surly replies. When the warmth hit me, they had stopped trying to talk to him. We must have been inside the tower, but my vision was beginning to blur and I was aware only of the change in temperature. Someone cleared their throat ahead of us and said, 'Vaysh?' It sounded cultured, yet mocking; a voice of command.

'Phade,' I heard Vaysh answer softly. He would have inclined his head, just enough for politeness.

'What's this you have here then?' Someone brushed back the furs from around my face. 'Ye Gods! A corpse, and, by the devil, it stinks!'

'Thank you, Phade, if we could be shown to our rooms?' Vaysh's voice; patient, soft, like the snow.

'What's going on here, Vaysh?'

Silence.

'Vaysh?!'

'Did Thiede tell you we were coming?'

'Yes; he didn't say why.' (Sneering)

'That is Thiede.'

'Yes, that is Thiede! Well?'

'You shall see when it is time.'

I heard Phade laugh. 'Oh no, not more of your mumbo-jumbo clap-trap!'

'The mumbo-jumbo clap-trap, as you so elegantly put it, that is responsible for your being here at all Phade, if you'll forgive my reminding you.' Phade's laughter stopped.

'Oh, Vaysh, Vaysh! Still humourless, still the ice-maiden!'

'I'm not female, Phade.' I could hear the rustling as he unclasped his fur cloak. 'Our rooms, Phade?'

'This way, this way.'

Phade wanted to stay while Vaysh undid my wrappings. He was full of morbid curiosity. 'Why is he like this? What happened? Is he dead?'

'No, he's not dead.' Vaysh's hand rested upon my swollen cheek for a moment. It may have been a gesture of reassurance or that he just wanted to note my temperature. I was heating up too quickly; my face burned and deep within the furs, my fingers began to tingle ominously. Vaysh stripped me down and rolled up his sleeves to perform all the distasteful duties of cleaning me. I could smell that the water he used was scented with pine.

'I don't like things like this going on here. Why did Thiede send you here?' Phade said.

'This town is on our way,' Vaysh answered. They continued to argue mildly; Vaysh, I'm sure, deftly sidetracking Phade's questions, but I no longer listened to them. All my awareness centred on the heavenly softness beneath me. It felt as if I was slipping down, slowly, into a cloud of feathers. Comfort; I had forgotten it existed. Vaysh's voice came close to my ear. 'Pellaz . . .' It was just a whisper. 'You will sleep now; it is time. We got here in time . . .' Obediently, I let myself go into the feather darkness and there were no voices there.

CHAPTER

3

My truth, my destiny . . .

It was a noise that woke me. I do not know what. It had gone when my eyes opened. I looked at the room for a moment. There were stone walls, hung with tapestries, like a medieval castle from the picture books. A fire spat and fizzled somewhere to my left; perhaps it was that which had woken me. I became aware that my skin was itching and my hand shot to my stomach to scratch. I could move! Startled, I sat up. Just like that. My head swam for a moment, the room tilted, but then energy and strength surged, with alarming confidence, right through me and my vision cleared. Something grey and papery littered the bed around me. It crumbled to dust when I touched it. I felt marvellous; strange, but marvellous. Swinging my legs over the side of the bed, it was no effort to stand. My toes buried themselves in thick fur. Of course, I went straight for the shine, the glaze, of the mirror. It hung on the wall beside the bed, framed in rather tasteless gilt gargoyles. Golden light spun into my eyes and I raised my hand. My golden hand. I could not look; it filled my chest to look. This . . . Thiede's essence. This was what he had made me. The gold that was a reflection of the dancing motes in his eyes. He had made me a god!

There was an adjoining room, which, although nothing as grand as a bathroom, contained a pitcher of cooling water and a large porcelain bowl. Clashing winds moaned outside and made the curtains shiver. It was colder in here. I washed my face and relieved myself in the primitive toilet facilities I found behind a curtain. Three candles peopled the room with eerie shadows. I became aware of someone moving around in the other room, and thought it might be Vaysh, but just peeped round the door in case it wasn't. A Har I did not know was inspecting the bed, picking at the grey stuff and sniffing it. His nose wrinkled with aversion. He had thick, black hair and was dressed in brown leather and fur. From the hooked, imperious nose and hooded, sulky eyes, I presumed it to be Phade.

'Where is Vaysh?' I asked and he jumped, his hand flitting to the knife at his hip. He narrowed his eyes. For modesty's sake, I had wrapped myself in a towel I had found in the other room.

'What ...? Who ...?' Phade had drawn the knife. I walked a little way into the room and his face lit up with gold flecks. He glanced nervously at the bed and then back to me. He pointed at the bed, mutely, and I nodded. 'You've changed,' he said, a little lamely. Straightening up from his position of defence, with some embarrassment, he tucked the knife back into his belt. 'What is going on?' he asked, in a voice that told me he expected the most outlandish explanation.

'I don't know,' I answered, and he shook his head in disbelief.

'If *you* don't know ...!' he exclaimed and then muttered, 'Thiede!' as if that explained everything. 'Whenever life looks as if it might become *ordinary*, or even *safe*, up pops the omnipotent Thiede and everything gets weird again!' He threw up his arms and grimaced at the ceiling.

'Ah well, it is our luck, I expect, to be born out of weirdness!' Did I say that? It sounded like the Pellaz who was dead, and as I am very fond of him, I was glad to hear he was still around. I smiled, and then a dozen representatives were sent down from my brain, bearing angry questions. 'I want to see Vaysh,' I said, surprised that I was gritting my teeth.

Phade nodded; his face was also grim with displeasure. We were accomplices in our censure of Vaysh, that was clear. 'Yes, so do I!' he said. He went to the door and bellowed an order. I heard footsteps scurrying away outside. Phade turned back to look at me. 'He's worked a fine old magic on you, hasn't he!' he remarked. 'His mightiness, the great Thiede. If you're one of his creations, he's more powerful than I gave him credit for.' I only shrugged. All this seemed rhetorical. 'Only a few hours ago you looked a week dead and now . . .' he shook his head, awed, and exaggerating this because he never liked to feel less than anyone, 'you shine!'

'Something happened to me,' was all I could say, facile as it sounded, coming from so resplendent a body. But it was all that I knew and I did not care to go into any detail.

Vaysh stalked in without knocking. He was dressed simply and elegantly in dark green. I could see now that his red hair was dyed. His expression did not change in the slightest when he saw me.

'Yes?' he enquired, looking at Phade. (He had, of course, been told that Phade had sent for him.)

Phade made an exasperated noise and slapped his thigh with one hand. 'Vaysh, I hope we didn't disturb your rest . . .'

'No, I wasn't sleeping.'

'Vaysh, will you just step out of your ice-castle for one second and look! Look! Your travelling companion has . . . hatched! We thought you should be told.' Any sarcasm in Phade's voice glanced off Vaysh's composure.

'It was expected,' he said. 'It was time. An hour or two early, perhaps, but . . .'

'Vaysh, you have to talk to me,' I butted in. His eyes slid over me like needles of ice.

'Ah Pellaz, you've found your voice.' It is very difficult to hate anyone who is as beautiful as Vaysh, but his detached and disdainful manner made it easier. He turned once more to Phade. 'Would you leave us please?'

Phade was not used to being addressed in that way. Clearly, no-one ever told him to leave anywhere. 'No, I will not! I don't take orders from you, Vaysh! This is my home and you're in it at my pleasure and don't you forget that! I want to know what's going on!' I suppose it was reasonable enough. Vaysh swivelled his withering glance over our host.

'It is not necessary,' he said politely. 'I hate to be blunt, Phade, and I am not totally ignorant of your position, but it really is none of your business.'

'And I hate to be blunt, Vaysh, but what goes on in this place *is* my business! We all dance dutifully to our lord Thiede's tune, of course we do, but I want to know how all this affects me, and my people.'

'It doesn't.'

'Why here? Why? Thiede has his own strongholds.' He wagged a finger under Vaysh's nose. 'I am suspicious, oh freezing one, very suspicious. I do not trust Thiede, you or any of your magical charades!'

Vaysh sighed. 'Phade, I know the hour is late, but I am sure you are a busy Har. This is your little kingdom, I'm sure you have things to do.' Vaysh picked up a crimson robe of heavy velvet from a chair and draped it around my shoulders.

Phade would not be put off. 'You can't speak to me like that!' he objected, but he did not sound sure of that.

'You're only curious, Phade,' Vaysh told him. It was impossible to anger him. 'Suspicions! Worries!' He made a derisive noise. 'Thiede helped you take this little town, and without him you would still be foraging round the country. Now tell me you don't trust him! When I tell you that what has happened here tonight is nothing to do with you, I speak with Thiede's tongue. Do you understand?'

For a moment or two Phade stood his ground. Then he hissed through his teeth and walked out, leaving the door open. Vaysh calmly shut it.

'Pellaz, you have been chosen,' he said.

It was late. I had slept, but Vaysh had not, yet we talked till dawn. He told me everything, nearly everything, without emotion or opinion, just fact. Thiede had waited a long time for this, he told me; since my inception. He had decided then what to do with me. And what was that? I wanted to know.

'Do you know who Thiede is?' Vaysh asked.

'No, should I?'

'It doesn't matter.'

Thiede had divined my possibilities, perhaps from the moment he had seen me laid out on the inception slab. He had seen within me an appealing unity of power, sanity and beauty. He had encouraged these qualities, in his own inimicable way, and made me what I am. Now it was intended that I should be put to work; I must fulfill my purpose as all things in Thiede's sphere of influence must fulfill their purposes. When he had taken aruna with me (if such a holocaust should be called that!), he had raised me to Nahir-Nuri, blistered away my lower caste.

'You are Efrata now,' Vaysh said. 'All thoughts in your head, you must voice to me alone. You need no-one else. You are apart from the others, all the others.'

'What *is* the purpose of all this?' I asked him. He seemed almost reluctant to answer me.

'I shall take you to Immanion,' he said. A single sliver of pain pierced my heart, and my head and my limbs went cold for a second. Vaysh looked at my face cold-bloodedly; it was likely he knew all about me, about Cal, everything. Those who walked in the white temple in the waste had seen it all: my tentative fumblings with the powers Thiede had transfused into me; my helpless idealism and finally, my discovery of love. To Vaysh, I was like an animal, whose habits have been observed until nothing is a mystery to the observer. It is an attitude that has never completely left him. Both Thiede and Vaysh know me better than I know myself. Vaysh said so easily, 'I am here to serve you', and he knew that was his purpose in the scheme of things, but there is nothing remotely servile in him. Sometime, someone (Thiede?) had sterilized his soul. What is within Vaysh is truly a monster, clothed in flesh. Only his eyes betray him. He watched the memory of Cal haunt my eyes and said softly, 'Yes, Immanion. Wraeththu are your people, Pellaz. Thiede has given them to you and you to them; you will become their king.'

I must have stared at him like an imbecile for some time. All questions were frozen within me. 'You are to become their king.' It sounded final and beyond argument. For this purpose

Thiede had groomed my flesh and tempered my spirit. Through suffering he had tried to raise me above the rest; he knew my mind, my feelings, my character and my weaknesses. I could hear myself asking, 'Why?', but no sound came out. Perhaps Vaysh couldn't even answer that. Was it because Thiede had incepted me, or had that happened because in some mysterious way, Thiede had already decided what he wanted to do with me? Now I was refashioned, remoulded and improved. Physically, a perfect sovereign; I couldn't dispute that. But what was so terrifying was how much of this wonderful new me was Thiede's construction, Thiede's virtues, and how much my own emotions and opinions? I couldn't swear that I remembered perfectly how I was before. Too much had happened. That I still possessed sanity under the circumstances was remarkable. Something very cold and hard must live inside me. My flesh was numb, but I really couldn't tell if I was pleased or horrified by what Vaysh had said. All I could think was, 'Well, so this is my fate.' The words formed quite clearly in my head, several times. I had been awaiting its breath on the back of my neck for a long time. It should have been a relief to discover that it was not merely death.

Vaysh asked me, 'Are you shocked? Are you surprised?' but there was no real interest in his voice, not even envy. Perhaps he had to report back to his master. (Yes, Thiede, he took it well.)

'Why?'

'Why not? It's what Thiede wants and that's the only reason I can give you.'

'What if I don't want to . . .'

Vaysh laughed at this. One thing that could delight him. 'By Aghama, you're pathetic! Yes, by Aghama.' This obviously meant something to him for he positively bubbled with laughter.

'You have no choice, Pellaz. Can't you see that. This is your purpose, you have no control over it. I doubt he'd even kill you if you tried to refuse; he'd just alter your mind. You're helpless.' Hadn't I always been?

'I shall see Immanion,' I said, uselessly, suddenly, hopelessly missing Cal in a great wave of loneliness. Why do things have to fade? Why does reality only have to exist in the present second?

We have no real proof that our memories are real. Once events occur and pass, they might well have never been.

Vaysh stood up and went to look at himself in the mirror, touching his hair. If he had lived before, in another time, he would have been a woman and a legend. It was not inconceivable that he should have been in my place, if he had possessed a conscience. I think I guessed then; this process had not always been successful, and I had not been the first.

'How shall we travel?' I enquired, and he tore his eyes away from his reflection.

'On horseback, as before. There is no fuel in this part of the world and anyway . . . things have changed, Pellaz. You must get to know yourself. The horses, Thiede's horses, are as different from man's horses as we are from men . . .'

'He *bred* them?!' I interrupted. Nothing seemed too bizarre for Thiede now.

'Not exactly. He brought them here from . . . they are . . . now you are ready, you shall see. The journey will not take long.'

I watched his shrouded expressions, wondering. 'What's your level, Vaysh?'

He smiled then; one of those rare frozen grimaces. 'Oh, I don't know. I don't think I have one. More than Ulani . . . not quite Nahir-Nuri.' He clasped his shoulders with his hands. 'It's nearly dawn. I must rest. We shan't leave until tomorrow now.'

'I'm not tired,' I said.

'Oh, Phade's people will be around soon. Get them to see to the bed.' We both looked at the drab, papery waste, some of which had blown onto the furred floor. Vaysh started to leave, but I called him back.

'What is it?' He was impatient to get out.

'Shall I glow forever?'

He looked at my luminous face. 'On the outside? No, it is already fading.'

Not long after Vaysh had gone, one of Phade's people knocked at my door. He did not raise his eyes as he entered. Phade must have told of what he had seen. 'My lord Phade requests your presence at breakfast,' he told me. As with all the other tribes I had visited, he had brought me clothes. It is something that is almost a fetish with Wraeththu. Wherever you go your clothes are replaced with the prevailing fashion. The Har waited in silence whilst I dressed myself. I was still numb, from moment to moment fluctuating in feeling from normality to stark terror. In a petty gesture of defiance against their customs, I braided my hair in the Kakkahaar fashion, even though it was doubtful that it would even be noticed. This was a different country. The land of my birth was far away. I did not exist there anymore.

I expected a vast hall furnished by an equally vast table, but found Phade awaiting his meal in a small, comfortable room on the ground floor, warming his toes by a fire. He smiled and stood up when he saw me in the doorway. 'I am honoured!' he said, sweeping a mocking bow.

I sighed. 'It is your castle, Lord Phade, and as such, I suppose I should not be too surprised, or affronted, that you listen at your guests' doors.'

'Not me!' he exclaimed, and I raised an eyebrow. 'I have others for that duty.'

'Hmmm.'

'Please, sit down, make yourself at home. I'm no longer sure how to address you!'

I sat, resting my arms on the table. 'Oh please! This is more of a shock to me than to anyone. I don't want deference. I would prefer it to be ignored, if possible.'

'It's something you'll have to get used to, isn't it. King, well!' He laughed pleasantly. It sounded ridiculous, like some kind of child's game. Let's dress up and be kings and queens. I couldn't help wincing.

'What had Thiede done to you? You were in a terrible state when you got here,' Phade ventured hopefully.

'Please don't try to interrogate me,' I said. 'I don't want to talk about it.'

'God forbid!' he cried. I wondered how much Thiede trusted him. He remembered his manners and decided to steer the conversation onto safer territory. 'We haven't been formally introduced yet, have we? As you know, I am Phade, but formally, you are the guest of the tribe of Olopade.'

'Thiede brought you here?' I was beginning to feel hungry, and could hear my stomach complaining. I could not remember when I had last eaten.

'I suppose you could say that. The men that lived here were very wise. This town, Samway, it is a faraway place and its people were not like the men of the cities, the so-called advanced areas. They fought us in a strange, resigned way, and in the old way, (he tapped his head), with the power of the mind. Olopade have been groomed by Thiede for this kind of skirmish. When we came here, the men fled to the forests. We have not seen them since. Thiede may have followed them, of course . . .'

At that moment, the meal arrived and seldom have I welcomed the sight of food more. Phade asked me what I thought of Thiede, and I answered with reserve, although without untruth. 'I think he is probably the most powerful of Wraeththu and, although he is frightening, I do think we need him. We need order and Thiede knows that too. I don't think he is beyond cruelty, but he will eradicate it in Wraeththu as a whole if he can. He knows the truth.'

Phade nodded. 'Well answered!' he said.

'I hope Thiede thinks so,' I replied drily.

Phade laughed. 'You must learn to live with it; what kings really know freedom?' he pointed out and I shrugged.

'I may have been under an illusion before, about being free, but it was a comfortable illusion.'

'Yes, ignorance is bliss as they say!' Phade sighed, attacking his helping of fragrant ham.

'You have met Vaysh before then?' I enquired, with my mouth full.

Phade poured me coffee into an enormous mug; he had no servants in the room. 'Oh yes,' he answered, in a somewhat confidential tone. 'He's Thiede's right arm and sometimes comes here to cause discomfort in his master's name. He thinks I'm an inarticulate slob, I'm sure,'

'I doubt if you're alone in that category,' I said. 'My role seems to be defined as mere nuisance.'

'What a challenge though, to break through all that ice!' Phade remarked enthusiastically. 'Don't you think so? Is there a Har of flesh and blood within perhaps?'

'There might not, of course, be anything left without the ice,' I said.

Phade laughed. 'Vaysh would consider my thoughts almost blasphemy!'

After the meal, neither of us made a move to leave the table, content to sit and finish the pitcher of coffee.

'This is sometimes a lonely place to live,' Phade said.

'Too cold for me; I come from another land, it's warm there.'

Hard sunlight was falling in through the leaded windows. Hara were clearing snow from the yard outside.

Phade said, in a different voice, 'Do you know, last night it looked as if your skin was alight. Perhaps it was the dark . . .' He reached to touch my arm.

'No, it is fading.'

'You are leaving tomorrow?'

'Yes, tomorrow.'

He curled his fingers in the air, above my hand. 'Pellaz.' He said my name slowly, as if to pronounce it right, although it is not a difficult name. I looked up defensively. 'It is difficult to speak with you . . . in a normal way,' he said, and I sensed something of what was coming.

'You've had no difficulty so far,' I answered tartly.

'About some things . . .' His fist clenched on the air. I could tell he did not want to miss this chance; not many Hara like Vaysh and myself would visit him here. I did not blame him.

'Some things,' I echoed. I looked at his face, his hair, his dark-coloured arms. Some things. All people have a certain taste, a certain smell, an *ambiance*. Cal's presence was lodged within me in the ghost of his scent. Perhaps I feared the scent of someone else would exorcise it and then I would have nothing.

'Pellaz, I want . . .' Phade began, struggling.

'A night with the king of Wraeththu,' I finished for him.

He smiled ruefully. 'I can see your answer,' he said.

'I hope so; there are reasons . . .'

'Are you another cold-store temptation like Vaysh?' I shuddered to think that sometime he must have tried this with Vaysh. If he had, I could only stand back in awe of his nerve.

'I don't think so,' I replied, 'but then, I don't know his reasons.'

Phade leaned back in his chair; the coffee was finished. 'What a pity; you are a beauty.' I did not resent the patronizing tone of that remark as once I might. I knew Phade's position. He would remain here in a corner of the world barely alight, whilst I would shine like a star. I could only pity him. But if it had not been for Cal, well . . . maybe. Phade too, was a beauty.

I spent the rest of that day in Phade's library. They were not really his collection of books, having been there long before Wraeththu had come to the tower, but he was proud of them. He showed me the volumes that interested him most; heavy, dusty tomes on magical lore, slim pamphlets on herbalism and homeopathy, delicately illustrated with water-colours. There were large picture-books of the world. I pored through them, searching for the place from whence I'd come. Phade looked for me. 'It was probably here,' he said, pointing. I stared at the photographs of yellow dunes, red dirt and men smiling in the colourless fields. All the people I had known still existed somewhere (why were their faces so shadowed in my memory?), living, talking. Did someone else now walk the cable-fields each evening with Mima? Would she say to them, 'Here I remember most my brother Pellaz; the Wraeththu took him . . .'? Had my father decreed, 'He is no longer my son'? Now they were a continent's, an ocean's width away. When I'd woken up in Thiede's palace, I had left the country of my birth behind. A great expanse of water was between us now, yet I had never seen the sea! I turned the page. Here, a white house adorned the brow of a steep, green hill. Pink flowers turned their petal faces and shiny, dark leaves towards it. It seemed I was back there; yet the house was not really the same. Did Cobweb still yearn for the attention of Terzian? Did Terzian yearn the loss of . . .? Had the curtains ever opened again? I shut my eyes and quickly turned the pages once more. He could have gone back there; easily. Bereft, alone, seeking comfort. Or did he still seek Immanion? Would I find him there again? Phade said, 'Perhaps it is not a good idea, Pellaz, to look back.' Of course my distress must have been obvious. 'I can force myself to think of other things, but it is still there. The future is like tangled yarn, but the past is woven thread.' Phade put his hand on my shoulder, but I could not be touched by sympathy. I made another vow, and this one I would keep. There could be no other; I would find Cal again. I was sensible enough to realize that time undoubtedly would lead me to the arms of someone else; after all aruna is the life-blood of Wraeththu-kind, but my heart, for always, would be pledged to him.

Vaysh appeared at dinner, glacial and pale. 'I hope the coffin we provided was comfortable enough to meet your requirements?' Phade joked and I began to laugh. Vaysh fixed him with a withering stare.

'It has become a custom of the Olopade, then, to bury their dead in four-poster beds?' he answered, but it was not meant to be funny.

Phade reached out and touched his white hand, which he snatched away instantly. 'You really do ask for it, Vaysh,' he said, 'and what an effort it must be to keep this behaviour up. Why not let your hair down for once? I promise not to tell Thiede.'

I could tell Vaysh was confused, messing with his cutlery, eyes on the table.

'I don't know what you mean,' he said stiffly.

Phade looked at me, and we both grinned. Because of the way he is, it is virtually impossible to resist the temptation to provoke Vaysh. You always long for a reaction. The chinks in his armour are well hidden, however. Only someone very clever or very familiar with him can find them. So Phade and I spent the evening meal slipping lines to each other and laughing at Vaysh's expense. I supposed he noticed it, but he did not care. Maddened by his aloofness, Phade's remarks became rather too brazen. I too began to speculate about what lay within the ice.

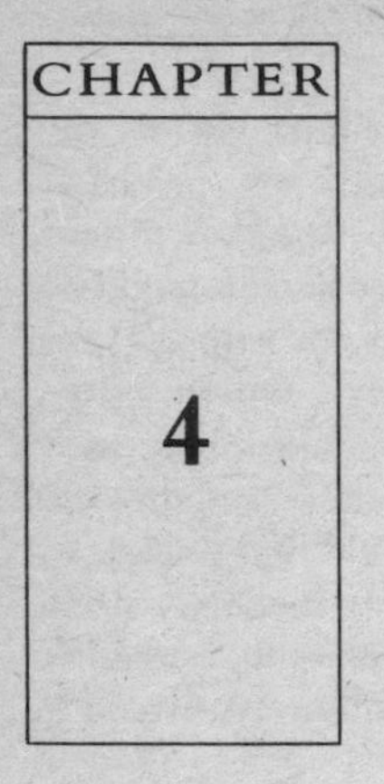

CHAPTER 4

On the nature of Vaysh and other journeys

Tomorrow we would depart Phade's tower. Travelling; it seemed I spent so much of my time wandering around. Perhaps I would feel uncomfortable settling down in one place. Once settled, it might be that the past would come back to haunt me with greater strength. I felt as if something hung there in the back of my mind, waiting to tarnish whatever happiness I might find. Is it safer to be unhappy? Nothing ever wants to take that away.

After dinner, I excused myself and went alone to my room. From my window I could see the virgin whiteness rolling out towards a shrouded forest. Mountain peaks rose above it. Would we go that way? I would not be sorry to leave this land. I have always hated being cold, and willingly dropped back the heavy curtains to turn once more to the fire. Phade's servants had prepared me a bath, but the ante-room had no fire and I was reluctant to undress in there. So I changed into a thick night-shirt and sat watching the fire. My hands rested on the padded arms of the chair and I disorientated myself by staring at them. These were not the hands that had worked in the cable fields nor taken up the reins of a horse for the first time. These were not the hands that had rested upon the warmth of another; he that was Cal. Those hands were mouldering somewhere in another country. Beneath the ground? Had he burned my remains? He believed me dead and perhaps I was. I did not know how Thiede had brought me back to the world, nor could I tell if I still looked the same. I could not remember! It might be that if I ever met Cal again, he would look at me with the eyes of a stranger. But I was Pellaz inside wasn't I? Confusion; everything was misting up. (This is the boundary; what is behind it does not concern you now. You belong on this side Pellaz ...) Even the memories of my former life were beginning to become indistinct, especially those of before I was Har. Faces were blurring; I could recall Mima only by her hair. I was suddenly terrified that even Cal would become erased from my thoughts. All the things I had learned, all the people I had met; so cherished. We need our memories; all of us. I dreaded that eventually Vaysh would become the only reality. Thiede's creature, my servitor and my guard. Oh, Orien had taught me well and I still remembered his words, those words that would never leave me: hide your tears, Pellaz. I have rarely gone against that advice, but that night I was alone, and the wind outside howled like a lost soul seeking warmth. No-one could hear me weep.

Vaysh woke me at dawn. He was already dressed to travel and carried a thick fur coat over his arm. I was glum and irritable as he supervised my dressing and made me eat an uninspiring breakfast of milk and oats. Perversely, at that moment I would not have cared if he had gone on without me. Let him take my place on the throne of Wraeththu. I would continue to moulder away in Phade's tower, hating the cold in this frozen wilderness. (Was there ever a summer here?) More than this, I wanted to go back. I had dreamed of Saltrock the night before; a Saltrock of brighter colours, greater charm. In my dreams it had been Seel, not Cal, who had quickened with desire against me, but it had not spoiled the illusion.

'Hurry up, I want to get out of here!' said Vaysh.

I was pulling on my boots, sitting on the bed, hair in my eyes. I replied in the only fitting, possible way, 'Oh, fuck off, Vaysh!'

slowly and with venom. Vaysh blinked and flared his nostrils.

'We have work to do and quite some distance to cover,' he said.

'I don't care!' I grumbled, pettishly.

'Are you always like this in the mornings, Pellaz?' A smile should have accompanied that remark, but when I looked up, Vaysh's face was expressionless, as usual. I wanted to make him angry.

'How much do you know about what ... about what Thiede has done to me?' I asked. Vaysh turned away so that I could not see his face as he answered.

'How much? More than you ... maybe. Is it important? It's happened, hasn't it? Would you prefer to be dead?'

A quick, cold anger flashed through me. I stood up and roughly grabbed Vaysh's shoulders. He tried to turn immediately; his hands came up and struck my wrists. I could almost feel his flesh crawling at my touch.

'Don't!' he shouted and I let go. His eyes were dark with the anger I had yearned for.

'My mind ... I'm forgetting things,' I told him. Emotions were pulsing in and out of his eyes as he struggled to control them.

'Forgetting things? What things?' he hissed and backed away about three steps, rubbing his shoulders. Even his own touch seemed repellent to him.

'Things that happened to me when I was alive!' I raved, and then, more soberly, 'When I was alive before.'

'Those things are not important,' Vaysh said.

I could have struck him. 'To you maybe not, but they are to me! I have to sleep, don't I? How can I sleep when my mind is draining away? Is it happening, is it really happening?!'

Vaysh stared at me impassively. 'I don't have to tell you anything, Pellaz. I have only to deliver you to the right place in one piece. I don't give a damn what you think or what you feel ... I don't give a damn about your precious, grovelling past. Don't you think that the only possible truth is that *he's* forgotten you already ...'

He might have said more, but I could stem my rage no longer. In a second, Vaysh was looking up at me from the floor. He looked confused, perhaps wondering how he had got there, and touched his lip. My blow had split it.

'Now,' I began patiently, 'I can't make you concerned about me Vaysh; I don't want to, but I do want answers. Now, let's try again. Is my memory going?'

Vaysh stood up, the back of his hand to his mouth. He walked slowly to the fire and I gave him his dignity and remained quiet.

After a while he said, 'I have something of yours,' and left the room. Absurdly, I had begun to shake. It was rare that my temper erupted to violence and it always scared me a little when it did. Vaysh's teeth had marked my knuckles and if I was shaken, at least so was he.

When he returned, he held something out to me. 'Take it,' he said. It shone gold in the firelight, on a leather thong, worn with use. A sacred eye. I could not reach for it.

'How did you get that?' I asked in wonderment.

'It came with you . . .'

With me? I stared at the pendant turning slowly on its thong. 'Orien . . . it was Orien's. He gave it to me.' Whether Vaysh knew of whom I was speaking, it was impossible to tell. He would not meet my eyes, nursing his cut lip with his tongue. I took the eye from him and it felt warm in my hands. How? How had this talisman made that impossible journey with me?

Vaysh answered my question. 'Someone made that trinket truly yours. Thiede took it from around your throat. It made him uneasy; he did not want you to have it . . .'

'Why give it to you then?'

Vaysh shrugged and folded his arms. 'Such a gift as that; even Thiede was wary of the charm. He gave it to me for safe-keeping. I was told that if you ever asked for it, I was to give it back to you.'

'But I didn't ask for it!' I protested.

'Didn't you?!'

I put the talisman around my neck where it rested with

familiar comfort. 'This is my past,' I said, and it was almost a question.

Vaysh's voice was dull, 'Your past? It is all in there, perhaps. Your body is new; nothing of your old life is relevant to it. Why should it adhere to events that no longer concern it? The talisman will give it back to you; that is its only purpose.'

'How?'

Again, he shrugged. 'Only your friend Orien knows that.'

My skin prickled. 'Does that mean ... does that mean that Orien *knew*?!'

'Maybe,' Vaysh replied with a sigh. 'Thiede respects Orien. That should mean something.'

'Vaysh, I want to know,' I said. I went towards him and he backed away.

'Know? Know what?'

'Everything. How did Thiede do it? Where did this body come from? It looks like me doesn't it? It does look like me?'

'It looks like you,' Vaysh answered, ignoring the first two questions. His voice sounded less harsh.

'You've seen me before?'

'Yes.' He went over to the bed and started packing the clothes Phade had given me into bags.

'Where, Vaysh?' He looked over his shoulder at me.

'Where have you seen me before?'

He turned back to the packing. 'Everywhere Pellaz, everywhere. I have seen through Thiede's eyes ...'

All the chill came back to my flesh; my hand curled around Orien's talisman. Thiede's eyes; my life a spectacle. I was staring at a heavy pewter jug that stood on a table by my bed. I was thinking of the weight of it in my hands and the impact of it against the back of Vaysh's bent head. I was thinking of me, fleeing the tower and running just anywhere; all of this. Luckily, I was not thinking hard enough.

Vaysh stood up. 'We must leave,' he said. 'Are you ready?'

We looked at each other without liking. He knew that I had the power, even the desire, to kill him, but he also knew just what had made Thiede choose me. I closed my eyes so that I did not have to look at him. 'I am ready,' I said.

Outside, the sun shone hard on the unbearable whiteness of the snow. Only the centre of the yard had been cleared. Phade, muffled in a wolf-skin coat, stood rubbing his hands by our horses. I was now in a condition to fully appreciate what magnificent creatures they were. Slim, long noses, intelligent eyes, dainty feet. They were draped with red travelling rugs, tassels dangled from their bridles. They did not appear to be laden with many supplies, however.

Phade came over to clasp our hands. 'It was a pleasure to meet you,' he said to me.

'We may meet again,' I replied.

'What? When you are king and summon me to your court as an underling?' he laughed.

'Maybe.'

Phade nodded good-humouredly and turned his attention to my companion. 'Goodbye Vaysh, may your snow-lined knickers never melt!' He smacked Vaysh heartily on the backside as he was half over his horse. The animal jumped back with a start and Vaysh had to pull its mouth sharply just to stay aboard. He looked furious.

'See that, Pellaz?' Phade guffawed. 'Emotion; pure and virgin loathing!' He laughed again and marched back to his tower, still waving at us.

We cantered out into the stinging, fresh air beyond the tower walls, heading towards the forest. I was wondering where we were going and how we were going to eat. We had brought nothing with us. Some three miles from the tower, beyond the lakeside town, Vaysh pulled his horse to a halt. We were on a snow-padded road, barely marked by tracks. Our voices seemed muted by the heavy clouds above.

'Why are we stopping?' I asked.

'I'm going to teach you how to ride that horse,' Vaysh replied, dead-pan as ever.

I laughed, 'What?!'

'Just listen. You are riding a horse called Peridot. It is like no other horse you have ever ridden. Speak to it.'

'Vaysh!'

'Just do it! Say Peridot and think the sound; like a calling.'

'Peridot.' I obediently sent out the name-shaped thought and felt it touch something disturbingly strange. The horse's head went up, its ears flicking back and forth. I had recoiled from the touch, but after the initial shock, tried again. My thoughts came to rest against an animal intelligence. It felt so different; frightening. The thought processes were so different. We made each other's acquaintance, Peridot and I. Animals do not look at the world like we do. It was a chastening experience to sense the way they do see things.

'We have to form a link,' Vaysh continued. 'I know the way we have to travel. We must communicate in the same manner for you to direct Peridot.'

I did not welcome that. I expected Vaysh's mind to be a chilly, dark, inhospitable land.

'I like this as little as you do,' he said frostily. 'But you must trust me now. Take the information from me. Peridot is experienced in this method of travel; he will know what to do.'

'Right,' I muttered, cold inside my furs.

'Now ...' Vaysh closed his eyes and for a moment, I just stared at him, before tentatively opening my mind to him. It was like an electric shock when we met and I pulled away. Vaysh waited with bitter patience. His thoughts were carefully protected; he exposed only the information we needed for the journey. I saw the place we would visit; I could almost feel the warmth, taste the air... 'Link to Peridot!' Vaysh's voice whispered behind my eyes.

Beneath me, the horse's silver haunches began to quiver. He too could smell the salt-laced air of a warmer climate. I joined my mind with his, two completely different intelligences linking and mingling, until I was half-horse and he was half-Har. I was blind, but I could feel Peridot begin to move; a great surging of white power. Contact with Vaysh became almost comforting. I was conscious of a gathering speed; the breathless impetus of flight. It was exhilarating. Air, vapours, formless, rushing, white noise poured through my skin. I could no longer feel the reins between my fingers. I had become inorganic movement; nothing else. I did not have to open my eyes that were no longer there to see. Two horses, two Hara; one unit. Together, we sped through unimaginable space, stars hissing through our hair, laughter of alien forms at our backs; they could not catch us. Colours upon silken blackness undulated before me, through me, round me. There were worlds and worlds, hanging like glistening beads in an infinite darkness. I saw my father stride across a purple sky ahead of me, dragging a sheaf of cable plants that had comets for roots. The vision shimmered and became Seel painting his eyes with kohl before a mirror. In the mirror I could see Saltrock behind him. Then it was darkness again, and pulsing seeds of light, things like seaweed flickering at the edge of my vision. It seemed we travelled an eternity; perhaps it was only a minute. Suddenly Vaysh exhulted: through, down, out! In a burst of light, I followed his directions and the world shimmered around us, scattering sparks and laughter. We were galloping down a hard, brown road, red sunlight behind us, warm air melting a frost from our lips. The horses' coats crackled with ice that broke and faded onto the road. Vaysh was smiling. We looked at each other and I smiled too.

Ahead of us, a walled town massed grey against an encroaching dusk. It was like another planet, air powdered with fragrant dusts tickled the back of my throat.

'Is this Immanion?!' I called.

'No, no!' Vaysh shouted back, still beaming like someone who was used to smiling.

'Where then?'

'Ferelithia!'

Vaysh slowed his mount to a trot and Peridot nudged up against them, snorting through his nose, his head curved right over his neck. He could not speak to me exactly, but his kind, horsy wisdom congratulated me on my first out-of-world journey. I buried my fingers in his thick mane and scratched his neck appreciatively.

'We shall have to rest now,' Vaysh told me. 'It's not safe to travel that way for too long.'

'Vaysh, that was incredible!' I exclaimed. Vaysh nodded.

'Pell, that is just the beginning. You have so much to discover. We have inherited a magical world.'

It was the first time he had called me Pell.

We trotted towards the town and Vaysh explained a little about the place. I learned that our other-lane jump had carried us many hundreds of miles south, although we still travelled over the same land mass. 'You will find Ferelithia different to most of the Wraeththu settlements you have visited before,' he told me. 'It is the home of the tribe of Ferelith. They're a showy and rather vain people, but much more advanced from Hara like, say, the Varrs ...' A grimace crossed my face accompanied by a dozen uncomfortable recollections. 'An unfortunate comparison, perhaps,' Vaysh added, and I glanced at him sharply. His elation after our mad ride had begun to dissipate; he had started to solidify again. 'Personally, I find the Ferelith somewhat frivolous and thus rather irriating, but I expect *you* will like them.' Accompanied by such a look of disdain as it was, this remark achieved everything it was intended to and offended me. But then, I looked at Vaysh's cut lip, which was still a little swollen, and began to feel better.

We must have looked ridiculous riding into the streets of that town, furred up to the eyes in thick coats. The air was so warm that both Peridot and I had started to sweat. Vaysh looked as cool as ever, but his horse shook moisture from his black neck. All the streets were lit with strings of multi-coloured lights, loud music, the like of which I'd never heard before, pounded from open doorways, along with the sounds of intoxicated merriment. Creeping plants, lush with heavy-perfumed blossoms, adorned many of the buildings, which were low and white and roofed with red tile. Vaysh struggled to undo the collar of his coat, looking down his imperious little nose at the Hara who were strolling and shouting through the balmy evening. Through the scent of flowers, I could smell the sea.

We rode up and down for some time, looking for an inn. Several that looked suitable Vaysh shook his head at. I was not sure whether he had economy in mind or comfort. Eventually, he decided on a dimly-lit, small hostelry we discovered up a quiet backstreet.

'We need to sleep,' he said, 'and everywhere else is too noisy. Ferelithia never sleeps!'

I was tired too, the journey had sapped my strength, but thought with regret of the cheerful lights and thrilling music back in the town centre. I did not know how long Vaysh planned for us to stay in Ferelithia, but I had seen enough of it to be eager to explore.

We tied the horses to a wooden bar outside the inn and went inside. A gleaming, red-tiled floor led to a low, stone-topped bar. Dim lighting revealed a group of Hara sitting round a table near the window. They all looked up as we entered and one of them stood up.

'Are you the patron of this establishment?' Vaysh enquired haughtily. The Har grinned and came towards us.

'I'm the landlord, if that's what you mean. A room is it?'

'Rooms,' Vaysh confirmed.

The innkeeper looked with interest at our clothing. 'Travelled far, have you?'

Vaysh glared at him rudely. 'We may stay a couple of days,' he said.

We ordered a meal and Vaysh told the innkeeper we would eat in our rooms. 'We would be pestered downstairs,' he said to me darkly, and then ordered the landlord to see to our horses. I was relieved to notice that Vaysh's high-handed manner provoked only amusement. Pausing at the door to my room, I asked him to eat with me. He thought about it for a moment and then said yes. God knows why I wanted his company; I was surprised when he agreed to sharing mine. We were served an attractive meal of smoked meat, rice and salad, accompanied by pale, yellow beer. There was a table in the room, but we sat on the bed to eat. Vaysh was silent and moody, consuming his food without pleasure.

'I'm sorry I hit you,' I said, hoping to lighten the atmosphere.

He pulled a face. 'I doubt it. I think you're still congratulating yourself for having done it!'

'You're weird,' I observed, 'and, I think, horrible.' It cheered me up considerably to poke at his reserve. 'What are you, Vaysh? Why are you like you are?'

He pushed his plate away, half finished. 'We can stay here a few days,' he said.

'What happened to you? Was it Thiede?'

He stood up. 'The way we travelled; it makes us tire easily. I'm going to bed now.'

'Oh Vaysh, sit down,' I said, in a cajoling tone. 'You haven't finished.'

He hesitated a moment, clenching and unclenching his fists. Then he said, 'Pellaz, I realize sometimes I treat you unfairly, even unfeelingly, but that's just the way I am. Also, I do not wish to talk about myself; ever!'

'OK,' I agreed, placatingly. 'I won't ask another question about your impenetrable self. Sit down, eat, tell me about me.'

He sat down. 'About you? What do you want to know?'

I laughed, 'Oh God, Vaysh, everything!'

'I've told you all I can,' he said. 'There's nothing more. Some things only Thiede knows.' He was staring at his food and then something made him grit his teeth and he threw down his fork. 'Pellaz, I can see you are straining towards some kind of camaraderie between us, but that is impossible!' I suppressed an obvious wince as he fixed me with his heartless gaze. 'You are very interested in what has happened to you; this is understandable. The future also fascinates you, but one thing you must realize, Pellaz, no matter how interesting it all is to you, it is only a bore to me!'

I suppose I should have let him stalk out after that, only more unpleasantness would follow if he remained, but it is difficult to act logically in the face of such excruciating indifference. I beat him to the door.

'You'll have to force your way out!' I cried, gleefully. Vaysh raised one hand to shoulder height. His fingers began to curl, his mouth to open.

'Just try it!' I snarled. Whatever words had been on his lips were never spoken. He could sense my counter-defence and thought better of attempting that kind of skirmish. His hand dropped to his side.

'I hope Pellaz, you are not going to make a habit out of tormenting me,' he said. I watched him as he slumped miserably back down on the bed, one hand clawing his red hair. 'Ask me questions, then, ask me!'

His defeat flummoxed me. 'I can't think ... well, OK, what happened to ... what happened to my old body?'

Vaysh made a choking sound that might have been a scornful laugh. 'Flirting with devils?' he asked, drily, leaning back on his elbows. Through that question, the balance of power had shifted.

'Just answer,' I muttered, turning away; I did not want to see his face.

'It was burned.'

I had started to shake. I knew what the real questions were, but could not voice them. I said, 'Tell me what happened to it after ... after I was gone.'

I could hear him laughing. 'Ah, I see, I am to be your crystal ball. Very well, I shall be generous. Are you ready? Turn around; I want to watch this.'

I thought, 'This is just another observation, this is unknown to him', but I turned around.

I wish you could see him as I saw him then. Dead loveliness that was inquisitive. A ghoul for the flesh of love.

'He wept for you, Pellaz. He soaked himself in your blood – for days. Sprawled in the rain and the mud until he was no longer rational; an unpleasant sight. Some time after, common sense got control of his hysteria and he burned what was left of you. Then, he went away ...'

My jaw was frozen. I could not say: where? Vaysh knew the question. 'We lost interest in him after that. He may have gone back north, or not, I don't know.' He stood up. 'I'm supposed to comfort you now, aren't I? Probably that is what Thiede expects of me, but ...' I moved away from the door to let him pass. 'Why be cruel to yourself?' he said. 'Forget it, forget him; you might as well.'

I know now that my pain pleased him, for reasons known only to himself. I let him leave to surrender myself to a nest of misery. In time it would not hurt so much, I was sure. Time fades everything to a degree; even the deepest wounds.

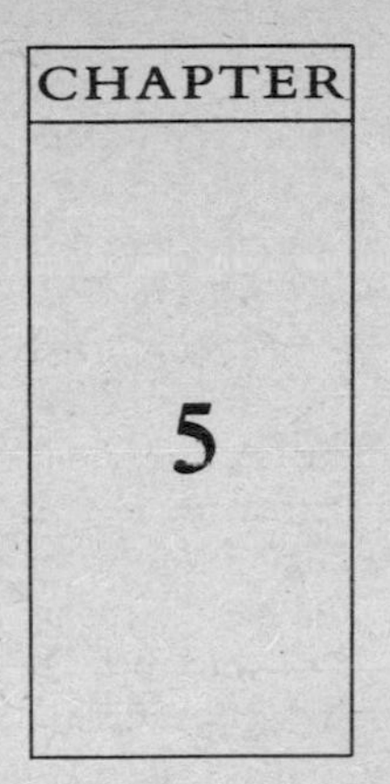

CHAPTER 5

New alliances and expectations; return of an old friend

The following morning, Vaysh being nowhere in sight, I breakfasted alone downstairs. The landlord waited for me to finish eating before sauntering over to my table. He offered me a cigarette. The smoke burned my lungs and I realized that this was the first time my new body had ever tasted it. I was subject to a subtle interrogation, which I equally subtly managed to side-step. The innkeeper laughed and called me a tease.

'Your companion has left money for you,' he said, once resigned to the fact that he would get nowhere with me.

'Oh, has he gone?' I answered abruptly. (Surely I could not have been abandoned!)

'He said he would be back to eat at noon. Why don't you take a walk around the town? There is much to see . . . spend the money. I would be happy to show you around.'

'No,' I said, 'Thanks, but I'll find my way about.'

The landlord seemed rather put out that I had declined his offer and handed me the money somewhat churlishly.

Outside, the day was already hot. I stood for a moment in the doorway to the inn, soaking up the sun. Already I had forgotten what it felt like to be cold.

The typical Ferelithian is a sociable and contented creature. This does not come as a surprise after spending an hour or two exploring the city. The thriving markets and their bright merchandise betokened affluence and by the amount of ale-houses and live music venues (all bearing colourful, exotic names), I could see the Ferelith spent most of their time in recreation. Utter strangers stopped and spoke to me when they recognized me as a new face. Street-vendors entreated me to buy their wares; sparkling, cheap jewellery and colourful, gossamer scarves. By the time I reached the town centre my mood was bordering on euphoric; friends could be made easily in Ferelithia and I could see no reason why I should have to spend another grim evening in Vaysh's company. I was intrigued by the amount of humans, most noticeably females, wandering around the streets of Ferelithia. Some even had stalls in the markets and were obviously enjoying a thriving trade alongside Hara. Had the two races learned to live in harmony in this part of the world?

It was in the market-place that I saw her, recognizing her almost instantly. That a woman should have been there at all was remarkable, but that it was her was just too much of a coincidence. A fragment of my past here in Ferelithia. She was looking at some coloured ribbons, a frown upon her face; the stall-keeper was bullying her to purchase. I hurried over, afraid that she would vanish, and tapped her on the shoulder. Her skin was dark brown and peeling. 'Hello Kate,' I said. She turned round with a smile on her face and I was surprised how much older she looked, but when she saw me her face dropped with bewilderment. She knew she had met me before but couldn't think where. 'Don't you remember me?' I asked and she shook her head slowly, still thinking.

'I'm sorry ...'

'Greenling. With Seel. You gave us guns ...'

Realization dawned across her face. 'Pellaz! Pellaz, isn't it? My God, you've changed! Sorry, I mean ...'

'Oh, that's OK, I know. What are you doing here?'

'What, at the moment? Oh, visiting friends. I'm a bit stranded ... waiting for a boat ... waiting for work ... you know ... low on funds. How about you? God, I can't believe this! I never thought I'd meet you here!'

'I'm just passing through really. The power of coincidence ... I don't even know how long I'm staying ...' I said.

She laughed. 'Long enough for a drink with an old friend, or shall I say acquaintance?'

'Long enough for that,' I confirmed.

She took me to a quayside tavern where we could see the sleek Ferelithian ships bobbing like impatient race-horses upon a dark blue sea. We sat outside at a canopied table, and Kate waved away my offer of Vaysh's money. 'No, I'll pay. I'm not that broke.' She was dressed like a man with her long hair clasped high on her head with gold circlets. But for her admittedly vestigal bosom, she could easily have passed for Har. She sat sideways in her chair, her nervous arms clanking with bangles. I could not remember her being that restless before, but of course it had been some time since I had last seen her. Now that we had said hello to each other, it was difficult to think of anything to say. I began with the obvious, 'I'm surprised to find a woman here.'

'Why?!' she snapped. 'I have no quarrel with Wraeththu, and neither have many other women ...'

'You are tolerated here then?'

She rolled her eyes and rocked back in her chair. 'God forbid! We're not back in the homeland now, Pell, thank heavens! There's quite a few women here. Ferelith like us, we amuse them, we have good friends. God knows womankind appreciates the vagaries of Man's nature just as much as Wraeththu. You've just got here I take it?'

'Mmm, yesterday.'

She nodded, poking out her lower lip. 'Have you any cigarettes?' she asked.

'For the first time in years, yes,' I replied, thankful that I had actually bothered to buy some of my own at last.

'Where've you come from, Pell?' she asked. 'You haven't stayed back home all this time have you?'

'No, not all the time ...' Something about the tone of "all this time" alerted me and I said, 'How long has it been Kate?'

She smiled, flicking ask over the table, twirling the cigarette in her hand. 'How long? God ...' she screwed up her eyes. 'Two years in Tahralan, some months in Lipforth ... god, I don't know ... what about five years?' She raised her eyebrows for confirmation.

'Five years?!' I slammed down my mug and ale slopped on the table.

Kate dabbed at her arm where I'd splashed it. 'OK, OK, maybe not that long ... four years something ... What's the matter, Pell?'

I looked at her; I could not explain. 'I didn't realize,' I said. 'Time goes so quickly doesn't it?'

'When you're having fun ...'

'That's not always the case.' Five years; I couldn't believe it. How much of that time had been spent in Thiede's care? I couldn't work it out.

'Where's your friend?' Kate asked and for a moment I thought she meant Vaysh. Then last night's wounds began to seep a little and the familiar cold numbed my head.

'Oh, you mean Cal ...' Just saying his name brought me sorrow.

'We got split up,' I explained and it came so easily after that. 'That's when I came over here; I don't know where he is now ...' (Now; five years later.)

'He really hated me, didn't he,' she said, pulling her lip thoughtfully and staring into her beer.

'He hated all women. It was nothing personal ... God, why do I talk about him as if he's dead?' Even in that hot, kind sunlight, I could not shake off the cold. I was shaking, my teeth were chattering. Kate was staring at my arms and must have seen the goosebumps.

'Do you miss him? Oh shit, yes, you miss him. Shut up, Kate.' She took a mouthful of her drink. 'He was gorgeous, can I say that?'

I laughed bitterly. 'You just did. Hell, it doesn't matter. I'd like to tell you about it, but I can't. At least I think I shouldn't ...'

'Where are you heading?' she asked, to change the subject.

I wondered whether I should tell her and then said; 'Immanion.'

She raised her eyebrows, swilling a mouthful of liquid thoughtfully. 'Well, well, how privileged.'

'Indeed. You must come visit me sometime,' I returned sarcastically.

'Sorry, I'm only jealous,' she said with a grin. 'Look, I know it seems terribly ill-mannered, but I have to go soon, but I'll tell you what, meet me for a drink tonight; you can buy me one back. I might be in a sorry state if I don't get this job I'm after.'

'I'd like that,' I said. 'I was hoping to find something to do tonight. I have a travelling companion who's about as lively as the grim reaper. Where shall I meet you?'

She quaffed the rest of her drink and wiped her mouth. 'There's a leisure-warren not far from here ...'

'A what?'

'A place to enjoy yourself, drink, dance, listen to music, whatever. It's called Temple Radiant ... not far, OK?'

I watched her hurry back into the crowd, heading for the harbour. I had not even asked her how she had got here.

Vaysh was waiting for me in my room. 'You've been gone a long time,' he said, in his flat, disinterested way. I did not welcome the prospect of Vaysh destroying my mood.

'I met a woman in the market,' I said. 'From Greenling. You remember Greenling, Vaysh, surely!'

He ignored the implication. 'What did you tell her?' he asked ominously.

'Nothing I shouldn't have!' I snapped. 'I was surprised to see her though. Is it fate, Vaysh, or did Thiede organize it for me?'

'Shut up, you fool,' Vaysh droned.

'Are all Wraeththu in this land kindly disposed towards women?' I asked, looking at myself in the mirror. I could see him behind me; his narrowed eyes.

'Some women are as pleased to see the decline of men as we are,' he said. 'It's a bleak prospect for them though and depressing for us. We have to watch them grow old alone. I had women friends once ...'

'Vaysh, one more word and I'll consider you good-natured,' I teased, making him pull one of his sour faces, of which he had an inexhaustive variety. I could still see him in the mirror. Sometimes, not often, Vaysh could be almost approachable and then he'd retreat behind a barrier of unpleasantness. He made disagreeable noises when I told him I was meeting Kate that night and then insisted on accompanying me.

'Ah, you just want to enjoy yourself,' I said. 'You're going to dance and get drunk aren't you?'

'I am not!' Vaysh snarled. 'I just want to keep an eye on you.'

We dined at the inn and Vaysh pointedly refused a glass of wine. He grumbled continuously whilst I tarted myself up to go out. The last time I'd had a social life was in Galhea; I was determined not to let Vaysh spoil our evening.

'Get changed, comb your hair,' I told him.

'I don't have to,' he replied haughtily, which was true. I had bought several brass bangles that afternoon and offered him one because I felt sorry for him. (Good humour often brings out a strange side to my nature.) Surprisingly, he took it. I had also spent a rather lavish amount of money on getting my ears pierced again, with half a dozen, heavy gold rings.

'The money's yours anyway,' Vaysh said. 'Waste it how you like.'

We discovered that Temple Radiant was *the* place to be seen in Ferelithia. I was surprised how much it cost to get in. Inside, it was almost dark; what light there was glowed purple or dark green. The music was so loud and so *strange*, strident, pounding; I wasn't sure if I liked it.

'Stop gaping,' Vaysh said.

'I've seen nothing like this,' I murmured inadequately. Vaysh sniffed.

'I used to come here, before,' he said.

Several rooms of varying murkiness led to the main auditorium. The furnishings were all of black velvet, leather and simulated animal skins. Black netting strung with painted bones hung down from the ceiling. Vaysh led the way into a room named Gehenna. I must admit I shrank at the door; its occupants, what I could see of them, seemed unpleasantly suitable for the name.

'Blend in, Pellaz; buy a drink,' Vaysh advised, firing his basilisk stare at anyone who looked at us.

'Where's Kate?'

'Buy a drink first ...' he said impatiently.

I didn't know what to order so Vaysh bought two glasses of something coloured neon purple that tasted like acid perfume on first acquaintance and increasingly pleasant after the first swallow.

The Ferelith were undoubtedly the most exotic and colourful race I had yet seen. Their hair, their clothes, their careful mannerisms combined to form a breathtaking glamour. '*Do* stop gaping!' Vaysh said. I saw several women who looked just like Hara; some of them may have been, it was impossible to tell. Vaysh pointed out Wreaththu of different tribes; most of them unfamiliar to me. Then someone touched my arm; a warm dry hand.

'Pell, you've come,' Kate said, sounding surprised.

'I said I would.'

'Yes I know, but ... this way.' She took my arm and hauled me into the darkness. I did not look to see if Vaysh was following. Kate and her friends had gathered round a table right next to the dance-floor; the music was deafening there. Coloured lights swept crazily through the smoke. I could see her mouth moving and presumed she was introducing us to the others. She couldn't stop looking at Vaysh. He was giving one of his virtuoso performances of astounding indifference, resting his elbows on the table, with his chin in his hands, looking bored. Kate was desperate to keep us entertained, although I would have been quite happy just watching the dancers. It was a strain to keep shouting over the noise. 'I got the job!' she bellowed and insisted on buying us more drinks. Restless as ever, she kept leaving the table to dance. Her friends realized the futility of trying to get acquainted with us, so most of the time I was left with only

Vaysh to mouth at. He looked sulky and lovely, and because of the drink, I remember trying to get him to talk to me. 'You're drunk,' he said.

Five empty glasses stood in sticky rings on the table in front of me when the music died down. My ears were ringing insanely; I felt pleasantly unsteady.

Kate leaned over. 'Soon you'll hear the *real* music,' she said, her face damp and flushed. 'Are you enjoying yourself?'

I nodded and smiled and could feel Vaysh looking at both of us with scorn. Kate waved at someone. 'Now be sociable, Pell, here's Rue. I want you to meet him,' she said with a conspiratorial smirk. The one she called Rue sauntered over to our table; white light from the stage at the other end of the room shone through his hair. 'Wait till you see this,' Kate hissed to me through her teeth. 'Hello Rue, mixing with the rabble are you? I'd like you to meet a friend of mine...'

That was where Kate faded out, more suddenly than she had intended, I'm sure. True magnetism is a hard thing to define, but Rue had it in abundance; shameless abundance. This was a classic example of what Thiede had once spoken to me about; instant gravitation. I suppose it was because he reminded me of Cal in a way; he had white-gold hair, but it was much longer. In looks, Vaysh could have outshone him easily (without the sulk), but what he lacked in symmetry of feature, Rue made up for generously with sheer sensuality and confidence. I could almost hear Vaysh thinking, 'Ugh, how common!' and that in itself delighted me.

'Rue, sit down,' Kate said, with the interested bustle of a voyeur, making room, patting the seat.

'I can't stay,' he said, and looked at me. 'Oh, hi,' he added carelessly. I must have mumbled something inane. He smiled and walked away, leaping up onto the stage and through some curtains at the back.

'A singer,' Kate explained and slid me a knowing glance. 'Did you like him?'

'Mmm,' I agreed, non-commitally.

Kate laughed, 'You can't stay in mourning for ever,' she

pointed out incisively.

'Kate, shut up.'

'You can't. I'm not psychic but . . .'

'Kate, shut up.'

'Why are you grinning then?'

'Kate!'

'Pellaz, how much longer do you want to stay here?' Vaysh complained in his usual chilly voice beside me. He had barely touched his first drink. I had forgotten he was there.

'You can go back if you like,' I said and we stared at each other for several excruciating seconds.

'Don't think about doing anything stupid,' he said with a sneer.

'What's stupid?' I asked delicately and he would not reply. 'Chaperone as well then,' I said in a low voice. He still would not answer. Then all the lights dimmed out and I could feel heat rising in the darkness. Vaysh shifted awkwardly in his seat; his bangle knocked against the table. A sound, like a hissing heart-beat prickled my skin. It built up slowly, louder and louder, and the crowd cheered and whistled. The excitement was infectious; Kate climbed up onto her seat. For a moment, silence, and then with a flash of white light and plumes of steam, drums rolled like thunder and Rue was bathed in a cataract of spotlights upon the stage. I stood up. Primal and thrilling, the music roared through my head. Rue leapt around the other musicians, sparks of light lasered off the chrome of their instruments. His voice was a scream then a snarl; he crouched to tease the nearest of his audience, leaping up; his body supple as a snake. Kate leaned down and put her arms round my neck. 'Dance with me,' she said. The heat of other bodies pressed against us and for a moment I held her close. She laughed in my face, mocking, bitter, and pulled away. 'Demon!' she said and then, in my ear, 'but what a way to die!'

I had danced, as a child, in the sand. My mother had said, 'What does he see that we can't? What does he dance to?' I had danced to the sky, reaching up for it, feeling a great and exciting void that had reached down for me. That had been so long ago but I could remember it vividly. I felt like that now. Before, the music had been only inside my head, now it filled my being and carried me. The sky had reached me.

At the end we cheered and shrieked and applauded; let it begin again. But the house lights came back on and Kate led us back to our seats. We were both drenched in sweat and exhausted to the point of collapse. I was surprised to see Vaysh still sitting there and steeled myself for the verbal assault. Unpredictable as ever he said, 'You dance very well.'

'Buy Kate a drink,' I said. It scared me when he was nice to me. He gave me a sour smile and disappeared, sinuously, in the direction of the bar. Kate sat beside me, attempting to organize her wet hair.

'I really needed this,' I told her and she looked at me quickly.

'I could see that,' she said. 'Your friend's a strange one isn't he?'

'He's not my friend!' I said, too harshly and she replied,

'Oh, really?'

Rue waited for quite a while before he came back to our table, as I had known he would. Outwardly tranquil, I was fighting the insufferable battle between guilt and desire. Could I forget so quickly? My feelings disgusted me, but I couldn't stop looking at Rue. He sat opposite me, the light behind him; his face was indistinct.

Vaysh leaned over and whispered in my ear, like a nagging conscience, 'You'll regret it Pell, you will.'

'Regret what? What are you talking about?'

'You know,' he said.

'What do you care?' I retorted.

'Remember who you are,' he said. 'Anyway, it's too soon. If you weren't drunk, you'd see that. Remember last night . . .'

I turned on him savagely, 'You love to make me miserable, don't you!'

He shook his head, 'Not particularly.' I sighed heavily. Rue was talking to Kate but he kept looking over at us.

'Look Pell,' Vaysh hissed, conscious of Rue's vigilance, 'we'll be here a few days. Just think about it.'

I glanced back at Rue. He felt my stare and looked into my eyes. I was torn two ways; it was not easy.

'OK Vaysh, let's go.' Vaysh was on his feet in an instant.

'Are you leaving? Kate asked, startled, seeing her plans disintegrate, whatever they might have been.

'Yes,' I answered, and could not resist adding, 'Where will you be tomorrow night?'

She seemed to relax then. 'Oh, the bar on the quay, probably. The Red Cat; where we went today.'

'Right, I'll see you there, then.' The message was not just for her but I did not look at Rue. Vaysh and I walked back to the inn in frosty silence.

This was it then: the monumental choice. That night, I sat up alone in my room, chain-smoking, drinking cold coffee and trying to think rationally. All the windows were open; the night was very warm. I kept going to stare down at the gardens and heady perfume wafted up to me. My mind was in turmoil. Ferelithia was a night-time world of crazy fantasy. All of it was new, untasted and exciting. I had spent so little time quite simply enjoying myself. Life with Cal had often been hard; many nights spent in cold or discomfort. Now I had arrived in a land of plenty clothed in new flesh that was hungry for life; a body that was radiant with the finest of Wraeththu beauty. Most of the time I was unconscious of it, but tonight I had seen it work for me. Rue's eyes ... Something prim and small argued inside me against the glowing vivacity. Didn't I owe it to Cal to restrain myself? Had I forgotten my vow so quickly? Ah yes, my eagerness countered, but I had not vowed celibacy had I? I was too sensible for that. I had pledged my heart to Cal and yet, only that was sacred. Oh, come now! the primness insisted, you have seen an attractive Har in a crowded, noisy place where everything was stimulating; music you'd never heard before, potent liquor, carefree Hara whose lives seemed enviably easy. It's not surprising you were tempted; it was just the atmosphere. I stood up and paced the floor. One thing I knew for sure, had known ever since my inception; Wraeththu-kind needed aruna. It was simply part of their existence and nothing to be ashamed about. Only love had made me feel shame. Perhaps this was the warning. Perhaps this was why Wraeththu scorned the relationships of men. Love means guilt means trouble. It was ridiculous; five years had passed. It was a concept that was almost too terrifying to think about and one, since Kate had made me realize it, which I had pushed to the back of my mind. Five years lost. Nobody knew; not those that had once cared for me. To them I was simply dead – mourned and forgotten. Just thinking of it chilled me. Mortal remains burned and rotted, skin, teeth, hair and bones. I looked down at my outspread hands. Had they heard of my death in Saltrock, in Galhea, at the Kakkahaar settlement in the desert? Did they ever speak of me? I summoned Rue's face to my mind's eye and sighed. He desired me. To him I was alive. It was inevitable that Cal had forgotten me, if indeed he still lived. I was just afraid; scared that in the arms of another, I would think only of him. 'Pellaz, you are nearly a king!' I told myself. 'Pellaz, you are Har. What you feel is natural to you and you must obey your instincts.' But I could not climb out of the guilt. Then there was Vaysh, his censure of my behaviour. To him aruna would be viewed as surrender at best and humiliation at worst, locked as he was in the ice-castle of his pride. I could not rely on his advice. Tomorrow, I would see; what will be will be. That was the only way out. Fate had me in her arms and I would not fight her.

After breakfast, I decided to take Peridot out for some excercise. Vaysh declined to join me; in his sullenness that day, he looked almost grey.

Peridot looked so pleased to see me I felt guilty I had not been to see him the day before. Vaysh's horse watched us mournfully as we trotted out into the sunlight. Now that I knew how to, I communicated with Peridot nearly all the time, passing over my thoughts on Ferelithia. To him, it was just bustle and colour and pleasing smells. I could feel his mild impatience at the chaos of my mind. I took him down to the beach and let him canter along the damp sand, through the wavelets. Ferelithia had reached my heart; I could have happily stayed there for ever.

Round lunchtime, hunger lured me back to the inn. I thought miserably of the sour face that would probably be waiting for me and was therefore gratefully surprised when I saw Kate lounging against the bar.

'How did you find me?' I asked and she tapped her nose and laughed.

'I wanted to see you. I feel a bit guilty about last night,' she said.

'*You* do!' I snapped, not meaning to sound so angry.

'Oh, I'm sorry Pell. I was a bit drunk and,' she shrugged expressively, 'well, you know. I shouldn't have said what I did about Rue or implied what I did. It was awful of me; after what you said about Cal... and what you didn't say! Is that why you left so early?'

'Oh Kate, you've done nothing wrong,' I said to ease the worried look from her face. 'I didn't leave because of anything you did. I just had to think.'

She nodded abstractedly, 'Yes, I understand. Anyway,' brightening, 'what did you think of Temple Radiant?'

I threw up my arms and laughed.

'Yes,' she said, 'I felt like that at first. That's because there's a little bit of peasant mentality lurking somewhere inside both of us, I suppose.'

'Speak for yourself!' I chided. 'It made me realize what I've been missing. Everything's been so hellishly serious lately.'

We ordered a light meal and went to sit at one of the low tables near the empty hearth. I kept thinking of what Vaysh had said about the future of women. Was Kate lonely? If I had known her better, I would have asked, but instead enquired about how she had ended up in Ferelithia. She grinned sheepishly and said she had run away from home. There had been no future for her in Greenling, other than becoming some man's wife, and whatever benefits that position had once offered seemed pointless now. 'I want to enjoy what's left of the world,' she said, with a wide sweep of her arm. 'What's left of it for me, anyhow. It will soon all belong for Wraeththu and, although I can't be part of it, I can still enjoy some second-hand thrills.'

'Have you ever thought, Kate, that it might be possible for women to share our future?' I asked.

'You obviously have,' she answered evasively and I sensed her embarrassment. 'You've touched a secret nerve there, Pell, you really have.'

'It just doesn't make sense sometimes,' I said.

'Oh, it does, there are reasons, Pell. Heavy, somewhat theosophical ones. Man before the Fall and all that. I'm just a spare rib and, I'm afraid, fearfully redundant. Woman is in you Pell; you know that.'

'You seem to know more about it than I do,' I observed.

'Well, that's obvious, isn't it. You don't really have to question things; you just *are*. I was full of frustrated anger at first. All of it seemed so unfair. Men, horrible things, seemed to have got away with lifetimes of mistreating women only to cheerfully phase us out with a timely mutation!'

'I must admit, that's how it seems to me,' I agreed.

'Well, it's not like that,' she said firmly. 'It's purely biological, I think. Males are easier to mutate; but the female *is* there. You can't see it very easily, perhaps, but it is there.'

'Why do we call each other 'he' then?' I argued.

'Oh God, I don't know!' she laughed. 'If it bothers you that much, think of something else. Think how easy it would be to get used to it!'

'Has anyone ever tried to incept a woman, do you think?' I asked.

She drew her breath in deeply and stared at the table. 'Oh, yes,' she said. Her voice was soft. I did not ask her to explain. 'When I die, Pell,' she continued, looking up with grave eyes, 'that's when I get my chance. You should know that.'

I shivered. Kate had accepted things so philosophically and worked out answers for herself. She had seen so plainly that which I had missed. We are all one. The bodies are different; but bodies are expendable. The soul goes on for ever.

Vaysh came to sit on my bed as I got ready to go out that evening. That he disapproved of my actions was obligatory; I only wished I could understand why. I was not so stupid as to think he was concerned for my welfare. He did not ask me any questions, just watched me steadily with blank eyes. Sometimes, I felt stronger than him; sometimes he reduced me to weakness. It was a constant struggle for supremacy between us; although for Vaysh it involved a deep fear of weakness. I just wanted to win for its own sake. I dressed myself in black leather and thin, white linen and was rather too lavish with the kohl. 'You don't need that,' Vaysh remarked coldly.

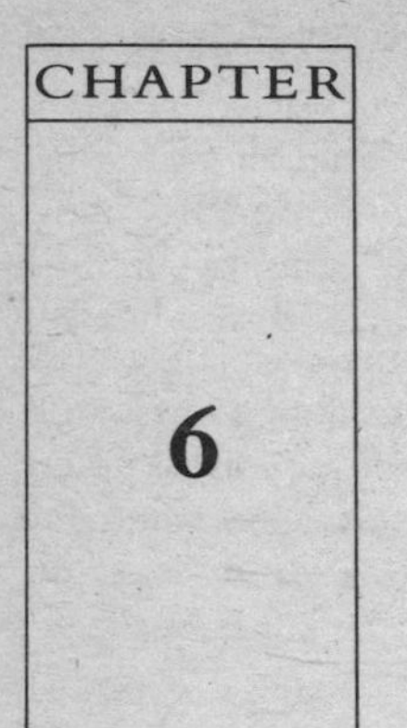

CHAPTER 6 *The sacred pearl*

The Red Cat was already busy when I arrived. The sun was setting in a blaze of colour over the calm sea and some Hara sat outside, laughing; the clink of glasses in the dusk. Not seeing anyone I recognized, I bought a mug of ale and sat down near the door. The room was much larger inside than I had anticipated and there was no sign of Kate. Absorbed in rehearsing a hundred different conversations, I did not notice Kate's friends sit down round a table nearby until they had been there for quite some time. Then one of them recognized me and called my name, beckoning me over. He had lilac hair plaited with feathers and earrings that brushed his shoulders. In fact, all of them were weighed down with gaudy jewellery. Two of them were musicians in Rue's band, which was named, somewhat esoterically, The Closets of Emily Child. They introduced themselves as Pharis and Amorel; the Har with the lilac hair was Karn. I had to fend off a rapid fire of quick-witted remarks and then a volley of salacious observations about Vaysh. Amorel asked, 'Where is he?' and I replied, 'It's still daylight isn't it?'

'Just . . .'

'Then he'll be in his coffin; ask later.'

I did not see Rue until he walked up behind Amorel and put his hands round his neck. They all seemed pleased to see him and no wonder. The light here was much brighter than it had been in Temple Radiant and, if anything, flattered Rue more. His long, yellow hair was spiked up and crimped down his back and his face was unpainted, his skin tanned. A loose, white vest complimented his colouring and the customary black leather defined with pleasing candour, the slimness of his hips. I was virtually drooling into my ale. He must have sensed my scrutiny; one of the others looked at me and laughed. I wished Kate was there. They all knew what was going on. Rue was still draped around Amorel. He narrowed his eyes a little before he smiled at me. I found out later that his eyesight was not that good.

Pharis said, 'Rue is short for Caeru, but we never call him that.'

'He sings well,' I said.

'He does!'

I guessed Rue was Ulani, but was unsure of his level; most probably Acantha. He did not look at me directly once after that first time.

Kate arrived about half an hour later. I had consumed several mugs of ale by that time and was feeling more relaxed. Pharis was discreetly trying to interrogate me and I was amusing myself by sidestepping his questions. This, of course, only intrigued him more. I was talking to Pharis, flirting and teasing, but all of it was for Rue. We still had not spoken to each other and the glances we exchanged had been furtive. Kate raised her glass at me and smiled. When Pharis got up to go to the bar, Rue slid into his seat and my heart leapt into my throat.

'What did you think of the show last night?' he asked me.

I felt about fifteen again and prayed it did not show, mumbling my way through some embarrassing fatuousness, trying to remind myself, 'You are not an idiot, you are a king, remember?'

Rue showed me a scar on his arm. 'The spoils of inception,' he said, 'where's yours?' I rolled up my sleeve to show him, then remembered I no longer had a scar. If I did, it was in a place that could not be seen.

He looked at me suspiciously. 'You don't have one.'

I shook my head. 'Not any more.'

'Why?'

'It's a secret.'

He rested his head on one hand. 'You're different aren't you.'

'Everybody's different.'

'Not like you.' He ran his fingers lightly over my arm. 'You won't be here for long, will you?'

'No, not for long.'

'Where are you going?'

'Immanion.'

'I should have known.' He took my hand and idly traced the lines on the palm. 'Such destiny.' He was only guessing.

Outside, the sky was pink and the air cooler. It was hot and noisy where we were sitting. The others had turned their backs on us.

'I'm going back to the inn now,' I said. 'Do you want to come?' My voice barely faltered. Rue just smiled and stood up.

We walked along the harbour and I could not think of anything to say. Rue threw stones into the sea; it was high tide. Ferelithia; the concubine of Wraeththu cities. Its ambience was that of lazy sensuality and its inhabitants were a reflection of that trait.

We came to a seat under a flowering orange tree. Rue sat down. I leaned on the sea wall and gazed at the horizon. For some reason, I felt nervous. Presently Rue joined me and our arms touched where they rested on the stone. 'Kate told me some things about you,' he said.

'Did she?' I must have sounded displeased.

'Yes. I lost somebody once, I know how it is. Don't feel obliged to do anything you don't want to ...'

'Kate had no right to say anything!' I grumbled irritably.

Rue sighed and I looked at his profile staring at the sea.

'Rue, if I seem wary, it's not because of that, it's because ... it's been a long time.'

He tilted his head to look at me and I took him in my arms. His hair smelled of musk and smoke. It felt unbelievably good to hold him, something I'd forgotten. Warmth and friendship. I frantically implored Heaven that Vaysh would not be still in my room when we got back. Hara walked past us; their voices muted. It was a place, a time, for closeness, and I did not want our simple embrace to end. But we started to get cold and Rue stepped back first. His eyes were saying, 'I know you are different and I will give you my best. I want to keep part of you here in Ferelithia.'

How thoroughly I took advantage of that.

Something about the atmosphere in my room, as if it held its breath, whispered, 'What shall happen here will be almost holy.' As before, the windows were held open to the night and heavy scents lingered in the air. We had taken a jug of hot coffee up with us from the bar. There was no sign of Vaysh; not even the faintest chill of his presence. We sat and smoked and drank the coffee. I ended up telling Rue all about Cal, right up until before, what I now termed, the 'first death'. Nothing more than that. In return, Rue told me something about himself. He had come down from the north about two years ago; Ferelithia seemed to be the goal of most Wraeththu in this country. More accessible than Immanion and very affluent. Its main trades, as in the Eastern cities of legend, were cloth-making and spice-growing. To the west of the city, a metal-work quarter was beginning to thrive. Work and money appeared to be in plentiful supply; there were no beggars on the streets of Ferelithia. In response to my query concerning the relationship between humans and Hara in the town, Rue explained that it had mainly been women drawn to Ferelithia. The hedonistic easy-going Ferelith had no quarrel with anyone who was not openly hostile to them and their first reluctant tolerance of humans gradually softened to acceptance. Times had been hard in the surrounding country for women, where many human settlements, divided by civil strife and suddenly deprived of the over-civilization they were accustomed to, had regressed in temperament and life-style to something like out of the Dark Ages. What equality females had once enjoyed had been taken from them by brute force. I could sympathize deeply with those who resented the reversal of function to mere baby-machines and male pleasure-fodder. It was not surprising many had preferred to take their chances with the Wraeththu. Not that the women I'd seen in Ferelithia were soft or frightened creatures, far from it.

Rue confessed he did not like to work, not in the labouring sense, but as he was blessed with a good voice made an adequate living out of singing for the band. I asked about the name, where did it come from?

'It's an allegory,' Rue explained mysteriously. 'It means many things; choose your own meaning.'

I like to think he guessed more about me than I told him. He knew I would go to Immanion as more than just a visitor. Half of me wanted to tell him everything, but I thought it would be unwise. Rue looked wistful when I skirted his questions. He wanted me to trust him, which I did, even on such short acquaintance, but trust was not enough.

The time came when our conversation came to an end. In the comfortable silence, Rue looked at me. We were sitting at the table.

'I was lucky to meet you,' he said and stood up, lifting the white vest over his head.

I told him he was beautiful and he held out his arms for me. We were about the same height. Sharing breath had never been so easy on the neck. I think it frightened him, what he tasted within me, for he tried to pull away at first, but I would not let him. It was too pleasant for me, soaking in his warmth, his misty, sighing waves. He tasted lazy and I wanted us to meld; see him from the inside out. When he broke away from me, he kept saying my name, half in fear, half in desire. When we had scrambled out of our clothes, I said to him, 'This body is virgin for you.' He smiled, thinking I was a romantic fool, but it was the truth. He was soume for me; selfless compliance, and it was like coming to drink at a cool, dark pool after endless torment in a searing desert. I wanted to experience every second to the full; my body had truly come alive again. I thought, 'After this, I will never be able to look at Vaysh seriously again.' Perhaps he had known that; known that by experiencing something he never could, I would disregard the hold he had over me. His words could wound me no longer.

At some point, I realized my purpose, *the* purpose, for what had happened here in Ferelithia, and it did not matter that it was probably Thiede's design. Rue tensed against me. He could tell something was happening but he didn't know what. 'Pell!' he said, 'Pell! What . . .?'

I put my hand on his face. 'Hush,' I said, 'relax.' I hope I did not cause him pain. Mostly, I think, he just found it strange, discovering parts of himself invaded that he did not know he had. I broke through the seal and his face flinched for a moment, but after that . . . Reality disappeared. With that unity we could have exploded the world. A microcosm flared in Rue's body, and I was the god that moved it.

CHAPTER

7

Journey's end and the shining city

I often ask myself what made me, what exactly made me, run away so quickly. I like to think I had noble reasons, but if I had, I can't remember them. It was just an instinctive reaction. I did not want this complication; I shunned commitment of this nature. There were greater things waiting for me, after all. I said to myself, 'It is Thiede's design that I should leave.' I have no doubt that he deserved the blame for many things that happened to me, and would happen to me, but not everything. Thiede had become my personal (and often convenient) incarnation of Fate. All events were accountable to him. I could behave as I wished and declaim, 'Oh, but it was not me; it was him!' and point the righteous, accusing finger. I can still do that now, if I wish. People will always believe me, liking as they do to believe the worst of Thiede. That is his fault. He has never exactly struggled to make himself either popular or trusted.

That morning, I woke to look at Rue's hair spread out over the white pillows; tangled and still damp at his neck, and knew instantly that I wanted to leave Ferelithia that morning; now, away from Rue. It was not, as Vaysh had predicted, because of regret; I regretted nothing. I just felt that I had fulfilled a particular path of my destiny and that was an end to it. Rue did not wake as I dressed, nor as I furtively emptied drawers of my belongings. We had had little sleep. Vaysh had left our bags under the bed. I hastily shoved all my things into them and pushed them back out of sight. I hardly dared look at Rue; I was afraid to wake him because I did not trust myself. I could not ignore the hundred screaming harpies in my head crying, 'Flee!' but Rue had surrendered himself to me for that one night of bliss; he had made me happy. I don't think he knew what I had done to him. Afterwards, he had only laughed and praised my prowess, although his eyes had been shadowed with vague doubt. He would think more about that today. As I stood there, looking down on his wild beauty, I said to myself, 'Rue, I will not forget you.' That would be no compensation, I know, but it was the simple truth. I could so easily have reached for him again, but something stayed my hand. It was not meant to be. Perhaps he would come to hate me, or perhaps he would be glad and remember me with warmth. He did not know yet, but the fruits of our passion would linger here in Ferelithia long after I had gone. Rue had got what he wanted, but in a way he could not have imagined. He hosted the pearl that would become my son.

Vaysh was still asleep and took some time to respond to my knocking. He gave me a sleepy, contemptuous stare from round the half-open door.

'Get dressed, Vaysh, and get the horses ready to leave!' I ordered, and did not wait to watch his surprise.

Downstairs, the landlord was just preparing breakfast. None of the other guests had yet come down. I ordered coffee and bread rolls and asked for paper and a pen. Sitting by the window, looking out into the morning mist of a new day, I wrote:

Dear Kate,

I have no doubt that you will come here asking questions or looking for me. Do not be angry that I did not wait to say goodbye, or condemn me for running out on Rue. It may puzzle you that I have said that, but in time you'll understand what I mean. I know that you've probably got plans for the future which may involve leaving Ferelithia, but I would like, if you can, for you to stay here for a few months and keep an eye on Rue. I know I've got a nerve asking you, but you remember once I said that you seemed to know more about Wraeththu than me? Well, this is something you won't have seen before and that's why I think you won't mind staying. Last night, Rue and I conceived new life. I'm afraid he doesn't know yet, and it's up to you when and if you want to tell him. I can't. I have to leave; I have no time. Finally, I want you to know that you'll always be welcome in my future home. Come to Immanion, Kate, and tell me how things went here after I'm gone. I shall leave money for you with the innkeeper, whom I hope can be trusted. I know all this sounds very high-handed and mysterious, but when we meet again, I shall explain. I believe you shall be able to find me in Immanion quite easily.

Your friend Pellaz.

I wrote it out about three times before I was satisfied. Sentiment or something like it made me keep the other copies. One of them is reproduced above. Whatever else I wrote for her I've forgotten.

Vaysh and I rode along the coast road away from Ferelithia. Yellow beaches alive with shrieking sea-birds led down to the sea on our right. To the left, grassy dunes hid the fields that lay beyond them. Would Immanion be as beautiful or as welcoming as this place we were leaving? My heart was heavy but I had learned long before not to look back and did not turn in my saddle for one last look at the sleepy, white town whose mantle of flowers blew a haunting fragrance to us on the morning breeze. Immanion was three hundred miles or so south-east of Ferelithia; a shorter jaunt than the one we had undertaken from Samway. Vaysh was impatient to cross over to the other-lanes. He was eager to conclude our journey, but I still wanted time to mull over recent events and could only do that on solid ground.

He reluctantly agreed to give me half an hour's respite and rode on ahead of me to sulk. I felt as if I was already out of this world; euphoric, yet at the same time a little sad. Soon my journey would end. On the other side of our next other-lane dash, Immanion lay waiting, waiting for me. So long ago, an ignorant peasant boy, (who thought an awful lot of himself), had set out upon an adventure into an unknown world. So much had happened since then. That boy was dead. I thought of the time when I had lain beside my brother agonising over that first fateful move towards a beautiful stranger whom I had thought of as just a man caught up in a glamorous, perhaps impermanent, craze. What would I be doing now if I had not braved reaching out to him? My life would have been ordered for a time, I'm sure of that, but eventually Wraeththu would have had to touch it. Perhaps a different face of Wraeththu to the one I had been incepted to. I had been offered the best. Some suffering had come my way, but the good things outweighed it.

Riding along that road, with the tang of the sea in my nostrils and the claws of the wind in my hair, my heart rejoiced. I thanked God for everything; for Saltrock, for Cal, for Rue. I would not have lived my life any other way. Perhaps we were not as different from Mankind as we liked to think we were. Many Wraeththu would travel the same path of selfishness and greed. Within myself, I could recognize vestiges of those inherent traits. It will always be a struggle to combat these things, but it is enough just for some of us to recognize that battle. I had work to do, for my race and for the world, and I was now prepared to take on that responsibility. Ah, is that a cynical eyebrow I see raised? You must think that I had just run away from responsibility, but as an excuse, and excuse it is, I can only say that I had no time to linger. Rue had been the right person, only the place had been inopportune. I followed the current of my destiny. It would lead to a vast ocean of infinite possibilities.

Before we left Ferelithia, I had asked Vaysh to collect my luggage from my room. He had given me a knowing look but asked no questions. No doubt he thought I was wallowing in the corroding mire of regret that he'd warned me about. I did not enlighten him. He smugly disclosed that Rue had been awake when he went in. Neither of them had spoken. 'He did not seem surprised to find you gone,' Vaysh said demurely, obviously under the impression that Rue and I had spent a tedious night of uninspired and passionless gratification. I did not want him thinking that.

'You could learn a lot from Rue, Vaysh,' I said. 'He's sensual, warm, and *very* experienced.'

'I don't need lessons like that!' Vaysh snapped, and I was satisfied to notice the self-congratulation drop from his face.

It was all so quick after that. A touch of minds, a shiver of power like white ice through the spine and we were up, up and slipping sideways into the otherworld night. Deadly chill smacked the breath from my lungs, a thousand screams echoing in a mind that clung to sanity only as a memory. In another world, so far from us, land shivered away from us in a shining, blurred ribbon, miles devoured, time become distance, become space. Sometimes, I felt the presence of others, whether fellow travellers or mere observers, I could not tell. I saw towers of light upon velvet blackness, pictures of the past frozen forever like photographs, but they were only memories. I could feel Peridot between my thighs, but I could not see him. He was sparkling dust. Vaysh was a curling spiral of steam, haloed by red hair. Once I think, he turned towards me for I saw twin stars that were the brightest jewels that were his eyes.

When we emerged once more, into the afternoon warmth of yet another land, we found ourselves careering down a gently-sloping, grassy hillside. Tall, white-barked trees with supple branches of pointed leaves that swayed like hair in the sussurating breeze, gathered together as if for company on the grass. Small, white flowers starred the sward. Where the ground evened out below us, a sun-speckled forest of widely-spaced trees was divided by a white-paved road. At intervals, statues stood like sentinels along its edge.

'Well,' said Vaysh, good-humoured again, at least for a while, until the madness of the other-lanes deserted him, 'the road to

Immanion, Pell.' The horses had slowed to a prancing walk and my heart began to pound. I did not know how I was to be received in the city. Did they know we were coming? Would the streets be thronged with cheering Hara and the air flutter with petals? I hoped we could make a quiet entrance. I could not organize myself to prepare for a public spectacle.

Immanion was not as near as I imagined, however. Vaysh and I had been riding along the white road for an hour or more before the trees thinned out completely and the fields and farms of Immanion's lands appeared. A faint whiff of the sea blew towards us from the distance.

'You are nervous,' Vaysh observed; a smile, straining to be expressed, hovered at the corners of his mouth.

'Yes,' I sighed. 'None of it seemed quite real until now.'

'You were too preoccupied,' Vaysh commented acidly. There was a familiar echo in his voice that made me look at him.

'Why does it bother you?' I asked. 'I presume you're referring to Rue?'

Vaysh's fingers clawed his hair; it was always a gesture that signalled his discomfort. 'To be honest with you, Pell,' and here he paused, his face twitching with reluctance. I dreaded what he might be about to say. 'I think it's because I nurtured you, made you live. You've always wanted to know this; here it is. Thiede materialized your flesh through the power of his will. Exact, precise and perfect. He remembered you well, didn't he? The only differences in you are that your slight imperfections have been smoothed away. Thiede said to me, the day he showed me what he'd created, "Vaysh, this is your charge. This is Pellaz. He will be your king. He will be your life." I was angry at first. For so long my home had been with Thiede. Now he was sending me away. I was not good enough for his purposes; now he had you. He was impatient with my bitterness. "Pellaz must always have you," he said. "Your fidelity must be complete." He did not mean, by that, that we should be close, the kind of close I can see you are thinking of; that was not my place. I was to attend your body like a servant, whilst you needed it, and after that, I was to be your confidante, your friend. After a while, it seemed as if it had been I that had made you. As if you had sprung from within me ...'

I could not think of a single, suitable thing to say. That Vaysh had opened up to me like this was enough to stun me to silence, but I knew his revelations deserved a response.

'Vaysh, I ... Why did you not speak before? I would never have guessed from the way you've ... behaved.'

His eyes were dark as they stabbed me with reproach. 'You know how I am; mostly dead inside. What feelings I have make me uncomfortable. Oh, it's something different with you; it has to be. Thiede's made you so much better than all the rest of us. You are his son – or as good as. Everyone wants you in some way, everyone! And you took that mouthy little roughy-toughie ...!'

'Vaysh!' I could not stop myself laughing. His opinion of Rue, though cruel, was not altogether inaccurate.

He smiled back at me in a thin sort of way. 'Yes, I amaze you don't I. Most of the time I'm jealous *of* you, with all your pompous warmth, goodness and beauty, which in itself is mind-numbingly sickening, but sometimes I'm jealous for you; all that you had with the incomparable Cal, and then with that ... well, there are no words for that. What on earth possessed you?'

I felt it would not be a good time to disclose that Rue, for all his unplaned edges, now carried my son.

Vaysh mistook my silence for something else. 'I see. Aren't you supposed to be elevated above all that now? I'd like to say, "You could have had me," but I can't. All that's gone now.'

'Why is it, Vaysh?' I asked gently. 'What has Thiede done to you?'

He gave me a sad smile. 'Oh Pellaz. You know. You've suspected haven't you? I'm burnt out. At best, barren and at worst gutted. No, you were not the first ...'

My stomach shivered and writhed. There but for the grace of God, or Fortune... 'I'm glad you told me this,' I said. It was inadequate, but I could think of nothing else at the time.

'I'm sure you are,' Vaysh replied bitterly.

I was beginning to understand the maelstrom of pain, frustration, panic and helplessness that was the essential Vaysh, but only a little. I was too privileged in my own circumstances to fully comprehend.

Then it was before us: white walls towering and crystalline, and the city itself; rearing like restless foam of sea-stallions into the cerulean blue of the sky. Towers, pillars and minarets convoluting, spearing, in a purity of grace. Immanion; first city of Wraeththu.

Vast gates in the walls were panelled with jet. They stood open. There was no guard. When I commented on this. Vaysh gave a dry laugh. Immanion did not need that kind of protection. No one would ever get this close who was not welcome. I wondered if Kate would ever be able to find her way here.

The streets were peopled by the most elegant and ethereal Hara I had ever seen. If a man had ever chanced to find his way here, he would believe he had found the kingdom of Heaven and was in the company of angels. A great atmosphere of tranquility calmed my thudding heart. It was hard to imagine the Wraeththu here cheering anyone. We rode into the city on our fine and magical horses, with their curving heads and proud steps, and the Hara we met nobly inclined their heads to us as we passed. I'm sure that many of them, (if they knew who we were), mistook Vaysh for their king and I for his companion. He looked impressively regal, riding just ahead of me. Immanion is a large city by any standards, but especially so to me as I was at that time. Riding through those evenly spaced wide avenues, I was overawed by the grace and symmetry of the white buildings around me, mystified by the utter calm and fragrance of the air. It seemed that Cal's dream had been based on reality, for surely I now rode along the streets he had once imaginatively described to me. Immanion felt as if it had stood a thousand years, yet, of course, its age was only the minutest fraction of that. How had Thiede done it?

Near the sea, in the heart of the city, a wooded hill afforded privacy to the half-seen building that rested upon its crown.

Vaysh pointed, 'Look Pellaz, forget the huts of Saltrock, the tents of the Kakkahaar, even the human cast-offs of the Varrs; this is your new home.'

It is not easy to describe. Not easy to do it justice. A list of words presents itself: elegance, space, height, echoes, gold, black, white crystal, silence, music. Terraces and rows of slim pillars. Patios of black and white marble. The palace had a name, as all places of fable should: Phaonica. It had a proud, female ambience. It was easy to turn to Vaysh though, and communicate without even speaking; 'I think I shall be very happy here.'

We rode up the hill and through the fantastic hanging gardens, past the cataracting fountains, the temples whose only function was ornament. Hara tending the grounds, lowered their eyes as we rode by, and made, with their hands, the genuflections of respect. I had come home.

My staff awaited us. Cordially, without fuss, our horses were led away and Vaysh and I led into Phaonica. Up a snowy crest of steps, between shadowed pillars, along lofty corridors, up more flights of steps. I could not take it all in. It was a fairy-tale place; sombre without brooding, shady without darkness. Naturally, the first thing that our attendants wanted to do for us, was to prepare the scented baths that would erase from our bodies the memory of our journey. Vaysh had been allocated a suite of rooms within my own apartments, which included his own bathroom presumably, for we were separated. My two servants were strange, elfin creatures with piebald skin, which may have been tattooed, and thick, black hair. They introduced themselves as Cleis and Attica. I was still gawping with wonder at my surroundings, but they passed no comment on my stupor. My clothes were removed with downcast eyes; fragrant oils poured into the bath-water. All the rooms were simple in design, high-ceilinged and with painted walls. The prevailing colours were dark red, brown and gold.

'What have you been told about me?' I asked the Har who lathered my hair. He was clearly not sure how to answer.

'Our lord came to us and told us to make these rooms ready for occupation. He has kept them empty since the palace was built. He said to us, "Your king is coming; I have chosen him." That was all.'

I did not have to ask who their lord was. 'Is he here,' I asked.

'We have not seen him,' was the careful reply.

They dressed me in an elegant costume of black gauze. My hair was crimped with hot irons, but when they asked what cosmetics I preferred, I shook my head. 'Nothing, thank you.' And what food did I desire? Anything, I wasn't bothered. Wine? Yes, anything. I kept getting faint reminders of Mur and Garis. Did I detect just the faintest shade of mockery in their ministrations? None of this felt comfortable. Thiede had said to them, 'Make sure you treat him well', and they were doing so, but it was Thiede who gave the orders, that was clear. I felt like a dressed-up doll to be exhibited in a position of prominence. 'Ah yes,' Thiede would say to his Nahir-Nuri peers, 'and this is my latest creation.' But I was Nahir-Nuri too, wasn't I? Although I felt no different. It was crucial for me to speak with Thiede as soon as possible, I decided. My role was vague. What must I do now?

I exercised my powers for the first time and asked Attica and Cleis to leave me alone. It was almost a surprise when they complied, backing, soft-footed from my presence. I spent some time investigating my rooms. There was nothing lacking. I found a bed-chamber which appeared to have been inspired from the pages of myth, two reception rooms, a library well-stocked with an eclectic array of titles, (the literature of both Man and Wraeththu), and several other chambers whose function had not yet been ascribed. Glass doors in the outer wall of my bedroom led to a marble terrace which overlooked the sea. I went out there and leaned on the wall. To my left the terrace led to another door in the white walls. It was open. Inside, I could see Vaysh brushing his hair at a mirror. He must have been able to see me in it, but did not turn round as I approached.

'Do you think Thiede is here?' I asked him and threw myself down on his bed.

'Don't be inelegant, Pellaz. As for your question, I don't know. But if he isn't, he soon will be.' Vaysh's steely defences were securely back in place.

'You look nice, Vaysh,' I said.

He threw me a look of practised disdain. 'I always *look* nice,' he said.

I was beginning to think more and more as Phade did; suffering an overwhelming desire to break through the ice. Vaysh was unconsciously seductive in his glacial loveliness, but he was also the only familiar face to me in Immanion. I was feeling insecure and needed warmth; Vaysh's manner was tiresome. I could not see why he should want to keep it up after our conversation on the road.

'I thought you were supposed to be my friend,' I teased him. He shook his head, but covered his face with his hair so I could not see him smiling.

'Remember who you are,' he said.

'And what's that, Vaysh?'

He looked up at me then and an unspoken thought passed between us. He shrugged. 'It has to be faced Pell. This is Thiede's world now. We all just dance to his tune.' (Phade had said that.)

'What if it's not our kind of music?' I asked.

Vaysh sat next to me. 'Don't talk like that, there's no point.'

He was dressed in green again. I put my hand tentatively on his back and the material was warm; which surprised me. He let me stroke him, like cats do when they're in the mood. It was possible to pretend, but I was sensible enough not to push it too far. I couldn't tell if he liked me touching him.

'What has Thiede got planned for me?' I asked.

'You will have to ask him.'

'I intend to. Do you suppose he is watching us now?' Vaysh looked over his shoulder at me.

'It's best not to think about that, Pell.'

'Make me think of something else then,' I said. It slipped out before common-sense could block my throat. Vaysh kept on looking at me, straining his neck, but I still could not tell what he was thinking.

'I thought you were in mourning,' he remarked. Perhaps he was trying to make me feel guilty, or perhaps he just wanted me to say that Cal was no longer important. Whatever the reason, it was pointless after what he knew about Rue.

'The truth is, Vaysh,' I said, 'that the time to mourn is sometime in the dead of night, alone, in bed. That's when I think, or get lonely. Nobody will ever take Cal's place, nobody. But don't think me shallow because I want company. I am Har; end of statement.' I felt him sigh, through my hand.

'I can't help you,' he said. 'I'm not even sure if I want to. Oh Pellaz, I thought I'd got myself in order! What are you trying to do to me?'

'I don't think you're as cold or unfeeling as you like people to think,' I suggested carefully. He did not comment. 'Perhaps,' I continued, 'living with Thiede it was easy to imagine that you were ...' He still did not move away. Every time I said something, I expected him to. I was desperate to bring out the real Vaysh; but my motives were not entirely unselfish. I could sense his confusion and only lay there, projecting all the sensuality Thiede had given me, tormenting him.

'I don't know,' he murmured, his hands clawing each other in his lap. 'I don't know ...' I still did not appreciate how deeply he had been scarred. Wriggling round on the bed, I put my head in his lap (his hands flew up to his neck), and stared up through his hair.

'What colour is it, naturally?' I asked, reaching up to put my fingers in it. Vaysh's face was so grave.

'Light coloured,' he said.

'The colour of light ...'

'No, just sort of yellowish, only darker ...' Evening light shadowed his face. He stroked my face with his cool, white hands. 'No more than this, Pell,' he said, in his softest, gravest voice. I closed my eyes and smiled.

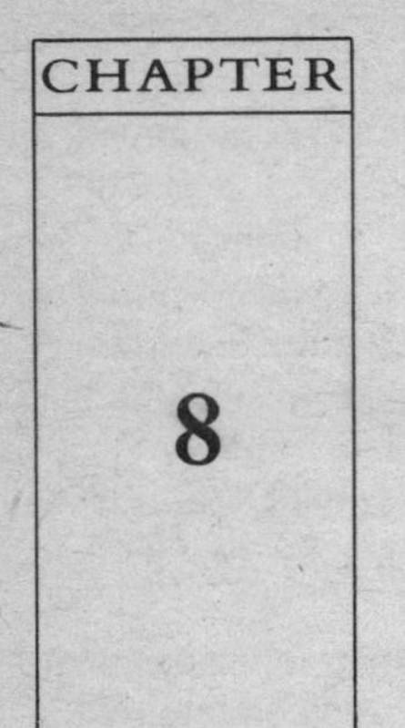

On the plans of the Hegemony and shattering ice

I could not remember where I was at first, waking up alone, opening my eyes to the swaying canopy above my bed. Then I smelled the air, purer than any other I had ever breathed. I had closed all the windows before retiring; someone had been in to open them. For a while I just lay there, staring at the fluttering folds of muslin over my head. My room did not catch the morning sun (an oversight?); outside the terrace was in shadow. I tried to imagine what it would have been like if Cal had been here with me; vividly picturing his cynical amusement. He would never have been comfortable here, not under these circumstances. I realized that when the time came for me to find him again, I would be ashamed to admit what Thiede had made of me. I feared his scorn.

Attica, or Cleis (I could not tell which, as they both looked the same to me), knocked on my door and entered the room without waiting for my answer. Breakfast awaited me. Would I dress first? I shook my head, reached for a robe to cover my nakedness and walked out ahead of him.

The table was decorated with flowers. Their incense perfume filled the room. Seating myself at the head of the table, I requested that Vaysh should join me. I was already eating by the time he sat down. As expected, the food was elegant and meticulously prepared, meticulously designed. Vaysh was robed in his favourite green and still sleepy. I had noticed it always took some time for him to wake up properly.

'Thiede will summon you today, I expect,' he said, helping himself to minute portions of the food. I put my hand over his wrist and he looked at it with interest.

'You no longer stop me touching you, I see,' I remarked.

He managed a bleak smile. 'I trust you,' he said. 'I wonder what Thiede will say to you.'

'I'm wondering what to say to him,' I replied bitterly.

Cleis and Attica brought us coffee in a tall metal pot and cleared away the food before we could help ourselves to more.

'They appear to be hurrying,' Vaysh observed. His meal had only been half-eaten.

Right on cue, the door swept open and my attendants all but threw themselves to the floor. Thiede, dressed in black and grey wolfskin, strode past them.

'Good morning Pellaz, Vaysh,' he announced. 'Ah coffee, good.'

He sat at our table and snapped his fingers. My attendants moved in a blur to fill his outstretched hand with a brimming cup haloed by steam.

'Do you like your new home, Pellaz?' He looked around him. 'I'm pleased with these apartments; they've turned out very well.'

I was silent, remembering all too clearly the last time we had met. It was difficult to equate that kind of Thiede with the one who sat here now though. Less awesome, he appeared to have put aside the trappings of terrible power; no-one could exist comfortably like that all the time. Thiede is very hard to look at directly, because his beauty is so alien and stark. It is easier to look at his nose (aquiline, with delicately flared nostrils, of course), or his amber eyes or his cruel yet smiling mouth, but difficult to take in everything altogether. He is taller than most Hara and his flaming red hair looks dyed, which it isn't. From the history books of Man, the nearest people I can compare him to are Salome and Alexander the Great combined in one body, with a dash of the witch Medea and the magician Merlin for good measure. He is deadly, but lovely, a little insane but clever. Shrewd Hara take great pains never to offend him although, mercifully, he rarely takes offence at anything.

Vaysh stood up and excused himself from our presence. Left alone with me, Thiede stared thoughtfully into my eyes for several harrowing minutes.

'I'm very pleased with you,' he said.

'You compliment only yourself,' I replied.

Thiede threw back his head to laugh. 'Oh, you have such spirit, Pellaz. You are ninety percent yourself and ten percent me, if that much. I expect you feel obliged to be annoyed at how I've taken control of your fate ...'

I did not answer. Thiede looked at me wryly. 'I shall arrange a coronation for you. That will be an excuse for a celebration. I do so like celebrations, don't you? Your title will be Tigron; Tigron of Immanion and of Wraeththu.' He folded his arms which had been gesticulating wildly.

'Forgive my ignorance, Thiede, but what exactly *is* my purpose? You are the true ruler of Wraeththu, that's obvious. Why do you need me?'

The smile never moved from his face. 'I need you because you will rule *well*, Pellaz. I'm not interested enough to spend all my time attending to the affairs of the little Hara. You must have seen; they are in such a mess. They need government, central government.'

I put aside further objections to comment on what I thought was his simplistic view of things. 'Thiede, I hate to sound pessimistic, but has it ever occured to you that the majority of the tribes of Wraeththu, who most need controlling, will fanatically resist anyone trying to wrest their autonomy away from them?'

He leaned forward and squeezed my arm. 'Ah, Pellaz, this is what I was looking forward to! Your rational little mind wrestling with the problems of administration!'

'Thiede, there must be a hundred Gelaming capable, and more knowledgeable than I, of becoming Tigron. I don't understand; why me? All this fuss, what you put me through, what is it for?'

Thiede affected an expression of being downcast. 'Pellaz, what must I do with all the power at my command? Call it a whim, if you like, but I had the desire to make you what you are. I wanted a new start, a new king, a stranger. Someone like you. You are still young, but I have always been able to see your potential.'

I leaned back in my chair. 'That is reasonable, I suppose. I hope you are right about me.'

'I am. Now, as to the problems of establishing order that you mentioned. For the most part, of course, our authority must be implemented by force; distasteful though such measures are to the Gelaming. There are trouble spots, that must be cut out, and swiftly. You will have under your control an impressively adequate army; you shall meet your generals later. Obviously, major decisions of a strategic nature must be left to them. The majority of our tribes, however, will welcome my organization. Everyone shall benefit.' He took a few mouthfuls of the coffee, staring out of the window. 'I must begin to spend more time here in Immanion,' he said. 'It is the jewel of Wraeththu cities.

'Thiede,' I began, having been thinking of it for some minutes, 'how much of my life is an open book to you?'

He carefully replaced his coffee cup on the table. 'You don't smoke much, do you.' He removed a slim cigarette case from a top pocket. 'This is one of the advantages of our hygiene-conscious bodies. They clean up after everything, even tar.'

He offered me one and I accepted.

'These luxuries were not always available to me,' I said, leaning forward to the flame he offered me. 'Why won't you answer me?'

Thiede fidgetted in his seat. 'Some sacrifices are necessary, for someone in your position, Pellaz.'

'Privacy being the first of them, I suppose?'

'The very first.' He inhaled deeply and blew perfect smoke rings at the ceiling. 'I had to study you, to be sure.'

'And since?'

He smiled and reached to pat my cheek. 'Not always, my dear, not always. You handled Vaysh with princely sensitivity last night, though. You have a knack of getting your own way with people, haven't you; of making them love you. I'm very proud.'

'Thiede, don't ever watch me with anyone,' I insisted, 'It can't be necessary now.'

He raised an eyebrow at my audacity. 'True, true; but I enjoy it. Vaysh is an interesting creature. Why didn't you reintroduce his miserable frigidity to the delights of aruna? He's not as disabled as he likes to make out.'

I cannot understand why I was still shocked by anything Thiede could say. 'I'm not going to discuss Vaysh with you,' I said. 'Whatever you did to him was despicable, merciless ...'

'How do you know that?'

'He told me ... some of it.'

Thiede sighed. 'Ah, well, what happened to Vaysh was an accident; unfortunate, but still ... He's yours Pellaz. Do as you like with him. Be liberal with the famous healing touch and the ever attentive ears ... A pleasing challenge, I'm sure.' He stood up. 'Take time to relax, this morning. Have someone bring you to my apartments for lunch. Then I can introduce you to your staff.'

'All of them at once?!' I cried.

'Oh, Pellaz, Pellaz; you are of my flesh, my blood, my essence. All these Hara are below you and you must believe that. They are naturally wary of you, but I have every confidence that you shall win them over.' He squeezed my shoulder. 'Until later then.'

After he had left me, Vaysh came back into the room. 'I listened at the door,' he said.

'You and Thiede have a lot in common, it seems,' I retorted, but I was not angry with him. Now I would not have to repeat everything, although some things I would have preferred Vaysh not to hear. 'I am not what Thiede thinks I am,' I complained.

'Think positively,' Vaysh replied. 'It is fairly safe to assume Thiede knows better than you.'

My attendants reappeared and enquired whether I needed assistance to dress. Why not? I thought. I sneakily enjoyed being pampered.

'It's your birth-sign,' Vaysh said scathingly.

I had found a box of jewellery in my bedroom and gave Attica and Cleis a different earring each. That way I could recognize them by looking at their ears. They thanked me effusively, the earrings must have been worth a fortune. I was no expert; cheap and expensive generally looked the same to me. Attica was the most talkative of the two. Because of the gift, he offered me some advice.

'It is not my place to say this, of course, but watch out for the one called Ashmael. He will try to trip you up.'

'What, literally?' I had visions of flying, head first, into Thiede's apartments.

Attica did not laugh. 'The word is, he disagrees with Thiede bringing you here. It is only rumour, of course, but many think he would have liked to see himself as Tigron of Immanion. No disrespect to you, my lord, but there are others who will say that he deserved the title; he is popular.'

'Thank you, Attica,' I said, awkwardly. Obviously, if spoiled, my two attendants were going to prove a fertile source of information. However, I was not blind to the fact that it could work two ways; I would have to watch my tongue. I asked them what their duties were and where they lived. It appeared that, since my arrival, their sole function was to attend to my needs. At present, they resided in a humbler region of the palace.

'It would be more convenient, I think, if you were to move into one of the empty rooms here,' I said. They exchanged a glance of surprise.

'You have means of summoning us if necessary, my lord,' Attica explained.

'All the same; I think it would be better,' I said.

The rest of the morning was spent investigating my rooms. Vaysh assisted me, looking into every drawer and cupboard.

'It's amazing,' he said. 'You have everything; it's almost as if someone lived here before.'

Thiede's apartments were similar to my own, except rather untidy. At lunchtime, I was conducted to his dining-room, nervous and wary; I had no idea what to expect. Thiede obviously had his own reasons for not briefing me more thoroughly. Perhaps he believed in throwing people in at the deep end. Half a dozen Gelaming Hara were already seated there and all went quiet when I entered the room. Thiede, at the head of the table, stood up, dressed simply, looking breathtaking, as usual. 'Tiahaara,' he announced grandly, 'May I introduce Pellaz to you.' This was met with stony silence. They all stared at me, but not one of them smiled. Thiede was not discouraged. 'Pellaz, you must get to know these Hara. They shall be working very closely with you.' A prospect that was not greeted with pleasure on either side.

He introduced them as Cedony, Tharmifex, Dree, Eyra, Glave and Chrysm. No Ashmael. I sat down, braced for a trying meal. It was obviously not going to be an easy task winning acceptance from this lot, that was clear. More than likely, they were all supporters of the absent Ashmael.

'How much do you know of governmental procedures?' the one called Tharmifex asked me. He had long, pink and black hair which contrasted rather strongly with his taciturn expression.

'Nothing at all,' I replied, thinking honesty was the best policy. Thiede was watching me through slitted eyes (what was he up to?), his head resting on his hand. Was he praying I would not let him down? This was a test of fire, which he could have made easier for me if he'd wanted to. Perhaps he realized his confidence in me was premature.

'Nothing at all, eh?' Dree remarked, throwing a weary glance at Thiede.

'He shall learn,' Thiede drawled, not moving his position. 'None of us came into this situation with vast knowledge, but we've coped. We need fresh minds, and this particular mind is of the finest quality.'

'Being your own?' someone asked; I didn't notice who. Thiede laughed theatrically.

'It gives you such sport to inject my motives with cunning, doesn't it!'

'I shall try to fulfill my purpose,' I said, realizing with shame how small and young my voice sounded.

'But do you know what it is?' This was Cedony, leaning forward over the table. I appealed to Thiede with my eyes, which he would not meet.

Tharmifex was seated next to me and turned in his seat to speak. Kind-hearted, he appreciated my difficulty. 'We have no end of problems to solve,' he said, taking the chance to assess me without appearing impolite.

'Thiede has told me a little about the outline of your plans,' I said. 'To unite Wraeththu into one nation. Is that possible?' Thiede's servant poured me wine, which was livid purple, and I sipped it nervously.

'The scale of this thing *is* vast,' Tharmifex admitted. 'But with co-operation from other tribes, not impossible. As a race, we desperately *need* organization. If something isn't done soon, it may be too late. We are a young race and for that reason, no-one has really become set in their ways. The way must be outlined as soon as possible.'

'I have travelled around a little,' I said. 'So I can understand some of the problems you're likely to encounter. I should imagine some tribes won't be that enthusiastic about the idea.'

'Mmm,' Tharmifex murmured eloquently. 'One thing I must stress though, we are not advocating mere oligarchy. The trouble with the world, or the civilized world as we know it, which at this time constitutes Almagabra and Megalithica, is that as throughout time, a few individuals of unscrupulous nature have seized power. They do not realize it, but they are a threat to Wraeththu existence. The Gelaming do not believe that we were put on this Earth to continue in the same way that mankind did.'

'It is time wasted,' Dree put in, 'that spent on pursuing selfish ventures. This world has been neglected. It needs attention, not further abuse.'

During these words, visions of the Varrs kept flashing before my eyes. but it was obviously not just of them that they spoke. 'What we wish ultimately to initiate,' Tharmifex told me, 'is a world council of tribes, although that term is a little deceptive. Our own country and the continent west are what we mean by that. That is where the strongest Wraeththu tribes exist. At the moment, we can plan no further than that. It will require more than enough diplomacy and planning to achieve results in these two countries. But if we succeed, we will have something to build on.'

The first course of the meal was brought in to us; savoury soup made of shellfish, and fresh, warm bread.

'How do you anticipate beginning this campaign?' I asked Thiede.

'Well, that depends on how long it takes us to get properly organized. Naturally, I have other matters to attend to as well ... Dree, where is Ashmael?' There was an uncomfortable silence. 'Oh, I *see*!' Thiede said archly. 'He is punishing me by his absence. If I was more suspicious, I would doubt his faith in my authority.'

'Thiede,' Dree cajoled. 'You know Ashmael, always a law unto himself!'

'Yes,' Thiede remarked drily, 'his contrived waywardness has not escaped me.' Thiede looked at me. 'Unfortunately, the Ashmael we speak of is a brilliant strategist, a fearless warrior and a cunning diplomat. You will need his talents, Pellaz despite the fact, (which I regret) that he may not be too willing to let you use them.'

'I know about that; I've heard rumours,' I said.

'Already?' Tharmifex grinned. 'Something tells me it will be quite entertaining when you two come to cross swords.'

'Metaphorically speaking, I trust,' Thiede observed. 'I will speak to him.'

'Again?!' This was Chrysm speaking. Of all of them, I found out that he was the least sympathetic with Ashmael. 'He is an infernal egotist! Because he had proved useful to you in the past, Thiede, he imagines you will condone all the absurdities of his behaviour!' Chrysm was younger than the others. They looked at him with mild displeasure; his face was red.

Thiede stared at him for a moment and then smiled at me. 'Ah, well, enough of that,' he said to change the subject. 'I've got some news for you, Pellaz; good news. An old friend of yours will be coming here to join your staff.'

My stomach lurched, but I should have known better. 'Who?'

'Seel, from Saltrock. I've always admired him. He has an enterprising spirit and these last few years have planed the edge off his temper.'

I had never thought him bad-tempered, but I was surprised at Thiede's choice. 'Seel? That's odd, I thought Orien, from Saltrock, would have been more suitable, if anyone.'

Thiede took a deep breath and looked down at his plate. 'Yes, you are right of course. Unfortunately ... Orien is no longer with us; he is dead.'

If you have ever received news like that, unexpectedly, you will appreciate how I felt; breathless and cold.

'How?' I demanded. 'What happened?' Visions of a smoking Saltrock blackened my mind.

'Well, I ... I'm not exactly sure,' Thiede said, still not looking at me (that alone should have alerted me.) 'Seel will be able to tell you.'

What I thought he meant was, 'I'm not exactly interested; Seel will be able to tell you.'

'Why does Seel want to leave Saltrock?' I asked, my voice too urgent.

'He doesn't. I want him to. He's wasted there. We need Hara of his calibre here in Immanion. Anyway, he won't be here for a while yet ...'

'We have to improve communications,' Tharmifex put in, impatient with what he thought were personal matters. Obviously, communication with Saltrock had proved a problem.

'Our technologists are working on it, Thar, as you know,' Thiede drawled wearily, as if he had said that a hundred times.

Tharmifex flashed him an irritated glance. 'I was about to

explain things to your protégé actually, our proposed Tigron. I believe he will need to know about these things?'

Thiede inclined his head, smirking at the sarcasm. '*Please*, carry on.' He leaned back in his seat and gazed out of the window. Tharmifex stared at him for a few moments before turning back to me.

'Clearly, in order to achieve any kind of union between the tribes of Wraeththu, we have to establish a reliable, far-reaching communication system,' he began. 'War, rioting, inexplicable dissolution; these factors have all contributed to virtually destroying those systems used by man, and as some areas no longer have access to the power supplies needed to run them, a completely new kind of communication network is called for. I'm sure I don't really need to tell you that we've not yet had the time to assess what may be salvaged of the world's technology and resources. It is a sad fact that many of the newly-incepted Hara neglected their education; events conspired against them. Their belief was what use is knowledge of the old world when they are full of the fire of the new. It was an exciting and frightening time when Wraeththu first stepped out into the light, so to speak. Anyway, the situation now is that we believe all the finest, most capable minds Wraeththu have to offer are being summoned to Immanion. The Gelaming have been scouting around for some years ...'

'Second to communication then, is education,' Dree put in. 'But that will have to come later, of course.'

Tharmifex nodded. 'Mmm. Fortunately, we think it will be possible to use our natural powers, those things that most Hara have been eager to explore and develop, to achieve things that Mankind had to carry out through science and machinery. Namely, our innate gifts for telepathy and telekinesis. Our technologists are working on an idea for communication involving the amplification of thought, the main problem being that over a long distance, this may not be effective for Hara of lower caste. We shall arrange, as soon as possible, for you to speak with the technologists, so you may understand more fully.'

'Representatives from Olopade, Unneah, Sulh, Colurastes

and Smalt will be arriving here soon for talks,' Thiede said to stem Tharmifex's enthusiasm. 'Once we have outlined our plans and are confident of their co-operation, we can begin to devise a programme for world domination!' He laughed. I suppose that was a joke.

'At no time, Pell,' he continued, pointing a curved claw at me, 'underestimate the scale of our proposal. It is vast, it will take time, and doubtlessly, lives as well. As Gelaming, we scorn the taking of life, but it would be naive to think we won't have to fight for our beliefs. Therefore, as with everything Gelaming put their minds to, our army is the best; the finest, fittest, fearless Hara you could hope to gather under one banner.'

Tharmifex laughed, unexpectedly. 'If our Lord Thiede could remove his tongue from his cheek for long enough, I feel sure he could impress upon you that we will be well prepared for what faces us when the time comes. I wish we had more time to educate you, Pellaz; we need years really, and I fear we shall have only months . . .'

'Are you joking?!' Thiede exclaimed. 'You'll have your years to indoctrinate him, Thar, you know that.'

'I only know that we anticipate having years of preparation; we have no way of ensuring that the Varrs and their kind will allow that.'

Thiede made a dismissive gesture. 'Trust me, Thar, we'll hold them off for as long as it takes. Don't be frightened of Megalithica because of its size; it's a mess.'

Tharmifex was clearly anxious not to continue this conversation in front of me. I had a feeling it was one that he and Thiede had had many times before.

'You must be able to talk to the other tribes' representatives as if you know what you're speaking about,' Tharmifex said to me. 'I'll give you a couple of days to settle in. After that, your education must begin in earnest.'

As we ate the meal, I assessed what I had learned. Of the hegemony of Immanion, Tharmifex and Chrysm seemed the most inclined to assist me. The others barely spoke at all, but I was aware of their scrutiny. Chrysm reminded me of Seel; the same eyes, I think. Tharmifex probably disapproved of me in principle, but was prepared to wait for me to prove myself, one way or the other. I discovered later that he was Thiede's oldest friend and was, therefore, obliged to agree with him to a degree. The others were all staunch followers of Ashmael. The Gelaming had long since got their own country in order and Ashmael had been mainly responsible for that. It was not a large country, Almagabra (as I had learned it was named); bordered to the north, east and west by mountain ranges, the south open to the sea. Being an old race, and therefore sensitive to the true nature of Wraeththu, Almagabra's human population had not struggled too violently to maintain a hold on their lands, discouraged more by superstitious awe than anything else. Ashmael had organized the survivors (and there were many), giving them control of land to the north. They were councilled, naturally, by Wraeththu, but governed fairly and left, for the most part, to their own devices.

'Their women are barren, however,' Tharmifex told me. 'So we envisage a time when their ageing population will become something of a burden.'

'How come the women are barren?' I asked.

'Well,' Tharmifex replied. 'That is something that rests only in the hands of God.'

I looked at Thiede, who glanced at the ceiling, whistling casually.

Gelaming technology is a strange marriage of the barbaric and splendid and advanced science, or para-science. Their architecture is classical, rhythmic and spacious, reminiscent of a much earlier time in the world's history and they have a fondness for labour-saving gadgets which sometimes sit uneasily in the lofty, camerated chambers of their homes. As with all civilized Wraeththu, the Gelaming have a love of beauty and harmony in their environment, and a great affinity for ceremony and ritual. Everybody seems to talk in long, carefully-constructed sentences. Slang is rarely used. Cal would have considered them elitist and too concerned with appearances of all kinds.

I spent several hours in Thiede's dining-room, watching and listening, and was in a thoughtful mood as I followed Thiede's servant back to my own apartments. There were so many people I had to meet and at the moment I was ill-equipped to discuss with them the things they felt so passionate about. Thus the thought would spring to their minds: where is Ashmael? Why is he not taking charge? It was easy for me to see why, even if the Gelaming couldn't. Thiede would have had a hard time controlling Ashmael as Tigron. Whatever meandering rubbish he fed me about my being 'right' for the part, I knew the truth; he wanted only someone he could manipulate; someone whom he had formed, moulded, someone who was nearly himself.

I dismissed Thiede's servant at the doors to my rooms. They were huge, but opened silently. Beyond them, a skylit corridor led to the main salon, punctuated by doors to different chambers. The floor was pale, green marble. Large, dark, shiny ornamental vases filled with rushes and feathers stood in alcoves; statues posed unselfconsciously, half in shadow. I was anxious to discuss with Vaysh all that I had heard. His comments, though dry, were always sensible. I could feed all my confused thoughts into him and get them repeated back to me in some kind of order. I expected to find him in the main room. He had planned to spend the afternoon there, reading. I saw someone lounging on a low couch, idly leafing through one of Vaysh's books, but it was not Vaysh. He paused a moment (too long for politeness) before glancing up. I was presented with a face both elegant and bored, an expression laden with challenge.

'You must be Ashmael,' I said, walking over to the couch so I could look down on him. 'What are you doing here?' It was not the wittiest thing I could have said, under the circumstances.

'I'm here to see you, of course,' he answered in a culturèd voice, flavoured by an accent I could not identify.

'You were expected at Thiede's for lunch, I believe,' I said. 'I've just come from there.'

'I know,' he drawled, sitting up, putting down the book, stretching. 'There is a rumour going round, that Thiede actually *made* you. Is it true?' He did not concern himself with hiding his contempt.

'Believe as you like,' I countered. 'It is of no importance to me.'

'You're pretty, yes; pretty. That's not enough, you know.' He stood up and towered over me by some inches. 'Don't think I'm unaware of why Thiede has brought you here. You won't be Tigron; Thiede will. He's too selfish or too greedy to surrender any of his power.

'You're just his puppet, you know. A glamorous sovereign for the people to fawn over so they won't get in Thiede's way. But it will be his words on your tongue all the time.'

'Listen,' I said in a low voice, but unconsciously moving away from his invasion of my space. 'I'm not going to play any of your fucking games!'

His face hardened, almost imperceptibly. 'Where do you come from? What antediluvian tribe spawned you?' His calm disdain was electric. His eyes steadily sought to hold my own; it was a simple technique, the most primitive of occult attacks.

I turned my back on him. 'If you don't like the situation, I don't give a damn. Think what you like of me and enjoy it! Now get out!'

'I'll leave when I choose to,' he said defensively. I mustered my strengths and turned back to face him.

'No, you won't. Attica!' I knew Ashmael would be loath to squabble with me in front of a servant and praised the moment when I had asked Attica and Cleis to move in with me. I could feel Attica hovering uncertainly behind me. 'Escort Tiahaar Ashmael to the door,' I said.

'You will regret this, I think,' Ashmael said quietly.

'Save your complaints for Thiede, I feel sure he will be interested,' I said with a smile. Ashmael uttered a furious snort and stalked out. Attica visibly flinched as he passed.

Perhaps my hostility had been too immediate. That, in itself, was a victory for Ashmael. Maybe I should have handled him differently; attempted to win him over. He was a forceful opponent and very strong. One show of weakness on my part and he would defeat me. I sat down on the couch, alarmed at how much I was shaking. I must learn to control myself, discipline my inner strengths. If I couldn't then I deserved to be beaten. This was no game of social etiquette; this concerned the future of our race. I needed the test to prove myself. To be Tigron, I had to be stronger than all the rest. Yet I was not too naive to recognize the seeds of truth in Ashmael's words. I was young and my position was uncertain; obviously not one from which to make a stand, because I knew so little. All I could do was be alert and absorb what I could.

Vaysh put his head round the door; his face was white. I imagined I understood why.

'He's gone,' I said.

'Thank God!' Vaysh came into the room and sat down on the edge of a chair opposite me. 'I must confess, Pell, I'm displeased, grieved, to find Ashmael here. I had hoped he might have moved on.'

'Do you know him then?' It was disquieting to see Vaysh upset.

'Once, once I did.' His hands were clawing his hair. 'A long, long time ago and I was different then. It was ... very awkward when he just walked in here.'

I went to kneel by Vaysh's chair. 'How intriguing, are you going to tell me more?' Vaysh sidled away from me.

'You sound like *them*.'

'Vaysh, this is not like you.'

'No.'

'Are you going to tell me?'

'No... At least... not now.' He clenched his jaw and swallowed. 'How did your meeting go?'

'It's difficult to tell,' I said, standing up because my knees had begun to ache. 'How many of the Gelaming hierarchy do you know?'

Vaysh shrugged. 'Not many. Tharmifex; he's OK. Cedony; he's a bit of a dreamer and worships Ashmael but apart from that, alright. The others I know by sight but that's all. I should imagine the ones to cultivate are those two and Dree; he has a big say in everything, but he's not that easy to get on with. Oh … and Ashmael, of course. I'm sorry Pell, but I think you will need him. If he's still here … well …'

'Hmm, you saw how we hit it off.'

'I didn't but I wouldn't worry too much about that. He doesn't bear grudges for long.'

'It's more than that,' I argued.

'Not really. He's bound to come round once he's seen more of you. You're not what he thinks you are, whatever that may be.'

'Even I'm not sure of that!' I said.

Vaysh scratched his brow. 'He won't be like this for long; once he starts fancying you, which is inevitable, I'm afraid …'

'I thought you disliked him!'

'I didn't say that, Pell. He's not the angel of Immanion for nothing. He's probably hurt because Thiede doesn't think he's fit to be Tigron. It might be hard going for a while, but he'll get fed up of being vile to you; I know him.'

'How well?'

'Well enough.'

There was that strange echo again in Vaysh's voice. Maybe I was just feeling very perceptive. 'Is he your Cal, Vaysh?' His eyes flashed up to meet mine, briefly, and then away. 'Was it the same for you?'

He did not know whether to speak or not. I could understand. The act of speaking your thoughts realizes them, somehow. Some thoughts are often best left unvoiced. He stood up and paced the room, wringing his hands, picking things up, looking at them, putting them down again, opening his mouth to speak, and closing it again. I tried to imagine how I would feel in his place, but the picture would not come. Vaysh's panic was infectious. Then he stopped dead, in the middle of the room, fists clenched by his sides.

'Pell … I don't have to tell you. You've guessed enough. Leave it at that.' He was the colour of chalk; his hair livid about his face.

I feared for his sanity. 'That's alright,' I said in a gentle voice.

'Don't say anything.' I sat down again on the couch. 'But if ever you do feel you have to ... I'll always listen.' I thought that would be an end to it for now, but Vaysh sat down again, next to me. He looked ill and some small part of me was selfish enough to consider getting up and walking out. I wasn't sure I could handle him.

'Pell, I'm scared,' he said. 'I'm so scared.'

Hating myself for wanting to leave, I put my arms around him. His rigid body collapsed against me; he was cold and trembling. This was not the Vaysh I knew.

'Scared, of what?'

'Breaking up ... disintegrating.' He made a sad little sound that was half moan, half laugh.

'What do you mean?'

He raised his head and looked at me. 'When I lived in the cold place, I could be like that; cold. What had happened to me meant nothing to me. I made myself strong. Now I've come back to the real world, having to face things again. Myself, for one. You're half to blame, Pell.'

'Shit,' I said and he almost laughed.

'I mean ...'

'No, no, I know what you mean; and you're right. I wanted to crack the ice, Vaysh, I wanted to get in at you. But you heard what Thiede said this morning; ice preserves doesn't it?'

He lay with his head on my chest, chewing a lock of my hair, thinking about what I'd said.

'What did Ashmael say when he saw you?' I asked. Vaysh's glassy eyes did not flicker.

'Say? What do you think? A long time ago, I died in his arms.'

CHAPTER 9

This news may not be welcome . . .

Some days later, Tharmifex came to visit me in my rooms. I had seen nothing more of Ashmael and little of the other members of the hegemony. Vaysh had kept mainly to his room, listening to endless tapes of mournful music, but I had spent a lot of time with Thiede. He lavished attention on me, showing me the city ('Here we shall build the finest theatre . . .'), dreaming aloud about how things would be when the Reign of Peace arrived.

'You have missed so much of it, Pell,' he said, as we walked among the trees. 'All the horror; the worst of it was over by the time . . . you were found. But *I* saw it; terror, panic, gluttony, fear and worse things besides. Boys dragged from the blackened ruins of their homes; firelight caught on steel and their screams as Wraeththu blood rained down upon them. That was often the way at first; that was why so many died. Inception, by its very nature, demands the discipline of ritual, of an educated mind; the other way was messy and for so long it was the favoured way, because of our hate.'

'I cannot imagine you young,' I said.

'Perhaps I never was,' he answered.

I loved to talk with Thiede and, although my opinions amused him, he always listened carefully to me. 'Hara are not like that,' he would say. 'How you see them, Pell, perhaps that is how they should be; but they are not.' We never spoke of my time in the other country. There was so much I wanted to ask him, but the subject seemed taboo. Perhaps when Seel came, it would be different.

Tharmifex brought me a gift; a spotted cat the size of a dog. He said he liked cats. 'They never embarrass themselves,' he said. Tharmifex, unlike Thiede, was not loath to talk about the tribes from across the sea. Gelaming call that country Megalithica; a somewhat tongue-in-cheek title, I suspect. Megalithica it still is. Tharmifex would frown a lot and say things like, 'Time is running out. Once tribes like the Varrs have wiped mankind and all the weaker Hara off the surface of their lands, they will be at a loss for what to do. That's when some bright spark among them will suggest a coalition between them, and that's when they'll all turn their eyes towards the east and Almagabra and Immanion.'

'Why are some Wraeththu like that?' I asked. 'We happened; and our purpose was to change the world, yet so many Hara still follow the same path as Mankind.'

'To understand that, Pellaz, you must understand something of the nature of humankind,' Tharmifex explained. 'Although there are two sexes, man has his female side and vice versa. In earlier times, the feminine principle was not denied and the world lived in a happier, peaceful age; a water age. All that changed and then, at the end, men came to uphold a rigid patriarchy; to be feminine was considered 'unmanly'; all men were afraid of that. The age of Fire had come. So they buried the femininity in their souls, subjugated women, whom they feared, and took away their power. Women, too were encouraged to think like men; motherhood was virtually scorned by all intelligent females, a kind of last resort when a woman was too stupid or uneducated to do anything else. Power, material power, was worshipped as a god; all other religions squeaked in comparison. Love between men was held in abhorrance; after all, feminine bits of the soul could then start leaking through and the warmakers feared that more than anything. Women, being discounted as worthless, were not as censured for seeking affection amongst their own kind (so long as its purpose was for the titillation of men!); they could do no damage to the myth, to the Fire God. Man could not grasp the truth; the power of sexuality and what it meant. A potent force was degraded to something animal, something steeped in guilt. Violence became the only true force.

'Warmaking is a strange disease, Pell, and goes hand-in-hand with greed. The majority of Wraeththu are those who have taken the Harhune; the changing. They are no longer men, physically, but the Harhune does not mutate the mind; that we have to learn. Until a new generation of Wraeththu children grows up, we shall always have this problem.'

'But Thiede's power is great,' I said. 'Surely he will be able to quell the trouble?'

'Eventually, yes; but we are anxious to avoid as much conflict as possible.'

My education continued along these lines. One day I asked, 'And what of Man, is he no longer a threat to us?'

The world is large, Pell,' Tharmifex replied, somewhat enigmatically and sighed. 'Ah humanity! How convenient it would be to regard them merely as ticks upon the back of Wraeththu!' Sometimes it seemed to me as if the human race had ceased to exist; Thiede never mentioned them.

'In Megalithica,' I said, 'we travelled for miles and miles and miles and there were no men there; only green stuff growing back over their towns. What happened to them?'

'Death's angel assumes many guises,' Tharmifex answered mysteriously.

'Were they all killed by Wraeththu, the *other* Wraeththu?'

Tharmifex shrugged. 'It happened; they were decimated, but Wraeththu were not entirely responsible. Panic, disease, melancholy; all of these things and many others too, claimed casualities,' he said, 'but you are mistaken if you think men are beaten. To the east of Almagabra and in the northernmost parts of Megalithica men still have control of their lands. At present, they are still disorganized, demoralized, thoroughly shaken up and afraid, but once they have finished licking their wounds (and they *are* a remarkably resilient race), they will stand up again and think about reclaiming their world. We must remember what happened when Wraeththu was very young; men ignored us until it was too late and we were too strong. Man's time is over, but I'm afraid he will be loath to agree with that. Do not underestimate mankind, Pell; they are tough and tenacious. We were lucky that they were in such a mess when we came into the world; that gave us a start. Now we must discipline the rogue tribes of Wraeththu; without unity men could inflict enormous damage on us when the time comes.'

Thiede had importuned most of Almagabra's population to assist in the building of Immanion, although Tharmifex did say to me that buildings had once had an unnerving habit of mysteriously appearing one morning in places that had been but rock and rubble the night before.

'Immanion came into being surprisingly fast,' he said. 'We had a brilliant architect working for us (not willingly, but his enthusiasm overcame his reserve), a man; I can't remember his name. I recall him saying to me once that the stone that some of the buildings were made of was like nothing he'd ever seen before. He said it looked (quote) "man-made", glossy and hard, but like nothing he'd ever worked with. At night it glows with a soft and barely noticeable radiance . . . Thiede's magical city!'

We laughed, but there was more than a grain of truth in that.

Thiede, though rigorously tidy in his government of man, was not a tyrant, and he paid his human labour fairly, if not extravagantly. By the time I came to Immanion, the humans had been sent back to their own lands in the north; Thiede did not want them lingering in the city once the bulk of the construction work had been completed.

Almagabra was effectively shielded by mountains on all sides (apart from the southern sea coast), which the Gelaming guarded zealously. Beyond Almagabra, especially to the east, Tharmifex told me, unrest seethed in an unknown and blasted territory. It was said that dark clouds obscured the sun in those places and that men had become lunatic and raving. What Wraeththu that lived there had submerged themselves in cultures of extreme eccentricity or, it was even suggested, had mutated further from the image of mankind than ever thought possible. Doubtless Thiede knew most of the answers, but as he wanted everyone's attention centred on the west, he was not forthcoming, and evaded conversation on that topic. The Wraeththu of Megalithica, Varrs and Uigenna especially, posed a more immediate problem; the mysteries of the east would remain veiled for some time yet.

Representatives from the co-operative tribes would be arriving in Immanion in time for my coronation. 'They shall see the new beginning,' Tharmifex said. I wondered if Seel knew yet who was to be crowned Tigron, and if he didn't, the expression on his face when he saw it was me! He would ask me about Cal and I would ask about Orien. Our meeting was not destined to be a joyous occasion, I felt.

News kept filtering through to me about Ashmael's pronouncements concerning my competence. The meeting place for the hegemony was a grand building near Phaonica named the Hegalion. Attica told me that once Ashmael had stood up and publicly argued with Thiede, accusing him outright of having me crowned Tigron for his own selfish reasons. 'You look down on us all,' he had said. 'None of us, in your opinion, are fit to lead Wraeththu but yourself!' Thiede, apparently, had taken this outburst with surprising calm. Until I was officially Tigron, I had no legal right to sit with the hegemony. Thiede explained to them, that when given the chance, I would be able to prove my worth easily. The hegemony was divided, but privately; publicly, they had sense enough to stand by Thiede.

I confided to him that I feared Ashmael's antagonism would cause too much damage to my reputation before I got the chance to speak up for myself, but he refused to take it seriously.

'Deep down, they all know I am right,' he said. 'Even Ashmael, though it would cause him a good deal of pain to admit it!'

I was not so optimistic.

'I have not heard bad of you from anyone but Ashmael,'

Attica said to me one evening. 'It is Thiede that they think is wrong, not you. They do not blame you.'

Only Tharmifex seemed to support me; Chrysm would commit himself to neither side.

I begged Thiede to let me be present at the next meeting in the Hegalion. 'Let them speak with me; let them know me!' I insisted, but he would not agree.

'By taking our time, by not panicking, we expose their wheedlings for what they are,' he said. 'You must not present yourself at the Hegalion yet. Ashmael is attempting to force you to do just that, and at the moment, he will only make mincemeat out of you.'

One morning, as I sat scanning the newsheet of the city, a Har I did not know was conducted by Attica into my presence. He asked leave to speak with me and I agreed, requesting Attica to bring us refreshment. Orders were beginning to fall easily from my tongue. My visitor would not sit down, but told me his name was Phylax.

'Ashmael has sent me,' he said.

'For what purpose?' I asked him.

He looked uncomfortable, standing there and I wondered if Ashmael had had to force him to come.

'Your presence is requested for dinner this evening,' he replied.

Curiosity may have killed the cat, but it also opens many locked doors. After a suitable pause, I agreed to attend. When I told Vaysh about it later, he called me a fool.

'Ashmael means to humiliate you,' he said. 'It's too soon.'

Thiede visited me in the afternoon, but I decided against letting him know about Ashmael's invitation. I felt sure he would forbid me to go.

I expected to walk in on a roomful of Ashmael's cronies, ready for sport at my expense, but there was only Ashmael. He lived in a residential area of the city, the home of many high-ranking Hara of Immanion. The house was low and spacious, framed by spreading evergreens. Phylax and I had ridden there through the perfumed evening, along the moth-garlanded avenues. Phylax had hardly spoken; I was an unknown quantity to him. He had called for me at sundown to show me the way, but it was clear that I intimidated him.

Ashmael was like a combination of Terzian and Cal; Terzian's elegance and refinement and Cal's cynical good humour. It is almost too absurd to describe his appearance. He was, as you expect, one of Wraeththu's finest, and very comfortably knew it. He offered me a drink, politeness itself. Phylax sat down by the door.

'Tharmifex speaks well of you,' Ashmael said to me.

'I can't see why that should sway your opinion,' I answered, and he feigned surprise. 'Ashmael, I'm perfectly aware of your feelings towards me and my position. If it's any comfort, I don't think they're entirely unjustified, but you must know yourself why Thiede has done this; you're not stupid.'

He laughed, very quietly. 'Well, Pellaz, you do believe in striking the first blow, don't you. But I didn't bring you here, sorry, *ask* you here, to squabble. Tharmifex has given me the sharp edge of his tongue over my behaviour, so, I'm to make amends!'

That was too glib. I was still suspicious, but said nothing.

We dined on a terrace behind the house, talking mechanically at first, of inconsequential things. Then the wine began to flow more freely and I was given every chance to exercise the wit of my conversation. Phylax sat uneasily at the table, and his edginess, more than anything else warned me that Ashmael might not be as innocent of motives as he appeared.

'I look forward to working with you,' he said and raised his glass.

I smiled. 'Ashmael, perhaps I've spent too much of my life looking over my shoulder, but I can't get rid of this sneaky feeling that you're up to something.'

He laughed, perhaps too loudly. 'I've done my bit, being pleasant, haven't I?' I did not answer but looked enquiring.

'Alright, Pellaz, Tigron of Immanion and whatever else,' he said, 'I'll be straight with you. I don't know yet whether you're a pathetic and squeaking idiot, as I suspect, or an angel of salvation as Thiede would have everyone believe. I didn't like it when Thiede told us about you; petty, I know, but we can't all be perfect. I'm still not sure if I'm right to allow you even one chance to prove yourself, but only time and working with you will reveal your true nature...' He poured himself more wine.

'By that time, Ashmael, it may be too late to get rid of me, if your suspicions prove correct,' I pointed out.

He shrugged and waved his arm at me. 'Tharmifex is not a complete fool. If he's willing to give you a chance, so am I. I've had my say, to no avail. So, I'll give in gracefully for now. However, there *is* one thing I wish to discuss with you...' He looked at Phylax, who was virtually writhing on his chair, and turned on him savagely, 'Oh, go inside! You know what has to be said, but you don't want to hear me say it, do you!' he raged.

'That was harsh,' I said, once Phylax had gone. Ashmael leaned forward on the table. I could smell the wine on him and thought he had drunk too much.

'No, not harsh. He would just prefer some things, things that happened to me before, to remain buried.'

'Oh, ... I see.' (Was this the reason then for the sudden change of heart?)

Ashmael looked up at me, resting his chin on his hands. 'Yes, you do, don't you! Did he tell you?'

'Ashmael,' I said, 'have I got this right? Have you asked me here, your rival, your political opponent and a virtual stranger, to talk about Vaysh?'

'Well, it's given you something to think about, hasn't it?'

I dismissed this remark as rhetorical. 'Surely you can ask Thiede about this ... why me?'

Ashmael sprawled back in his chair and put one foot on the table. 'Do you want to listen to this? I *am* rather drunk.'

'I might as well.'

'Well thank *you*, Pellaz! It comes as a relief to find that I can come to the Tigron with my problems! It was a shock when I went to your rooms and found Vaysh there. You must know why. Are you chesna with him?' he asked quickly. 'Is this rather embarrassing to you?'

I shook my head. 'No, to both questions,' I said, and Ashmael shrugged.

'I had to ask. Anyway, I didn't say anything to him other than, "Where's the master, then?" or something like that. It didn't sink in at first. I remember thinking, "My god, he looks just like Vaysh!"; it's been some years, you see. Of course, he just shot out of the room as if I was the devil, and I sat down and waited for you . . . not long. Afterwards, I began to think about it and then I mentioned it to Tharmifex. I couldn't say anything to Thiede. What if it hadn't been Vaysh? Thiede would have thought I was cracking up; and it's not a very good time for him to be thinking that, is it!'

'Tharmifex told you then?'

'Yes, all that he knew . . . sickening . . . terrible.' Ashmael rubbed his face with his hands, drank some more wine. 'Whatever you think, whatever you thought, that wasn't the only reason for my asking you here. I hadn't made up my mind whether to mention Vaysh or not until you arrived.'

'And the grape unleashed your tongue?' I suggested.

Ashmael snorted derisively. 'That too, I suppose. Tharmifex has spoken forcefully for you; to me personally and to the hegemony. Thiede would say nothing; that's his way. I suspect he knows the outcome of everything in the world already . . .'

'Vaysh said you'd come around,' I said, to bring him back to the subject.

'Yes . . . about Vaysh,' Ashmael's face twitched uncomfortably. 'Does he remember me? Is he the same? Should I speak to him?'

I paused eloquently before anwering him. 'He does remember you . . .'

Ashmael looked at me stonily. 'You have answered all my questions by that,' he said bitterly.

'You mind is as quick as they said it was,' I said, smiling hopefully.

Ashmael did not smile. 'Why shouldn't I speak to him? He was . . . and here's a Wraeththu heresy . . . he was *mine*.'

'I wouldn't advise it; not yet,' I said smoothly. 'I don't think he could cope with it yet.' I realized afterwards that this was ultimately a lie; I don't know why I said it. I should think the truth was, Vaysh really did want Ashmael to speak to him, but I did not.

'Oh God, Thiede can be a monster, he really can,' Ashmael murmured, his eyes shining.

'It was an accident,' I said.

This was like being an observer to a situation I could imagine happening about me some day. Then too, people would doubtlessly try to keep Cal away from me. I said, 'Ashmael, you said it's been years since ... how do you feel about Vaysh now?'

He shrugged. 'Feel? I can still smell his blood, even now. He was so beautiful, so alive. Losing him was like losing life. Everyone worshipped him ...' I had gone cold, although the night was warm.

'But now, how do you feel now?' I insisted.

'Now?' Ashmael wrinkled his brow. 'Now ... something lives in a body that looks like Vaysh, but is it him? I watched him die and spent a year demented with grief. Now? What can I feel? Vaysh is dead.'

Was this the way it would be then, when Cal found out that I still lived? Would he be angry because all his grief and rage had been misdirected? Would he feel cheated? That night, I tossed and turned in sheets that turned to wet rope against my body. I could not sleep for the thoughts that tormented me. Several times, I was on the point of going to Vaysh, but I did not want to answer the questions he might ask me about Ashmael. My thoughts turned to salt in my eyes. I could see Cal so clearly; time and absence had not blurred the memory of his face. I remembered the times we had sought each other's warmth in the dark, in the dangerous open country and by the stranger's hearth. The velvet texture of his skin, the flame of his violet eyes; all of this was lost to me. There could be no other to touch my soul as he had; no-one. Beauty could make me twitch (and laughter), but in my heart, in the deepest fibres, there was only him. Was I condemning myself foolishly to an eternity of loneliness? It was a possibility, but only if I stopped believing.

Seel arrived earlier than expected; Thiede brought him to my rooms. Vaysh and I were poring over some ornate and ancient maps in the library. They illustrated where dragons and trolls may be found and it was with amusement we discovered that one of the locations was right by Phade's tower. Gradually and carefully Vaysh and I had developed an easy friendship. Sometimes he was still staunchly unapproachable, but the cruel tormentor of our journey to Immanion had gone. His acid remarks were no longer tinged by hatred. We never spoke of how it had been before.

Seel had not aged in appearance, but as Wraeththu hardly do, this was not surprising. We began to greet each other as strangers, but then I threw my arms around him and the ice was broken. He still had about him a faint fragrance of soda.

He laughed and said, 'Well, Pell, who could have guessed it would all have come to this?'

Later that day, over dinner in Thiede's apartments, I asked about Saltrock.

'Oh, it is bigger and better now,' Seel replied in response to my questions. 'I could have done more there, but not much. Thiede has impressed on me strongly how much work there is to be done elsewhere.'

Thiede smiled gently at the cold edge to Seel's voice.

I waited until the last course was cleared away before asking about Orien. 'He was murdered,' was all Seel would say. I could tell he did not want to talk about it, but he had only made me more anxious to know what had happened. He asked me nothing about Cal, but that may have been because Thiede was there.

Time passed slowly in Immanion; every day was golden. I was invited to gatherings at Tharmifex's house and Dree's; in the latter case I sensed the invitation was wary. Delegates began to arrive from different tribes; they could easily be recognized by the expressions of bewilderment or wonder on their faces. To many Hara, the splendour of Immanion seemed but a dream.

The time came when my coronation was but two days away. After that, talks would begin in earnest and there was a feeling in the air as of a holiday drawing to a close and the party that would mark the last night. Costumiers came to fit my regalia; an outstanding creation of black and azure feathers. My jewellery was made all of turquoise and silver. Seel wandered in to visit me, smoking a black cigarette and leaning against a table to watch the outfitters at work.

'You're still a wonder of the world Pell, and still to me that absurd little urchin who trailed after Cal into Saltrock burning with ignorance.'

I could not move my head to look at him. 'I had hoped you'd bring Flick with you,' I said.

'Did you?' His voice was bitter and I jerked my head, to a chorus of complaints from pin studded mouths.

I feared the worst. 'Is he . . . alright?'

'I don't know!' Seel stubbed the cigarette out angrily in an empty wineglass.

'Don't know? What do you mean? Did you quarrel?'

Seel took a deep breath and something about his expression angered me deep inside. 'Pell, there's something you should know, but I didn't want to tell you before the coronation . . .'

I was silent for a moment and then said, 'Why?' Presentiment rattled my brains; I could feel the cold creeping in towards me. I knew already whom it would concern.

'Send these peacocks away, Pell,' Seel requested, 'It's now or never.'

The outfitters looked at him with displeasure, but silently gathered up their things. I changed back into a loose robe and told them to come back later.

'Sit down,' Seel said. He knew where I kept my liquor and went to the cabinet. 'Drink this.' It was a generous measure.

'Seel, what's all this about?' I asked, fighting my body's urge to start shaking. His face told me enough.

'God, where to begin?' He threw up his arms and walked to

the window and back again. 'Cal came back to Saltrock,' he said. If I could have shrunk back into the chair, let the chair swallow me, I would. If I could have blocked my ears … and yet, of course, I wanted to know. 'He would say nothing except that you were dead,' Seel continued, still pacing. 'We all tried to do what we could for him; he had lost far too much weight and spent most of his time out of his head; drink, drugs, whatever. I know grief has to work itself out. I was as supportive as possible. Flick took it very hard. He's very fond of you and it scared him to see Cal like that. One night, Orien was round, and to try and comfort Cal, he said that he thought you were involved in something none of us could understand. The fool! Cal's face went very strange. He just looked at Orien as if he'd said he'd killed you himself. He did not shout, his voice went very low. He said, "What do *you* know about it, Orien?" By this time, Orien was regretting what he'd said; perhaps it hadn't sounded the way it was meant to. He shook his head and tried to mumble his way out of it. That was when Cal went wild. He grabbed hold of Orien and pushed him up against the wall. He was babbling that he'd had enough of witches and savagery. He blamed Orien for what had happened to you, in very graphic terms, and … Thiede. Well, he was right about that! Flick and I managed to pull Cal away, and then he appeared to calm down. When Orien had gone home, Cal apologized to me, but he said that he knew something had happened at your Harhune that had marked you somehow, and that Orien and Thiede were responsible. He asked me if I knew anything about it and I said no. Well, I didn't. We all had our suspicions at the time but … Anyway, I think Cal believed me, although he did look at me hard for a few minutes. He looked at me and he told me that he loved you. Loved you … I felt terrible; his eyes were … He was so, so *haunted*. I have never seen anything like that and I didn't know what to do, how to handle it. Cal said he wanted to be alone that night, so I was with Flick. We heard nothing. Next morning, we woke up and Cal was gone. Next morning he was gone and Orien was dead; hanging half-gutted from the roof of the Nayati …'

At some point I had buried my face in my hands. I cried, 'It was *me* that did that!'

Seel squatted down beside me and pressed me to him. 'No, it was not you. Some kind of craziness did that. The same kind of craziness that made men kill; obsession.'

'Yet he called it love . . .'

'It was obsession; obsession and sickness. Perhaps he's never been truly well . . . since Zack . . .' I knew that was not true.

'Flick . . .?' I said; dreading further revelations.

Seel sighed and stood up, rubbing his arms. 'Flick . . . well, for a few days, he was just so quiet, listless, like there was nothing left inside him. I tried to make it better, say things . . . but there was so much to do. He left me a letter when he left Saltrock; it was a very nice letter, but he still went. I was left to clear up the mess. Everyone looked so wild and scared; things like that just don't happen at Saltrock. But then they started to forget, life goes on . . .'

I could feel the warmth of Orien's talisman against my skin. I should have known he was dead. I should have known it.

'Seel,' I said, 'I'm cold . . .'

We embraced and he said nice things to me to make me weep. It took some time. 'I didn't want to tell you,' Seel said, 'and yet I did; *so much*!'

My tears were silent and I said, 'You hate him . . .' Seel's arms tightened around me.

When Vaysh came in and found us like that, he thought it was something different at first. Then I stepped back and Seel turned away. Vaysh saw my face and I saw the fear come into his. I said, 'Tell Vaysh, Seel, tell him for me,' and went away to my bedroom. I could hear Seel's voice begin again, but not the words. My curtains shivered in a slight warm breeze, the day outside was golden. I lay back on the bed and put my arms behind my head. The aftermath of grief and weeping is almost sensual in its piquancy. Words composed themselves in my head. I could hear birds outside, singing on the terrace, see the pools of light beginning to edge towards my room. The day was black.

CHAPTER 10

He began it all . . .

Even when we think we are safest, we never are. Darknesses are everywhere. Both Vaysh and myself had become the victims of cruel shocks since reaching Immanion. We spent the following two days getting helplessly drunk together, licking each other's wounds by intoxicated ramblings. 'You must put it behind you Pell,' Vaysh advised, 'there is nothing more you can do.' Nothing more? Banish my fury, the fury I thought I felt, and the seething frustration? Some part of me kept saying, 'This is not right; this is not Cal.' It had crossed my mind that it might just be another of Thiede's games. What better way to drive all thoughts of Cal from my mind? But commonsense told me that no-one could have acted as well as the way Seel would have had to. Could he really have acted out so convincingly telling me that the Har I loved had butchered the mentor and friend of my early Wraeththu days? Thiede was capable of such an obscenity, but I was sure Seel was not. The worst thing was, although I lamented and cursed the cruelties of Fate, scored by misery, some deep part of me was never touched. That part watched dispassionately, a core of cool rationality. It waited for the surface pain to pass; at night I could feel it lurking somewhere in my heart and it appalled me.

On the morning of my coronation, I turned aside the measure of hot liquor that Vaysh offered me. Two days had purged me. My tolerance, my trust and my eternal hope had been battered numb, but some deep and healing well of strength overflowed within me and kept me sane, kept me safe.

They dressed me in the morning; the ceremony would begin at noon. Vaysh and I looked at each other and our eyes were full of granite exhilaration. We shared dark secrets but the terrible things we knew only fed our strength. There was a strained, tense atmosphere in the apartments that day, voices sounded muffled, as if on the eve of a great battle. Within us was the knowledge; we had both been singled out for greatness, Vaysh and I, and the harvest of the greatness had been emotional flaying. Yet neither of us blamed Thiede. He controlled us, bonded us to loyalty; now we had nothing, now we had everything; now we had nothing. It was endless.

We went out into the sunlight and for the briefest moment, the shade of Saltrock blurred my eyes and the solemn, soaring temple up ahead became the wooden-roofed Nayati and the angels that lined Immanion's streets became the cheerful and scarred pioneers of another town. Vaysh sat by me in the splendid open carriage that was drawn by eight silver horses. He was the colours of alabaster, verdigris and rich henna, and among the feathers at my side, he held my hand.

Among the echoing columns, silvered by floating incense, I spoke before the hegemony of Immanion and the priests and the most exalted citizens, the sacred oaths that would bind me to them for evermore. Thiede's eyes, full of satisfaction and pride, watched me with ophidian constancy. He must have known what Seel had told me, yet there was no sign. He trusted me to be strong and indifferent. I was Tigron and I was changing. He would say to me, 'You must listen to your wisdom now, Pellaz. See what the world really is and how we must cut out the dark and rotting places.' He could never be termed benevolent, Thiede my holy father, but he knew what the Great Rightnesses were and no petty compassion would stand in his way of realizing them. From below, among the little Hara that toiled and scrabbled and tried to understand what they were, I had stepped up to stand beside him, to take my place upon the dais of Knowledge and of Power. Wretchedness and fear were no longer equal to me. Tranquillity smoothed my cares. I had lived and died and resurrected; resurrected to immeasurable power. I could no longer be patient with the twitterings of passion and pain.

When the last words had been spoken, the last thurible cast above my head, Thiede came towards me and took my face in his hands. I did not tremble when I felt his breath upon me; I was equal to it. 'I have brought you through pain,' his voice echoed in my mind. 'Give me back some of the life I quickened.'

It had not been planned, I was sure of that. Silence thickened among the congregation, yet I could feel their eyes upon me. I was heavy with silver and turquoise; feathers folded around us like wings.

The altar of inception, in that most sacrosanct of Wraeththu temples, is tasselled with gold. Power was red behind his eyes and his red, red hair fell into my mouth and eyes. 'Pellaz, my jewel,' he said, with a voice he had never used with me before. As with all Wraeththu temples, the place of inception could be veiled. Tumbling, black muslin shot with sparks, pooled to the floor, and it seemed we were alone. Tharmifex stood within the curtains. He looked at us once and we looked back with frightening unity. He twitched the curtains aside and stepped through. I climbed up onto the table and stripped the feathers from me. The Chosen One. He came to me and his heat was just Har, nothing more. I cried out once, but not with pain. His eyes never left my own; he wanted to read everything there. When the moment came, it shocked me like electricity, switching on, opening up to a greater current. His flame hair crackled with static dust and I could see his face, so vulnerable in ecstasy. A god trapped in the anemone folds of aquatic soume. I could control him and make him writhe, and I did.

There was great feasting that day. The streets of Immanion were alive with celebration and so packed with Hara; many had come from afar for the occasion. Thiede and I led the way back to Phaonica. Chrysm came up to me and embraced me.

'A coronation sanctified by aruna!' he exclaimed. 'Will this become a custom?'

Now, it seemed, Immanion's reservations about me had been thoroughly quelled. I basked unashamedly in the admiration. This was my home, these were my people; for once everyone seemed happy.

Once evening had folded into dark, Thiede took me to his chamber of office. I was feeling dizzy with happiness and more than a little drunk.

'Pell,' he began, 'you might think it is too soon to discuss this matter, but it is important, especially as we may all be called away from Immanion in the near future to deal with potentially dangerous concerns.'

I listened, still smiling. Thiede pushed me back into a chair and leaned on his desk in front of me. 'Pell, you must know that as Tigron, we must be selective as to who shall host your heirs. Had you thought of that?'

I shrugged. 'I can see that, even if I hadn't thought about it.'

'You know, of course, that often Hara are committed enough to each other to become chesna . . .?'

I could not keep the edge from my voice. 'I think you could say I am aware of that.'

Thiede nodded and tapped his lips with steepled fingers. 'You need a partner, who is mostly soume, at least publicly, who shall host your seed. This Har will also have to be trusted with domestic government in our absence, that is, government within our own lands.'

I laughed. 'What you are suggesting, Thiede, sounds almost like a marriage!'

Thiede did not laugh. 'I suppose in a way, it could be seen as that. You need a consort, and you shall be united in blood at the temple to show our people that you are of one mind.'

'Who?' I demanded.

'I haven't decided yet.'

Anger shouldered aside the effects of alcohol. I could feel myself burning. It was not just that Thiede, as usual, was organizing my life for me; I was becoming used to that. It was that he expected me to commit myself in blood to another. I knew I could not do it; such a union would be a lie.

'Are we men then now?!' I stormed, 'that we have to marry amongst ourselves?'

Thiede flapped his hands at me. 'Pellaz, calm down, calm down. What I'm suggesting is not a stifling fidelity which might be alien to you. This is merely a political arrangement.'

'But it's barbaric!' I cried. 'I can't believe I'm hearing this!' I stood up. 'And how many concubines will I be allowed? Is there a harem quarter in Phaonica?'

'Oh don't get emotional, Pellaz!' Thiede said impatiently. 'Tomorrow, you will see the sense in what I say. There is no reason why you should not do this.'

I read the challenge in his eyes immediately. Maybe I should have kept quiet. 'Oh, I *see*. This is a test is it? Am I over Cal? Is that it?' Thiede said nothing. 'It really bothers you, doesn't it,' I said bitterly.

'Pellaz, he is not worthy of you. I should have stopped that relationship a long time ago, and would have done, if I'd guessed how deep your feelings ran. Don't you remember what I once said to you about how dangerous such feelings are? You must have seen within him all the time the possibility of . . . He was Uigenna once; the fruits of that inception can never be truly eradicated.'

'Why did you have to say this today?' I asked, but all I felt was anger, not pain. Thiede was not oblivious of that.

'I know, perhaps I should have waited, but I had hoped that this discussion would not become an argument about Cal.'

'Thiede!' I cried. 'That is bullshit!'

He twitched a corner of his mouth and walked to behind my chair. I sat down again.

'What if it was Vaysh?' he said slyly. 'Would you be so angry then?'

'Thiede,' I said in a patient voice. 'We both know that it cannot be Vaysh.'

'Yes, most unfortunate.'

'But even if it could be, I would still say no. I can't. If you cannot understand that, I'm sorry. I will let you choose a consort for me to host my sons, and I will gladly hand over the reins of power to that Har should I need to, but I will not, certainly and most definitely not, mix my blood with his in a vow of any kind involving spiritual communion. And that is my last word!'

He let me walk to the door. 'Pellaz, all that I have given you; it could all be so easily taken away . . .'

I turned with my hand on the door handle. He had spoken so quietly I was not sure if I had heard it.

'Thiede,' I said in a weary voice and shook my head, 'are you incapable of compromise?'

He looked seriously at the ceiling in a comic display of deep thinking, then back to me. 'Compromise? Are you joking?' He laughed. 'Oh, Pell, get out of here. We've reached a stalement for now, that's clear. We'll talk again some other time. Tomorrow.'

I went back to the party, but my heart was no longer in it. Cal's ghost had intruded once again. I could almost see him, standing in a corner of the room, among the tall ornamental plants, smiling, his hair matted with blood. But whose blood; mine or Orien's? I wanted him out of my head; that time was the closest I ever came to really hating him. He'd thought he'd had a murderer at his mercy. Did he feel elation as he tore Orien's life from him? (One for you, Pell.) Orien, no murderer, who had nurtured the seeds of my wisdom and kept my past in trust for me. My hand wandered unconsciously to the talisman. Cal, you fool! You blind, stupid fool! They thought he was mad, but I knew better. I had looked through the door with him, beneath the Kakkahaar sands, and seen Lianvis take life for power. We had seen that and we both knew, knew what lurked in the shadows of Wraeththu consciousness. Because of that, he would kill for me.

Back in my apartments, sounds of merriment still reached me through the open windows. I was feeling mellow and sad, but in a hazy, wistful sort of way. I was not unhappy. I went out onto the terrace to stretch against the cool, diamond-studded night. Tomorrow ... Something was over now, but I couldn't explain exactly what. The music sounded mournful below me. The gardens were in darkness, but thronged with rustlings and muted laughter. I looked along the terrace. Vaysh's window-door was open and a low light burned inside the room.

He was lying on the bed, half conscious. Two empty bottles stood upon the table where the light glowed. Nothing was knocked over. I went over and sat down beside him. 'Vaysh.' I shook him and he made a sound. 'Vaysh.' His eyes opened and I could see the redness.

'Pell, get out of here,' he said.

'No, no.' I took him in my arms and he wept anew. Vaysh was soume, more so than any other Har I had ever met. The female was strong in him. He seemed made to be my consort, yet Thiede had scoured him barren; such justice.

'What is it?' I asked.

'His eyes,' was all he said, but I knew. To someone, what lived in Vaysh's body was not Vaysh. 'What am I, Pell? Why am I still alive?'

'Oh, Vaysh, Vaysh,' I murmured and put my mouth upon his brow. His skin was hot and dry.

'I am a monster!' he said and tried to pull away from me. 'You try to make me feel better, but I know, I know there is no hope for me. What hope is there for someone who can only repel, who makes Hara back away in revulsion?'

'That's not true,' I told him lamely. I put my hand in his luxurious hair and touched his neck.

'Isn't it? Isn't it?'

For the second time that night I looked into eyes that offered me a challenge, but this was a hesitant, fluctuating challenge. At any moment, it might be withdrawn.

'You're beautiful, Vaysh,' I said. 'And because you're shamefully drunk, I intend to take advantage of you.'

Outside the music had died away and the horizon was grey with the promise of dawn. Vaysh lay in my arms; we had pulled a sheet over our nakedness for the air was cool with dew. I thought he was asleep, but he put his hand upon my face.

'Pell,' he said, 'I'm going to tell you something that no-one else knows; or hardly anyone. It may mean nothing to you or it may explain everything. It's about Thiede.'

I propped myself up on one elbow and leaned over him. 'What?'

He smiled wistfully, seeming anxious about continuing, perhaps wishing he had not spoken. 'We've had no time for gods really, have we?' It did not require an answer. Vaysh touched me quickly again and turned his head away. 'Perhaps I should not speak,' he said softly.

I took his hand. 'It can't be that bad, Vaysh.'

He shook his head. 'No . . . not bad, but I may be betraying his trust. Then again, he may want me to tell you, I don't know. Do you remember me once asking you if you knew who Thiede was?'

I didn't, then. 'Vaguely,' I said.

'There is one Wraeththu Har whom everybody knows . . .'

That disclosure implied nothing to me.

'Thiede is known to everybody?'

'Yes!'

'What do you mean? How is this important? He is notorious, I know. I've always known that.'

Vaysh snatched his hand from my own. 'It's more than that!' he hissed. 'He is . . . he is the Aghama, Pell!'

'Aghama? What?!' I even began to laugh.

'Pell!' Vaysh's nails dug into my shoulders. 'Don't laugh! Can't you see? He is the most powerful, the first, the last, the eternal. He began it all, Pell, everything. Wraeththu *is* Thiede! We are all his; like cells, like atoms of his own body! Aghama, Pell, think about it . . .'

I was silent for a while. I thought about it. Only the creaking of the palace walls and the call of early sea-birds broke the calm. I could not even hear Vaysh breathing, though I could see his chest rising and falling quite quickly. I did think about it. I thought of a wooden shack back in Saltrock that they call the Forale-house and sunlight coming in through a high window, falling onto Orien, where he sat cross-legged on the floor. Orien's hair shining around the edges, full of light, his mouth moving. I envisaged once again, after so long, a steaming, grey city, half rubble, dark and soulless and a mutant child-man scrabbling through the ruins, looking behind him, frightened and alone. Homeless, powerless; nothing. Thiede? Could the urbane, sophisticated, potent creature I knew ever have been so helpless? The first Wraeththu. On reflection, who else could he be? Through suffering we rise . . . I had been stupid not to guess. Had Orien known? In the beginning, once the Aghama had established his new, feral race, he had slipped into anonymity (changed his name? His appearance? Some people must know him, surely?). Perhaps he had been tired, needed time to recuperate, to plan. Perhaps he had simply become bored. Thiede divulges his inner feelings to no-one, except himself.

Wraeththu speak of the Aghama sometimes, not as often as they should, bearing in mind what he should mean to them, but when they do, it is in veiled terms of his still being involved in manipulating our race. A misty figure; part god, part monster. They are not wrong. The Aghama vanished from the chaos of Megalithica and built his stronghold here in Immanion. He had made the city the nerve-centre of his operations, the heart of Wraeththu, and the communication lines he sought to install would become the veins and arteries, our thoughts the life-blood. Had Thiede once needed peace? Was that why he had come here? Could he ever be allowed to experience it? He had never been human.

I lay back on the pillows and held Vaysh against me. Now I could hear him breathing; the sky beyond the window was faintest pink and gold.

Today, I would tell him; tell him that I knew. I could not anticipate his reaction, but I could imagine relief in his eyes. Together, we would walk outside and look towards the far horizon, where the sleek ships prance upon the skirling waves, and we would see the sky and we would see the future. It lay that way, didn't it? So much, so much; I wanted to know it all. I wanted to live the past through his eyes to understand what was to come. His blood, the primal blood, ran in my veins. His essence was my essence. He could see everything in the world and I would look through his eyes and see it too. I knew what to look for.

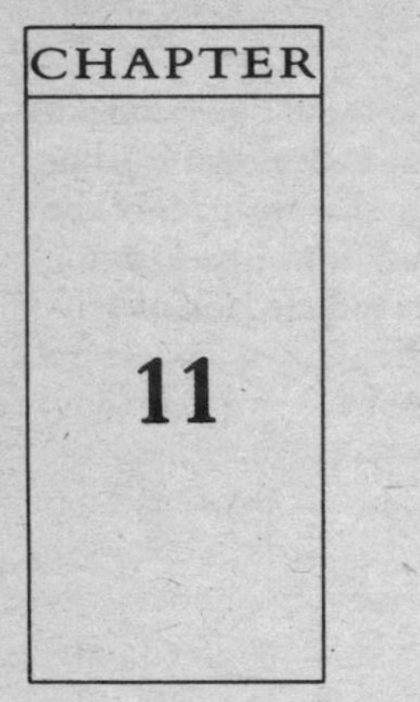

Ending

It has taken me many months to complete this statement, and of course, other things have happened to me since the time where I wanted it to end. Parts of it I decided to rewrite; Vaysh pointed out to me the places where I'd been too vague or too hurried. Essentially, the writing of these pages has been an exorcism for me and surprisingly, a relaxation; one thing to look forward to every evening, even if I never actually get the time to write anything, which does happen. A year has passed since Vaysh told me the truth about Thiede, and already the Pellaz who lived then (and who began to write his story), seems such a callow, ingenuous person. I have been educated well. I am Tigron, and even if it suits some Hara to continue calling me Thiede's puppet, I have proved my worth, both in the Hegalion and among our people. I have pursued the desire to be thoroughly Gelaming with single-minded zeal. My ears are always alert; there are few things in Phaonica kept secret from me. Vaysh says I look taller, and it is true that I do *feel* taller. If the ghosts of my past have not yet laid to rest, at least I have learned how to silence them.

Thiede appears to have been right about the amount of time we shall have to prepare ourselves for the war against the Varrs (because no matter how euphemistically our invasion of Megalithica is referred to – that is what it boils down to), but we have learned that the self-styled supreme commander of the Varrs, known to us as Ponclast, has begun to turn back to the Path. The Varrs' weakness has always been their lack of self-development; now there are rumours that Ponclast seeks to rectify that. This news was not well received by the Hegemony. We shall have to move more carefully now. Ashmael has proposed that we should transport three divisions of the Gelaming forces to Megalithica and establish a garrison in the south. Around this base would be constructed a barrier that no enemy could penetrate; a shield of natural force. It is essential now that Gelaming personnel obtain a hold in Megalithica. We have supporters there who will need our help. I often hear Terzian's name mentioned nowadays; he is almost respected in Immanion. Every time I hear it, some part of me goes cold. It is because some instinct tells me, no matter how hard I try to ignore it, that Cal is in Galhea. He is with Terzian. I can sense it, and even now, if I dwell on it too deeply, I am filled with rage. Thiede knows for sure about this, of course, and in time will probably tell me. I suppose I am as close to Thiede as anyone can get, but he enjoys keeping secrets and I know he is still concerned about my feelings for Cal. I have hidden them very well. It angers me to say that I still love him, for I know it *is* a weakness and I can't afford that kind of weakness, but after all that you have read, surely you can understand. I feel that Cal and I will meet again, but I'm not sure about what will happen between us when that time comes. I've changed so much and I fear that living with the Varrs will have changed him greatly too. When Thiede reads this, as he will, he will be furious and we will probably argue. Occasionally, he makes some casual reference to finding me a consort, but because we are all so preoccupied with more important issues at the moment, I can generally avoid that one. Somehow I feel that the subject will be brought up again fairly soon.

Yesterday, Thiede and I travelled through the other-lanes to a small Wraeththu town, north of Immanion. I can't remember its name. Thiede thought we deserved a peaceful afternoon after a hectic morning of arguing with Ashmael in the Hegalion. (He thinks we are dragging our feet over when to move our people to Megalithica. He is too impatient.) I was in no mood to let Ashmael rant on and the debate got quite vigorous. Once I cracked a joke at his expense and everyone laughed. The atmosphere in the Hegalion had been sour when we left.

We found a quiet cafe and sat outside in the sunshine, drinking tart, sparkling wine. Thiede was amused by a fanciful statue that had been erected in the town square, supposedly in the image of the Aghama. It looked nothing like him. The Har who served us our wine thought we were just high-ranking Hara from the city. He spoke to us about the Tigron, whom he'd heard had more spirit than Thiede had bargained for and that they quarrelled incessantly. Thiede caught my eye and smiled. We confirmed or denied nothing. The Har went back inside the cafe.

'Well,' I said, 'Is that true?'

Thiede shrugged. 'Sometimes you *do* say too much, but not enough that I regret my decision in bringing you here.'

'Will we move to Megalithica soon?'

He looked away. 'Not *you*, Pell.'

'Why?'

'There's no need.' Thiede has a knack of bringing down a cloud of silence that no-one dares break. He did it then. I watched him stare across the sleepy square, absently rubbing his glass with his fingers, frowning at the statue. Eventually, he said, 'That isn't me, Pell,' meaning so much.

'Yes it is,' I replied, meaning even more.

He laughed, drank, laughed, drank some more. 'I suppose you're going to put this in your book are you?' he said.

Everything of import, Thiede, everything.

Extract from 'Immanion Enquirer', a weekly news journal, five weeks after the completion of Pellaz' manuscript

A press release from Phaonica today confirmed rumours that have been circulating within the city for over a week. It appears that yet another total stranger will ascend to the throne of Immanion, as Tigrina, consort to Tigron Pellaz. Without doubt, this is the decision of Lord Thiede, but it is stressed that the proposal has been given the full approval of the Hegemony.

It has been reported that a Ferelithian Har, whose name has been given as Caeru Meveny, accompanied by a Harling of indeterminate age and a human female, applied for an interview with the Tigron ten days ago, after travelling by sea from Ferelithia. Palace sources now reveal that the Ferelithian shall be crowned Tigrina in one month's time, and take the bond of blood with the Tigron. No comment has been forthcoming from either Pellaz or Thiede, but we are given to understand that up till now, the Tigron has refused to grant an audience with his proposed Tigrina or even acknowledge his presence through a third party. An employee at the palace has disclosed that the strangers have been allocated a suite within Phaonica itself and have described the child as having 'weirding eyes'. No confirmation has been forthcoming, but it is the widely held belief that the Tigron has been cited as the father of the child and that its hostling has come to Immanion in order to demand recognition and status for his son.

As the voice of the people of Immanion, this publication requests that the Tigron should make a public statement to clarify this matter as soon as possible.

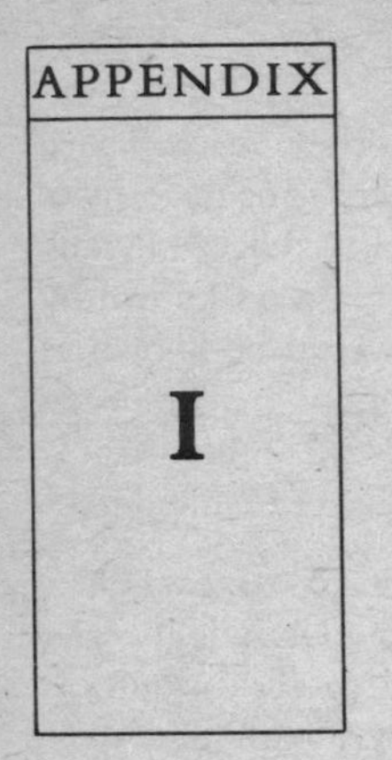

Wraeththu caste system

Wraeththu Hara progress through a three-tier caste system; each tier consisting of three levels.

KAIMANA (Kī-ee-marna)

Level 1: Ara (altar)
 2: Neoma (new moon)
 3: Brynie (strong)

ULANI (Oo-lar-nee)

Level 1: Acantha (thorny)
 2: Pyralis (fire)
 3: Algoma (valley of flowers)

NAHIR-NURI (Na-heer Noo-ree)

Level 1: Efrata (distinguished)
 2: Aislinn (vision)
 3: Cleatha (glory)

Natural born Hara have no caste until they reach sexual maturity, when they are initiated into Kaimana. The majority of them rarely progress further than Level 2 Ulani: Pyralis. Wraeththu of Kaimana and Ulani caste are always known by their level, i.e. someone of Acantha level would be known as Acanthalid, of Pyralis, Pyralisit. Once Nahir-Nuri has been achieved, however, the caste divisions (mostly incomprehensible to those of lower caste), are no longer used as a title of address. Wraeththu of that caste are simply called Nahir-Nuri.

Caste Progression

Training in spiritual advancement must be undertaken to achieve a higher level. Occult rituals concentrate the mind and realize progression. Progression is attained by the discovery of self-knowledge and with that knowledge utilizing the inborn powers of Wraeththu.

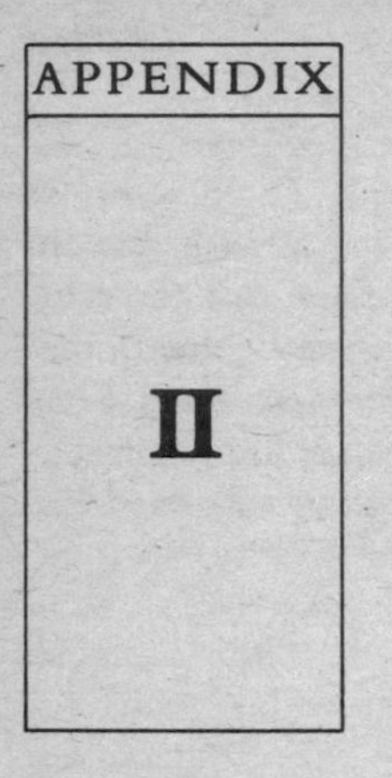

Wraeththu special abilities: a comparison to Man

The differences between Wraeththu and humankind are not vast in number, and not even apparent (in most cases) to the naked eye. Biologically their functions are similar, although in the case of Wraeththu many basic design faults present in the old race have been removed.

A. Digestion

Wraeththu digestion is not wildly disparate from that of human-kind, although it is unknown for Hara to become over-weight whatever amount of food is ingested. Their bodies are so well-regulated that excesses of all kinds are merely eliminated as waste. Perfect body-weight is never exceeded. This thorough system cleansing also extends to most intoxicants or stimulants. Narcotic effects can be experienced without side-effects. Because of this, few poisons are lethal to Wraeththu. It has been rumoured that the Uigenna tribe of North Megalithica are fluent with the use of poisons effective against their own kind, but this has yet to be proved.

B. The Senses

Wraeththu senses of touch, sight, hearing, smell and taste are marginally more acute than those of mankind. But the sixth sense is far more well-developed. This may only be due to the fact that Wraeththu are brought up (or instructed after inception) with the knowledge to glean full use of their perception. This is a quality which has become dulled in Man. Some Hara can even catch glimpses of future events or atmospheres; either by tranquil contemplation or in dreams.

Again, it must be stressed that this ability is not a fundamental difference from humanity, as all humans possess within themselves the potential to develop their psychic capabilities. Most humans, however, are not aware of this.

C. Occult Powers

This is merely an extension of becoming acquainted, through proper progression, with one's psychic senses.

Magic is will-power; will-power is magic. Self-knowledge is the key to the perfect control of will.

Obviously, this particular talent may be used either for the benefit or detriment of other beings. As all Wraeththu are firm believers in reincarnation and the progression of the soul (see *Religion*), most are sensible enough to realize the dangers of taking 'the left hand path'. Others, however, still motivated by the greed and baser emotions of human ancestors, are prone to seek self-advancement through evil means.

D. Life-span

In comparison, to Mankind, Wraeththu appear ageless, but this is not strictly the case. Har bodies are not subject to cellular deterioration in the same way as human bodies, but on reaching the age of 150 years or thereabouts, they begin to 'fade', vitality diminishes and the dignified end is welcomed as the release for the soul and the gateway to the next incarnation.

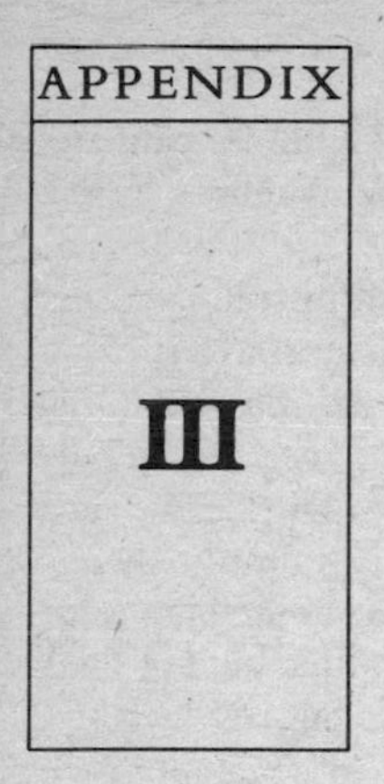

APPENDIX III *Wraeththu sexuality*

A. Reproduction

Wraeththu are hermaphrodite beings, any of whom have the capacity to reproduce on reaching the caste of Ulani. This is mainly because Hara of lower caste have insufficient control of the mind, which is required to attain the elevated state of consciousness needed for conception. Experienced Hara can guarantee conception whenever it is desired.

Conception can only occur during the act of aruna (Wraeththu intercourse); Hara are unable to fertilize themselves. The inseminating Har is known as Ouana (Ooow-ana), and the host for the seed, soume (Soow-mee). This corresponds roughly to human male and female, although in Wraeththu the roles are interchangeable. When conditions are propitious (i.e. when the desired state of consciousness is achieved through the ecstasy of aruna), ouana has the chance to 'break through the seal', which is the act of coaxing the chamber of generation within the body of the soume to relax its banks of muscle that closes the entrance, and permit the inner tendril of the ouana phallus to intrude. This act must needs be undertaken with patience, because of the inner organ's somewhat capricious reluctance to be invaded by foreign bodies or substances.

Aggression or haste on the side of ouana would cause pain and distress to soume (or possibly to both of them) caused by the inpenetrable tensing of soume muscles.

Once the seed (aren) has been successfully released, the chamber of generation reseals itself and emits a fertilizing secretion (yaloe) which forms a coating around the aren. Only the strongest can survive this process, weaker seed are literally burned up or else devoured by their fellows. During the next twelve hours or so, the aren fight for supremacy, until only one of them survives; this is then enveloped by the nourishing yaloe which begins to harden around the aren to form a kind of shell. By interaction of the positive aren elements and the negative yaloe elements, a Wraeththu foetus begins to develop within the shell.

At the end of two months, the shell is emitted from the body of its host, resembling a black, opalescent pearl some 6″ in diameter. Incubation is then required, either by the host or any other Har committed to spending the time. After 'birth', the pearl begins to soften into an elastic, leathery coating about the developing Har-child. Progress and growth are rapid; within a week, the pearl 'hatches' and the young Har enters the world.

Wraeththu children, on hatching, already possess some body hair and have moderately acute eyesight. Familiar Hara can be recognized after only a few days. Though smaller in size, the Har-ling at this time is comparable in intelligence and mobility to a human child that has just been weaned. Wraeththu children need no milk and can eat the same food as adults within a few hours of hatching. Development is astonishingly rapid within the first year of life. Har-lings are able to crawl around immediately after hatching, and can walk upright within a few days. They learn to speak simple words after about four weeks, and before that, voice their demands by exercising their voices in a series of purrings and chatterings. Sexual maturity is reached between the ages of seven and ten years, when the Har-ling is physically able to partake in aruna without ill effect. At this time, caste training is undertaken and the young Har is also educated in the etiquette of aruna. Sexual maturity is recognized by a marked restlessness and erratic behaviour, even a craving for moonlight. Aruna education is usually imparted by an older Har chosen by the child's hostling or sire. This is to prevent any unpleasant experiences which the young Har could suffer at the hands of someone who is not committed to its welfare.

(N.B. Those Hara who are not natural born, but incepted, are instructed in aruna immediately after the effects of althaia (the changing) wears off. This is essential to 'fix' the change within the new Har.)

A physically mature Har, when clothed, resembles closely a young, human male. Hara do not need breasts for the production of milk, nor wide pelvises to accommodate a growing child. They are, whilst obviously masculine, uncannily feminine at the same time; which is a circumstance difficult to describe without illustration.

B. Aruna

The act of sexual intercourse between Hara has two legitimate types. Aruna is indulged in either for pleasure; the intimate communication of minds and bodies that all Hara need for spiritual contentment, or else for the express purpose of conceiving. Although it is a necessity for Wraeththu, the amount of physical communion preferred varies from Har to Har. Some may seek out a companion only once a year, others may yearn for aruna several times a week. It is not important whether a Har enjoys most performing ouana or soume; again this varies among Hara. Most swap and change their roles according to mood or circumstance.

The phallus of the Har resembles a petalled rod, sometimes of deep and varied colours. It has an inner tendril which may only emerge once embraced by the body of the soume and prior to orgasm. The soume organs of generation, located in the lower region of the body in a position not dissimilar to that of a human female womb, is reached by a fleshy, convoluted passage found behind the masculine organs of generation. Self cleansing, it leads also to the lower intestine, where more banks of muscle form an effective seal.

C. Grissecon

Grissecon is sexual communion for occult purposes; simply – sex magic. As enormous forces are aroused during aruna, these forces may be harnessed to act externally. Explanation other than this is prohibited by the Great Oath.

D. Pelki

There are only two legitimate modes of physical intercourse among Wraeththu. Pelki is for the most part denied to exist, although amongst brutalized tribes it undoubtedly does. It is the name for forced rape of either Hara or humans. The latter is essentially murder, as humankind cannot tolerate the bodily secretions of Wraeththu, which act as a caustic poison; pelki to humans is always fatal. Because aruna is such a respected and important aspect of Wraeththu life, the concept of pelki is both abhorrent and appalling to the average Har. Unfortunately, certain dark powers can be accrued by indulging in these practices and this only serves as a dreadful temptation to Hara of evil or morally decadent inclinations.

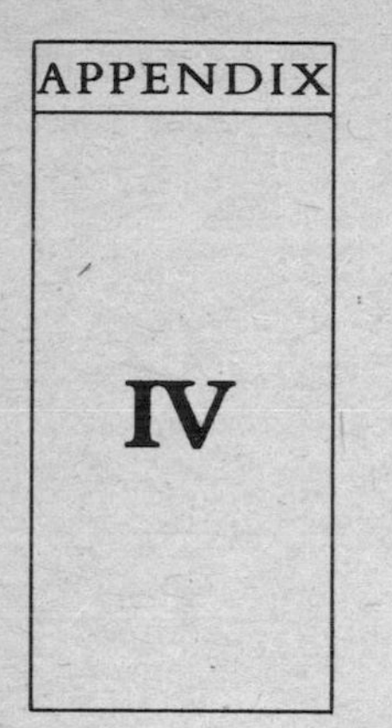

APPENDIX IV Wraeththu religion

At the time of Tigron Pellaz' reign in Immanion, the religious beliefs of Wraeththu were widely disparate.

Obviously, the faith of the Gelaming is the most widespread, and the most organized. They believe that the power of the deity is expressed within each individual, and that to lead a religious life, is to strive for inner peace, tolerance towards others and development of Wraeththu's innate powers. They are fond of ritual and extend their beliefs to the existence of unseen intelligent forces, who have a direct influence upon the lives of earthly creatures. Other tribes practise pantheism, dualism and diabolism, depending on area and lifestyle. A separate volume could be written on the intricacies of each religious practice, but to summarize, it may be said that all Wraeththu religions revolve about the occult aspects of the Wraeththu race.

Glossary of Wraeththu terms and principal characters

(pronunciation indicated where not obvious)

Acantha	First level Ulani.
acanthalid	Har of first level Ulani.
Aghama (Ag-am-ar)	Title of the first Wraeththu.
Aislinn (Ayz-linn)	Second level Nahir-Nuri.
Algoma (al-goh-mar)	Third level Ulani.
algomalid	Har of third level Ulani.
Almagabra	The land of the Gelaming.
althaia(al-thay-ar)	i) A period of three days or so, during which a newly-incepted Har mutates from human to Wraeththu; ii) (slang) bad time, living hell.
Amorel	Ferelithian Har, friend of Rue.
Ara	First level Kaimana.
aralid	Har of first level Kaimana.
aren	Wraeththu seed.
aruna	Sexual intercourse between Wraeththu for purpose of pleasure, spiritual enlightenment and the sharing of essences.

Ashmael	Gelaming Har, a member of the Hegemony of Immanion. His talents as a diplomat and strategist are renowned.
Brynie (brî-nee)	Third level Kaimana.
bryniesit (bri-nee-sit)	Har of third level Kaimana.
Caeru Meveny (Ki-roo)	Ferelithian Har who was hostling to Pellaz' first son. He later became Tigrina of Immanion.
Cal (*Calanthe*)	Companion to Pellaz when he travelled in Megalithica, before being summoned by Thiede to Immanion.
Cedony (Sed-on-ee)	Gelaming Har, member of the Hegemony.
Chrysm (Kry-zum)	Gelaming Har, member of the Hegemony.
Cleatha (Klee-a-tha)	Third level Nahir-Nuri.
Cobweb	Consort to Terzian, rescued from the Irraka by Pellaz and Cal.
Colurastes (*Kol*-yur-*ast*-eez)	Wraeththu tribe of North Megalithica, also called the Snake People.
Dree	Gelaming Har, member of the Hegemony.
Efrata (*Eff*-ra-ta)	First level Nahir-Nuri.
Eyra (*Ay*-ra)	Gelaming Har, member of the Hegemony.
Ferelith (*Fe*-ruh-lith)	Wraeththu tribe of Western Almagabra, pleasure-loving.
Ferelithia (*Fe*-ruh-lithya)	City of the Ferelith.

Flick	Saltrock Har, companion to Seel Griselming.
Forale (For-*al*)	A period of fasting undertaken by initiates prior to the Harhune.
Forale-house	Building where a Forale takes place.
Galhea (*Gal*-ay-ah)	Varrish town in Megalithica, governed by Terzian.
Garis	Saltrock Har, whose task is to prepare initiates for inception.
Gelaming (*Jell*-a-Ming)	Highly developed Wraeththu tribe, founded by the Aghama.
Glave	Gelaming Har, member of the Hegemony.
grissecon (*griss*-e-kon)	sexual intercourse between Wraeththu to harness occult power.
Har	One who is Wraeththu (p1. Hara).
Hara	See *Har.*
harhune	Ceremony performed whilst converting human to Wraeththu. Inception.
Harling	Wraeththu child.
Hegalion (Heg-*al*-yon)	The chambers of the Hegemony.
Hegemony (*Heg*-em-onny)	The ruling body of Immanion, consisting of seven Hara and presided over by the Aghama and the Tigron.
hienama (*hi*-en-*arm*-a)	High-ranking Har whose blood incepts converts to Wraeththu. A shaman, sorceror.
hostling	Wraeththu parent; he who hosts the child within his body.
Immanion (*Im*-an-yon)	First city of the Gelaming.

inception	That process which transmutes human to Wraeththu form. A tranfusion of Wraeththu blood.
Irraka (Ir-*ark*-a)	A feeble Wraeththu tribe of North Megalithica.
Ithiel	Terzian's equerry.
Kaimana (Ki-ee-*mar*-na)	Primary caste of Wraeththu, consisting of three levels.
Kakkahaar	Wraeththu tribe of the southern desert in Megalithica, given to dark, occult practices.
Kate	Human female friend of Pellaz, from Greenling in Megalithica.
Lianvis (Lee-*an*-viss)	Leader of the Kakkahaar, he gave Pellaz caste instruction to first level Ulani.
Megalithica	Western continent wracked by civil war and conflict of all natures. The birth-place of Wraeththu.
megalithican	Pompous, warlike mien.
Mima (Mee-ma)	Human sister to Pellaz.
Mur (Merr)	Saltrock Har whose task is to prepare initiates for inception.
Nahir-Nuri (Na-*heer*-*noo*-ree)	Supreme caste of Wraeththu, consisting of three levels. Individuals of this caste are adapt occultists; highly developed.
nayati (Ni-*yah*-tee)	Temple, place of worship or gathering.
Neoma (*Nee*-*oh*-ma)	Second level Kaimana.

neomalid	Har of second level Kaimana.
Olopade (Ol-oh-pard)	Wraeththu tribe of Cerdagne, a country north of Almagabra.
Orien Farnell	Saltrock shaman, first teacher of Pellaz, murdered by Cal.
ouana (oo-ar-na)	The male principle in Wraeththu. Active sexual role. Masculine generative organs. Fire.
ouana-lim	Masculine generative organs; especially phallus.
pearl	The shell around a Wraeththu foetus.
pelki	Rape.
Pellaz	Later, Pellaz-har-Aralis, who after receiving training from Thiede became Tigron of Immanion.
Phade	Leader of the Tribe of Olopade and his hospitality was enjoyed by Pellaz and Vaysh on their journey to Immanion.
Pharis	Ferelithian Har, friend to Rue.
Phesbe	Town in Megalithica inhabited by the Wraeththu tribe of Irraka.
Phylax	Gelaming Har, companion of Ashmael.
Pyralis	Second level Ulani.
pyralisit	Har of second level Ulani.
Rue	See *Caeru Meveny*
Saltrock	Wraeththu settlement in southern Megalithica.
Samway	Town in Cerdagne, inhabited by the Olopade.
Seel Griselming	Wraeththu leader of the Saltrock community, later summoned to

	Pellaz' staff in Immanion.
Sheh (shay)	Alcoholic drink distilled by the Varrs. It has a faint taste of cinnamon.
shicawm (*shee*-cawm)	Ritual shaving of hair during inception.
soume (*soo*-mee)	The feminine principle in Wraeththu. Passive sexual role. Feminine generative organs. Water.
soume-lam	Feminine generative organs.
Spinel	Leader of the Irraka.
Swift	Varrish Harling, son of Terzian and Cobweb.
Terez	Human brother to Pellaz.
Terzian (*Terr*-zee-an)	Leader of the Varrs, famed for his cold nature.
Tharmifex	Gelaming Har, member of the Hegemony, who was also responsible for the bulk of Pellaz' education on reaching Immanion.
Thiede (*Thee*-dee)	The instigator of Wraeththu, who brought about Pellaz' coronation as Tigron in Immanion and was instrumental in the uniting of Wraeththu tribes.
Tiahaar (*tee*-a-har)	Form of address indicating respect.
Tigrina (tee-*gree*-na)	Tigron's consort. Presiding earthly deity of the water principle in Wraeththu; this term can also be derogatory to mean suppressed masculinity. The power of soume.
Tigron (tee-gron)	Ruler of Wraeththu. He presides, with the Aghama, over the Hegemony of Immanion.
Uigenna (Yew-ee-genn-a)	Fierce Wraeththu tribe of North

	Megalithica into which Cal was incepted. They are famed for their cruelty and their experimentation with poisons.
Ulaume (Oo-law-mee)	Lianvis' creature, once of the Colurastes.
Ulani (Oo-lar-nee)	Secondary caste of Wraeththu, consisting of three levels.
Unneah (Oo-nay-ar)	Tribe of North Megalithica, of which Cal was once a member.
Varrs (Varz)	Warlike Wraeththu tribe of North Megalithica.
Vaysh	A protegé of Thiede's, who became Pellaz' companion and aide.
yaloe	Fertilizing medium found in the soume-lam of Wraeththu.